Immaculate Deception

A Novel

First Edition Design Publishing

Immaculate Deception

A Novel

Written by
Donald Tucker

Also by the Author

The Two Edge Sword
The Complex

DEDICATION

This novel is dedicated to all of the children who have been either physically or sexually abused in the name of religion!!

ACKNOWLEDGEMENTS

Thanks to everyone who have provided input in the publication of this novel.

A very special thanks to my wife Wendy, who has always been by MY side to give much needed support.....

And my complete admiration to Carol, my confidante, who has been with me through this entire literary journey.

Preface

When I first set out to write *Immaculate Deception*, my intention was to deliver an action-packed page-turning thriller about counterfeiting crimes that involved the Roman Catholic Church. However, it was not until I started to delve deeper into background material about the Church's nefarious activities that I realized their counterfeiting activities were merely the tip of the iceberg. The number of sex crimes that priests, even cardinals, had committed had reached epidemic proportions. As I continued to read on, I felt a chill running down my spine. It was the same malevolent feeling I used to get as an agent when I was investigating a major criminal case.

It was well-known fact that the Vatican was one of the wealthiest institutions on Earth. Yet with the current number of lawsuits related to sexual abuse and other forms of corruption, the coffers were now almost depleted. Total debt of bankrupted dioceses was already in the billions of dollars. How could a financially destitute Church continue to pay the court settlements for these lawsuits? They appeared to have found an easy solution. In the name of "sins or transgressions that could be forgiven," they decided to simply sweep these crimes under the carpet.

By the year 2013, cover-ups and "rituals of forgiveness" had become standard operating procedure. The Vatican merely transferred abusive priests to other church properties without notifying the proper authorities they were housing bona fide sexual perverts still on the loose.

At a certain point I realized I needed to include details of this travesty in my novel. The work would be a blend of fiction and non-fiction that would include graphic descriptions of the Catholic Church's sex rings, rituals, blackmailing activities and other abuses against innocent young boys, and girls as well. I would not hold back on the visuals or any of the lurid details. The reader needed to know exactly how these "priestly" sadomasochistic pleasures played out. I also needed to show the reader how members of the Catholic clergy were able to avoid court sentences that would have sent any non-Catholic to prison with potentially multiple felonies and in some cases, homicide as well.

Catholic, Protestants, Jews and Muslims are aware of these crimes. Notice I refer to these acts not as "sins" but as crimes. The difference between the two terms is noteworthy. A Catholic person who commits a sin goes to confession and is forgiven. Yet make no mistake about it: these are hard core crimes, linked to big money and big business.

I ask in this book just as I ask my fellow citizens of the world: why are these Catholic sinners/criminals not being punished for their illegal activities? Have the eyes of the world become blinded? The United Nations Committee on the Rights of Child (CRC) has finally forced the Vatican/Holy See to deal with its shoddy record on child abuse. It has given the Church until January 2014 to provide a detailed report, answering specific questions and providing confidential records regarding its handling of child abuse investigations. The new Pope appears to be in agreement with the U.N. and has expanded the Vatican's legal system to allow broader prosecution of sex crimes on Vatican grounds. *On Vatican grounds.* Has something important been deliberately omitted? What about prosecution of sex crimes on *grounds worldwide*? A priest with the Holy See's diplomatic corps has told the Religion News Service that the U.N. is being manipulated by enemies of the church.

Ireland's Prime Minister, Enda Kenny, launched an unprecedented attack on the Vatican, accusing it of downplaying the rape and torture of Irish children by clerical sex abusers. Kenny said in parliament that the Cloyne report... had exposed the Vatican's attempt to frustrate the inquiry into child sex abuse. Kenny said the rape and torture of children had been downplayed or "managed" to uphold the institution's power and reputation.[1]

With the whole world watching, *Immaculate Deception* delivers a climactic scene staged at the Vatican that builds to a wildly orgasmic struggle of good vs. evil that ultimately explodes in a graphically unforgettable *coup de grace.*

This novel is my passionate outcry against crimes that have continued to go unpunished. It is my hope that it will stir the same degree of passion in you so you will join with me in helping to bring sanity to the clergy and the courts that allow these illegal activities to continue. Our children are still being abused. *This has to stop.*

May God Be With You,
Donald Tucker, Phoenix AZ

---

[1] http://www.theguardian.com/world/2011/jul/20/irish-prime-minister-attacks-vatican

Table of Contents

1
Decisions

It was a typical Chicago "lake effects" day in mid-February. Blustery, raw, 24 degrees Fahrenheit with a sub-zero wind chill factor that cut to the bone. Yesterday's heavy snow on less traveled streets had frozen into icy ridges, making driving on the side roads treacherous and unpredictable.

At least once a week U.S. Secret Service Agent Wes Charles got together to shoot some pool with Benny Portera, one of his informants.

Wes could think of other ways he'd rather spend a Saturday afternoon, but Benny couldn't make it yesterday. His '78 Lincoln clunker was in the shop and wouldn't be ready until today, so Wes had to take whatever time he could get. Long ago he'd learned that sometimes, like most of the time, the job had to come first. Benny was Wes's lucky penny. He always seemed to have the right connections.

The pool hall, "Larry's," was a drafty nondescript looking barn at the end of a street of foreclosures and empty lots. Half of the interior to the left of the bar and restaurant was partitioned off for rentals—a tattoo parlor, smoke shop, loan center, and pawn shop. It was the kind of place where losers and desperados, often the same species, hung out trying to make deals or meet the right joe to pull them out of their current crisis. Almost every customer was too focused on their problems to pay much attention to a faceless Secret Service agent who could easily pass for one of them.

Facelessness, like invisibility, was another of Wes's arts that over time he'd perfected. He also had the color thing going for him; it helped that most blacks, Asians and Hispanics were look-alikes to the whites.

According to Benny Portera's Italian birth certificate, his real name was Dario Taccini. Dark-haired, medium height and muscular with coarse features and a Mediterranean complexion, he had six different passports and residencies in several Middle East countries where he'd worked as a mercenary until 2008. Wes picked him up on counterfeiting charges

1

linked to a Mafia money laundering scam. His connections were impressive.

"So this guy Masella, Tony Masella, is looking for a printer." Benny picked up his cue stick.

And?" prodded Wes, rattling the ice cubes in his drink before downing the rest of it.

"You don't think we could find one for him, do you?" Benny's hand shook noticeably on the cue stick. *Click!*

Wes leaned forward, positioned his cue and aimed. *Click-click-click!*

"Do you?" Benny straightened, sucked in his breath and waited nervously for Wes's response.

Wes moved around the pool table, said nothing and pretended to study the hit.

A printer to print counterfeit money! Tony Masella was one of the kingpins of the entire counterfeit operation that Wes and the Chicago USSS counterfeit squad had been trying to take down.

Like Benny, Masella was also Cosa Nostra. Apparently he was involved in a group that went several layers deep and extended to every Laundromat throughout the world. Mafia games like this one often started here in good old Chi, working with some interesting national banks that were partially owned by the Vatican.

Masella had almost been picked up before in connection with a Catholic charity organization that was passing counterfeit bills. According to the bank where customers had turned them in, the bills showed up in toy stores, supermarkets and clothing stores near Adams and Thomas streets. A month before, at a bank on West Chicago Avenue near Loyola University, some $100 bills had been turned in with the same serial numbers. They were produced on an ink jet printer whose encrypted yellow pixels tracked back to a printer purchased by Masella. After that incident apparently he'd smartened up and started to use other chumps to do his dirty work. He'd also learned that the counterfeiting had to be done on an offset printer where there was no way of tracking ownership.

Wes ordered another round of drinks for both of them and let Benny win the next two games while he weighed the odds of how the courts would look at a case like this.

If Wes was locating the printer and was indirectly in charge of the counterfeiting, it was certainly going to set off some alarms.

If it went to trial, and chances are it would, Wes knew it would be more than a "how"—how it was done. It would also be "who." Who was sitting on the bench. Some of the courts had their own political agendas. If the media got involved—and because of the size of the case, of course they would—anything could happen.

Here's what it looks like, Agent Charles. You print up the money for the sonofabitch and deliver it to him. As soon as he takes possession of it, you grab him.

"You printed the money, Agent Charles, and you handed it to him. Right? A setup with a printed invitation?"

Wrong!—but how else could he close in on the guy? How else could he bring down the whole fucking operation?

"It's bigger than both of us, Wes, m'boy," said the voice in his ear.

Masella must be desperate if he couldn't find an offset counterfeit printer himself and he was asking one of his brothers for referrals. Masella trusted no one except himself. It was the kind of risk Masella didn't usually take.

What the hell. He might as well do Benny a favor. Besides, he needed to keep him happy. Benny was proving to be a valuable informant. He'd already helped them get one counterfeiter behind bars.

"We can do it." Wes laid down his cue stick.

Benny's tan tee shirt had dark spots underneath the armpits and his forehead was beaded with sweat. He was usually pretty cool, but this was a big fish and there was too much in it for him to lose. Shit. If everything worked out, he had his own plan.

On the way out, Wes glanced over his shoulder as he always did when leaving a place, and caught a glimpse of a short bald-headed man with deep-set eyes, sunken cheeks and a large misshapen nose, directly behind him.

The man had a sinister look about him... where had he seen him before? Then he remembered. Adam Csonka was his name. He was a former priest with a colorful history. His clerical name used to be Father Bartholomew.

At the exit the man headed to the left, to the men's room. Wes stepped inside to the hallway of video games and waited for Csonka to emerge. Before he drove away, just in case, Wes took a photo of his vehicle and captured the plate numbers.

2
Happy Anniversary!

Sunday, February 14, 2010 – The Elite Restaurant - Chicago, Illinois

"Happy 30th Anniversary, Agent Charles!" Kim Taylor Charles lifted her champagne glass. "Earth to Wes Charles, come in... come in...!"

"Oh, yes... yes, Sorry, Angel. Happy Anniversary!" Wes lifted his glass and his pinkie simultaneously, a signal for Kim to roll her eyes and flash him one of her dazzling smiles. "Gawd. Will you ever grow up, darlin'?"

"I hope not," snorted Wes, toasting her in return before tackling the bread basket with gusto. "Mmm, *mmm.* Just squeeze this bread, baby... fresh from the oven. Let the butter melt quick and sweet over every one of its parts."

"So your mind is doing the details of the Who-Who case when we're out celebrating our once in a lifetime anniversary dinner at one of the most exclusive restaurants in Chicago, courtesy of the United States Secret Service—"

"That," retorted Wes, a broad grin of sweet satisfaction spreading over his face, "is Miracle Number Three."

"And Miracle Number One?" Kim forked up an oyster.

"What's that called?" Wes poked one of his forks into her appetizer. "I mean the fancy name."

"Oysters, hon. O-Y as in 'Oy vey,' and 'S-T-E-R-S' as in 'gang-sters' and 'bank-sters.' Miracle Number One?"

"Did anyone ever tell you that you're beautiful, witty, clever—brilliant in fact, and—"

"—even more beautiful than when we first met, 32 years ago?" Kim shook her head, clicking her tongue and laughing. Her laugh was like velvet, rich and seductive, straight from the soul. "You know what, Wes? I fucking love you!"

"Miracle Number Two," he continued, admiring the neckline of her pale green silk dress, mainly the cleavage, "that I, a po' black boy from So'Side Chi, am sitting here in one of the city's top banana restaurants where not so long ago was the unwritten sign over the door, 'No Niggers Allowed,' 'scuse me, Ma'am..."

"Gotcha. And Number One, Mr. Successful?"

"Is that you and I, two senior U.S. Secret Service Agents, have stuck it out as long as we have, and are still on the streets instead of pushing pencils behind boat-size desks. And there's more: that we're blessed with two brilliant children, male and female respectively, who are the spittin' images of their parents..." Wes paused.

"And—?" Kim waited, already knowing what was next.

"—that as soon as we polish off this expensive meal we will return to the office, to our Styrofoam coffee and stale Dunkin' Donuts, and the Who-Who case."

"So what did you find out about those counterfeit bills? Did they do the forensic tests again in D.C.? Has any more of the stuff turned up anywhere else in the country? Agent Charles, what do you know that you've been too selfish to share?"

"Confirmed *fugazy*. Fucking Fake," said Wes. "They have the same identification marks as the ones we've been finding over the past three months. Also, some bank documents that W-2 and the forgery squad have been looking at may be linked somehow."

"Bank documents?"

"Remember W-2 told us about some bonds they traced to a bank trading program? Bank statements, Certificates of Deposit, Proof of Funds... all kinds of stuff."

"W-2" was their son; Wes, Jr. nicknamed "W-2," who'd joined the Chicago office forgery squad six months ago.

"It's too soon to tell and it's going to take much more work before we can find actual proof. But the main thing is, W-2 confirmed the bonds are as FF as the Parker Brothers money we sent to D.C."

"As for the bills, according to Agent Ji Song in D.C., the forensic tests picked up problems with the watermarks on the larger ones. And Old Hickory on the 20s would turn over in his grave if he knew he was the rock star of so many counterfeiting takedowns."

Wes did some serious work on his shrimp cocktail before continuing. "Do you know that since the time I've been a member of the counterfeit squad, the number of counterfeit cases have quadrupled?"

"No surprise." Kim forked up another oyster. "All those crooks out there need to make sure they keep us busy, especially you. Slow down, Wes. Give them a break!"

"Look who's talking. Anyway, the operation appears to be a much larger one than we thought. Tentacles everywhere. So it may take awhile before we actually know what we're dealing with. First things first."

He reached across the table and squeezed her left hand, running his thumb and finger over her wedding band. "The good part is, like I've been saying for the past...*how many years*? ... We're in this together."

"Thirty. Thirty years. I know, darlin', two agents that lay together stay together. Don't look behind you to the left at that bald-headed man with an escort. He keeps stealing sideways glances in this direction like he knows you."

"Is the escort male or female?" Wes buttered another chunk of bread.

"Male. How'd you guess?" Kim forked up another oyster. "Mmmm. These really are delicious. You want another one?"

"Don't tempt me. Remember we still have a whole lifetime ahead of us." Wes leaned back as the waiter arrived with their salads. "I saw them when they came in. His name is, or was, Father Bartholomew. Adam Csonka. A Hungarian priest, who was, as they say, defrocked or forced to resign. Same thing. Right before you joined the counterfeit squad, in '79 I think it was, the Catholic Church paid off a judge in the Seventh Circuit. A pissing shame, but one of these days..."

"The Mississippi will run backward and the sun will stand still. Never trust the snake in the tree. Did you say 'pay off a judge'?" Kim smiled sweetly at the waiter.

"More parmesan for your salad?"

"Yes, please."

She pulled out her iPhone to check for messages. "So the D.C. report is what the meeting's all about. And reason to call in the forgery squad as well. Is W-2 going to be there? I haven't talked with him since he came back from New York."

"If Rachel's there, W-2 will be there. I wonder when he'll have enough courage to ask her out. Did you catch those hang-dog eyes of his whenever he looks at her?! I think I need to set up some coaching sessions with him. About the Mississippi. I believe in 1812 during an earthquake the Mississippi River near the Ohio River started to run backward when a thrust fault created a sudden dam several feet high near the bottom of the river loop near the New Madrid. Significant Trivia 101. And about that snake," grinned Wes, "the only one I've ever trusted is that evil critter in the Old Testament that tempted Eve. Thank God for small favors."

"Otherwise, you wouldn't be here," sighed Kim. "*We* wouldn't be here. And we wouldn't have jobs."

"All true. And I have to admit, sweetheart, your arrival in our office that windy Chicago day in March of '80 changed the climate overnight. It took at least a month to get the guys to Focus and Function every time you—"

"And you? How long did it take *you* to start functioning, darlin'?" Kim touched the neckline of her dress, her fingers pausing at the lowest point. A gentle reminder that for the first three months after she joined the counterfeit squad, Wes had deliberately avoided her like the plague.

"You were dangerous. A threat to my virginity. I ducked. Or at least tried to...until that fateful day in the surveillance van."

At the time Wes's personal life was still rocky. Even though he'd been divorced from Terri for a year already, it had been a nasty breakup and he was still recovering. Fortunately, it was Terri and not Wes who'd been caught cheating, forcing her to retreat and accept her rightful desserts— child support and a house that was paid for, but no more.

Nevertheless, Terri had made a point of alienating their daughter, Charlene, from her father. Not that he'd done much in the way of parenting. How could he? A Secret Service agent owed his life first and foremost to the country and he could never forget that for a minute. During the time they were married, Wes had been sent on numerous presidential and dignitary protection assignments and he was out of the country almost as much as he was in Chicago.

––––––––––––––––

Two years before Kim came to the Chicago USSS, Wes had been asked to be on a committee to explore the possibility of hiring the first Secret Service female agents. Wes, the only black agent on the committee, was appalled at the hostility of the white agents toward females.

"What makes you think they can do the same job we do?" whined Bruce Melkin.

"We've survived all these years without them, why do we need them now?" argued Reggie McPherson.

"You know what women do best," retorted Wayne Cooperman, one of the senior agents who'd been married and divorced three times. "They cry. And that's what they're supposed to do. They're supposed to be soft and squeezable like tub toys. Not hard like pricks. How else can we be their protectors? Men are hunters and women are—"

"You guys are so fucking 'ha-ha' funny it cracks me up," Wes broke in. "How about giving women the same rigorous training we're forced to go through, in order to prove just how soft and whimpering they are? Did you ever see a woman give birth? Did you ever see her in labor for two straight days?"

"Wes, that's not fair and you fucking know it," countered Reggie, polishing off his beer and snapping the lid off another. Reggie's arguments were even more humorous than Wayne's, since his wife, Lee, was a black belt in Taekwondo and one of the best instructors in the city. Domestic feuds in the McPherson household were non-existent. If they ever disagreed or argued—God forbid!—Lee would kick him in the balls before Reggie could even say "boo" and it would be over.

"What happens during a chase, or when they get into a fight?" sneered Wayne. "Or when they've got a gun or a knife at their throats? They shit and piss in their pants!"

"What happens to a lot of men when they've got a gun or knife at their throats?" Wes stalked out of the room to cool his rage. Were these guys living in the Stone Age, or what? Women were minorities like blacks. Like Jews. Hindus. Hispanics. Asians. Gays. Lesbians. They needed to be given a chance.

He was even more shocked by some of the attitudes of white agents' wives. Their biggest bitch with hiring female agents had nothing to do with whether they were capable enough to do the job. It was all about fear and what could happen on the job. Often their husbands had to work late hours on surveillances, and when they were out of town they'd be sleeping in the same hotels with these female agents. By necessity they'd be spending so much time together. In their minds, only the worst things could happen.

What a lack of trust, thought Wes. What kind of a marriage was that?

Wes had won the argument, or maybe time was in his favor. Civil Rights, Women's Lib... what the hell. What a hypocrite he was.

In 1980 four women had applied for jobs and two were accepted. Kim Taylor was one of them. With her advanced Intel training and her skills in code-breaking, she'd been placed on the forgery squad. Then a year later there'd been a vacancy on the counterfeit squad. Wes was the only one who spoke out against bringing her in. What was his reason? Argued the rest of the agents.

Lack of experience?? The counterfeit squad was an elite group; they only accepted experienced agents who could cut the mustard.

Bullshit. Kim was an expert shot on the pistol range. She'd done well at physical self-defense and had made way more than the average number of arrests. In truth, she was quicker and brighter than several of the male agents. It wasn't the female issue after all... or maybe it was. And not because Kim Taylor was too drop dead gorgeous to be tough enough to blow the guts out of someone if she had to; or drag them by the hair while she twisted their arms out of joint and cuffed them. No, that wasn't the issue at all.

The issue was Wes Charles's own insecurity. Cover-up for an alpha male who'd picked up the scent of an alpha female: a sharp shooter with a mind that never stopped. Quick on her feet and quick to think on her feet when she had to. Too tantalizing for his alpha male instincts, both upper and lower. Certain physical parts were already testifying to this fact whenever Wes thought about her. Whenever she was in close proximity, it was exactly the game change he didn't want.

Kim was his kind of woman and he knew it from the moment he'd first laid eyes on her. Those big brown eyes, gorgeous brown skin, creamy brown voice...

She proved herself as he knew she would. But there were other factors, like those mini-skirts and half unbuttoned blouses that may have performed well for Agent Taylor but behaved poorly for Agent Charles. Long legs, short skirts, black hose... "Pray for me," muttered Wes under his breath that day they were in the surveillance van together on a counterfeit case.

Although she denied it afterward, Wes knew Kim was playing him.

Agent Frank Reece was in the van that day with them and when Kim bent over to take her turn at viewing through the one-way window, the two men leaned down from behind and bent their heads so one of their ears touched their shoulder. In this contorted position with both leaning over in the same direction and trying to look up where the sun didn't shine, their ears touched and they bumped heads.

Frank let out a snort and Wes didn't have to do anything. His grin and other personal effects gave him away. Kim tipped her head and smiled, the expression on her face registering total satisfaction.

Damn, she was good. Wes inhaled sharply. *Too good for his own good.*

Agent Taylor turned away from the window and motioned to Wes, lifting one eyebrow and curving her lips provocatively. This was way too much and needed to be addressed. Now.

Agent Charles was in charge of the surveillance operation. "Here, Frank." Wes handed him some bills. "There's a McDonald's about three blocks from here, on Greenwood and Beckley. Bring us back some grub. Three whoppers, three double fries, we've still got coffee in the thermos. Extra ketchup. Keep the change."

"Sure! Back in 30." Frank pocketed the bills and exited out the back of the van. Wes was already coming up behind Kim, pretending to look out the van window. Kim moved her butt back into him as he touched her shoulders then slipped his hands around her breasts. The nipples were hard.

"We shouldn't be doing this," she murmured, but Wes didn't seem to hear her as he pulled up her blouse. She was still packing so he removed her glock from her belt.

Pressing his face against her cheek, he started planting slow tiny multiple kisses on her neck. As he let his tongue take over he felt her body tighten; her breathing grew heavier. Reaching beneath her skimpy skirt, he pulled down her panties.

She pressed against him, stroking his leg. "So... Agent Charles?"

"Kim, I've wanted you from the first day I saw you."

"But you need to know," she retorted, her arms around his neck, nibbling his ear, "this cannot be a one shot deal. I am very attracted to you."

"And it's mutual, in case *you* want to know." His hand moved over her thighs, stroking, caressing... "but I can't make any commitments. Do you want to stop?"

As he removed her panties, she kissed him hard, and then pulled away. "One time and one time only and if you won't make a commitment don't ever touch me again or I promise, I'll blow your fucking head off."

"Music to my ears, darlin," he murmured. "Kiss me again and don't stop. What ever you do... *don't...stop!*" She backed her butt hard against him, feeling his thrusting manliness. He gave her short breaths on her neck, followed by brief kisses and let his tongue glide on her earlobe.

She reached back, pulling his head down, giving him the hardest wet kisses as she moaned for more. She spread both of her legs to give him immediate access. He pressed into the small of her back and entered her slowly. A sweet, but intense mutual explosion occurred as they both enjoyed the pleasure of each other. If this was the only time and the last time, they made the most of it.

When Frank returned with two large McDonald's bags and started unwrapping the goods, even the meaty smell of hot hamburgers couldn't camouflage the unmistakable odor. Frank looked around the van, smelled under his armpits and glared at the two who were hastily reassembling themselves as they eyed him with sheepish intensity. "Goddamn," he muttered. "Smells like a Ho house in here."

"I think we parked the van over a sewer hole," said Wes, fastening his belt buckle.

"Yeah, right," muttered Frank, opening the bag and distributing the goodies. *It shoulda been me,* he mourned to himself.

3
Loose Ends

Wes knew the job came first and so did Kim. Or maybe there was another reason why Wes deliberately avoided contact with Kim whenever possible. Her last words before both of them took off for Nirvana still rang in his ears. He had visions of Kim parading around the office with his head on a stick, the way it was still done in more primitive areas of the world. This woman meant business. She was mean on the streets and had a reputation for getting the job done quick and easy like bathroom cleanser. Down the drain, into the clink.

In an office as tight as the counterfeit squad and with Kim and Wes the two top agents for making cases, at a certain point the rubber had to meet the road, no puns intended. Exactly because Kim *was* such a good agent, she'd ended up with Wes in Dallas in '81 on the FLESO case with Marc Green, Mitch Gordon, Shane Burke—and Wendy Weisman.

Wendy. Agent Weisman from the DEA, New York City, a stunning redhead with satiny skin, adorable freckles and the kind of personality that left no room for compromise. Either you disliked it with a passion or adored it with a passion. Wes was smitten from the moment she'd sashayed into his life that day in Dallas in her svelte black suit and six-inch heels. Her looks, laugh and devil-may-care attitude, whether making a case or eating a whole apple pie in one sitting was the kind of femme fatale that meant danger for anyone like Wes who thrived on it. No emotional baggage, no fake airs, no whimpering or whining... and she was also an agent. She understood that the agent's lifestyle was one of necessity, not choice.

There she stood by the side of the sedan where only two seconds before, she had been sitting next to him. Then before he knew what was happening, the tan vehicle leaped forward, banged into the car door and Wendy was tossed up in the air and down into his lap and she was dying...

What good was winning a case when you lost one of the best agents in the business... when you lost the woman of your life, *of your future*?

Agent Kim Taylor was there... but he didn't care. All he could think about was Wendy. Yet if it hadn't been for Kim, he may never have known how much Wendy loved him. It was Agent Kim Taylor who had made it happen, Agent Taylor who'd given both Wendy and Wes a heads up about the way they felt about each other. Then graciously, selflessly, she stepped out of the way.

After all these years the sadness was still there like an emotional scar whose tissue had eventually grown over the pain of loss and regret. Yet strangely enough, Kim had cloned into Wendy. No person is replaceable, yet the two women had many of the same qualities: bright, quick, clever and intelligent—and both were babes.

In the short time they'd worked together on the Dallas case, taking down Kevin Riley & Co., Kim and Wendy had become comrades, sharing the same love for adventure and love for Wes. In retrospect, Wes wasn't so sure Wendy would have been as generous as Kim. Even when she ordered a whole pie, it was hers. No one got even a snitch. (Did her gorgeous figure suffer? Never.)

Maybe it was an ethnic or environmental thing. Jewish by birth, Wendy was an only child; her father was an attorney and her mother, the daughter of an industrialist who spent most of her time running charity balls. Wendy had never known what it was like to wear hand-me-downs or live on food stamps.

Kim, on the other hand, was the youngest of four siblings. Her father had flown the coop when she was an infant and her mother cleaned houses to pay the bills. Kim had grown up in the slums of Newark, New Jersey, one of the armpits of the Northeast. From childhood she'd learned how to defend herself against guns, knives and open zippers.

Even so, Wendy had rejected the silver platter/country club lifestyle and dozens of marital offers—*shidduchs,* Wes learned they were called in Yiddish. She'd nurtured her chutzpah, which was part of her charm, and never hesitated to ask for what she wanted. Because of her background and sense of entitlement and simply because she asked, she believed it rightfully belonged to her and her alone.

Instead of returning directly to Chicago after FLESO, Wes booked a flight to LaGuardia to attend Wendy's funeral. According to Jewish custom, it would take place directly after the body arrived in New York and was prepared for burial.

As soon as he checked into the hotel he called the Weismans, who sent a taxi to bring him to their Lower East Side condominium on Orchard Street.

Suzanne and Abe Weisman greeted him with warm hugs. Apparently Wendy had spared them no details about the future man in her life. In a matter of minutes, Wes felt as close to them as if they were his own parents.

Suzanne Weisman was an older replica of her daughter, both in appearance and personality. "I know why Wendy fell in love with you," she was quick to tell Wes. "I would have fallen in love with you, too, if I were her age."

"I would have fallen in love with you, too, Wes, but you've got the wrong parts," quipped Abe, a tall, clean-shaven athletic-looking man with a Brooklyn accent. It was evident that Abe wore his heart on his sleeve. His eyes were red and swollen from crying.

The five-bedroom tenth floor condominium was appointed with expensive avant garde custom-designed furniture and accessories. The walls were covered with modern art and in the living room and den were glass cases filled with ancient pottery, fragments of manuscripts and Middle Eastern sculptures. The Weismans were prominent Zionists.

Wendy had attended Brearly School and Swarthmore, graduating with honors and joining the DEA after graduation. She'd told Wes shortly after meeting him that all her life she'd always wanted to be a law enforcement officer.

"A strange wish," Suzanne shrugged now as Wes mentioned it," but we never stood in Wendy's way."

"As if we could," added Abe, smiling sadly. "She did have a mind of her own."

Abe broke down and cried when Wes started to talk about Wendy's excellent skills and how lucky they'd felt to have her as part of their FLESO team in Dallas.

The Reform Jewish funeral would be held at Temple Emanu-El on East 65th Street, where the family had been long-time members. Wes wasn't surprised to find a large ethnic mix of people attending, including several Afro-Americans and Africans, Europeans, Asians, Indians, and Hispanics.

Suzanne and Abe had asked Wes to speak, but he declined. They understood. By the time they reached the end of the ceremony and the cantor sang the 23rd Psalm while the casket was wheeled out of the sanctuary, Wes was eager for the whole event to be over. It was too much for him. He'd always loved the 23rd Psalm. It was his mother, Grace's favorite. Now, to hear it sung at Wendy's funeral...

As the coffin was lowered into the ground, the rabbi repeated so aptly from Psalm 91: ... *"Thou shalt not be afraid for the terror by night; or for the arrow that flieth by day..."* Wes touched the black ribbon pinned to his lapel, identifying members of the family.

Ironically, in the midst of his sorrow and throughout the day, he thought about Kim. He had no reason to do so, except that he knew she, too, was mourning Wendy's death. Somehow he felt Kim belonged here with him. Was she not an integral part of this?

Wes had stayed on to sit *shiva* (mourning) for the first of the three days when friends and family visited Suzanne and Abe. Even though Wes proudly wore his black ribbon, the Weismans had a tacit agreement to introduce him as a close friend who represented the law enforcement agency where Wendy's services had recently been contracted. That was enough of an explanation. Few would have known or cared whether she'd worked for the DEA or USSS, but they would have made it their business to learn about his religion if they knew an intimate relationship was involved.

In fact, many of the Weismans' friends would have been shocked to learn that Wendy had been planning to marry a Christian. A black Jew would have more or less passed the test, especially since Israel was now populated with many Black Ethiopian Jews as well as Middle-Eastern Jews of color. That she had been planning to marry a *goy* (non-Jew) was a totally different story. Amazing pretzel logic, thought Wes, smiling sadly.

Upon returning to Chicago, Wes was immediately assigned to protection detail and was away from the office for several weeks. After he returned, Kim made a point of keeping her distance. When the two met during staff meetings, they acknowledged each other more as sister and brother: two colleagues who had gone through an unforgettable experience together that had left its indelible mark on each of them.

And then it happened.

In law enforcement or any type of detective or intelligence work, the name of the game was to discover a person's price. In this particular case, the counterfeiter, Calvin Tacit, had a fetish for black females. Working out of Chicago, Tacit had part ownership in a number of casinos and resort hotels in the Middle East, Europe and Asia. The safe where he kept his reserve supply was in his home office, a massive English Tudor estate in Evanston, Illinois on Lake Michigan near the Northwestern University campus. It was guarded by two Rottweilers, a cadre of servants and an elaborate alarm system.

Tacit would do his pickups at the college library, student union or one of the coffee shops where students gathered with their laptops to take advantage of wifi.

Effortlessly, Kim slipped into position with a student ID and everything on campus she would be familiar with as a graduate student in anthropology. As soon as they'd isolated some of the places where Tacit was most likely to show up, she was there. The first meeting was innocent, a dinner date.

The second meeting was an invitation to Tacit's estate. Once inside, Kim had done videos and stills of the interior that were immediately transmitted to the rest of the squad, and obediently followed Tacit to the bedroom where he unbuttoned her blouse and proceeded to slowly and sensuously move his lips over her breasts.

As soon as they landed on her right nipple, he passed out. Kim had smeared both of her nipples with a highly toxic chemical.

Wes, Shane and Marc were waiting in a van outside the gate. Shutting down the remote that alerted security, the dogs and servants, Kim signaled "all's clear" to the team and unlocked the gates. She also emptied the revolvers underneath the bed and dresser.

By the time Tacit came to, a naked Kim was seated next to him on the floor. "What happened?" she asked him. "Am I too much for you?"

Tacit was furious. Lunging for her, she ducked, whirled around and let him come at her once again.

"I'm going to kill you!" Tacit screamed, his fetish getting the best of him as Kim spread her legs and let out a belly laugh.

Reaching underneath the dresser, Tacit pulled out a revolver and aimed it at her.

Bang! Behind him a gun went off.

"A beautiful piece of work, Wes!" Kim reached for her clothes.

"Yes," said Wes, admiring her plump, well-formed breasts before bending over Tacit to cuff him.

They worked together like a well-oiled machine, Wes told her later. "Like KY-Jelly maybe?" Kim hooted.

"I was thinking more along the lines of WD-4," retorted Wes.

After that incident they grooved in, went out to lunch together, laughed, tossed off some drinks and went dancing...

"This isn't just sex or soul food, is it, Wes?" murmured Kim into his ear. "I mean, I want you to know, just like I'm not the one night stand type, I also don't do rebounds."

"I've never been a rebounder, either," Wes was quick to reply. "When I'm on the court, I own it. And when I go for a basket, it's a hoop the first time. But we've got a problem, Kim. Remember your threat?"

Kim pulled away from him, her eyes filled with mirth. "I can't believe I ever said that to you, Wes. Are you sure?!!"

"Oh, I am very sure," declared Wes, holding her closer. "As sure as the fact that I'm well aware I may not be here tomorrow if I should so much as dare tell you I love you and I want to spend the rest of my life with you."

The dance ended and they started back to their table. "Wes, whatever I said I take back... and I fucking mean that." Kim turned to face him. "Neither of us will ever forget Wendy, but I can live with her memory if you can."

A warm wave of love and gratitude swept over him. He hadn't expected a speech like that. He pulled her close, kissing her tenderly. "Somehow, Kim, as selfish as Wendy was about apple pie, I think I can almost feel her generosity blooming as she grins at the two of us and says, "Go for it, you two! Chalk it up to fate. I love you both!"

"Wes," Kim whispered, looking up at him later that night, "do you remember the expression on Frank's face when he came back from McDonald's with the hamburgers and opened the door of the van and got a whiff of us?!"

They both laughed heartily.

The Lord is my shepherd, I shall not want. He leadeth me beside the still waters... he restoreth my soul...

Wes finished off the rest of the bread in the basket, closed his eyes and smiled contentedly. "Life is good, m'love. Are you ready for at least another fifty years together?"

"Starting with tonight's meeting, Agent Charles?"

Wes's smile turned to a frown. Leave it to Kim to be already onto the next course. God, she was good. That's why he loved her so much.

"Besides the forgery squad, is The Boss going to be there too?" asked Kim.

The Boss was Special Agent in Charge (SAIC) Larkin Fuller. He was also affectionately known as The Brush, an intentional non-sequitor, since he shaved his head daily and was the furthest thing from a door-to-door broom salesman or *any* kind of salesman. A nasty-ass sonofabitch with no sense of humor or social graces, Fuller was genuinely despised by most of the agents. He'd risen through the ranks solely because of his political connections. Everyone knew he should have been canned long ago for his overt bigotry that had ample opportunity to air itself, thanks to Agents Wes Charles and Kim Taylor. Taylor had not one but two strikes against her: she was also a female.

Every six months, The Brush redecorated his office with a different theme. Last December it was Hawaii, with travel posters and fake flora and fauna: nerium oleanders, orchids, lilies, heliconias, jasmine, etc.

Since The Brush had never been married, there were rumors of his sexual preferences. Only rumors, no proof. "Any day now," was one of the office taglines that tripped off the tongues of every agent after another mano-mano meeting with The Brush about forgetting to turn off the lights in the men's room, or twist the window blinds to the right instead of the left.

The waiter arrived with their coffee as the pianist rippled his fingers over the keyboard and launched into a medley of popular songs. When he came to "My Way," Kim fastened her eyes on Wes, placed both palms flat on the table and leaned forward. "You know what, Wes?"

"What, m'love?"

"I have the hots for you right now and I can't wait another minute. I think it must be the champagne or maybe it's just you."

"But aren't we too old for this, darlin'?" Wes dropped his napkin on the carpet, bent down to retrieve it and reached under the table.

"Logistically," said Kim, moving his hand higher on her leg and shifting in her chair, "as soon as we finish our Godiva Hazelnut Crème coffee, if we head immediately for home we have just enough time for a quickie before we're due at the office."

"Fuck the coffee." Wes motioned to the waiter to bring him the check.

Kim tucked her arm in Wes's as the two circled the outside ring of tables, avoiding Mr. Ex-Priest and his boyfriend. With their usual finesse, they slipped out of the restaurant unnoticed.

The secret to being invisible, Wes Charles was fond of saying is, "just pull in your aura." Since the rest of the agents except Kim had no idea what the hell he meant by such New Age psycho-babble and Wes had no intention of sharing, the comment usually got tossed into the ethers.

There was more truth to the statement than Agent Len Eastwood, one of Wes and Kim's colleagues on the squad, cared to admit. In fact, it "scared the living shit out of him" when he learned by accident from one of his cousins who was part of a military remote viewing unit, that invisibility was one of the more common guerilla warfare tactics that our Asian brothers and sisters had been practicing for centuries. Eastwood was so left-brained he had no place to put this information.

They didn't make it home after all. Their SUV was roomy in back and it was too much fun taking off each item and draping it over the front seat as they sank into orgasmic oblivion, enjoying the same recklessness and abandon that had first put an edge on their relationship that night in the surveillance van.

They did make that case and got credit for it. So did Frank.

4

'Don't Mess With Wes'

February 14, 2010 – USSS Headquarters – Chicago, Illinois

The All Night Meeting turned out to be a surprise anniversary party for Kim and Wes, with the entire office personnel of agents and staff attending. The party planners, headed by W-2, included the five other agents from the counterfeit squad: 5'4" Shane Burke, "Wonderman Elf," with brown curly hair, thick glasses and gnome-like features; 250-pound computer geek "FIM" Foot-in-Mouth Marc Green; slim, tidy, reticent Len "Sherlock" Eastwood; "Comrade" Kevin Gerr or "Babyface Gerr," who resembled a graying Pillsbury doughboy; and Romeo "Rombo" Bonemo, a huge hulking meaty-faced guy with fists and a swing who resembled the Mongo character in *Blazing Saddles*.

The crew had outdone themselves, and for good reason. Wes Charles was the star of their operation and everyone knew it. Highly respected by his peers, hands down, in every undercover case, Wes was the man.

Quick, sharp and slick, whenever an agent got in a tough situation, needed help or just wanted someone to talk to about law enforcement, their first action was to "call Wes." If they needed backup, "call Wes." If a door had to be kicked in, Wes would be the first through the door. If a rogue needed to be grilled for a confession, the script was: "Let Wes have a few minutes with him."

Predictably some of the other agents were jealous, but they knew better than to "mess with Wes." Besides, he was so likeable, how could they hold anything against him? With a great sense of humor and penchant for playing practical jokes, it wasn't long before Wesley Charles became a legend both in and out of the office.

After his first marriage had gone sour, Wes didn't have to search for replacements. The female clerical staff adored him. What was there not to like about this strong, tough, good-looking dude? Printed in invisible ink across their ample chests was a "Choose Me" banner that Agent Charles had no difficulty reading. What a Garden of Earthly Delights he was dwelling in, he would marvel, grinning to himself as the bevy of goddess-es fought to take *dick*-tation from him and follow *UP* on his instructions.

Wes played them all like a mellow French horn. His stories always in-ferred something sexual or had a sexual connotation. The goddesses ate it up, always wanting to be the first to hear the latest.

One of the secretaries named Cynthia, a perky brunette with dimples and a pug nose, happened to be exceptionally well-endowed.

She was a cute thing, thought Wes. No taller than 5'2" with well-designed curves, her derrière wiggled invitingly when she tripped around the office in her strappy stilettos. The main attraction, however, was in front: boobs to die for, effectively displayed through low-cut blouses and tight V-neckline sweaters. Two round, luscious-looking cantaloupes. Two missiles on the landing pad ready to take off.

"Cynthia," said Wes tentatively, chewing on his pen and interrupting his dictation to her, "they couldn't be real."

"Real, sir?" asked Cynthia, gazing at him with her large baby blue eyes. "You mean this information you just dictated? The details of this case? The evidence?"

"No," said Wes, staring hard at the heart-shaped locket nesting in the valley between the two large perfectly shaped mounds exposed almost to the nipples through the opening of her ruffle-trimmed blouse. "I mean those breasts."

"Excuse me, sir?" Cynthia turned scarlet.

"Cynthia, Wes pointed a finger, "they could not possibly be real. They are too large, too round and too perfect."

Cynthia was a very proud young lady. The idea of someone accusing her of having breast implants or plumping up her breasts with anything fake was a gross insult.

"Excuse me," she retorted," but they are *mine* and *all mine!*"

With that, she stood up and clack-clack-clacked out of the office.

Wes buzzed her desk. "Forgive me, Cynthia, I didn't mean to accuse you of something you'd never think of doing. Actually I was just admiring your breasts the way someone admires a famous painting. The way a viewer at an art gallery when looking at a genuine Rembrandt or Picasso says, 'I can't believe it's real!'"

For the next two days Wes deliberately ignored Cynthia or acted over-ly officious and impersonal when she took dictation or did some filing for him. Then, at the appropriate moment while Cynthia was seated in front of him and reviewing her notes, to make sure she understood what he'd just told her she needed to research, Wes exclaimed softly, "Amazing. Just amazing!"

"Sir?" Cynthia looked up.

"I just know I'm right," declared Wes, staring at the front of her open blouse.

This time, without a moment's hesitation, Cynthia stood up, tripped over to the office door which was partially open, closed it firmly and locked it.

Then she clack-clack-clacked over to the desk, positioned herself next to Wes, unbuttoned her blouse and lowered her bra straps. Fully exposed and bobbing up and down in front of him were two large round pink Beauties, each decorated with butterscotch colored nipples that were rapidly growing hard.

"Here! Do you see or feel anything fake about these?" she demanded, placing one of his hands on each breast.

Wes was caught totally off guard. With considerable difficulty he managed to heroically pull himself together so he could take full advantage of this unexpected opportunity.

Gazing into her baby blue eyes, he crooned, "I just want to tell you, Cynthia, I believe you, but I also want you to know that my hands will forever be in love." Then, slowly and tenderly he kissed her on the lips and removed his hands.

At that point, Cynthia was a goner just as Wes knew she would be. With the door locked and the office emptying out for lunch, she was all his if he wanted her.

Closing her eyes, she waited for Wes to proceed.

Nothing. Silence.

She opened her eyes. Wes appeared to be totally absorbed in reading his emails. He started to type a reply to one of them.

Misty-eyed, her fingers shaking, once more Cynthia replaced her treasures in their respective containers and rebuttoned her blouse.

From then on Cynthia's skirts became tighter and shorter. Often her sweaters and blouses were sheer enough for Wes to enjoy prominent nipple display. Every so often during her secretarial duties she would pause and drop a hint that she'd be willing to repeat her previous validation and remove (her clothing) all trace of doubt from Wes's mind—if he happened to be still interested.

Often these comments required additional focus, concentration and self-discipline for Wes to continue with whatever chore he had just assigned to his dick, er his secretary.

Then along came Kim, followed by Wendy. And then Kim again, for a marriage that instead of destroying Wes's playfulness, redirected it. Kim was also worldly enough to celebrate both of Wes's brains.

The anniversary party honored Agent Kim Taylor equally. Her colleagues highly respected her work as well, partly because many of them still couldn't believe she could perform what was traditionally considered "men's work" skillfully and often better.

Now in their mid-fifties, Agents Taylor and Charles made a handsome couple. They'd reached the point in their relationship where one started a sentence and the other finished it. They even had some of the same facial expressions and gestures, which often happen when a couple is good together for a long period of time. Few people would have been able to pull off an intimate relationship like theirs, especially in law enforcement.

The entire office had been decorated with balloons and streamers. The anniversary cake was from Il Giardino del Dolce and the ice cream from iCream Café. Corks popped on bottles of Taittinger Comtes de Champagne Blanc de Blanc 2002.

Included in the gifts were citations from the POTUS and every branch of law enforcement. Even The Brush showed up for ten minutes. Wes and Kim were touched. They knew it had taken a lot of guts for Larkin Fuller to let down his hairlessness to celebrate the wedding anniversary of two slaves whom he probably believed were incapable of experiencing authentic human emotions such as love.

Fuller's racial prejudice even surpassed Agent Kevin Gerr's, which was borderline KKK. Gerr's parents were white supremacists from Memphis, the city where Martin Luther King was assassinated.

Fuller had made peace with the Blacks long ago when it became evident that the U.S. Secret Service could not complete many cases without its devoted cadre of Black undercover agents operating in the ghettos of this country's crime-infested cities. Yet he couldn't help adding: "they created it, so now it's up to them to clean it up."

Before leaving, Fuller remarked as only Fuller could: "Well you two, with all those citations, I guess you've now got something you'll have to live up to."

"I didn't hear that remark," Kim said to Wes later.

"What remark?" Grimacing, Wes pinched his nostrils together and swatted the air to remove the stench.

What a schmuck Larkin Fuller was, thought Kim. No one could even match Wes's record! Over the years, he'd taken down more crooks than most agents anywhere in the U.S.

Wes slipped into bed next to her. "Kim, remember you asked earlier when we were still at the restaurant about the latest information from D.C. and I answered that the operation is a much larger one than we thought?"

"Okay," sighed Kim, rolling over and snuggling close. "Tell me."

"Maybe there really is more to come... and maybe The Brush is right after all," said Wes softly, running his fingers through her hair.

Kim bolted up in bed. "Wes, you're keeping something from me. Sleep is out of the question. My curiosity is aroused, so before anything else gets aroused, out with it!" she commanded.

Wes let out a sigh as she handed him his robe. That's the way it was with the two of them, and why they were so good together, they reminded each other often.

"Do you know what entrapment is?" asked Wes, following her to the kitchen where she was already reaching for two mugs and the coffee grinder.

"Of course. But I don't know of anyone who has ever been accused of entrapment, do you? I mean, isn't it like baiting someone to commit a crime and then calling them on it? Isn't it like if they had no intention of committing the crime—if it was not premeditated—but if an agent sets them up to do it, the agent can end up in prison?"

"More or less."

"Like 'more' rather than 'less'?" Kim tossed him a look over her shoulder. Was this the kind of challenge—possible prison sentence if he failed—that would make the Tony Masella case large enough to match Wes's appetite and ambition?

Apparently. As Wes proceeded to fill her in on his meeting with Benny Portera yesterday, he became more animated, pacing the kitchen, waving his hands—and presenting several scenarios.

"The good part about it is that I don't even have to bait the rod to make the fish bite," Wes finished his story.

"And the bad part?" Kim already knew what he was going to say.

"I have no intention of passing up this chance."

Even if it could cost him his career if things didn't turn out right, thought Kim. Long ago they'd learned that the banks and courts had their own ass-kissing parties going on with Congress, and a group of middlemen serving as patsies when necessary.

And if the Mafia was also involved, anything was possible.

5

Jesse the Jester

May 19, 2009 – Chicago, Illinois

They all had their stories: some of them sweet and heartwarming, others real tear-jerkers and still others that were nothing short of gut-wrenching.

The small stories could be about the mother who couldn't afford new ballet shoes for her gifted 12-year-old daughter who'd grown out of her old ones and who received a call from the dance studio telling her an anonymous donor was providing both shoes and lessons.

Medium-size stories about full scholarships to universities for students who came from some of the worst ghetto areas of the country. Or larger stories, such as the several hundred thousand dollar purchase of a painting rendered by a "starving artist'" and gifted to a major art museum. This was the boost that was needed to launch the artist's career and that allowed her to quit her McDonald's job so she could devote all her time to creating new works.

Then, even larger stories: food, clothing and shelter for AIDS victims who were unable to survive on the government's limited rations, yet were too ill to hold down a job... Money for unwed mothers whose boyfriends had deserted them as soon as they learned they were pregnant... Vocational training programs in nursing, hospice care, pre-school management, restaurant/hotel management for prostitutes...

Anonymous donations were sent to cancer victims, inviting them to try a new and different therapy. "You have nothing to lose and everything to gain," they were told. Those who accepted the money and became committed to the program were shocked to discover the therapies actually worked.

Jobs, free health care, counseling, food, clothing and shelter were all part of Jesse's program. No one got anything free. The price they paid was commitment to better themselves and their condition through awareness: discovering what needed to be changed and then, with the help of

Jesse's Better Day non-profit organization, taking the necessary steps to mend and heal.

Who was the person or group behind all these good deeds? Who was the Good Will Ambassador who had carefully researched the ills of American society and chosen which people were suffering the most and needed the most help?

Even more important: where was all this money coming from? If one had a list of all the individuals and groups that had received funding, the total amount must have been staggering.His name was "Jesse." "Actually, it's short for Jester," he liked to joke.

If they didn't believe him, it didn't really matter, just as Jesse didn't really care if many people associated his name with "Jesse" in the Old Testament—the father of King David, son of Ohed and grandson of Boaz and Ruth—or that the name originally meant "wealthy," or "Jehovah exists."

It was also common knowledge among Christians that Jesus was a direct descendent of King David, with the same bloodline. If Jesse appeared to many as a Messiah, so be it. Jesse could care less. It was the work or the cause that mattered. The country was falling apart. People were suffering. Sick. Starving. They needed help.

Jesse had no illusions about solving the world's problems. He realized he was only one among many, an ant in a colony of millions of other ants. The most he could do, he felt, was to set an example for others. If he could be true to himself and follow his heart, the energy and intention that went out from the core of his being would continue to widen the circles of influence. Others would receive it and because it was powerful, positive and life-affirming, they would embrace it.

It was a law of physics. Nothing saccharine or "Kumbaya" about it.

If some people thought he was a crackpot, so what? Jesse really didn't care. One of his favorite sayings was, "What other people think is none of my business."

"Hel-lo, HEL-LO!!" Jesse would come barreling through the door of an orphanage, foster home or children's hospital ward in his polka dotted balloon pants clown costume, pointed cap with a tassel and start juggling ten pins or rubber balls; or twisting balloons into lions and seals and puppy dogs; or doing magic tricks; putting on marionette shows; dangling a puppet on his knee and doing a ventriloquist routine...

The kids loved him. They'd crawl into his lap or follow him around the room like a Pied Piper... they couldn't wait for his visits! They also knew that Jesse never left without giving them a present. Sometimes it was a gift for each of them and other times it was something for all of them to share, like a giant-size television, painting easels and paints, an aquarium, indoor greenhouse... huge world globe that lit up and talked... or for the yard outside, a sandbox, batting cage, tricycles, bicycles, skateboards...

Soon Jesse developed a number of other costumes and roles besides Jesse the Jester: Peter Pan, The Jolly Green Giant, Uncle Remus, Paul Bunyan, and Mickey Mouse...

All that remained of the former Daniel Hanas had been pushed to the back of his psyche: Right now he had no use for his extraordinary computer skills, genius abilities in math, and advanced training in banking and finance.

If someone were to ask Daniel Hanas how he got started doing good deeds for people, he'd have to tell them that honestly he couldn't remember. Probably he'd come up with something like: "I think I was born wanting to help people."

As a child, he loved to give things away to others. If someone gave him candy and a friend didn't get a piece also, he'd give his candy to them. When he had a bicycle and his school friend's parents couldn't afford one, he gave his own bicycle to them. This often caused embarrassment for his parents. Marya and Emil Hanas had to retrieve Danny's giveaways and apologize to the family, telling them it was just Danny's habit to want to share things.

Danny was the middle child, the only boy. The Haneses lived in Akron, Ohio where Emil Hanas was a foreman at a tire factory and Marya Hanas was an elementary school teacher. Danny's maternal and paternal grandparents were originally from Hungary and since Hungarian, German and French were spoken at home, at an early age, Danny was multi-lingual.

Danny was a small, undersize child with pale skin, blue eyes and coal black hair. "A runt," his classmates would say. Yet for some reason, bullies left him alone. Maybe it was because there was nothing wimpy or whiney about him. Fear was often the red flag that incited bullies to attack, yet instinctively they knew Danny wasn't afraid of them.

Maybe it was even simpler than Danny's apparent fearlessness. Maybe they realized he wouldn't be able to produce the victory they needed for their next performance. This silent understanding continued through his growing years to adulthood. Rarely was he accosted or put down by his peers. Apparently they also realized he had nothing to offer them except friendship and good will.

He was everyone's friend: gentle, kind, and very smart. He was especially good in math and won several math awards during his elementary school years. Predictably he was also a computer geek.

Upon graduating from high school in 1979, Danny won a full scholarship to McGill University in Montreal. One of his roommates, a wealthy boy from New York whose father was on Wall Street, introduced him to a group of men who were interested in Danny's skills. After graduating cum laude, he was offered a management position in one of the major investment banks.

What a stellar career for any young man! By the mid-'90s, Danny was wealthy, successful and married to Rhonda Kellerman, a Harvard Law graduate. Soon they had two children, Maya and Max, both bright and gifted. It was a dream life, a dream career—or at least for the first 46 years of Danny's life. Then, a change started to occur. It was subtle at first... so subtle, only Danny himself would have been aware of it.

Often changes do not have to be triggered by illness, a natural disaster or personal tragedy. Nor do they have to be related to what is often referred to as "midlife crises."

Danny's situation was more complex. Throughout the entire process of growing up, Danny was present—yet after the school years were over and he was already well into his adult life, he was at a loss to know exactly what had taken place.

It was as if his life had been on auto-pilot, like he had been positioned on a conveyor belt that had taken him from one predictable point to the next. All he had to do was perform, and since he knew he could easily do what was expected of him and felt no compunction to do otherwise, he kept traveling on to the next "station" and the next, and the next...

This perception of himself and his life had never occurred to him until May 15, 2009 on his forty-seventh birthday. It was as if an alarm clock went off inside that caused a sleeping part of him to open his eyes, stretch his limbs and start waking up.

By nature, Danny was a curious person, a collector of information. His bank position was highly demanding, but after awhile it had become routine and somewhat boring. In the evenings and on weekends he loved to browse on the Internet and watch videos on ancient history, early civilizations and miscellaneous phenomena that were often considered "conspiracy," "propaganda," or just "junk" by most people.

Danny was too intelligent to believe everything he viewed and read. He soon learned that everyone had different theories and different source information, with more than enough proof for anything that needed to be verified. This was the part that was confusing. Clearly, it was possible to manufacture any "truth," if truths were relative and not an absolute, as Plato, the great Greek philosopher had taught... yet *how could that be?*

Ultimately he concluded that the more he learned, the more he realized he didn't know. It was much easier to ignore the past, enjoy the present and not worry about the future. Some people were even bold enough to say the present is all there is... and maybe that's where all the trouble for Danny started.

Like the drivers of the tourist buggies in Central Park who placed blinders over their horses so they could keep the buggy moving on the narrow path around the park, Danny suddenly realized the drivers of his life—parents, church, school, corporate executives, government, etc.— had placed blinders over his eyes to keep him on the straight and narrow path called Life. For the most part it was not a conscious act. They didn't know what they were doing because *they already had blinders over their own eyes.* The blinders were like a computer software program that was running them.

On May 15, 2009, Danny tore off the blinders. What he saw was so shocking and traumatic; one could only compare it to the experience of a veteran coming home from a war during which he'd served as a killing machine in strategic attacks against "the enemy"—in the process, possibly witnessing the death of some of his buddies. Once he was back in the U.S., reality hit. No one seemed to care *what* he'd done or what kind of a hero he was.

In fact, to the amazement, anger and dismay of most vets, except for a few faithful friends or relatives, most Americans didn't even care if they lived or died. When these war heroes returned, their job was gone and often their wife (husbands) or girlfriends (boyfriends) had walked out on them. Often these vets returned with bullet wounds, lost limbs, chronic diseases, and serious repercussions from exposure to hazardous chemicals. All this in addition to the stress and emotional trauma from the devastation they'd wreaked or witnessed first-hand.

Wherever Danny Hanas went he saw people in need. And when he poked beneath the surface of his current lifestyle, he saw graft, corruption, and deliberate manipulation of the system for the benefit of the "haves" at the expense of the "have nots." The information he'd been reading on the Internet was not "all conspiracy." Highly respected journalists and reporters with sterling reputations were sacrificing their lives to blow the whistle or tell the truth. In the process many were "suicided" or simply went missing.

The picture was far different from the one that had been painted for him when he'd been trotting along like an obedient peon, albeit a wealthy one, on that narrow, carefully manicured path that had been set out for him.

Although he'd been dimly aware of the direction in which the country was headed, he'd never given it much thought until now. For the first time Danny understood the game of war or "the war industry." He also understood the game of banking and finance from the other side of the tracks. He heard people using the expression "too big to fail" and laughed it off. Why should they fail? What were they doing wrong?

By 2008 the housing, credit card, student loan and derivatives bubbles had ballooned out of proportion and predictably they collapsed. The Federal Reserve kept the interest rates at zero, making it easier to get loans, as they continued to print more money. Consumers could be counted on to feed their spending frenzy. The success quotient of the American Dream was equated with acquisition: houses, cars, boats, clothes, shoes, gadgets, etc., etc. The addiction of buying one's happiness with yet another credit card or loan was totally out of control. When it came time to paying the monthly bills, often even minimum payments weren't possible... especially with a whole stack of credit cards that needed to be fed.

Danny now realized that as a bank executive he was not part of the solution but part of the problem. The banks and corporations—often the same entities—were in control of everything. It was an octopus. The game was to create the problem—the war, lack, pollution, disease—and then come to the rescue to fix things. The solution usually required contracting the same agencies responsible for the problem to come in and do the cleanups work. Solve one problem to create another.

He found himself clamming up at the office or at informal gatherings. He was savvy enough to know he was the odd man out, but he soon found it uncomfortable to be around people who were, in his opinion, only "sheep" who were catering to a system that was greedy, corrupt and self-serving.

Danny had always been candid and outspoken. Now he realized he couldn't exist in a fishbowl. It was a Catch-22. The water was never changed. The fish were feeding on their own excrement.

His wife, Rhonda, held the same views as his colleagues. Why shouldn't she? She was also a product of the system. The daughter of a wealthy corporate executive, Rhonda Kellerman had known nothing but privilege. Danny loved her for her brilliance and enthusiasm. An attractive 5' 11" brunette with high energy, an athletic body and intense brown eyes, she was a Type A female who knew what she wanted and usually got it.

At social functions, Rhonda was a pro at working the room. She was also an expert at planning and giving parties; she always said the right things to the right people. Her client base consisted of the wealthiest and most influential; her legal documents were impeccable and she won 95% of her cases.

Danny also loved her for her sex drive. Rhonda wasn't a "not tonight, darling" type of woman. On the contrary, she enjoyed taking charge of their intimacy. Candles, incense, costumes and props... she was exciting and fun.

None of these parts of their relationship bothered Danny. It was something more than that, and much deeper. He realized for the first time that they were strangers when it came to basic beliefs. Did he really know her?

Did he really know himself?

For example, he didn't like the way Rhonda put down people who were poor and struggling... or how she turned away clients who couldn't pay her high fees... or how she chastised the homeless who sat on the sidewalks with baskets or cups or stood at expressway exits baking in the sun as they feebly held up their cardboard signs.

"Why don't they get a job and stop asking for handouts?" She'd shake her head, her mouth curving into a frown. Or: "Why doesn't the city get rid of these pests?" Her lack of compassion hit the awakened Danny like punches in the gut. Had she really said that... *and did she really mean it?* Of course she did!

Were they selective about their friends?

Yes, they were.

Was the Country Club they belonged to considered exclusive with restricted membership?

Yes, it was.

Were they, in fact, part of the "1%"—the Elites who were despised by the 99% or the middle and lower classes?

Absolutely yes. They had it all: expensive cars and homes—one in Highland Park, Illinois and a second one in Palm Springs, California—tax shelters (offshore bank accounts and investments in the right places)... Hammacher-Schlemmer, Tiffany, Prada, Gucci, Armani, Givency, de la Renta...

The more Danny saw, read and researched, the worse he felt, physically, mentally and emotionally. He started to lose weight; his skin turned even paler than normal and most of the time he felt weak and lethargic. No one knew what was wrong with him. After visits to several specialists and countless batteries of tests, Danny was smart enough to realize that only he had the answer to what was going on.

He cancelled the next round of medical musical chairs and decided to take a leave of absence from work so he could go away somewhere by himself.

When he broke the news to Rhonda, she was openly relieved. "Choose your place, honey, and stay as long as you need to. No one has to know where you are. The main thing is that you have a chance to get your health back."

When she pronounced the word "health," there was a quiver in her voice because, like Danny, she had no idea what she was talking about. All she wanted was resolution: removal of the dark cloud that had settled over their formerly blissful life. For three months already their sex life had been non-existent. Family fun times had disappeared. Rhonda was tired of making excuses to the children, who were old enough to know something was wrong.

What Rhonda didn't tell Danny before he left was that she loved him. Nor did she suggest any type of relationship therapy for the two of them in lieu of Danny leaving, because as far as she was concerned, the problems were Danny's, not hers.

Something was going on with him; it wasn't another woman and it wasn't burnout. Nothing that simple.

She didn't like the Internet websites and blogs he read, or the comments he'd been making more recently about "Austrian economics" and someone named Ludwig von Mises and the Mises Institute... about the "real story behind such and such "or "the truth that was being covered up by so and so." And then he talked about the "fear mongers," "Illuminati," "Bilderbergers," "Committee of 300," "underground concentration camps," and—horror of horrors—the *Nazi's*—who, Danny said, *still existed in this country. Nazi's!*

Rhonda abhorred loose ends. It was a good thing the country had decided to spread Democracy throughout the world. After all, it was the only form of government that worked. Developing nations had a great deal to learn from America.

She was extremely glad all the wars the U.S. was involved in were far away, and the Viet Nam war was over. If the country ever had another military conscription, she'd find a way for their son Max to be exempt. Although it was important for the U.S. to have a global presence and defend Democracy whenever necessary, defense was a job for other people's children, not theirs. There was plenty to do right here to hold down the fort against Terrorists.

It would be good for Danny to go away. Then when he returned, things would get back to normal.

Three months later when Danny called her from London Heathrow and told he was due to land at O'Hare that evening, Rhonda scuttled the children to friends' houses for overnights, brought out her Agent Provocateur lingerie, scented candles and had the cook prepare one of Danny's favorite dinners.

At 6PM the man who walked through the door looked like Danny—a tanned, healthy and relaxed version—but after only five minutes of conversation with him, Rhonda realized he was a total stranger.

"I'm sure Alan and the rest of the staff will be eager to see you," she chattered nervously, after Danny was finished asking about how she was, catching up on the news about Maya and Max, yet not responding to her with more than short "yeses" and 'no's."

"I won't be working there anymore," said Danny as calmly as if he were telling her he was switching toothpaste brands.

Rhonda blinked, crossed and uncrossed her legs, ran a hand through her hair and finally lost it. "What do you mean, *you won't be working there anymore*, Danny?" she rasped, her eyes flashing. "Isn't this something you and I should talk over first? How can you make a decision like that all by yourself?"

Danny wondered if he heard her correctly. "Rhoda," he said evenly, "do you feel you would need to consult me if you decided to leave Shaeffer & Bloom law firm?"

"No of course not. But it's not the same."

"Oh and how is it different?" Danny glanced around the living room. They were seated on a new black leather eight-sectional sofa with two recliners. The coffee table, easy chairs, drapes and window dressings were new. When he left, the color scheme was orange, coral, beige and white. Now everything was maroon, gray, yellow and black. "You redecorated," he said.

"Thank you for noticing," said Rhonda. "What makes you think the bank will give you a referral if you resign?"

"I haven't thought about that," said Danny evenly. "What did you do with the old furniture? Actually it wasn't that old."

"I don't know what I did with it," snapped Rhonda, close to tears, "and I don't care. The delivery van took it away when they brought the new pieces. I don't ask questions like that and I never have."

"That's right," said Danny, "you never have. What was wrong with the other furniture?"

Rhonda stood up. "What time would you like dinner?"

"Any time is fine. I'll just get myself unpacked and—"

"Don't bother," shrieked Rhonda, rising to her feet, neck veins bulging. **"Get out! I've had enough!"**

Rhonda strode to the foyer and stood next to his luggage, cheeks flushed, eyes flashing.

"So our relationship depends on my position at the bank? Is that what you're telling me, Rhonda?" Danny tried to put his arms around her.

She shrugged him off. "Is that so terrible? At least it's honest."

Yes, it was honest all right. Sucking in his breath, he picked up his luggage, strode through the kitchen to the garage entrance and piled it into his Mercedes. Without saying another word, he opened the garage door, backed out and drove off.

"So where's your beard, your Birkenstocks and your backpack?" joked Alan Brockmeyer, the bank president, when Danny appeared the next day, trim and debonair in a navy silk suit and paisley tie. Looking infinitely better, Brockmeyer had to admit. Whatever Danny had acquired during his furlough, he wanted some of it.

"I've got some tofu and a wok in my bike basket," returned Danny good-naturedly. That got the laugh he'd expected.

"So you're ready to return to work? I have to admit, some people are dispensable. You are not, Danny. We missed you."

Brockmeyer waited for a mutual response from Danny, that he'd missed the bank, his colleagues, etc.—or at least a humorous rebuttal about being too busy drinking coconut juice from a gourd, entertaining all the native women, etc., etc.

Instead, Danny said, "Alan, I have to congratulate you. You run a tight ship."

"Why thank you, Danny!" beamed Brockmeyer. Now in his late fifties, Brockmeyer was a 6'5" well-preserved former Big Ten football linebacker in college who still had a full head of silver-gray hair and chiseled features that were none the worse for wear. He was at his best when he beamed. In fact, of the dozen or so expressions he wore for various appearances, beaming was one of his specialties.

Seconds later, Brockmeyer's hazel-colored eyes narrowed as he rubbed a hand over his chin, trying to assess where Danny was at or what he was up to. *Trust no one who delivers unsolicited compliments.* Brockmeyer was also a good blocker and excellent tackler.

"I haven't received a better offer anywhere else, and I could never match the offer I've had here," continued Danny.

"Had? Past tense?" He'd missed the play. The ball sailed past him. "How much do you need, Hanas? If you want a raise, or a bonus or better benefit package... for God's sake, let me know!"

"None of the above," said Danny smoothly.

"So, what—?"

A glimmer of apprehension bordering on fear now entered Brockmeyer's eyes. He sucked in his breath. The expression on the bank president's face took Danny back to his grade school playground days and the bullies who used to gang up on the pale skinny kid, hovering over him as they tried to figure out how to intimidate him.

"I'm working on some software patents," said Danny, "and if I want to bring them to market, it's going to have to be a full-time effort."

"Ahhh, I see!" smiled Brockmeyer, relieved. The lines on his face changed to his Sunday dinner "Pass the rolls, will you, dear?" expression.

"I've learned a great deal while I've been away," Danny couldn't resist inserting the knife just a little to the left of the jugular vein.

"I'm sure you have!" Brockmeyer fidgeted with his letter opener. "Well, I wish you the best, and if there's anything we can do to help besides er, offering you our severance package, which I'm sure, you'll find more than generous..."

Brockmeyer was scared all right, thought Danny. They were all scared. Just like any bully, the "too big to fail" slogan may look good to the public and be catchy enough to satisfy the media, but the actors in this tragic drama were already seeing the handwriting on the wall.

Danny had enough information on the bank and on Brockmeyer to have them shut down in a heartbeat—if he chose to blow the whistle on them. Yet why bother? Why implicate himself and endanger his life when they would implode on their own? It might take a little longer, but it was bound to happen. Anyway, he already knew if he made a move he might end up with a rope around his neck and his feet dangling over the Grand Avenue or LaSalle Street Bridge.

Why take risks when he didn't have to? It reminded him of one of his favorite childhood stories about the three little pigs. The first pig built a house of straw. The big bad wolf huffed and he puffed... and he blew the house down, eating the first pig.

The second pig built a house of sticks. The wolf huffed and puffed and blew the house down, eating the second pig.

The third pig built a house of brick. When the wolf came flying down the chimney, the pig captured him in a cauldron of boiling water. Brockmeyer was a tough old bird. Danny had no desire to cook him for dinner.

Predictably, Rhonda filed for a divorce. College expenses through graduate school for both children were already taken care of in offshore bank accounts. Danny contested nothing and they parted amicably. As far as Rhonda was concerned, he was a misfit in her past, so good riddance. Onward and upward. As an attorney she was making a six-digit income, sufficient to live in style. Anyway, she was still young enough to find someone else.

Danny moved into an apartment near the University of Chicago and changed his name to Jesse Jay.

Although Rhonda didn't know it, Maya and Max stayed in touch with him. Daily he wrote loving emails to each of them. He didn't care if they shared these emails with their mother, but apparently they chose not to. In every email they wrote back they told him how much they loved him too.

6
Merry Christmas!

July 15, 2009 – All Saints St. Anthony Church - Chicago, Illinois

Jesse's list of charities continued to grow. Soon he found himself in an uncomfortable position. There was so much more he wanted to do, but he was running short of financial resources. Even though he was a good fundraiser and had managed to bring in substantial amounts of money to Better Day, his non-profit foundation, it was never enough.

One summer afternoon while Jesse was playing "Santa Claus in July" to underprivileged children at All Saints St. Anthony church on Chicago's South Side, he noticed the church's program director seated at the back of the room.

After the program was finished, the tall blond, athletic looking man came over to Jesse and extended his hand, smiling graciously. "Mr. Jay, I'm Father Ira. I want to thank you so much for this wonderful visit!"

"My pleasure, Father Ira," said Jesse. "I love the kids! I wish I could do even more."

"Do you mind my asking how you raise your money?" asked Father Ira.

"It's all by private donation. People see what I do and they give me money. I've never approached any corporations, but it may be my next step."

"Do you have a minute?" asked the priest.

"Yes, of course."

Father Ira motioned for Jesse to follow him to his office, waving a hand toward the two easy chairs in front of a natural stone fireplace. "Make yourself comfortable." He seated himself opposite Jesse.

Jesse glanced around the spacious, tastefully appointed wood-paneled room lined with tall bookcases filled with leather-bound volumes. On the walls were Alex Grey drawings from the Chapel of Sacred Mirrors. Jesse was mildly shocked to see Grey's artwork in the office of a Catholic priest. Few people knew about this amazing work, and even fewer people appreciated it, considering it "psychedelic," "marginal," or just plain "scary."

Beneath the plaque of a "Love is a Cosmic Force" reproduction was an Alex Grey quote: *"God is the divine artist and the universe is the continually evolving masterpiece of human creation."*

"As you know, the Church has always been devoted to humanitarian causes," began Father Ira. "You don't have to look very far to realize this country is going to hell in a hand basket. The economy is in terrible shape and the people are suffering. It's bigger than just the U.S. government. It's the global bankers who are the problem, and in this country they're determined to wipe out the middle class. This is causing havoc and creating an even greater need for welfare programs and people like you, who know how to administer them."

Jesse was amazed that the priest was so outspoken. "Yes, I do know a great deal about the situation," he admitted, "and you're right on the money. Things are bad and getting worse."

"I used to serve as a chaplain at several of the county prisons in the area," continued Father Ira. "In our group sessions often I asked the prisoners what I felt was a thought-provoking question that would cause many of them to look at their lives differently. The question was a simple one. I asked them: 'Why do you think you're here behind bars?'

"I always received the same answer. Every one of them said, 'Because we happened to be the ones who got caught.' It's an international operation. Some call it a 'cabal.' The bankers are criminals." He fastened his clear blue eyes on Jesse. His gaze was kind but penetrating. "I'm guessing that's why you resigned from your position. Yes, I know who you are, Mr. Hanas, and that's all right. I admire your courage. You got out before it was too late. Excuse me if I'm being too candid."

"I admire your candor," Jesse responded without flinching.

"Of course, we're not going to let them get away with it, are we? We're going to fight back." Father Ira sifted a hand through his long blond hair and rubbed his chin thoughtfully. "We have been working with a man who has one of the only successful high yield trading programs. He has special connections with people in Hong Kong and Zurich. He got in touch with me because one of the requirements for use of funds is that 50% of the money made from the trade programs is used for humanitarian purposes. When he locates investors for the trade program, he also looks for humanitarian projects. It occurred to me after watching your wonderful presentation today that he may be able to help you also."

Father Ira's "we" did not slip by Jesse unnoticed. *We're not going to let them get away with it, are we?*

"I've heard of bank trade programs, of course," said Jesse, "but I've never explored them to the point of being able to talk intelligently about them. From what I understand, they're surrounded by a certain amount of secrecy. They're not open to everyone."

"Yes, you're right about the secrecy," smiled Father Ira, "and for a good reason. Too many people have been burned by working with secondary agents and con artists instead of 'going direct' or having a direct contact at the very top. So tell me what you do know about the programs and I'll see if I can fill you in on a few of the details."

"It is my understanding that top world banks are authorized to issue debt instruments like bank purchase orders—BPOs, standby letters of credit—SLCs, or Bank Debenture Instruments—BDIs," said Jesse, feeling his cheeks grow warm.

Actually, he'd heard some scandalous tales about these programs, but since disinformation was rampant these days and one never knew where it was coming from, until now he hadn't really given the matter much thought. "Each bank instrument has a market price that is established at the time the bank issues them. As I understand it, you have to have the right contacts as well as initial cash resources, of course, in order to participate."

"That's right," said Father Ira. "And you're right. You do have to have a strong working relationship with so-called 'insiders.' That's where our man shines—of course, with a little help from us."

"So your 'man' is able to place the investor's money, let's say ten million or a hundred million I believe is needed, on a trade platform. It is secured by a bank guarantee or Certificate of Deposit, usually issued by one of the major banks," said Jesse. "This money is used to buy the instruments at a discount. They are then sold to other banks at higher prices. Sales continue until eventually the instruments are sold to an end buyer. I believe this kind of trading is referred to as 'forfeiting.' The key to successful forfeiting is having that end or 'exit' buyer. The exit buyer pays the final price that is now higher than the original price but still below the face value of the bank instrument. Usually the exit buyer is a trust fund, a foundation, insurance company—some group that is seeking a reasonable yield investment."

"Well, you *do* know a great deal about the programs. Good!" said Father Ira. "We are one of the benefactors of this particular trade program. When a trade closes, or when there's an exit buyer and the trade actually happens, we receive a portion of the payment."

"Surely that must be a significant amount of money, since by that time the trader is dealing in many hundreds of millions—billions!" exclaimed Jessie. "But—forgive my ignorance—the Catholic Church doesn't need money from outside sources, nor does the Vatican need bank trade programs, does it? I thought it was extremely wealthy."

"It may appear that way," sighed Father Ira, "but actually our re-sources can hardly cover what's needed to wipe out poverty, disease, drug and human trafficking... you know the list. And now with what's happening to the U.S. economy, we will need even more money to sup-port the disenfranchised. Then there are the lawsuits. If you've been fol-lowing the news over the past several years, I'm sure you're well aware that the claims are outrageous. They far exceed our budget. Plus, the church is losing parishioners. We just can't afford that kind of loss."

Jessie nodded. Like most Americans, Jesse knew about the Catholic Church's pedophile cases. Condemnations of priests, bishops, even cardi-nals were splattered all over the media. In the United States alone, he re-membered the statistic that over 3,000 civil lawsuits had been filed against the Church. Some of the cases resulted in multi-million dollar set-tlements with many claimants.

As if reading his mind, Father Ira said, "Settlements of sex abuse cases from 1950 to 2007 totaled more than $2 billion, and five dioceses got bankruptcy protection. Several Catholic dioceses have already declared bankruptcy due to sex abuse cases. And this is only the tip of the iceberg."

"So who is this man who has the trade program?" asked Jesse.

"His name is Martin Seligman. All you have to do is make a list of the charities that need funding and send him a brief description of each. Mar-tin has a huge data base of prospective clients, er, contacts. When these wealthy people hear about the good works that are linked to their in-vestments—we send Martin reports of the money we've been given—they feel very good about working with him."

Father Ira leaned forward and placed a hand on Jesse's arm. "The Church provides credibility, and you will, too, when you start to receive money from the program."

"So am I missing something?" asked Jesse. His head was spinning.

"I don't believe so." Father Ira picked a thread from the sleeve of his robe and rolled it into a ball between his fingers. "There are two parts to the program. Number one, the banks use the investment money from Martin's clients—money that doesn't leave the investors' bank but is held in escrow for a year and cannot be touched—as an asset or as collateral. The bank can borrow against that money. The loan is deposited in the Vatican bank accounts, of which there are several here in Chicago. As a former banker, you may be aware that the Vatican Bank is not a 'true' bank. There are no check books. It is more a fund deposit and transfer situation than a bank. And the Vatican itself is a sovereign state, which means that every transaction is international."

The Vatican was a sovereign state and therefore immune to the laws of another country... it was above the law! Once the loan against the investor's principal was placed in the Vatican Bank's checking account, it became money that never had to be paid back. The paperwork disappeared down the rabbit hole.

"The second part of the program involves actual printing," said Father Ira softly, waiting to see how Jesse would receive this information. When he didn't respond, the priest continued, "For our administrative costs, we need something that looks like real money, that's not just a computer entry. But of course, we don't pass that printed money ourselves," he added quickly. "Some of our members are happy to print and pass it for us, since it takes care of their own interests and keeps the other traders happy."

The other traders... drug traders possibly? So that's where The Brothers come in, thought Jessie. *Very clever. You take a cut of their counterfeit money and cover them in the courts whenever they need you. This keeps your Catholic hands and their Catholic sins clean, Father Ira...*

"You see, we don't even need exit buyers, do we?" chuckled the priest. "We just need money from the principal. We can certainly keep you busy, entertaining our children, as well as seniors and adults who are hospitalized and need some extra cheer. It's a large Archdiocese. After you submit your list and they're approved, we'll arrange for you to have a debit card."

Jesse's eyes blurred as he stared at the paisley design on the Oriental carpet beneath his feet. Mazes. Labyrinths. Layers upon layers. That's what the church had always been about. Since the beginning of time it had been that way. In AD325 the Council of Nicea called by Roman Emperor Constantine the First set the guidelines for what eventually developed into the Christian religion. Like the Vatican Bank, it was all a fabrication, a way to conduct business, and business was all about bottom line profits.

The Golden Rule: *He who has the gold makes the rules... and gives himself permission to break them as well. The banks and the Church make the money and make the rules. Both are above the law.*

Father Ira smiled congenially. "The goal is to get crime off the streets. People should have plenty of money. They shouldn't have to steal or sell their bodies, or end up addicted to some harmful substance. Everyone should have an opportunity for the good life and we want to give it to them."

"So tell me, Father Ira, have any of Martin's trade programs actually happened?"

"Maybe," shrugged the priest, "but it's really not important, because there's always another one immediately following. And most of Martin's investors are willing to wait and keep spinning the roulette wheel until it lands on the winning number. May I offer you some wine?"

"Water will be fine, Father," said Jesse.

Jesse had just returned to his apartment when the downstairs door buzzer rang.

"Hi Dad, it's us, Maya and Max." Maya's voice.

"Hi Guys! Come on up!" Jesse buzzed the door open.

He met them at the door, giving both of them big hugs.

"So...?"

"No, she doesn't know," said Maya, a tall pretty 16-year-old with long black hair and big brown eyes. "We took a cab."

"Its okay, Dad. It's our fault if we get caught," 14-year-old Max reassured him.

They clung to him. "We miss you."

"I miss you too."

"You know what, Dad? It's a different world now from the one you grew up in. We read a lot. We see a lot."

"We're in the midst of a terrible economic crisis, aren't we?" Maya's expression was so serious; Jesse wanted to reassure her that everything would be all right. But he couldn't, because he knew he couldn't lie to her.

"Yes, we are, Maya. You and Max are luckier than most. Are you guys' hungry? Do you want to call up for pizza delivery? What did you tell your mom about where you are?"

"She's in Washington with *him*," said Max.

"Him?"

"The new man," Maya said. "Mom's had a string of them but I think this one is going to stick. He's got money and he's a politician with a big job in government."

"So who's staying at the house with you?"

"Grandma. She moved in right after you left. You know, Grandma's a trooper. She said it was fine, that it's just between us."

"Don't you think you should give her a call?" Jesse was proud of them, and relieved that at least they didn't have to lie about visiting him. He'd always gotten along well with Marcia, Rhonda's mother. A CPA, she'd divorced Horace, Rhonda's dad when Rhonda was 15 and had never remarried. Unlike her daughter, Marcia had always been very liberal and outrageous, a lot of fun to be around. She'd chosen not to retire but only worked during tax season. The rest of the time she followed the international music festivals.

"I'm going to go to the University of Chicago so I can be near you," said Maya. "I'm going to major in political science."

"I don't like Evergood," said Max. I think he's a jerk."

"Evergood is—?"

"Mama's new man," said Maya. "Evergood Krug. Anyone who has a name like Evergood must be Everbad. Max and I call him Everbad Crook. He's sarcastic and he drinks a lot and he's got a wicked temper."

7

Abyssus Abyssum Invocate ('Deep Calleth Unto Deep')

Tuesday, July 21, 2009 - Offices of the Archdiocese – Chicago, Illinois

Father Ira always looked forward to his meetings with Father Elmo Rigardi, one of Cardinal Francis George's secretaries of finance.

Cardinal George was head of the Chicago Archdiocese and a native of Chicago like himself. The cardinal was very popular among church members, and rightfully so. He took special care to meet with them personally to address their concerns. Currently president of the United States Conference of Catholic Bishops, the cardinal had become a major international figurehead of the Catholic Church.

Offices of the Archdiocese were located in the center of Chicago's financial district at Three First National Plaza on 70 West Madison Street. If one googled Three First National Plaza, one would find no reference to this fact. This may seem strange, since the Catholic Church was such a powerful American institution.

It may also seem puzzling that the name "First National" bore no connection to the First National Bank of Chicago, which was never housed in this building, although it merged with Bank One in 1998. Then in 2004 Bank One merged with J.P. Morgan Chase and established headquarters in Chicago. Chase, now known as one of the Big Four that together held 39% of all U.S. customer deposits, was one of the banks the Vatican used in the U.S. and Italy for conducting its business.

At one time a walkway existed between Three First National and the Chase Building next door. The Chase Building used to be called the Bank One Building; its name was changed in 2007. Currently, Hines, a privately owned international real estate firm, owned and managed both properties.

Under Church provisions and Illinois law, the Catholic Archbishop of Chicago was a Corporation Sole. The Archbishop of Chicago was also the treasurer of Church funds for the entire western hemisphere.

"Our charity outreach program continues to grow, Father Elmo," reported Father Ira, as soon as he had been ushered onto the secretary's spacious suite of rooms, and served coffee and scones.

"I'm very glad to hear that," said Father Elmo, a mild-mannered gray-haired priest in his mid-seventies. "You're doing fine work, Father Ira. Cardinal George mentions you very often, particularly in relation to the work you're doing at the Orphanage and with the Boys' Clubs. What can I do for you to aid your cause—or your causes?"

Father Ira had come prepared with his shopping list. "I think the most important thing you can help us with is to make sure the media covers our events. The church needs good press, as you well know, and charities are one way of reassuring all people, not only Catholics, that the church is not a corrupt institution."

"Of course." Father Elmo nodded. "I couldn't agree with you more. "So many rumors are flying around... it's difficult to put a stop to them, especially when they're attached to lawsuits. You do know how many of the dioceses are in serious financial trouble as a result of these claims."

"Yes, of course," said Father Ira, "which is why our charity outreach program is so valuable. As we raise money to support our good works, we also raise exponential amounts of money for the Church. As you know, we have been able to help many churches take care of their operating expenses."

"Yes, charity is the church's best friend, and public relations—some people are bold enough to call it media manipulation—is a special art," smiled Father Elmo. "I like to compare it to hypnotic trance. You can only have one thought in a single moment. If you are experiencing pain but not thinking about it, the pain will go away. Charity and good works are the best way to refocus or trance the public away from these misdemeanors. They are rampant everywhere, as you know—even among some of the, er, most prestigious members of the clergy."

Both men fell silent. Damage control was a major challenge, a full-time job for the Catholic Church and the Chicago Archdiocese in particular. They now had two leaky vessels: bank corruption ever since the Marcinkus scandals in the '70s and '80s that had exposed Vatican counterfeiting and money laundering operations, and the alarming pandemic of pedophile lawsuits. Every time they settled a case or covered it up, another one hit front page news. Added to this were the growing numbers of suicides among young Catholic boys who had been sexually abused and who could no longer live with their guilt afterward.

During the last decade, Catholic churches had lost five percent of their membership, and according to statisticians, the number would have been even higher if not offset by the impact of Latino Catholic immigrants.

Father Ira leaned forward, breaking the silence. "Father Elmo, I would like to ask you for another debit card, for a Mr. Jesse Jay. He is an entertainer, another 'Mr. Rogers' who has captured the hearts of our children. Just as important is the fact that Mr. Jay is a financial genius who was a bank executive for several years before he launched his non-profit foundation."

"He is a Catholic?" asked Father Elmo.

"No, he is not. But then, Martin Seligman, one of our key financial agents, is Jewish, as you know."

"Yes. Well." Father Elmo waved his hand dismissively. "Mr. Seligman is a special case. I think we agree that his important function is delivery of more opportunities for er more public relations. Incidentally, has Mr. Seligman's trade platform begun to perform yet?"

Father Ira did not respond.

"I thought not. There's one thing I must warn you about, my friend." Father Elmo lifted one eyebrow. "No one must link bank trade activities such as Mr. Seligman's to the Catholic Church. That is the type of publicity we do *not* want.

"Also, we need to make sure that the sellers and buyers of the, er, printed money are well entrenched in their urban ghettos. And when they're arrested, as they will be eventually, they must find ingenious ways to restore their operations. One way is to make sure their prison sentences are as short as possible, especially if they are expert printers and they know how to work the streets.

"Yes, of course," Father Ira reassured him. "Our Sicilian brothers are professionals in that area. We have nothing to worry about. They have never let us down, as you know."

"Time is of essence," continued Father Elmo. "We need literally billions in order to pay off these lawsuits as soon as possible. At the same time we must keep the churches financially solvent for their day to day operations. In more ways than one, ink is the blood of Christ," he joked drily, standing up and shaking Father Ira's hand.

"In Hebrews 9:22 it says: '*Sine sanguinis effusione non fit remissio.* (Without shedding of blood there is no remission.') And I John, Chapter 7 says: *Ego Johannes dicit quod 'sanguis Iesu Christi, Filii eius, emundat nos ab omni peccato.' Deus agens eligit purgatio peccatorum, ut erat in primis eligit sanguinem Filii sui.* (The blood of Jesus Christ his Son cleanses us from all sin. God, in choosing the cleansing agent for our sins, chose the very best that He had, the blood of His own Son')," responded Father Ira.

"*Ut Deus tecum sit* (May God be with you,)" said Father Elmo.

8
Sex vs. Chocolate Cake

Wednesday, July 22, 2009 – St. John Cantius Church – Chicago, Illinois

Father Ira called Jesse the next day and suggested they meet the following Monday at St. John Cantius church, located on North Carpenter Street, not far from the Kennedy Expressway. "Twice a month I give guided tours here. It's one of Chicago's famous Catholic landmarks."

Jesse knew very little about Catholicism. He'd grown up in Western Pennsylvania, where his parents belonged to a Quaker church. Rhonda's parents were non-church going Unitarians. Both he and Rhonda had tacitly agreed to dispense with a religious education for the children. Neither of them felt any desire to be Sunday churchgoers or participate in any type of religious activity. As far as they were concerned, said Rhonda, it was good enough to say they were Christians who lived according to the Ten Commandments.

During his overseas trips, Jesse had dutifully visited some of the world's greatest cathedrals and he'd also attended a funeral at St. Patrick's Cathedral in New York when one of the bank executives had passed away.

Once inside these structures, Jesse's sensitive nose picked up an odor that was a combination of mold & mildew, incense, and candle wax— and guilt. Like a rotting corpse, it gave off its own noxious stench.

The human dilemma was rotten and rotting. It was toxic. Man was born of original sin. Doomed from the start. These poor sad Soldiers of the Cross carried their heads under their arms wherever they went. No wonder many of them gave up at a young age on getting it right. Weekly confessional worked better than Mr. Clean to absolve them of their narcissism and promiscuity.

Every week drink yourself into a state of oblivion. Beat your wife and your kids—and *if you are a priest, play with the boys...* After weekly confession, life was fresh and clean again. Weekly laundry. *Tabula rasa.* Blank slate for yet another seven days of transgression. "How lucky we are to be

51

able to suckle the teats of Mama Guilt (Mother Church)! All it costs is membership dues and coins for the cup."

As for elitism, the ecclesiastical hierarchy was just as bureaucratic and rigidly structured—and just as forgiving and permissive for those at the top—as in the corporate world of banking and finance, or any other "corporate world."

Jesse also didn't care much for self-righteousness, which seemed to be built into every fundamental religion. Most sects thrived on proselytizing, which was, after all, just another business venture. The sales pitch or script for garnering investors needed no clause about a money-back guarantee. Only those who converted could be "saved."

Jesse had never felt the need to be saved. He was fine just the way he was.

The handsome blond priest was standing at the far side of the sanctuary surrounded by a group of school boys and their teacher. He motioned for Jesse to join the group.

"The Saint John Cantius is an example of the Polish Cathedral style church," Father Ira was saying. "The church building's design is by Adolphus Druiding. It was founded in 1893 by the Congregation of the Resurrection and had an active membership for many years until the Kennedy Expressway broke through the Polish area of Chicago, causing many residents to relocate. Actually it was scheduled for closure in the 1960s and '70s, but then it became part of a Catholic traditional revival movement."

Father Ira paused and smiled at Jesse to acknowledge him. "Today the church has a rich program of sacred music and the building now houses the Chicago Academy for the Arts."

Jesse's eyes wandered around the sanctuary. It was an impressive interior, with eight massive Corinthian capped stone columns supporting the vault.

"The floor is not only a beautiful contemporary work of sacred art but it is also designed as a teaching tool," continued Father Ira. "The medallions inlaid into the main aisle tell the story of salvation: Star of David—Jesus was born as a Jew; Three Crowns—with the arrival of the Three Kings Jesus was made manifest to the world; Instruments of the Passion—Christ's suffering for our Salvation; Banner—the Resurrection; Star—Christ is the Light of the World. This floor, the only of its kind in the United States, has already won three national awards."

Father Ira was flushed and excited as he completed the tour and received a loud round of applause. The school teacher accompanying the group thanked the priest profusely, handing him a check, which the priest acknowledged with a dip of his head and steepled fingers. "I'll see you tonight, John?" Father Ira asked him before they parted.

As soon as the group had filed out, the priest motioned for Jesse to follow him down a long corridor to a semi-darkened room furnished with comfortable chairs and a conference table. He pulled out a chair at the table and sat down. Jesse seated himself in a chair opposite.

"I enjoy coming here to give these tours," said Father Ira, "and I especially wanted you to see this church for a personal reason. I sensed you hadn't been inside before, even though you may have seen it many times from the Expressway."

"You're right," said Jesse. "I've never been inside."

"I grew up in this neighborhood," said Father Ira, whose real name he told Jesse was Philip Tuma. "I lived around the corner from this church. There were seven of us. I had three sisters and three brothers. My parents both worked. They came from Poland right before the U.S. entered World War II. My uncle brought them over. We lived on day old bread and left-overs."

Jesse knew what "left-overs" meant. Dumpster digging was common in these neighborhoods.

"I entered the church in order to have a roof over my head and take some of the burden off my family. Several of us did that. My brothers worked the streets, ended up in prison or ran away. My two sisters worked as waitresses and paid the bills from their tips and blow jobs—excuse me if I offend you. But they survived and I guess that's what mattered, God bless them."

Jesse noticed he did not make the sign of the cross, as was customary for most priests when they mentioned God or referred to blessings. Many things about Father Ira were unique. Jesse found it fascinating that he'd openly admitted his reason for becoming a priest.

"Both of my parents died within a year of each other. Cancer and heart disease. It's life." Father Ira shrugged, smiling whimsically. "I've been the luckiest of them all. *They* say I sold my soul to the church. I say I sold my body to the church. There's a big difference."

"Yes, you are helping others," said Jesse, not knowing what else to say.

"More than that, my friend, much more than that. I'm helping myself, believe me. When I saw my parents struggling, when I saw my siblings take to the streets, when I saw my two sisters living off whatever favors they could get, as if they were nothing more than gypsies or bag ladies, I realized I'd found a better way."

"But you took vows, Father Ira," Jesse pointed out. "And every day you perform a certain set of rituals. Your whole life is centered on so-called marriage to the church."

"You also took vows when you married your wife," said Father Ira. "Some people never get divorced because it's easier not to. And furthermore, love has many dimensions and can be worn in my sizes. I love the Church and I am devoted to serving it. I love the rituals and I love the life. I love my life. In that sense, one can say the Church and I are one."

"Do you think God loves some people more than others?" asked Jesse cautiously.

"Of course not!" chuckled Father Ira, breaking the somberness of the mood. "Now let's get on with the business at hand. We are very old-fashioned with all of our operations. Not that we don't believe in high tech. Computers are accurate and efficient for the bookkeeping and accounting part, as you know. And that's what's propping up the banks, as we discussed during our first meeting."

"Yes," said Jesse. "So, 'old-fashioned' meaning—?"

"Plates. Negatives. It is a very exacting process and must be done by experienced offset printers."

"And digital printers aren't good enough," prompted Jesse. "Why is that?"

"For one thing, most amateurs don't know it, but the inks and color balance are slightly off. They don't match actual money colors. They're skewed just enough to fool the counterfeiters."

"So you have a number of expert offset printers who make the plates and negatives." Jesse was impressed.

"Not specifically 'we,' shall we say. Let's call them our Brothers." Father Ira opened his briefcase and removed some documents, placing them on the table. "And incidentally, the strategy is to burn the candle at both ends. The Vatican through its banking connections has large holdings in UNICOR and the prison industry. You may or may not have known that."

The priest eyed Jesse intently to see how that information registered. Jesse's expression remained unchanged. He offered no comment as he came over to the other side of the table to examine the documents.

"Here are the items that are included in the package that each investor receives. These can be printed by anyone on any computer, since they are just generic documents.

"And it is my experience as a banker," said Jesse slowly, "that most of these documents are so abstruse, they are beyond average comprehension."

"Exactly!" beamed Father Ira. "You are an entertainer, a magician. You know how easy it is for the hand to trick the eye. The ear can also trick the eye. The visual of the house in Beverly Hills or Bali or Hawaii takes over. As you know, sex is all in the mind. Not that I know anything about *that*," he added hastily, blushing to his hair roots. "Food is perhaps, er a better example. A piece of chocolate cake is savored even more in the imagination."

"Actually I prefer sex over chocolate cake," said Jesse, hoping to get a laugh, which he did. He was rapidly getting the whole picture. Was it his imagination that this room was wired?

Of course it was. It was already too late to escape. He had visions of being found in an alley, his throat slit or a bullet in his chest. Or maybe body parts dismembered and tossed into a Polish dumpster.

"In exchange for underwriting many of your non-profit projects with the new debit card, which will be ready in a week—I'll call you and perhaps we can arrange to have lunch together—we are asking you to supervise the preparation of the packages for Martin Seligman's clients. I'll have a key made for you and you'll have your own office on the ground floor level of the church. You will have an assistant to type out the documents, and a graphic artist as well as a proofreader. Let me know if you need any other staff members.

"The first task is to review these documents to make sure everything is in order. Make whatever changes are necessary. This shouldn't take too much of your time. Once the documents are prepared, when Martin sends us the name of a new client, we send them a package from a post office box."

Jesse's head was swimming. "Do you know what I like most of all about you, Father Ira?"

The priest waited. He was a handsome sonofabitch, Jesse couldn't help thinking. *Did he use makeup or was that a natural beach tan... from where? Certainly not Chicago at this time of the year!* The sex remark wasn't an idle one after all.

"Your honesty," said Jesse, gliding into overdrive.

"Thank you," beamed Father Ira. "I believe we have a mutual admiration society."

The priest gathered up the documents and placed them back in his briefcase, indicating the meeting was over. "*Ut Deus tecum sit.* (May God be with you)." He unlocked a side door that led directly to the parking lot.

Jesse enjoyed the long drive to his apartment. The sun had disappeared from the wintry sky; another storm was brewing. He was comfortable and toasty in his Mercedes. It purred like a kitten. *A pussy.* He placed a CD in the player. *Bach Brandenberg Number Four.* He'd always found Bach's music uplifting.

What the hell. Did it really make any difference where the money came from if he could put it to good use? The Catholic Church was Mother's Womb and a godsend for him. Under their protection he'd be able to help many more people and create greater awareness. Maybe he could beat the cabal after all. With enough "money" he'd be able to find a way to clean up the air and water, provide free energy for everyone, deal with the Monsanto GMO issue that was destroying people's food, and bypass the system altogether.

Did he really care whose money he used… and what was money anyway? As a banker, no one could fool him about *that* anymore!

The Catholics weren't such a bad lot after all. Or at least some of them. And the Church was invincible, was it not? Just like the banks… 'TBTF'…Too Big To….

9
Martin's Vineyard

"So when is it coming in?" asked Barbara, pouring another cup of coffee and bringing it to her desk as she waited for Martin to answer.

"What's the big hurry, Sweetheart? What are you wearing right now? Let me guess. Pink lace bikini panties, matching lace bra... I hope it doesn't have any wires. Wires are bad for your breasts, you know. Very bad."

"I'm all wired up, Martin," purred Barbara, who had described herself to him countless times already as a 43-year-old busty blue-eyed blonde with gorgeous legs, all of which was verified by a photo scan of a model advertising teeth whitening in a Valpak coupon mailer. "I'm so big in front if I didn't have something to hold them up, do you know where they'd be? Do you want to come over and hold them up for me?"

"Ha ha ha! Ho ho ho!" Martin laughed heartily. "You are so funny, Barbara! That's what I like about you. God *damn,* you're good. I love your sense of humor. I love you! Sweetheart, guess what? I've got good news for you. You'll be coming here next week! Do you have your suitcase packed yet? Don't bring any clothes. We'll buy everything when you get here."

"Here" was Palm Beach, and "buy everything" referred to the boutiques and galleries on world-famous Worth Avenue.

Barbara knew Martin Seligman had a post office box on "The Island" as he fondly referred to it, because she'd sent him some books he wanted her to order (and pay for), but a post office address was just a box. She had no physical address for him. Although he'd mentioned a "house on the ocean," for various reasons, until they actually met, he said he couldn't tell her more.

Barbara was supposed to understand this and many other things. For references, Martin had a long list of people to call. She'd spoken with two of them, Lorraine Lemure, who owned gold mines in Nevada and who ranted for 45 minutes straight about how horrible the country's public education system was—Barbara could agree with her on that one—and at the end of the conversation told her that she'd known "Marty" for ten years. "He's a great guy," she said. "A lot of fun. I met him when he had a financial planning company in Denver."

The other reference, Dorrance Peterson, was head of a venture capital company. Dorrance told her that Martin had given him several good tips that had led to good investments. "He said stay away from fiat money and invest in gold. He sent me to Lorraine Lemure, a woman who owns gold mines in Nevada. Lorraine said—"

"What about performance?" Barbara interrupted Mr. Peterson. "He's done the bank trading before, right?"

"Oh, many times," Dorrance reassured her. "I never had the capital to invest myself, but now that I've met Lorraine—"

"Neiman-Marcus on Worth Avenue is our first stop," Martin was saying. "The bikini department. All the sales ladies know me there. I'm not like most men. I like to go clothes shopping with my women. And you're my woman now."

Barbara put her cell phone on speaker and swiveled around in her desk chair to check her emails.

"Either the guy's a fake or he's a pervert," commented her brother, Homer, when she made the mistake of telling him about Martin. She could count on Homer to be stodgy, conservative and dull, like his life. He was the manager for the local hardware store. Light bulbs for Homer were not ideas or bursts of imagination, but the glass kind that screwed into fixtures. And as for screwing... yes, well. Between the times when his wife, Penny, wasn't driving a school bus, all 300 pounds of her ate everything in sight. One of these days Barbara predicted she was going to eat Homer if he got in the way.

"The first tranche is due next Wednesday," said Martin. "Four Billion. And then after that, 4 Billion every week for 1½ years."

Walmart's had sent her an email that they were having a sale on vacuum cleaners. Her Hoover was burping and belching, definitely signs that it was getting ready to croak.

"It sounds wonderful!" said Barbara, checking the sale prices for an upright with attachments. She'd never heard of a "tranche" before until Martin mentioned the term. She looked it up and learned that it meant a "slice" or piece of the whole. Lemon meringue or cherry? When related to securities, it was a type of bond payment that was doled out over time. That was as much as she understood or wanted to.

"Today I put a bid on a house on South County Drive. Not far from Mar-a-Lago."

"From where?" asked Barbara. She gazed out the window at the large snowflakes starting to pile up on the row of parked cars in front of the apartment complex. It was still mid-winter in Washington. A white cuff already lined the top of the dumpsters that had been pulled onto the driveway for the trash collectors. Barbara shivered. Today was pick-up day. *Trash. Pick-up day.* The words repeated themselves. Is that what she was to Martin? Is that what she was to herself? A trashy pick-up? Why did she put up with him?

The answer to that question was easy. Martin Seligman was one of the sharpest financiers she knew. Not that she knew many—like whom else did she know who did what he did? No one. And that wasn't such a terrible thing. According to Martin himself, he was the *only* person who had managed to connect with the right people to set up his own bank trading program. "They chose an unknown person. Imagine that!" he crowed. "Not a billionaire like Warren Buffett or David Rockefeller, or –"

"Donald Trump," Martin was saying. Barbara jumped. "Mar-a-Lago has become an exclusive club since 1995, and I intend to join. You will be my first guest."

"That's wonderful, Martin. You're right. I do need a new wardrobe."

"Do you have some more pictures of yourself, Sweetheart?"

"I'm in every Philadelphia Cream Cheese ad," said Barbara, typing in her password for her bank balance.

"Ha ha ha! HO HO HO!" Martin went off again into gales of laughter.

As she checked her savings account, her heart skipped a beat. She was getting too close to the edge. Her mother's inheritance money was almost gone. It was time to look for a better job. An assistant librarian's salary was hardly enough to pay her bills and she was tired of trying to stretch every dollar just for rent, food and utilities.

She knew she never would have fallen for all of Martin's crap if he hadn't come so highly recommended by her cousin, Jack Gimpper, who was a gem dealer in New York. "He comes off as a nutcase, but let me tell you, Barbara, *he knows everyone* and they all say the same thing about him. He's for real. At one time he had one of the largest brokerage agencies located in the Three First National building in Chicago. A big office, 200 employees."

Jack knew Barbara was desperately looking for money to fund her literacy project. It was such a worthwhile project. Give books to inner city schools. Create more lending libraries. Pay college students to come to the schools to read to the kindergarten and first grade children. Place digital book making machines—Espressos they were called—in every college student union and let students print books at a discount, subsidized by her literary foundation.

As chairman of her foundation, Martin told her Barbara could have headquarters in Palm Beach, with annual fund raisers at The Breakers. "We'll go on cruises together and fly wherever we want to go—wherever YOU want to go—in my private plane. I want you on my Executive Board. I'm going to buy a home in Ecuador. Have you ever been to Ecuador?"

"No, I haven't," said Barbara wearily. "I understand it's beautiful."

"It's Paradise!" shouted Martin. "And Portugal. What a gorgeous place! You'll love it!"

She wondered if Martin had been to Ecuador and Portugal himself. Was there a way of finding out if he'd ever closed a bank trade program?

According to the experts, there was not. The entire operation was so clandestine one didn't even know who was king of the mountain, where that person lived and how the operations actually worked. But they *did* work. Several people could attest to that.

Who were those people? What were their names?

Barbara didn't like unanswered questions, especially when they involved finances. She should have started job hunting a long time ago. Why was she hanging onto this, she asked herself too often. Was it only because she was afraid of losing out on a good thing?

It was like buying a lottery ticket. If you didn't buy one, how could you ever win? And if you did buy one, what were your chances of winning?

It was also more or less like the game of life, she decided, her mouth twisting into a frown. Damned if you did and damned if you didn't. She'd never bought a lottery ticket for the same reason she'd never married. Many relationships, two abortions, even three live-ins. At age 51, that was quite a record. She still bleached her hair blonde but now it was short and she needed to lose some weight, maybe 30 pounds or more. With money she could take care of herself better, get rid of the wrinkles and puffiness around the eyes, have some liposuction done...

If she wanted to be honest with herself, the literacy project was just a way to get a large tax-free income stream and have fun for the rest of her days. Was she being punished for her honesty? Is this why nothing was happening?

"People don't talk about bank trades for a reason," Martin was saying for the hundredth time. "Do you know what that reason is?"

"Because they don't exist?" Martin loved it when she played devil's advocate so he could keep delivering his lines.

"Yes, you're right, Sweetheart! That's exactly the reason why." He was so smooth it was painful. Was his cock as smooth as his tongue? Would it be painful? Did she really have to find out in order to get that unlimited debit card?

"Do you know how many sharks there are out there, Barbara? Take a guess. Go on, take a guess!"

"Probably 50%. Or maybe 75%." Barbara downed the rest of her coffee and checked her watch. She was due at the library in fifteen minutes and with the snow falling this fast, she'd already be late. Roads would be slippery, cars stalled...

"Of course you have! I'm sure you have!" crowed Martin. But I want to tell you, Sweetheart, you're wrong. You're fucking wrong! Ninety-nine percent of them are crooks. Lightweights. Talkers."

So how do I know you're *not just a talker too, Martin?* "Martin, I have to go, I'm going to be late for work."

"How do you know I'm not just a talker like the rest?" Martin persisted, reading her mind. "Because I told you I'm not. Would I tell you something that's not true? Look how many years I've been in business. If you want to doubt me, I'll give you some numbers to call. You want some numbers to call? Let me tell you some of the things we're doing."

"I'm going to be late for work, Martin. I'll talk with you later... 'Bye!"

She'd heard the Martin's spiel so many times already, she knew it by heart. Occasionally there was a variation, but the rest of the script usually went as follows:

Martin had a special relationship with a Mr. Wuang Li Xaou. He called him "Xaou" for short, pronounced like "Chow," and he was located in Hong Kong, or Singapore, or the Philippines. Mr. Xaou was working with a Mr. Henri Gendarme, who was a Swiss banker.

Two years ago, Mr. Xaou gave Martin his own trading platform.

"What did I do to deserve this? Who am I? Just a little guy. Somehow I think the Man Upstairs wants me to do His work for Him. I don't understand it. Maybe I shouldn't even try to. I'm just...."

Martin suddenly realized the phone was dead at the other end. He dialed Lester Worthington. Martin was proud of the fact that he was never without someone to call. There were always plenty of people waiting to hear from him because they all knew he had the goods. Even if they didn't *believe* he had the goods, when he finally started to produce and could prove he was the Real Thing, *then* let them talk about him behind his back! He'd show them all, and *then* watch them come crawling!

"*I don't need the fame and glory,*" he told himself. "*I just need to make it happen. I just need to prove myself once.*"

"Hello Les, are you ready for the good news?"

"Hello Martin, how are you? Where are you?"

"Whaddya mean, where am I? I'm in Palm Beach!" yelped Martin. His eyes swept over the pyramid of papers on his tiny metal desk. Besides the folding plastic strap lawn chair he was sitting on, the only other furniture in the room was a cot with a plastic crate next to it that served as a night table.

He shared a bathroom and kitchen with three other tenants in a house on South 'J' Street in Lake Worth. The town of Lake Worth used to be the red light District of Palm Beach County. Although some of the places still existed, the county had cleaned it up somewhat, but it was still seedy with bars and flop joints. Ironically—or maybe not so ironically—Lake Worth was also cluttered with churches. Hypocrisy attracted the self-righteous; God knows, religion had its share of preachers who thrived on judgment and condemnation of others. Sin was Big Business.

The town's proximity to Palm Beach worked well for Martin. It was only temporary anyway, he reassured himself. It was easy to be anonymous here, as long as he had enough money to pay his bills. Sabrina, his estranged wife, had cut him off four months ago and reluctantly he'd asked Father Philip Tuma, aka "Father Ira," one of his most prestigious connections, for some help.

Father Ira was head of several non-profit organizations for the Chicago Archdiocese. It was a well-known inside fact that Chicago was the seat of Vatican banking, for better or for worse. In addition to being extremely wealthy in its own right, it was rumored that the Vatican was one of the most powerful money laundering operations in the world.

Martin couldn't care less if the rumors turned out to be true. What mattered was his connection to the Vatican that he could casually drop on his clients—in confidence, of course. In the middle of one of his conversations—"and believe it or not, we've just signed in the Vatican as one of our clients... I'm not at liberty to tell you how much they're putting onto the platform, but just know it's a goodly amount that starts with a capital 'B'...", etc., etc.

Added to this was mention of Father Ira's humanitarian projects—without disclosing his name, of course, or even that it was linked to Chicago. It was important for his client to know that half the proceeds from the trade program, once it began—which would be any day now—went to worthy causes.

He dialed Father Ira's phone number and left a voice message. When the priest called him back, excitedly Martin told the priest his good news.

At just the right moment in the conversation, Martin paused and purred, "You do understand, Father Ira, that the service I'm performing for you doesn't come free. I do have expenses."

"Yes, of course, Martin. Of course."

"I don't need much. Just a couple thousand every month. It's really auxiliary income. And if you could send it in cash..."

"I understand. No problem. We'll send it FedEx. Will you be there to receive it?"

"If I'm not, I'll have one of my assistants sign for it. And do send on the new list of projects so I can have them approved."

As soon as he hung up, Martin breathed a sigh of relief and mopped his tears and sweat with his tee shirt. All this fucking hardship would be over once the first tranche came in. He'd pay Sabrina back. No animosity. A divorce would be out of the question, of course. No legal entanglements. She was a bitch and could easily pull a fast one.

He'd give her a place on the ocean to rattle around in and do whatever she liked. Decorate, redecorate... an unlimited credit card... he'd show her how generous he could be. The way to get back at someone who was deliberately stingy and who talked about you behind your back was to kill them with kindness.

Martin liked the sound of that last phrase, especially the emphasis on "kill."

He never thought he'd get to the point of having to live off Sabrina. It was all her fault. If she hadn't given up on him, they'd still be living together in their house in Boca. Actually, it was her house. It was part of her divorce settlement. Martin told her he could have gotten more for her from her stingy ex, but Sabrina was so eager to get out from under him (how comical *that* one was; Harold had been impotent for years), she took whatever she could get, and ran.

"I'm in love with you, Martin," shrilled all 5-foot-one-inches of Sabrina. Blonde French twist, baby blue eyes, size 36D, tiny waist and muscular legs... Except for her large white teeth and overbite, she was gorgeous. He could live with the overbite, ha ha!

"I want to be filthy rich and I know you're going to make something big happen for us," repeated Sabrina too often.

After five years, Sabrina got tired of waiting for that something to happen. He didn't blame her, but it wasn't his fault either. He used to be a pretty good lover himself, at least Sabrina and all his other women thought so.

"These things take time," he kept reassuring her, referring both to his erectile dysfunction that had happened in stages after the first year of marriage with Sabrina, and to the fact that no money had come in.

"Like twelve years?" Sabrina would snarl, baring her teeth. Three months after they were married she discovered Martin had engaged in nefarious bank trade activities several years ago, long before they were married.

"Martin, when was the last time you made an honest dime actually working?" she shrieked at him one day, shortly before walking out.

"So what's the ocean like today?" asked Lester, who was in Shaker Heights, Ohio. An affluent suburb of Cleveland, in February it suffered from the same nasty-ass sub-zero temperatures as all the Great Lakes cities... Chicago, Detroit, Buffalo, Rochester... Martin shivered every time he thought of Chicago and its paralyzing winters. He hated that city with a passion, yet he knew he needed it with the same desperation that the large leafy green shade trees needed all that moisture.

"The green might come from a different source, but who says you can't fool Mother Nature, ha-ha," Martin was fond of joking when talking about money growing on trees. No one understood the joke, yet they laughed anyway. It was always good to humor Martin. He was the kind of person you didn't want to have as an enemy.

He could blow up and be such a sonofabitch, you'd be ready to slam down the phone in his face. But you didn't—maybe because deep down you felt sorry for the sucker. You felt sorry for yourself for being such a sucker and falling for his crap. He wasn't worth all that energy, and yet...

Lester Worthington was a European car dealer with a hefty income and sizable investments.

"The ocean! Ha! It's beautiful from my window but I doubt if I'll get a chance to get any closer to it today," retorted Martin. "I'm so busy right now with buyers, I'll be lucky if I finish with all my calls by midnight. Are you ready to invest?"

"As soon as your attorney sends me the paperwork. Five million ready to go into your account to do the trade. That's what you said, right?"

"You've got it! I'll have the documents faxed to you by mid-afternoon today."

"Nothing leaves my bank account for the 12 months that I'm in. Is that correct?"

"Yes, yes," said Martin impatiently. Lester was getting to sound like a parrot. What was he so worried about?

"Nothing is ever lost, Les. It's not like other trade programs where they take your money and rip you off. But we do need to give the banks and traders 12 months. You understand that part, right? Four billion a week for two and a half years!"

"Sounds good to me. Let it roll!" declared Lester. He'd always wanted to be part of a trade program and after this one started, there were more to follow, Martin promised. What the hell.

As soon as Father Ira finished talking with Martin he dialed Tony Masella.

Tony was at a lube shop getting an oil change. *My baby's getting all lubed up,* he sang to himself. His phone lit up for an incoming call. "Hey! How's my favorite father confessor?"

"I didn't see you at Mass last Sunday, Tony."

"Well, you know, I was busy."

"Busy doing good works, I trust? **When** can I expect to see you at church again?"Father Ira started the coded language between them. "We're having a big gathering on **the first of the month.** About **100 thousand people** are expected, give or take a few."

"You've got to be kidding," retorted Tony. "That many?"

"Considering that the entire U.S. population of the Roman Catholics is now well over **50 million**, it could happen."

"I'll try to attend. You do know how busy I am."

"Make time for yourself and for your religion," said Father Ira. How's **Patty?**"

"She's doing well. Her friend's about to **deliver** her baby, so she's been busy doing errands for her."

"I have another call coming in and **hundreds** of emails to answer. Stay in touch, Tony. Good to talk with you."

After the phone clicked, Tony swore under his breath. By the first of the month Father Ira wanted 50 million in 100 dollar bills for a commission of $100,000 and he'd just lost his best printer. He'd up and quit, just like that. Got scared. Two bad things happened when he wasn't using an inside printer or doing it himself. Besides having to find another one, he had to make a plan to get rid of them afterward. Usually that cost money. Trust, or lack of it, had a price.

On top of that, he was dealing with an abscessed tooth. Damn thing was killing him. The pain went right to his eyes and up the side of his right cheek. It was starting to swell.

At 43, Tony Masella was already starting to look wasted. His complexion had a grayish cast and his eyes were disappearing beneath puffy dark circles. He was starting to look like a raccoon with mumps. He frowned at the swollen cheek and jaw in the mirror. The last thing in the world he wanted to deal with right now was a tooth extraction, and the tooth was right in front. *Damn!*

Nothing was easy in this world and it wasn't getting easier. Tony let loose with a string of invectives. Father Ira wanted the money by the first of the month.

In Lake Worth, Florida, storm clouds were gathering. The sky was dark and fierce looking.

"Nothing that's worth it in this world is ever easy," Martin reminded himself, checking his bank balance, a personal account that Sabrina had forced him to open. The bitch. He was down to $57.34.

He logged off and chewed on a hangnail. Damn thing. He didn't want to tear the skin. If only he could get a manicure like in the good old days...

They were cutting it close. Xaou had all the traders lined up and he was giving them four more days to complete the work. That would take them to the first of next week. He didn't dare ask Xaou what happened if the traders decided they didn't have enough to do the deal. The $5Millon from Lester Worthington should put it on roller skates, yet one never knew...

10
Sabra

Monday, February 15, 2010 - Chicago

When it came to women, W-2 wasn't the needy type. He'd always had too much going on in his life for bar pick-ups or one night stands.

In high school and college he'd had more than a few girlfriends, especially when he was on the varsity football team. Gorgeous babes who were only too eager to fall into his bed. Yet none of them ever sent lightning bolts through his groin. *That's the only kind of woman a 5-star stud like me should fall for*, W-2 told himself. *A goddess worthy of my erection.*

Now that he'd settled on a career and a job, he decided it wouldn't be so bad to have someone special in his life. Not just anyone... someone special.

Where would he find her?

"Just let it happen," his mother advised. He trusted her. Wasn't that how it happened with her and his dad?

Kim was fond of describing the moment she'd first laid eyes on Agent Wes Charles. "It was a good thing it was during off hours," she joked. "I was a basket case. A group of the forensics agents were having coffee at Sally's across the street and in walked three of the members of the counterfeit squad. One of them was a tall, handsome dude whose middle name was 'Charm' the minute he opened his mouth and started joking around with us. At that moment, I swear to you, the earth moved underneath the booth where I was sitting. If only it would have swallowed me up so I could avoid looking into his eyes because he was staring right at me with a look... *oh, I knew what that look meant!*

"I managed to escape to the Ladies' Room where I sat in a stall and shook for over an hour, I swear, before I could bring myself to return to the table. I was a basket case!"

"Actually it was less than five minutes. I timed her," Wes corrected her, waiting for W-2 and Loretta to laugh.

"It'll happen. Time will tell," Kim advised her son, giving him a hug.

And then time *did* tell.

He would never forget that first day when Agent Rachel Nahari entered the office. He couldn't take her eyes off her. She was a babe all right. And so much more. Besides looks and a bod she had brains, personality and a delicious laugh, rich and melodious like his mom's...

The game was up. He'd won and he'd lost. He was smitten. A prisoner, a goner.

That day after work, as soon as he'd unlocked his apartment door, he threw off his jacket and turned on his desk computer. It was the search he'd been waiting to do all day that couldn't be done at the office.

Rachel. A Jewish name. Hebrew, said Wikipedia. In the Old Testament, the wife of Jacob. Daughter of Isaac. Rachel and Leah.

Rachel Nahari. An Israeli from Ethiopia—just as dark-skinned as he was! Like all Israeli's, male and female, she'd served in the army. That's where she'd picked up her shooting skills. She was good all right. Very good.

Tall, long black hair, huge brown eyes, Grecian nose, gorgeous smile and dimples. Built. 36D? DD? Maybe. Solid, athletic; runners' legs.

She'd shown up at the Secret Service forgery squad offices without any advance notice. At least his dad could have warned him. Or Agent Taylor. *Leave it to Mom to lock me out of my fantasies!*

Rachel put American babes to shame, with the exception of the one quality they had that she apparently lacked. Most American women fawned all over him. Six-foot-two, U of Iowa varsity linebacker who could have played pro. Gorgeous body, gorgeous looks by all standards, mostly his own.

"And an ego that never stops," his sister Loretta would add, giving him a playful punch in the chest.

"Rock hard, Sister," he'd retort.

"Macho macho... Type A, all the way," she'd chant.

"And wouldn't you love to have a man in your life just like me?" he'd taunt back.

The truth was, thought Loretta, her older brother was right. Wes, Jr. or "W-2" as they called him was a spittin' image of Wesley Charles, Sr., and like all daughters only even more than most, Loretta was wildly in love with her dad.

"Maybe I love you so much because I'm the spittin' image of Mom," she liked to tease him. "How did W-2 and I get to be perfect copies of you guys? Like clones?!"

"Maybe God decided he had a good thing going," was Kim's quick response, giving her daughter a hug.

Wes and she were so proud of Loretta's accomplishments. Kim had been a fashion model for *Ebony*, but she'd never thought about taking her good looks to Hollywood. After getting her B.A. at the University of Southern California in Cinematic Arts, Loretta enrolled in the Master's Program of Film and Television Production. As an undergraduate she'd already produced two Indie films and had been asked to be the lead actress in another.

"Without any acting experience!" she gloated. Her parents didn't want to point out that she was the daughter of two professional actors. That's what undercover work was all about. It was in the genes.

Both of their children had the same values as their parents. When W-2 had turned down two pro football offers and chosen to do graduate work in criminology, Kim and Wes were secretly elated. A football career was glorious, but they wanted so much more for their son.

"Dare I say that money isn't everything?" Kim chuckled when W-2 told her he'd said no to a whopping six-digit starting salary—far more than Wes and she could ever make combined, as Senior Secret Service agents. "If you can't say it, I will," said Wes, Sr. coming up behind her and placing his arms around her. "Money isn't everything. Have we ever wanted for anything? Even our overseas trips get paid for!" That drew a round of laughter.

"You're right, Wes," agreed Kim. "We have never wanted for anything." He didn't have to convince her about this but he did anyway, just because.

The morning after W-2 received his M.S. degree in Criminology and Criminal Justice from Arizona State University, while they were having brunch at Chompie's in Tempe, one of W-2's favorite restaurants, W-2 dropped the news that he'd applied for a position with the U.S. Secret Service.

"I want to train under you two." With gusto, W-2 attacked his hot pastrami sandwich.

"So you can be close to home cooking?" Kim teased him. "Although I know you're going to miss Chompie's!"

Both she and Wes were surprised and elated about W-2's decision. Nepotism wasn't permitted in the same unit, but there was a vacancy in the forgery squad and it wouldn't be difficult to put in a request.

In addition to graduating with honors and making Phi Beta Kappa, W-2 was also a computer geek. With a family background of law enforcement and two parents who lived and breathed their jobs, there wasn't much he needed to learn.

"Two successful kids. We must have done something right," was Kim's favorite statement.

"We always do," was Wes's predictable response, delivered with just the right lilt at the end.

The history of the Ethiopian Jews was intriguing. They were said to be the descendents of the Tribe of Dan; their DNA had the same Y-chromosome characteristics that one found among all Jews everywhere. The Ethiopians were "soul black," like Afro-Americans. Both were from the same area of the world.

Color issues had the same stigma in Israel as in any Caucasian dominated culture. The Zionists who settled Israel were from Germany and Western Europe. According to several forums and blogs on the Internet, when the Ethiopians immigrated to Israel, they'd experienced their fair share of prejudice, like the Yemeni and Middle-Eastern Jews of color. They were treated like second-class citizens.

The Israeli military draft—as soon as children reached the age of 18 both males and females had to serve for two years—usually leveled everything, especially when these newer immigrants excelled, as Rachel must have. Most Ethiopian Jews changed their names to more "acceptable" Israeli ones. W-2 wondered what Rachel's real name was.

Rachel had already been working at the Agency for two months and W-2 was starting to get pissed off. Not even a friendly "hello" could he get from the woman! What was wrong with him? Did he have BO? Halitosis? Horns?

According to his dad, who was in expert in F matters—'F' for female, Wes reassured him—Avoidance meant Attraction. "Just wait, son," he promised. "She'll come around."

And exactly when was that going to be? Like next Halloween?

Maybe he needed to take some lessons from Wes, Sr. According to rumors (and who's to say they weren't true?) in the days when his dad was fancy free, by the time he finished working the office, not a woman had been left untouched. Literally a Golden Globes performance.

Rachel acted so cold toward him. Why was he such a turn-off? Or maybe she was scared. Jobs do that. He'd experienced enough bureaucracy already in his life to understand how important it was to cross every 't' at the beginning—especially when an employee was dealing with possible color issues. Rachel's challenge was BTx2—Big Trouble Times Two. She was also a female USSS agent.

In his off-hours, W-2 continued to research the Ethiopian Jews, the history of Judaism and specifically, the Ethiopian Jews in Israel. Some of them weren't even allowed to immigrate because only the father and not the mother was Jewish. Blood. Bloodlines. W-2's mouth twisted in disgust. One of these days the bigots would find out what scientists and other more conscious individuals already knew. The world was a hologram. We are all one. But no, that was too much to ask yet. It was too early for many to give up the belief that the earth was flat.

Talk about suffering! And marginalism! Yet somehow the People of the Book always seemed to come out smelling like a rose. The accomplishments of the tiny state of Israel put most other countries in the Middle East to shame. Of course, W-2 knew there were reasons for that. But still...

At his parents' anniversary party, Wes, Sr. had cornered Rachel and beckoned for W-2 to come over and join them.

"I may need the help of both of you very soon." Wes gazed deeply into Rachel's large brown eyes.

How did he do that? W-2 wondered enviously. He made it look so *easy*.

"As you know, we're working on a large counterfeit money case—the Masella case. Those bonds and other bank instruments that were turned in to your office and that you two discovered were counterfeit may be linked to the Masella counterfeit money.

"Rachel and W-2, you are the experts. The rest of the squad is good, but not like you two. You know how to make the new software sing. The rest of the staff doesn't know diddley-squat about how to do such advanced work."

Wes glanced over at W-2. "Tomorrow morning, be at the office at 8:30. I want to show you what I have. I need both of you on my team. I want the two of you to work on these documents together."

Rachel's large brown eyes were fastened adoringly on Wes, Sr.

"Yes, sir!" said W-2 with almost too much enthusiasm.

In the next instant, Wes vanished, leaving the two of them standing awkwardly together and staring at their plates of half-eaten cake and melting ice cream.

"I think it would be a good idea if we put these down and found a place to talk," suggested W-2, relieving Rachel of her plate. "I've been eager to learn more about you, but you—we—we've been so busy."

"That is a good idea," said Rachel shyly, following him out door and down the hallway to one of the vacant offices.

The next day before the meeting with The Brush, as promised, Wes asked W-2 and Rachel to come into the conference room. He also asked Kim to join them. As soon as the door was closed, Wes opened his briefcase and produced a sheaf of documents. He laid out the top set on the table for W-2 and Rachel to examine.

"These are the bank instruments I was referring to last night," said Wes. "They came into my hands after one of my contacts gave me more information about Tony Masella and the fake $20s and $100s that have been showing up around town. Some of the same names are appearing on these documents as in the data we've been collecting on Masella. It's possible, but it's too soon to tell, that we're dealing with much more here than just funny money."

W-2 and Rachel had already put their heads together and were examining the documents. Kim and Wes exchanged glances.

"The plan as I understand it," said Kim, deferring to Wes, "is to deal with the immediate issue, which is for the counterfeit squad to bring in Masella. Then we have something—or someone—to work with. Once we have him behind bars we can interrogate him."

"Right," said Wes, "if he'll talk. Meanwhile, we need the forgery squad to examine these documents. Before showing them to the whole squad, I wanted you two to give them a look-see."

Rachel was already taking notes and examining some of the seals on the documents. W-2 was right behind her, leaning over her shoulder.

"Two peas in a pod," thought Kim, watching them. *"Amazing!"*

"God, let them be good together," prayed Wes.

11
Pazzo Pazzo
(Crazy, Insane)

Monday, February 15, 2010 – Office of SAIC Fuller – Chicago, Illinois

"So, Wes, sit down, sit down." SAIC Larkin Fuller was watering his ferns on the other side of his Hawaiian style executive pagoda, his back to Wes as he entered. "Excuse the clutter, we're in transition again." (*We*"? wondered Wes. Who besides Larkin was "in transition" in Fuller's office?)

Larkin turned around, frowning at Wes. "We're thinking of creating a country in Central America. Possibly Panama."

"Yes, sir, that would be a pleasant change," said Wes, almost losing his balance as he fell into one of the hammock chairs. "Sir, I won't take much of your time."

"You know I prefer that you take none of my time, so it must be important." Fuller turned and frowned at Wes, his nostrils flaring. With horns on either side of his head, thought Wes, he would look just like a hippopotamus.

"Actually, sir, I have something to propose to you regarding the Masella case that if we pull it off, would be a hell of a feather in our caps."

"Agent Charles, we are not Robin Hoods. We don't wear fucking feathers in our caps," snarled Fuller. "There's only one place in this profession where a feather is appropriate. I think you get the picture. Continue."

"Forget the feathers metaphor, sir," Wes said quickly. "I just need your permission to contract a counterfeiter to print some money."

"YOU **WHAT?**" yelled Fuller. "So is **that** all you came to see me about, Agent Charles? Just a little fucking illegal project like printing up some fake money? Are you *pazzo*? And I suppose you want the Agency to chew it down like grass and pass it out through our anuses or maybe juice it through our tits. What the hell are you talking about, printing counterfeit money, Charles?"

"None of the above," said Wes smoothly, ignoring Fuller's rage and waiting for him to calm down. The man was a rage-aholic and Wes had just pushed one of his "Howdy Doody" buttons.

Fuller started pacing from one end of his tropical island to the other, almost knocking over a fake ficus tree as he lifted his fist and pointed it at Wes. "And what's this about 'we,' Agent Charles? There **is** no 'we,' is that clear? It is **just you** and always **just you**, because this would be wrong, **fucking wrong**. So I suppose you already told your informant you'd get Masella a printer for him, didn't you? God *damn!*" he glared at Wes, standing over him now.

Wes wasn't intimidated by Fuller. If The Brush ever got physical, one slug in his bread basket and he'd be flat on the floor. A tuna wrap. But it would never happen. The Brush knew better than that, which is why Wes was confident he was going to get his way.

"Sir, I'd like to discuss a few more things regarding the case," Wes continued.

"There is nothing to discuss except for the fact that what you're suggesting is fucking illegal," repeated Fuller. "And incidentally, I'm not sure you heard me correctly. I want you to be aware of the distinct fork in the road. Can you see the sign posted in bright red letters, Agent Charles? It reads 'WE'—meaning The Agency—and 'YOU'—meaning Wes Charles— part ways. We will take no responsibility for any of your shenanigans. Is that clear?"

"So does that mean it's a go?" Wes didn't even raise his voice. The words just rolled out, smooth and easy.

Fuller sat down again. "Exactly what do you have in mind, Agent Charles?"

"I'd like you to check with U.S. Attorney Berger to see if there's another way to do this. The informant did not approach Masella. Masella asked the informant if he knew of a printer."

Wes paused to take the temperature of The Brush's rage. When it was once again below boiling point, he continued. "Frankly sir, I consider it an opportune moment to reel out the rod and bring 'em all in. You know how long we've been trying to get the right hook on this case."

Again Wes waited. The fisherman metaphor was a good one for The Brush. A good Christian, he even had a fish decal on his vehicle license plate. That was what the tropical island shit was all about. He couldn't wait to retire so he could spend all his time in a boat drinking beer and pulling hooks out of half-dead fish.

"Masella can find another printer," said Wes, baiting the hook once more. "Someone we don't know."

"Shit." The Brush picked up the watering can. His bald head was beaded with sweat and his left eye was twitching. Often one can get the whole package of a person just by observing the hardware around the jaw. Fuller's jaw was wired square and mean. "Mumser" was the word that popped into Wes's head. Where had he heard that word before? It was Yiddish for "sonofabitch." *Wendy. Agent Weisman.*

"Get out of here, Charles. I'll see what I can do."

U.S. Attorney Michael Berger was a political creature who liked feathers, especially when they were linked to leather and lace. It would take only one whistleblower to ruin his career, but no one wanted to do it to him. He was such a nice guy and besides, he had a bull dog for a wife. Margery Berger, also an attorney, was a ruthless litigator and must have been hell on earth to live with. One couldn't help feeling sorry for the poor sucker.

"I have a feeling Mr. Berger is going to like your plan," said Kim. "Especially if the media gets behind it and gives him and The Brush all the credit. How do you feel about that?"

They were driving home together from the office, since Wes's vehicle was in the shop. She turned sideways to look at him.

"Do I have to answer?" Wes chuckled mirthlessly. "I'm going to call Mitch as soon as we get home."

"Mitch Gordon?" Kim looked at him incredulously.

"None other than the Big M, Babe."

Agent Gordon had been called out of the office on a special assignment in New York. Tall, black and wiry, without his beard, mop of hair and shades, he and LA Lakers star player Kobe Bryant could pass for twins. Mitch moved with the same speed and he had a skill on the streets that came naturally. Like Wes, he'd also grown up in a ghetto and knew the lingo, the gestures, and the movements. And like Wes, his timing was impeccable.

Kim knew what Wes had in mind. It was a brilliant idea. Gordon would pose as the counterfeit agent who could arrange to have the money printed. As case agent, this left Wes free to make decisions if anything went wrong.

Wes dialed Mitch's number. "How's it going, man?"

"I'm in Tahiti right now, sipping a teetie."

"That bad, eh?" snorted Wes. "How about Hackensack or Nyack, downing a Jack?"

"Shit, man. You've got something for me. *I knew it!* I can smell it on the tip of that follicle that just floated through the phone. What do you want me to do? Why is it you never call to tell me I won the lottery or you've got a woman for me that's as toni as Kim?"

"It's coming, man, its coming, just give me time." Wes loved Gordon like a brother. They made a good team.

"So you mean I've still gotta earn it?"

"When can you be here?"

"Like tomorrow? Have you already unhooked me?"

"I'm working on it. I've already submitted the requisition. Based on the size of the case, they're not going to say no."

Wes was right. His request was immediately granted.

He was relieved. Gordon wasn't easy to work with, but that came with the package; it was also what made him such a good agent. Both of his wives had left him. Women liked at least a little attention, and if they didn't understand what went on when an agent was making a case, they were easy touches for jealousy. Imagination ran wild when their man was out all night or came in late half drunk.

"Maybe he's been choosing the wrong kind of women," said Kim when the second divorce was final. "Sometimes men look in the wrong places because they've never learned how to use any other search engine besides the anatomical one."

Kim was already thinking ahead. Rachel Nahari had a sister who was seven years older. Like Rachel, Esther was a slim dark-skinned beauty who was now also in the U.S. Rachel had attended Columbia for a degree in Sociology and Esther did her graduate work at MIT in quantum physics. They were very close. Esther had just moved to Chicago where she'd accepted a teaching position at Northwestern University.

"Gordon will be back in town on Wednesday," Wes reported later that day.

"Good," said Kim. "We'll do Jimmy Green's tomorrow night and ask W-2 and Rachel to join us."

Jimmy Green's Sports Bar on State Street in the South Loop was Gordon's favorite eatery in Chicago. He was stuck on their Kick-Ass Crafted Burgers and usually ordered a Smokehouse Barbecue and a Windy City Willy with a large pitcher of beer on tap. It took a lot of food and drink to fill his tank.

"That's just what I was thinking, Babe." Wes checked his watch. Midnight. "And now I have another thought."

12
Ribs & Beer on Tap

Tuesday, February 16, 2010 – USSS Office – Chicago, Illinois

Before Gordon arrived, Wes gave himself a refresher course on entrapment. In criminal law, entrapment is defined as "conduct by a law enforcement agent inducing a person to commit an offense that the person would otherwise have been unlikely to commit."

And, here was the catch: "In many jurisdictions, entrapment is a possible defense against criminal liability."

Depending on the law in the jurisdiction, the prosecution may be required to prove beyond a reasonable doubt that the defendant (person printing or passing counterfeit bills) was not entrapped. Or the defendant may be required to prove that he *was* entrapped as an affirmative defense.

The word "entrapment," meaning "to catch in a trap," was first used in the United States Federal Court case of *People v Braisted (13 Colo. App. 532, 58 Pac. 796).*

In case law, the court looks at two tests, subjective and objective, to determine whether entrapment has taken place. The subjective test considers the defendant's state of mind. Benny the informant asked Wes for a printer to print counterfeit money. This clearly indicated predisposition to commit the crime.

Wes participated in the crime by finding the printer for making counterfeit money. Before that time, was the printer a law-abiding person? Had he *never* committed the crime of counterfeiting? The answer to both of these questions was no. Tony Masella had already been involved in counterfeiting. He was slippery. Until now, Wes and the agency had been unable to put together a plan for arresting him and shutting down his operation because he worked through intermediaries.

In all the cases cited, the issues of entrapment were shady. Clearly, the decision rested with the courts. In Wes's case, this only added to the risk, inviting the possibility of the courts getting it wrong. He'd already attracted attention with his civil rights case in the year 2000 involving discrimination among Secret Service agents, i.e., numerous instances of bypassing black agents for deserved promotion. Or, when awarding status positions, showing priority to white agents—even when records indicated a black agent was the most deserving candidate.

The other unspoken factor involved working undercover to make cases. Black agents often worked "undercover with no cover" because white agents either were too chicken shit to put their lives on the line or just because they *were* white, they stuck out like sore thumbs in black or ethnic ghettos. Often the black undercover agent caught the criminal but the white agent made the arrest—the white agent getting the accolades for making the case.

Wes was well aware that discrimination worked both ways. It prevented white supremacy scenes that may have taken place with The Brush a long time ago, yet also opened the door to the type of scrutiny regarding his case work that no top notch agent was eager to entertain. They needed freedom to act on their feet at all times and not be shackled by anal "R & R,"—bureaucratic Rules and Regulations.

He called a meeting on Thursday at the office with Gordon, Kim, Shane, Marc, Len, Kevin and Rombo to discuss a plan of action.

As expected, Marc was all over him for trying to get the Agency in trouble. "I'll be honest with you, I don't like this."

"You don't have to like it, Bud," Gordon retorted. "You're not doing the undercover work." Gordon and Marc had never gotten along well. They had a natural aversion to each other. Maybe it was a body size thing. Marc was a 250-pound lummox and Mitch Gordon was a loosey goosey, all skin and bones, who could have played Ray Bolger in the Thirties version of *The Wizard of Oz*.

"We're all in this together, right?" muttered Green. "You need me, we need we."

"Wes, I think we've got something big here. An opportunity we can't pass up," said Len Eastwood, surprising all of them. Usually a stick in the mud, Eastwood actually seemed genuinely excited about the plan. For Eastwood to be excited about anything was a major event.

"How so, Len?" asked Kim, eager to get Eastwood's take. Eastwood also had a mind like a steel trap. Nothing got past him.

"From what I know about Masella or whatever his real name is—"

"He's got half a dozen," interrupted Green. "We've staked out a connection to the Chicago Catholic Archdiocese and The Clan."

Eastwood nodded. "If our hunches are correct and if everything adds up, this is a big operation. National. And if it's connected to the Catholic Church and Cosa Nostra—"

"—all roads lead to Rome," put in Gerr, "and they're loaded with road apples."

This got a laugh from all of them. Kevin Gerr's ex-wife was a Catholic and she'd fought for and won custody of their three children who were being raised Catholic. Rombo, Italian by birth, laughed hardest. One day, on some kind of Italian holiday, he'd brought in some delicious lamb sandwiches that his mother had made. He also brought in a lamb's head that he placed in computer geek Cuthbert Wilcome's desk drawer.

A couple hours later, when Cuthbert opened his desk drawer to find the head of a lamb glaring at him, he let out a yell that could be heard throughout the office and up and down the stairwells of the other five floors in either direction. It was one of the many memorable stories that had become part of the Chicago counterfeit squad's repertoire.

"So who's in the truck and who's on the ground?" asked Shane, after several more minutes of discussion.

"Gordon, you're the 5-star printer who meets with Masella. I'll have my informant set up the meeting. And incidentally, you'll be wearing a wire."

"A *what?*" repeated Gordon, whipping around to glare at Wes. "Did you say a condom?"

"A wire, man," Wes repeated. Part of the deal of loving Gordon like a brother was putting up with an ego that never stopped. "We can't take any chances, Bro, we can't fool around. This case is shaky enough as it is. We need to get as much shit as we can, in order to keep the The Brush and the USA involved."

"Hey Gordon, having a playback of you and Masella talk shit about the printing is going to make this case a slam dunk," added Kim. "We need to impress them and you're a master at that."

"Kim's right," Rombo chimed in.

Wes put in a call to Bennie Portera, his informant. "Yo, Bennie. When?"

"I'll call you back."

Bennie rolled off Natalie/ Roselyn/ Patricia's sleeping body and lit a cigarette. Patting the prostitute on the rump, he threw on his clothes, locked the motel room behind him and headed for the Denney's pay phone a block away.

Two phones calls later and the plan was in place for the following afternoon. Gordon would meet with "Paul" at Jocko's Sports Bar on the South Side, off 47th Street, near Lake Michigan.

By mid-afternoon it was almost dark. Near the lake the wind was fierce. Huge gusts picked up the trash and sent it sailing down the street, onto the broken sidewalks and against barbed wire and concertina topped chain link fences. It was a godforsaken area of the city. Streets tight with four-and five-story walkups, at every corner a convenience store, bar or smoke shop, windows slathered with Spanish, Chinese, Arabic and Korean graffiti. Dirt- and cinder-crusted snow banks lined the streets, adding to the gloom.

Jocko's was next to a vacant lot on one side and a coin laundry on the other. The letter 'J' of the neon tube was broken and the light flashed on to "ocko's." All the windows had grills and were frosted over to darken the interior for daytime customers.

The street lights went on as Kim parked the surveillance van in a back alley. Wes, Gordon, Rombo and Shane were in the van and Len and Kevin were parked a couple streets away. Marc was on the computer back at the office making the backup A-V.

"I feel like a fucking stoolie," fumed Gordon as Wes wired him up and they tested it from the restaurant interior. Wes knew better than to toss anything back at him. If he were Gordon right now he'd probably feel the same way. He also knew Gordon was well aware that the decision had nothing to do with him.

"*Yeah yeah yeah*, everything always for the Agency," Gordon muttered good-naturedly to himself.

As he entered the semi-darkened restaurant he was met by a blast of warm air and blaring TVs mounted on the walls over the bar and throughout the restaurant. Only two people were at the bar. The restaurant, down a few steps and to the right, was almost empty. It was too early for dinner.

Gordon slid onto a bar stool next to a fellow wearing a baseball cap and service station uniform, eyes glued to the TV.

A light blue Dodge Ram matching the vintage and description of Tony Masella's vehicle rattled around the corner near Len and Kevin's SUV. The agents signaled to the surveillance van.

The Dodge sputtered to a stop in the parking lot and a medium-height man wearing boots, a black knit cap and bomber jacket climbed out and headed toward the restaurant entrance.

Kevin and Len pulled their vehicle into a parking space on a side street directly next to the restaurant and entered separately after Masella had opened the front door and disappeared inside.

Gordon swiveled around on the bar stool and made eye contact. Masella wandered over. Gordon thrust out his hand. "How's it going? Peter."

"Paul," said Masella, giving him a firm grip in return.

"The fish and chips any good here?" asked Gordon (Peter).

"Not bad. Ribs are better, if you like ribs."

The waitress, a plump matronly woman with frizzy blonde hair in a too short uniform that humped over her behind and a name tag that read "Sheila" led them to a table at the back, away from the TVs. Neither of the men removed their outer jackets, caps or shades.

"What's on tap, Sheila?" Gordon (Peter) asked.

"We've got some Finch's."

"I'll have the ribs and whatever else comes with them," said Gordon (Peter) (as long as it's not you, honey.)

"Make that two." As soon as Sheila left, Paul placed his palms on the table and looked over at Gordon (Peter), sizing him up. He pulled off his shades and Gordon found himself looking into a pair of oily black eyes that were neither friendly nor human, but more the eyes of a wild animal on the run against predators and against himself, the biggest predator of all. One side of his cheek and jaw were swollen.

"So you've got a job that needs to be done," said Gordon (Peter), removing his own dark glasses.

"Can you do it? Benny said you're a printer."

Gordon broke the tension, leaning back, unzipping his jacket. "Yup. That I am. Brochures, pamphlets, stationary, business cards... but what you want printed is dangerous. Illegal. I could go to jail."

"We both could go to jail. How do I know you're not the police?" Paul did a quick scan of Gordon's (Peter's) expressionless face. Nothing.

Reaching over, Gordon (Peter) felt the front of Paul's shirt. "Don't play that shit with me. How do I know you're not trying to set me up? Are you wearing a police bug?"

"Are you?"

As Paul leaned forward to feel Gordon's (Peter's) shirt, Gordon (Paul) pulled away and snapped, "If you touch me I'll kill you. *Don't be a fucking idiot!*"

Paul was stunned, as Gordon knew he would be. Wes and he used this technique often in the undercover business. It was a perfect tool for protecting their cover. The police wouldn't talk about killing someone.

"All right, all right!" Gordon (Peter) got the response he expected. They both settled down as Sheila came with their beers and left.

"What do you want?" asked Gordon (Peter).

"50 million in 100-dollar bills."

"50 million," repeated Gordon (Peter). He let out a low whistle. "You want me to—" His voice dropped off, letting Masella (Paul) finish. *Say it, man, say it, for the record.*

"I want you to print 50 million in counterfeit 100s."

Long pause. "What are you going to do with that much funny money?" Gordon was a pro. Now that he had the statement he needed for The Brush and the U.S. Attorney, he started to enjoy himself. Besides, he loved good ribs.

"That's none of your fucking business," snapped Paul. "Can you do it?"

"Yeah, I can print anything. Hell, I can print toilet paper with the Habsburg KK Coat of Arms if I have to," snorted Gordon (Peter), digging into his ribs as soon as Sheila put down the plate in front of him. "What do I get if I do this for you?"

"If you do a good job I'll pay you $40K."

The two set to work on the ribs. Gordon (Peter) finished off the first stack, mopped his face and reached for the second one. "That doesn't seem like a fair price. 40K for 50 Mill."

"Take it or leave it," said Paul, pretending to be totally absorbed in gnawing and chewing.

"Hell, its only funny money," muttered Gordon (Peter) between chews.

"If things go well I'll be back for more." Paul leaned back, wiping his hands and waiting.

Gordon (Peter) put down the rack of bones gnawed clean. "Who the hell are you? You own a bank?"

"You print and don't ask questions. Is that clear?" Paul glared at him.

"Okay, okay. I'm going to need some dough up front to buy supplies." Gordon (Peter) drained the rest of his beer and signaled to Sheila for another one.

"How much?"

"About 3 thou."

"I'll give you 2 and the rest when the job's done."

Gordon shook his head dubiously. "That's cutting it pretty close. The inks and papers are expensive, man. Shit. Okay, I'll see if I can get a good price for them. The trouble is, you need to use the best inks. I'm not sure you know anything about printing."

"I don't. That's why I'm paying you to do the work."

"I don't want to bore you, but I think I need to get you up to speed on a few things," said Gordon (Peter), warming up to his subject. "In order to make genuine currency, you use a photo offset process. You make a negative of the currency with a camera and then you put the negatives on a piece of masking material."

"Enough. I'm already bored," Paul snapped. "How long will it take you to get the job done?"

"If I work all night, about five days. I can start next Wednesday." (*Two days to line up the printer*, thought Gordon. *Good luck, Wes boy.*)

The two finished their meal in comfortable silence with intermittent small talk about the latest NBA basketball scores and who was going to win the title.

In the surveillance van, Wes, Kim, Shane and Rombo were watching and listening to the entire transaction. Silently they gave each other high fives. As usual, Gordon was putting on a first class act.

Gordon (Peter) drained the rest of his beer. "I'm a perfectionist," he said, dipping his napkin in the water glass and wiping his mouth and hands. "You'll like my work."

Paul removed his wallet and peeled out 20 100-dollar bills. "Count them if you want."

"Why should I?" retorted Gordon (Peter). "Why would you want to screw me?"

"Yeah, right," Paul frowned, motioning to the waitress to bring him the check.

The two men parted at the door. Gordon went to the rest room.

Agents Gerr and Eastwood waited at the bar for Gordon, then signaled an all clear and followed him out of the restaurant to the surveillance van.

"Great going, man!" Grinning broadly, Wes slapped him on the back.

"Get this piece of shit off me," growled Gordon, obviously pleased with his success. "Man, those ribs were good. I was just getting started. We have to remember that place."

"Yeah, sure. It'll be there for us for future counterfeit printing jobs," grunted Wes as he unwired him. The rest of the agents crowded close to offer their congratulations. As soon as they returned to headquarters and checked in, they took off for Angie's bar to celebrate.

"Tomorrow, tomorrow," sang Kim as they landed in bed around 1AM. "What time is the meeting with The Brush?"

Wes joined in, humming the final chorus as he pulled her close. "Don't know, don't care."

13
Seward's Folly

"Good job, Gordon," grumbled Fuller.

"Damn right it's a good job," said Wes to himself. What made it so difficult for this asshole to say something civil to a staff that works its butt off for him?

It was a rhetorical question. He already knew the answer.

SAIC Fuller caressed the top leaves of an avocado plant. "I grew this myself from the pit," he said proudly. "The trunk now measures seven inches."

"Very fine, sir," said Gordon. "Seven inches. My, my. That's quite an achievement!" He didn't dare look at Wes, who was about to lose it. The two had the same droll sense of humor. In former days when Gordon had been in the office, they'd always kept the laughs coming. The Brush was often the brunt of their jokes.

"I learned how to do it on YouTube. Some mighty fine videos on YouTube. This little Japanese girl had a whole windowsill of avocado plants. Imagine! You see, the trick is, you have to soak the bottom part of the seed in water for a day and then carefully remove its skin."

"Like removing a foreskin. Yes, sir, very important," said Gordon, his voice dripping with admiration.

Wes could no longer control himself. Fortunately at that moment, Ruby, the receptionist, knocked on the door to admit U.S. Attorney Michael Berger, a mid-thirtyish balding man with a paunch, wearing thick horn-rimmed glasses.

"Sorry I'm late, gentlemen." Berger looked around the office, removing his eyeglasses as if to make sure he was in the right place. "Well, Larkin, I see you've remodeled again!"

"Do you like it?" Larkin Fuller shook hands with Berger. "Very tropical for winter in Chicago, ha ha!" Fuller gestured toward Wes. "You know Agent Charles. And I believe you also know Agent Mitchell Gordon."

"Yes, yes, of course." Berger glanced peremptorily at both agents. Again, Wes and Gordon dared not look at each other. Berger's contempt for underlings was so palpable you could cut it with a knife, thought Wes.

"Agents Gordon and Charles have just played this recording for me." Fuller pushed the replay button of the Peter-Paul meeting the previous day.

At the conclusion of the recording, again Berger removed his eyeglasses and wiped them with a tissue. He was visibly impressed. "So you have what you need," he offered. "You have the statements by 'Paul' of his intention to print counterfeit money and you have his contract with Gordon, 'Peter,' the printer, confirmed by the exchange of money. That's good."

"And that's enough, isn't it?" declared Fuller. "It is undeniable conspiracy. We can stop right there and pick up Masella on those two charges."

Wes steepled his hands and let his eyes bounce between the SAIC and U.S. Attorney. When Berger didn't respond, Wes jumped in. "Actually sir, in my opinion, this case is not big enough with just a conspiracy charge. It will not get us what we're looking for."

"And exactly what *are* you looking for?" glared Fuller, as if he didn't already know.

"Agent Charles is right," Berger came to Wes's rescue. "The case is nothing on a conspiracy charge alone. We need to lock up these guys and put an end to this, once and for all. We already have enough Intel that indicates Masella is not a lone operator. He's part of a network, and until now we haven't had a chance to catch any of them. Catching Masella on counterfeiting charges would give us the kind of lead we've been looking for."

"So I need to put *my* office, *my* counterfeiting squad and *my* reputation on the line, to run the risk of entrapment. Is that it?" Fuller was now red in the face. He'd started pacing the office between the waterfall and grass hut.

"We all put our reputations on the line with this case," Wes reminded him. Gordon nodded silently.

"We need to take possession of the entire gang," agreed Berger. "Agent Charles is right. What good is it if we just get them on conspiracy? The case needs some balls."

That was the last straw. The Brush was furious. "And who's going to get called in on this if the operation fails?" he raised his voice.

"The operation will not fail," said Wes firmly, eyeballing Berger.

"Yes," said Berger, maintaining his mild tone. "I believe Wes—Agent Charles—is correct. If these two men are on the case, you can count on it, Fuller. *It—they will not fail.*"

The irony of it was too much for Wes and Mitch. Nothing was ever lost on these two men. They knew they were, after all, disposable. As good as they were, the Agency could always pick up more black stooges and train them to risk their lives undercover. As for Larkin Fuller, the Agency had been looking for a good way to get rid of him for years already. What did they care if the case went down?

Attorney Berger opened the office door to leave and Gordon followed him out.

"Agent Charles, wait!" ordered Fuller. Closing the office door, Fuller rose to his full 5 feet 6 inches before Wes.

"This is my office, and no agent is going to tell me what to do. Is that clear? Do you hear me?" He waved a fist at Wes, the blood vessels on his forehead and shaved scalp protruding.

He really is an ugly sonofabitch, thought Wes. Especially when he's angry. "Sir, I'd like to—"

"WHO DO YOU THINK YOU ARE?" shouted Fuller.

"This is the way I see it," Wes tried again but was outshouted.

"JUST WHO? ANSWER ME. WHO THE HELL DO YOU THINK YOU ARE, AGENT CHARLES?"

Fuller's voice was now so loud it could be heard throughout the office. Mitch, Kim, Len, Marc, Kevin, and Rambo looked up from their desks and exchanged glances.

Kim strode down the hallway to the water fountain outside the SAIC's door. She didn't want to miss a word of this one because she already knew what was coming.

On the other side of the office complex, W-2 had also heard Fuller bellowing. Word traveled fast. All the agents in the office had already learned what was on the agenda that morning, confirmed by the appearance of U.S. Attorney Berger. W-2 met his mother in the hallway and pretended to loiter a short distance away, riffling through some papers he'd brought with him.

"DID YOU HEAR ME, AGENT CHARLES?"

"I'm sure the whole office heard you, sir," answered Wes.

The Brush ignored him and continued: **"IF YOU DON'T WANT TO WORK UNDER MY COMMAND, I CAN HAVE YOUR ASS TRANSFERRED TO ALASKA!"**

"Alaska," thought Wes. *"Maybe I can get a pet polar bear. Nope. Too cold for Kim. She doesn't even like Chicago in the winter."*

"Agent Fuller, sir, please. I respect you as my boss, as the agent in charge in this office. I have put my life on the line to make cases for you. I have had guns at my head, traveled all over this fucking country working undercover in some of the worst conditions, in the worst areas and for some of the biggest racist assholes in the Secret Service."

He was winding up. Kim had already turned on her wrist recorder. This was going to be a speech for posterity. She leaned against the wall, thoroughly enjoying her husband at his best.

"I have been out there by myself and proven myself again and again. Over and over. I've made some of the biggest cases ever made in this fucking office!"

He was on a roll. Mitch came over to stand next to Kim and the other squad members. Even Kevin and Len were cheering him on. It was about time someone stood up to The Brush.

"Who in this office has made the most arrests, the best cases, and put this office on top of the Federal Law Enforcement pole? Me, dammit, ME!"

Fuller had fallen silent.

"If you don't want me in your office, transfer me. Tell headquarters to transfer me, but I'll bet you they won't send me to Alaska! I'm too good of an agent.

Wes let that sink in before he continued.

"And let me tell you one more thing. I hope this isn't because I'm Black, because that's what I'm getting from this conversation!"

That did it. Wes's last jab landed right in the solar plexus.

Fuller fell back into his Eames chair, flushed and defeated, a TKO countdown in the second round. "STOP!" he shouted weakly. "Just go and make the case, dammit, and get out of here. Keep me advised."

Wes shut the office door firmly behind him and strode down the hallway to his office. Kim caught up with him. "Agent Charles, may I be the first to congratulate you!" Later she'd have the pleasure of replaying the scene for him and acting out the parts. Kim had a knack for dialects and one of her specialties was mimicking The Brush.

W-2 ducked into his office before his father saw him.

"That was quite a speech!" Rachel was standing by the door with the other agents. "Someone needed to say it and I'm glad it was your dad!"

"Oh. Yeah." W-2 grinned, hoping Rachel couldn't tell how he was quaking inside. *Damn, she's gorgeous!* "He's the man all right," he added lamely, wishing he could think of a clever comeback.

14
Gutenberg Redux

Monday, February 22, 2010

As soon as Wes recovered from the blowout with The Brush, he called Johnny K., another informant who owned a print shop in Cicero, the heart of Chicago's Mafia district. Johnny had done some expert work counter-feiting some government checks. Thanks to the teamwork of W-2 and the forensic squad, Wes's hunches about Johnny had proven correct and he'd arrested him.

Johnny was a moody fellow, tall, stoop-shouldered with large hands, gangly arms and mousy brown hair. His face had aged beyond his 52 years, possibly from acid tripping and chain smoking. Now he was in his mid-fifties but looked older.

He met Johnny at the print shop, located in a mini-strip mall on South Canal Street near Taylor, next to a Circle K, a car wash and Taco Bell.

"Here's the deal." Briefly Wes described what he needed.

Johnny was livid. "You gotta be kidding! Absolutely NOT! What kind of an idiot do you think I am? All of you guys oughtta be put away yerselves, coming up with schemes like this! Why the hell would I want to get into more trouble?" Eyes flashing, Johnny waved his hand toward the door, gesturing for Wes to leave. "Meetin's over."

"I'm not so sure about that, bud," drawled Wes, patting his hip pocket and not moving. "Are you looking to do more time? Even though there's free room and board at the joint, I've heard the food is only mediocre. And as for the company—"

"Shit," grumbled Johnny. "You guys are all the same."

"So can you do the job?"

"Yeah, I can do it." Johnny pointed to the giant Gutenberg press visible through the open door in back. "That thing can do anything I ask it to."

Wes motioned for Johnny to open the counter bar and let him through to take a look at it up close.

It was a formidable beast, all right. He was sure Johnny was right, that it could do whatever he told it to.

Wes turned to Johnny and shook his hand. "We're in business. Write down the list of supplies you'll need and I'll have them for you tonight."

"Shit." Johnny reached for a scratch pad and started scribbling product names and brands of inks, papers, and other items.

As soon as he left the print shop, Wes called Mitch. "Hey man, go see a good flick or shoot a few hoops. We're gonna be busy for the next few days."

The printing had to be done at night, since they could only work during off hours when the shop was closed to customers.

On Wednesday, February 24, Wes and Mitch appeared promptly at 5:15PM at the delivery entrance in the alley behind the shop, with several bags of supplies.

A sour-faced Johnny K. unlocked the door and let them in. "Jeezus," he muttered, blasting them with his foul nicotine breath. "I never thought I'd be doin' somethin' like this for the Feds."

"Be impressed," said Mitch, sidling up next to Wes, shaking Johhny's hand and showing him his badge.

"We brought food and drinks and plenty of smokes." Wes was well armed against any excuses to interrupt the all-night operation. He handed Johnny a carton of Marlboro's.

"Ben Franklins are the specialty *du jour*," said Wes. I need $50M in $100 bills with at least five different serial numbers," Wes instructed Johnny.

"500,000 in 100s," Johnny whistled under his breath. "That buys a lotta burritos." He set to work making images of the bills, then developing the negatives and making the plates.

It was one thing to learn about how to counterfeit money and another to actually watch someone doing it. Two negatives of the portrait side and one negative of the back side of the bill were developed and dried. Then, using opaque on one of the portrait sides, the next step was to touch out all the green—the seal and serial numbers—and replace the serial number with a new one. The back side didn't require any retouching because it was all one color.

Each of the three flats was a different color: black and two shades of green that were made by mixing the inks.

Burning the plates was a three-stage operation for each of the flats. This produced four images on each plate, with an equal space between each bill.

It was a tedious process, soon requiring another carton of Marlboro's. Wes took the negatives and plates home with him each night for safe-keeping.

The Brush was as nervous as a first-time expectant father pacing in front of the hospital delivery room. Day and night he rang Wes to check on progress. "What's going on? Any problems? How're you doing? You coming along all right? Any hitches?" etc., etc. Maybe Alaska should be the next theme for Fuller's office. Icebergs, frozen tundra, a dog sled for a desk. Real huskies for The Brush to yell at. *Now there's a concept.*

By the end of the week Johnny had finished the negatives and plates.

"Sunday's our printing day," Wes told Gordon. Both men had to admit they were excited. They were involved in making a case that would set a precedent. They were making history. As for the risk, life was risky. You could be walking across the street with a green light and a car could come speeding along, drunk driver, yada yada... Life was a bitch. And the best part of it would be the look on The Brush's face when they pulled it off. As for U.S. Attorney Berger, he'd stand a good chance for another four-year appointment.

At 6:30AM Wes picked up Gordon. They stopped for coffee, Danishes, donuts and a couple more cartons of cigarettes and arrived at the print shop at 7AM.

The hours slipped by; Johnny worked, loading paper in the press, printing the black plate first, mixing the inks for the serial numbers and the back side, printing, testing, mixing exactly the right colors, cleaning the press to print the other side...more testing and printing...

"So what's wrong with these?" demanded Gordon, when the latest batch of bills appeared perfect but to Johnny still didn't pass scrutiny.

"Wrong color. Too dark." Johnny shoved them into the shredder and started over, printing, testing, and mixing the inks...

After ten hours the three men were getting on each other's nerves. Wes didn't want to think about what might happen if Gordon didn't deliver on schedule. They were cutting it close.

"Sorry, guys. I need to have a good product," Johnny tossed another cigarette butt in the overflowing ashtray. "I'm a perfectionist."

"You know, Bud, this shit won't hit the street," Wes reminded him, standing over his shoulder as he shredded the latest attempt. "Your 'perfection' will never be seen or exposed. You will never be a Michelangelo!"

"Geez. You don't fuckin' understand, do you?" muttered Johnny. "How could you? How could *anyone* understand?!"

Gordon started to pace the shop. "This guy's got problems," he muttered to Wes. "We need to get the show on the road."

"Go to sleep," Wes advised, sweeping the counter clean and offering it as a bed. "We'll take turns."

Finally, around 3:30AM Monday morning, they were finished.

Wes examined the bills closely, riffled through them and felt a pressure valve release inside his head. They did it! The bills were more than passable. They were perfection. Fifty million dollars worth of beautiful looking funny money.

"Good work, Johnny," Wes praised what was left of him. "Yeah, great work, Johnny," added Gordon, giving him a high five.

The bags under the informant's eyes added another twenty years to his exhausted looking face, but his eyes were bright and the lines around his mouth were smug. He knew he did good work and he was proud of it. To him, that's all that mattered.

Wes and Gordon placed the bills, negatives and plates in a large box which they carried outside to their unmarked van. Gordon slept while Wes drove them to the office. It was close to 5AM when they wheeled into the garage.

The two men barreled out of the van, locked it, checked the doors and headed for the office where they promptly fell asleep at their desks.

"Hey, big man!" Kim tapped him on the shoulder. Gordon was still asleep and no one else was around. She nuzzled her nose in his neck. "You smell like cigarettes and coffee and Man," she murmured. "The Brush just landed in his Hawaiian heliport. Give him a minute to water his orchids and avocado plants."

"Hell no!" Wes bolted upright and ran a hand over his chin stubble. He went over to Gordon's desk and gave him a shake.

"Msymyzgg... whassup?" Gordon rubbed his bloodshot eyes and stared at Wes. "Jeeze, you look like shit."

"So do you, man. The Brush is here."

Kim watched the two with amusement as they headed for the rest room with their toilet kits.

By the time they emerged, Marc, Shane, Rombo and Len had arrived. The four agents pretended to busy themselves at their desks as they waited for the curtain to come up on the next act.

Nervously clasping and unclasping her hands, Ruby approached Wes's desk. "Agent Fuller is ready to see you."

The past week in the office had been a morgue. The Brush was so uptight about the Masella case; everyone had been going about their business keeping their mouths zipped up and staying out of his way.

The door opened before Wes even touched the handle. Agent Fuller nodded officiously in the direction of the elevators and the garage.

On the way to the van the three men said nothing. The tension was thick enough to cut with a knife.

Wes unlocked the van and flipped the lid off the box. He had to admit, the stacks of 100s looked pretty damn good. How fitting that Franklin himself, known to be one of the best printers in Philadelphia, should be memorialized two centuries later as part of hundreds, maybe thousands of USSS counterfeit sting operations, thought Wes. He could imagine the editorial that would have appeared in his *Poor Richard's Almanac!*

The Brush was visibly pleased. "Shit, Wes, your printer did such an excellent job with these counterfeits, they're better than passable. You need to keep your eyes on this guy. He may get into the counterfeit business."

Wes and Gordon deliberately avoided eye contact. Such a dumbshit remark deserved no response.

"Now go get his ass," ordered The Brush, heading back to the elevator.

Wes and Gordon let Fuller get well ahead of him before they cracked a smile.

"Your call now, Mitch." Wes handed him a non-trackable phone that would throw the name "Peter" to the person who picked up.

Gordon dialed "Paul's" number.

He picked up. "Yeah."

"I'm finished with the job. Where do you want to meet?"

"How about on Chestnut Street near Rush?"

"Do you have my money?"

"Yes. You'll get your cut when I see the 50."

"11:30A."

Click.

The two men headed back to the office. Wes gathered the team into the conference room to map out a plan.

"Don't let those counterfeits out of your sight," warned The Brush as Wes was entering the conference room. "If we lose any of them, all of our asses will be grass and headquarters will be the lawnmower. Our careers will be over."

"The headquarters lawn mower will be trashed if it meets your fat ass!" thought Wes, nodding. He was glad none of the other agents had overheard Fuller's stupid comment. *When the Lawnmower Hits the Brush.* It would make a nice title for a movie or a novel. Or maybe *Brush The Lawnmower Man.*

All the vans were in place. The sky was cloudless, the sun was bright, and for the end of February it was surprisingly mild. The arrest would take place in broad daylight. *Perfect conditions for a good video*, gloated Kim, who was in the van with Wes, parked across the street from Gordon.

The prearranged signal for the arrest would be the moment Gordon removed a cigar from his jacket, lit it and started puffing.

As soon as Wes saw a beat-up looking light blue Dodge van rounding the corner on Chestnut Street heading toward Rush, Wes gave Gordon the "go" sign to drive up and park behind it.

From his rearview mirror, Paul watched Gordon exit his SUV. He opened the car door and strode back to where Gordon was waiting. Both men did a quick eye sweep of the street to make sure no police were around before Gordon lifted the SUV hatchback and opened the box.

It was a large box... a lot of bills. Paul had to practically climb inside the vehicle to do a cursory inspection. Gordon blocked the open hatchback with his body half turned toward the street.

"Looks good," Paul finally called out, his head emerging from the hatchback.

From the surveillance van Wes and Kim exchanged satisfied smiles. *Almost home.*

"Let's put the box in my trunk and then I'll give you your money," said Paul.

It took the two of them to lift out the box and carry it over to Paul's van. Paul unlocked the trunk and they hoisted it in. Gordon gave the box a final push as Paul reached into a corner of the trunk beneath the spare tire to pull out an envelope.

The bills were brand new $100s. "I hope these aren't counterfeit," joked Gordon (Peter) drily.

Paul busied himself with securing the box in the van, covering it up with a jacket and some other clothes while Gordon (Peter) counted out the money. It took several minutes to check through so many $100s, and because they were new, they stuck together. Gordon (Peter) made a point of deliberately counting them twice.

"Okay," he said at length. "We're good to go."

Removing a cigar and lighter from his jacket pocket, he cupped his hand around the tip and lit it. Inhaling deeply, he blew large smoke rings into the clear blue sky.

As if out of nowhere, G-cars appeared and screeched to a halt in front of and behind Masella's and Gordon's vans.

"United States Secret Service. You're under arrest!" Wes, Kim, Kevin, Rombo, and Shane surrounded Masella (Paul) and Gordon (Peter) and pushed them up against Masella's van, holding them at gunpoint. Marc was back at the office working the cameras with Len, who was in one of the G-cars.

"What the hell!" yelped Gordon (Peter) with just the right dose of shock and awe as his buddies yanked his hands behind his back and clamped on the cuffs.

Masella's face registered surprise and shock and then it went blank. The big man was going down. In his entire career as a criminal he had never been so hoodwinked. It was an insult to his talent and his style. Without a struggle he let the other agents cuff him, take possession of the van and the box of counterfeit money.

Kim opened the back door of the G-car for Wes and Masella.

Rombo climbed in after them. The defeated Masella looked like a hot dog squeezed between Rombo's bulk and Wes's brawn. He couldn't budge even if he'd wanted to.

Kim climbed into the driver's seat and waited for Kevin and Shane to push Gordon into the back seat of their van before she started the motor. In the rearview mirror she was amused when she saw Masella openly gawking at her. A gorgeous female broad and a black one at that, as part of the take-down! Wes also caught it. The two didn't dare look at each other. These moments of recognition were some of the precious parts of their relationship that both of them savored.

At the office, Rombo and Wes carried the box to the evidence room while Masella was processed for lock-up.

Wes eyed the box with satisfaction. "No need to inventory it," he thought. Mitch and he had packed it themselves as it came off Johnny K's printing press only a few hours ago. They already had a list of the inventory with the serial numbers and it was logged in. Piece of cake.

Or actually more than cake: a steak dinner on the house, for the entire counterfeit squad at Mike Ditka's. They were grateful that The Brush excused himself.

Wes, Kim and Mitch were amused. They knew he didn't like to be seen with people of color. They'd once overheard him saying to Kevin Gerr, who he considered a like-minded agent that he didn't want to tarnish his reputation. Gerr, of course, had no choice. Wes was in charge of the squad. Also, he had too much respect and admiration for Wes's undercover work and all the successful cases he'd made, to let The Brush's bigotry influence him.

15
Lock-Up

Tony Masella was furious. Benny Portera, that rat. Never would he have guessed that Benny would be the one to panic and go pussy. What the fuck happened? Did someone fuck with his mind? Chemicals? Drugs?

Benny was a slick guy, one of the cleverest crooks he'd ever met. A good Catholic who went to Mass every Sunday and said his fucking novenas, carried around a rosary... confessed every week to some fucking gay retard who once asked him to unzip his pants... That lying motherfucker had told him that his priest was the one who got the charges dismissed. Since when had the Feds become ordained priests?

Shit. Did he have any fucking idea what would be in store for him now? Freedom: Ha. Life on the other side all right. He'd make sure Benny's favorite Sky Merchant would execute the orders. *Credo in Deum, Patrem omnipotentem creator emcaelietterae.* (What does it mean)?

Masella placed two calls, the first to a crackerjack attorney, Eldon Howell, who didn't come cheap but would be worth everything it would cost. Anyway, he damned sure wasn't paying the shot on this one. By now, with all the money he'd printed up he should be living like a king. But no, Father Ira's business partner, Giuseppe Tubiano, "Peppi," that piece of turd, that fucking Botox pussyprick said it wasn't time yet. *Time for what, for Chrissake?*

"Just a little bit longer, Mr. Masella," Mr. Wonderment promised. "We just need to do this right and then you and your good wife, Patty, are going to have all the things you've ever wanted in life."

The other call was to Patty.

She was angry and drunk. "Shut up and listen to me." Tony cut through her hysterical rant. "You need to get the car back."

"I need to do *what?*" Patty shrieked. "Do you understand what I just said, you liar, you motherfucker, you douchebag, you piece of scum?? You promised me you were through with all this shit, that you weren't gonna do it no more. If we've got no car I can't get to work. I took the bus today and came in late and the boss said if I can't show up on time—"

"Shut the fuck up!" Tony shouted into the phone. "Listen to me! Call Agent Wesley Charles and tell him you want the car back. Take down this number. It's a direct line. Start calling him now and if you don't get him, keep leaving messages."

"I have no way to get to work," sobbed Patty hysterically.

"DID YOU HEAR ME, BITCH?" screamed Masella. "YOU NEED TO GET THE CAR BACK. DO NOT LET UP WITH THEM UNTIL YOU GET THE FUCKING CAR BACK. And then I want you to come over here and visit me. You understand? I NEED TO TALK TO YOU. DRIVE THE FUCKING CAR OVER HERE TO VISIT ME."

"I can't drive it to the jail if I don't have it," Patty wailed.

Shit. Masella tried one more time. He lowered his voice. "Patty, you WILL get the car back. First you need to call Agent Charles and ask to pick it up. Take down this number."

By the time he hit disconnect Tony was dripping with sweat. He smelled like a sewer. *Shit.*

Local and national media pulled out all the stops, giving the Chicago Secret Service Counterfeit Squad exactly the kind of publicity and attention that SAIC Larkin Fuller craved—and that Agents Wes Charles, Mitch Gordon and the rest of the team deserved.

Fuller's idiot grin made front page news of the *Chicago Tribune.* Inside pages showed Wes with the box of counterfeit hundred dollar bills. Fortunately, TV and the Internet by-passed The Brush and interviewed Wes. Mug shots of Tony Masella were everywhere and remained at the top of breaking news on Google for 48 hours. By that time the whole world knew what the crook looked like. His name was indelibly engraved on their frontal lobes.

Then, suddenly, as if it had never happened, the media moved on to other events: a late winter snow storm in the Dakotas; overturned school bus in Kansas, injuring 20 and killing the driver; 14-year-old girl raped in an Oakland, California used car lot; etc., etc. The Masella case disappeared altogether.

"Fickle media," was Kim's comment.

"No, actually I think it's more than that," said Wes.

"How so?"

"Time will tell. W-2 and Rachel have been doing a lot of research in their spare time. It's more than a hunch, Honey Bunch."

"So you think—"

"Yes," said Wes. "Someone silenced the media. And that 'someone' has even more clout than law enforcement and the U.S. Secret Service. Whoever has the biggest boots gets to trample the grapes into wine. If you haven't heard that piece of wisdom before now, guess what? I haven't either."

"Wine as in blood?" repeated Kim.

"You've got it."

"Then it has something to do with the banks."

Wes nodded. "That's only a small part of it."

"*In nomine Patris, et Filii, et Spiritus Sancti. Amen.*"

"Where'd you learn *that*?" Wes grinned.

"When I was five years old I had a Catholic girlfriend who lived next door. It means 'cover your ass, and look both ways before you cross the street,'" said Kim. "I think I'm getting the picture."

16
Triple Dip

"Did you hear the news? Tony Masella took a fallout."

"WHAT? "When? Who ratted?" Peppi took a puff of his cigarillo, his eyes resting on the electronic photo album of Father Ira on his desk. Each of the photos paused for several seconds, and then moved on to the next and the next, like a slide show. Peppi now had over 200 photos of the two of them.

He gazed at Father Ira in swim trunks, tanned and smiling into the camera... Father Ira bedecked with leis at the love-in, bare-chested, in a grass skirt, dancing with the natives... Father Ira and himself on the beach at sunset, barefoot and dressed in matching white embroidered surplices, gazing into each other's eyes... The photo album was turned on with a tiny remote that Peppi carried on his keychain. Otherwise it appeared as an ebony black paperweight.

"How soon can you come to Rome, *tesoro mio* (my sweetheart)?" he murmured into the phone.

"How soon do you want me?"

"Like tomorrow?"

As soon as Peppi hung up with Father Ira, he placed a call to Cardinal Cosimo Scatturo at the Vatican. He was put through at once.

"*Securim, Cosi! NUNC!*"

"*Imo.*"

"*Chi-Chi Portero. Benny Portero. P-O-R-T-E-R-O.*"

        "*Imo.*"

"*Nunc! Securim!*"

        "*Imo.*"

At once Cardinal Scatturo called the Three First National Plaza Archdiocese hotline in Chicago.

Peppi met Father Ira's plane at the Leonardo DaVinci Airport. "It was a sting. A setup," said Father Ira. After a leisurely dinner they were relaxing in Peppi's hot tub.

"The Feds again?"

Father Ira grinned at the slogan on the mug that Peppi just handed him: "Don't sweat the petty things... Pet the sweaty things."

It had been ten years already since the two had been together. Peppi owned an upscale dress shop on Via Condotti in Rome. As a celebrity designer, he could make his own schedule. Although it was no secret that he was gay, no one would have suspected he led a double life with a priest. Peppi would have been delighted if Father Ira decided one day to "defrock" and move permanently to Rome, but the couturier knew the priest enjoyed his other life in Chicago too much to give it up. At times he felt jealous, but what the hell? He had him whenever he wanted him, in more ways than one. Peppi knew his inside connections to the Vatican were far more valuable than those of a mere priest.

"I assume Masella has an attorney?" asked Peppi, climbing out of the hot rub and reaching for a towel.

"The best. Eldon Howell. Still, it's going to be like trying to nail Jello to a tree. Howell will argue entrapment and he'll take it to the Supreme Court if he has to. There's too much at stake here if the Feds win. They're hell bent on setting a precedent. The case will make major media, which means SS agents all over the country will crow like banty roosters just fantasizing about trying out this clever trick themselves. The agent in charge of the case, Wes Charles, is no dummy. He's a veteran, one of the best in the Agency. Also a native of Chicago."

"Anything new on Martin Seligman's trade program?"

"*Nessun.* He's brought in some more suckers, but a couple of them who've been waiting for over eight months are squawking. They're getting tired of Seligman's shtick."

"One can hardly blame them. Thank God that's his shit to deal with and not ours. Do you think there's something to it after all?"

Father Ira climbed out of the hot tub and waited for Peppi to dry him off. It was a ritual the two of them had initiated several years ago that added to the enjoyment of hot tubing together. "It's an interesting program but as I've said often enough, do we really care? Or, maybe the question should be, does it really matter? In the long run, who suffers? Surely not us. And surely not the people on the streets who get a chance to have a life because of us and our 'good works.'

"'*Know ye not that the unrighteous shall not inherit the kingdom of God?*'" quoted Father Ira. "'*Be not deceived: neither fornicators, nor idolaters, nor adulterers, nor effeminate, nor abusers of themselves with mankind, nor thieves, nor covetous, nor drunkards, nor revilers, nor extortioners, shall inherit the kingdom of God.' —1 Corinthians: 6.*"

Peppi grinned mischievously as he gently patted his friend's more sensuous parts. "So I guess no matter how you cut it, we're doomed."

Later when they were talking about the latest global happenings—uprisings, bank collapses, high rate of unemployment, etc., etc., Father Ira said, "I know this sounds pedestrian for me to bring up, Peppi, but sometimes I can't help thinking we're living in a fish bowl."

"I like the analogy of Russian Matryoshka Dolls better," said Peppi. "Or Chinese boxes. I have a sensitive nose. Fish bowls stink unless you change the water every few days. The tiniest Matryoshka doll is totally protected by layers and layers of Mother Church. Generations of lies and cover-up."

"The part that I like most about all of this," said Father Ira, "is the amazing *power* of the Church. It's like a total whitewash. Just mention the word 'Catholic' to a believer, and they genuflect inside or get down on their knees. The Church can do no wrong!"

"Astonishing, isn't it?" Peppi smiled wickedly. "It's called mind control and it's been going on for centuries. A good Catholic looks the other way. I heard rumors of a report that will be released soon by the Survivors Network of Those Abused by Priests. They call themselves SNAP and according to the statistics they've collected, nearly 60 percent of Chicago's Roman Catholic parishes have had a priest publicly accused of sexually abusing a child. This is your home city, my love!"

"It is like Teflon, is it not?" grinned Father Ira.

"Or vaseline..." Peppi reached for the priest's hand and started to stroke it. "Poor schmucks. It's all a game you know."

The next morning over breakfast, Father Ira stirred his coffee thoughtfully and looked up at Peppi, who was buttering a croissant and slathering it with strawberry jam. "Peppi, did you ever consider that even the game is an illusion?"

"Of course!" Peppi chuckled. "He who makes the rules rules the game. And he who wants to change the game changes the rules. It's all very simple and predictable."

"Tell me Peppi, speaking of change, to change the subject, what are you going to do about the rat?"

"Already handled. *In fact*, while we're talking..."

17
Stuff Happens

Wednesday, March 3, 2010 – Chicago Metropolitan Correctional Facility

"You're too clever to get caught, Tony. How the hell did it happen?"

Eldon Howell sat down across from Masella in the visitors' conference room of the Metropolitan Correctional Facility and fixed his steel grey eyes on his client. The attorney, impeccably dressed in a navy suit and open-necked pale blue shirt, was clean-shaven except for a thin mustache neatly bordering his upper lip. Those who remembered the actor David Niven in his prime would have immediately mistaken Eldon for the famous British actor, but with an American accent.

"It was a fucking frame-up," said Tony. "A sting."

"And you fell for it."

"Eldon, what I need to know is, is there anyone else besides Benny Portera who ratted? What can you do for me?" Masella looked bad. He had dark circles under is eyes and his left cheek and jaw were swollen. His breath smelled of nicotine and anger.

Eldon waited for him to continue. When he didn't, Eldon prompted, "I have no information, Tony, but I'll do what I can. You run a tight ship. What's going on?"

"There's always a price, a ticket," Masella fumed. "You know that, Mr. Attorney, better than anyone. Portera thought he could buy his freedom from the Feds."

"Far more important right now is focusing on your own freedom," answered Eldon mildly. "You're asking me a question that only you can answer. You know this racket better than anyone. It's always a matter of who's on first... isn't that so?"

"Thanks for nothing," snickered Tony, wiping his runny nose on the sleeve of his uniform.

"How's Patty doing?"

"How do you think Patty's doing?"

"She's a good woman."

"You mean because she puts up with all my shit?" Tony sniffed. "Take it straight from the horse's mouth, if she had something better, she'd be gone. But there's one thing I gotta say. She's straight. And besides, Patty's got nothin' ta hide, so leave her alone."

"I didn't think she *did* have anything to hide," said Eldon, making a note to himself to call Patty later.

As Eldon was accompanied by a guard to the exit, he was overcome by a feeling of despair, which was unusual for him. He had no illusions about Masella. He was a crook and should have been locked up long ago.

Agent Wes Charles was a good guy. He'd done a good job staking out Masella and now that he had his prize where he wanted him, he'd do his damnedest to make sure there'd be no contracts out for anyone else besides Benny who may have been involved.

Whoever had printed the stuff did quality work, no doubt about it. The hundreds could have easily passed on the street, especially since the banks these days were not as careful as they should be. They had other fish to fry.

By the time Wes arrived at the office the next morning, his voice mailbox was jammed with messages from Patty Masella, Tony's wife. She'd started leaving messages at 5AM.

"Mr. Charles, Agent Charles, I need your help." *Sob. Gulp. Shaky voice:* "I got no car. You took our car. Tony's in jail and I've gotta get to work. I got no money. Tony left me with nothin', the fucking bastard!" *Hysteria, sobs.* "I need to talk to you, Mr. Charles!"

Wes returned her call, reassuring her that he'd see what could be done. At once he wrote a memorandum to the property department describing the age, condition and mileage of Masella's '92 Dodge Ram. "It would cost the government more money to keep it and auction it off than to give it back to Mrs. Masella," he pointed out.

The next day, Wes received consent. He phoned Patty and told her to come to the office and pick up the car. "I've just done a mitzvah," he thought, not without a certain amount of satisfaction.

Wes leaned back in his chair and closed his eyes. If he were a cat he would be purring right now, he thought. But he wasn't a cat, he reminded himself. He was a tiger. Before he felt good about this case, he needed to get a solid win from the jury and a strong statement from the judge, so other agents wouldn't have to go through the same shit in the future. Entrapment was a bitch.

The phone rang from one of the larger TV networks, requesting yet another interview.

Wednesday, March 3, 2010 – Chicago office

Kim was the first to find the write-up in the police reports. She sent the Internet hyperlink to Wes, then knocked on his office door and placed the printout on his desk.

On March 1, Dario Taccini, also known as "Benny Portera," was found dead in his apartment, hanging by the light cord. Apparent cause of death was suicide; medical reports were still incomplete.

"Agent Kim Charles, did I ever tell you how much I love you?" exclaimed Wes, looking over at her after he'd finished reading the printout. "When shit like this happens, nothing else seems to matter except what *really* matters."

Kim understood what he was trying to express. "And Agent Wesley Charles, did I ever tell you how clever you are? Your hunches have been right all along."

Wes was already piecing things together. Flashing in front of him was the Elite Restaurant scene when they were celebrating their 30th anniversary. The two men, Adam Csonka and his male friend seated nearby, who had been watching them... Csonka had appeared at the pool hall two days before when he'd met Benny to check in with him.

"Wait here." Sweeping by Kim and giving her hand a quick squeeze, Wes went to the file cabinet, pulled out his file on Benny and brought it to his desk.

He leafed through the folder until he came up with the report on February 12, 2010: the photo of Csonka's vehicle and license plate numbers. The vehicle, a red 2007 Chevy Silverado pickup truck, was registered in Kansas with Kansas plates, under the name of Peter O'Flannery.

O'Flannery was a 68-year-old Caucasian male, a janitor at Smithfield Elementary School. His vehicle was repossessed in 2009. A series of phone calls delivered the information that the dealership had gone belly-up shortly afterward. The repossessed vehicles were auctioned off. It was still registered under O'Flannery's name, even though he was no longer the owner—and even though O'Flannery's motor vehicle license had expired eight months ago.

18
Slam Dunk

Monday, March 8, 2010 – Chicago, Illinois

Wes concluded it wasn't just a matter of chance that the Masella case had been assigned to AUSA (Assistant District Attorney) Dan Walter. A young man in his early thirties with unruly brown hair, large wet eyes and an adenoidal way of talking, Woody Allen came to mind.

Dan Walter's AUSA experience thus far involved filing one charge and negotiating a couple of plea bargains. Leave it to the fraternity boys to dump a case that involved something as tricky as potential entrapment onto the desk of a newbie. "Let the rookie take the lumps."

Wes wasn't in the mood to babysit anyone in order to get the guilty verdict he needed.

"It figures," said Kim, delivering one of her favorite quotes in a Texas drawl: "We service what we sell, 'cause what we sell needs service."

After the third pre-trial conference, Wes was losing his patience. "How many times do I have to repeat the same details about how the fucking case was made? Is the guy trying to trap me into some kind of etch-a-sketch moment? It won't happen!" he fumed to Gordon and Kim.

Finally on the fourth go-around, Wes decided to use a strategy he should have tried two pretrial conferences ago. It had always worked in the past and he was confident it would work now.

As soon as they sat down opposite each other he eyeballed Walter. "You know, Dan, I like you. You're a smart fellow and I can tell you're going to go places. You're the kind of brilliant legal counsel our government needs. You've done such an outstanding job in these pre-trial conferences; I'm going to put in a special commendation on your behalf. Here's the story once again about exactly what happened. I made a PowerPoint for you to make it even easier for you to follow along."

Opening his laptop, Wes clicked on the first PowerPoint slide.

"*One:* Tony Masella aka Paul, initiated the conversation with Dario Taccini, aka Benny Portera. Paul asked Benny to find a printer to print $50Million.

"*Two:* Paul met with an undercover agent, believing him to be a print-er, and again asked the printer to print $50Million in counterfeit bills.

"*Three:* Paul gave the undercover agent $2,000 to purchase supplies to do the job.

"*Four:* Paul took possession of the $50Million printed counterfeit bills."

At the end of the PowerPoint was a summary. Walter's constipated expression vanished. "Wes, I think I can win this case. I really do!"

"Good!" beamed Wes. "I'm glad you feel that way. I feel the same way, Dan. In fact, I *know* you can win it. You've got what it takes, man (boy)!" *God help us all.* Wes wondered how long it took his mother to get him toi-let trained.

Two days later, as Wes drove into the parking garage of the Everett M. Dirksen U.S. Courthouse at 219 South Dearborn Street for the Federal Grand Jury hearing; he was feeling right at home. When he'd first taken a position as a Secret Service Agent, his offices had been in this building.

The entire complex of steel, concrete and plate glass buildings known as the Federal Center had been designed by the renowned German archi-tect Ludwig Mies van der Rohe, last director of the Bauhaus contempo-rary art school in Germany. The courthouse was a handsome structure set at a right angle to the John C. Kluczynski Federal building. The top 10 stories consisted of fifteen two-story courtrooms.

Although one couldn't help admiring the two buildings that were fond-ly called "skin and bones architecture," as a law enforcement agent, Wes had another take. Skin and bones brought forth the image of dead bodies, piles of them. It was so easy to throw stones at glass houses, as witnessed by the Oklahoma City Federal Courthouse bombing.

Wes had once written a report about the need to consider advanced security as an integral part of the architectural plan for any federal build-ing. Aesthetics was one thing; practicality was another. Glass buildings invited trouble. Wes had coined them AWTH: Accidents Waiting to Hap-pen.

Maybe Alexander Calder's steel flaming red 53-foot tall "Flamingo" sculpture was supposed to ward off evil. Wes remembered reading once that the Egyptians believed that flamingos were living representation of "Ra," the Sun God. Calder's Flamingo "Ra" could be an ET masking as a Homeland Security agent protecting the building against bombs and ter-rorists.

The fact that the Federal Building was named after the late Everett Dirksen held much more value for Wes than Bauhaus or Calder acclaim. Dirksen had represented Illinois in the U.S. House of Representatives from 1933-1949 and the U.S. Senate from 1951-1969 when he served as the Senate Minority Leader. During that time he played a major role in helping to write and pass the Civil Rights Act of 1964 and the Open Housing Act in 1968.

A couple of times as a Secret Service agent, Wes was assigned to protect well-known dignitaries who had devoted their lives to promoting white supremacy. They were true believers.

As a law enforcement officer in service to his country, Wes sucked it up. Kim wasn't joking when she said undercover agents are born actors. There was a time in this country when a black man dared not look straight at a white woman *or* man. "We've come a long way, baby," Wes and Kim reminded themselves often. But still, not far enough, they would add.

Thank God for politicians and statesmen like Everett Dirksen, who fought tooth and nail for what he knew was just and right.

Wes's testimony was a slam dunk. After Wes produced the box filled with 500,000 authentic looking hundred dollar bills—50 Million Dollars of funny money!—the jury had a single response: lock up the crook (*asshole, messing with our currency!*)

Fifty million dollars of Monopoly money that could have been floating around the city was nothing to laugh at. It wasn't difficult for every member of the jury to envision a hundred dollar counterfeit bill landing in their own wallets. The name of the game as most people well knew, was Hot Potato. If you use it you can go straight to jail without passing "Go," and if you keep it, you eat it.

As anticipated, the outcome was a true bill delivered to the court by the Grand Jury foreperson that it had heard sufficient evidence from the prosecution to believe that the accused Tony Masella had committed a crime and should be indicted.

The court set the trial date eight months later, on Tuesday, November 16, 2010. In the interim, AUSA Dan Walter had several pre-trial conferences with Wes and Gordon. At the conclusion of one of the conferences, Walter dropped the mother lode. "You're not going to like this, but—I have a feeling you're not going to like this—I've been discussing the case with Attorney Berger and several of the senior AUSAs. I have a strong feeling you're not going to like this, but here it is anyway."

Dan Walter removed a spotless white handkerchief from his navy pin-striped suit jacket and wiped the perspiration from his forehead. "We've uh, well *we all* have concluded that it would be a good idea, Agent Charles, for you *not* to testify in the case. That means that you will not testify in the case, but just assist me. Just assist me throughout the trial. You know how it is."

Wes gave him a quizzical look. "I'm not sure I understand what you mean by 'you know how it is,' Dan. Won't this send a signal to the Defense that it's highly unusual for the case agent not to testify?"

Walter avoided eye contact. "You're right. I knew you weren't going to like this, Agent Charles, but maybe..."

"Maybe what?" asked Wes.

"Maybe... but we don't want to take the chance. Maybe it will send a signal to the Defense that it's highly unusual for the case agent not to testify, but we don't want to take a chance. A chance that, because you know everything about the case from A to Z, that the Defense will grill you on every detail from A to Z."

"Yes?" Wes prodded him.

"I know you can handle the grilling, but why should we take a chance? Why should we give them the opportunity to present something like some technicality that might make this case more difficult?"

Wes admitted they did have a good point. He wished he could have more confidence in Walter. If only he would learn how to speak without repeating himself. He was so *nervous*. Clearly, it was going to be a tough performance with the defense pulling out all the stops to try to persuade the jury that the Feds were cruel bastards, determined to create non-existent cases if they could, just to get more innocent well-meaning people behind bars. On the streets, hostility against "the Feds," "cops"— anyone in a uniform, with a badge, helmet, billy club or weapon—had passed the boiling point, and no wonder.

After the string of police brutality incidents during the peak of the Arab Spring overseas and the Occupy Movement in the U.S., it didn't matter whether the agency was CPD, FBI, USSS, DEA, CIA or any other of the alphabet law enforcement groups; "We the People" often lumped all of them together. It was no longer a "good guy-bad guy" cops & robbers game. Law enforcement depended on OFA (orders from above) as far as John and Jane Doe were concerned... and that order could even be a Henny Penny.

The sky was falling because it had been deliberately primed by a lawless upper crust of corporate executives. Corruption on the street was plain vanilla compared to the 67 flavors at the top that included everything from banks, politicians, courts, churches... If one searched hard enough, one discovered that every ice cream flavor was another corporation filed in a registry with a name in capital letters.

With no lines that could be drawn in the sand, every court case was given a prize if the attorneys could figure out a way to pin the tail on the wrong donkey. Blowback from stings and other covert operations—premeditated crime, or in this case, entrapment—would be a perfect ace card for the accused.

If the defense could get the jury to drink their Kool-Aid, i.e., "all law enforcement agencies and their operations are corrupt," they'd be halfway to heaven and back—on the streets again making and passing more of the same shit. Tony Masella's defense attorney, Eldon Howell, got paid big bucks—real money—to keep the counterfeiters out of prison, or at least get them a plea bargain so they could go back to earning a living again. Unemployment was a bitch, especially for criminals.

Wes had met Eldon in the courts several times; he had great respect for him. Trim, clean-shaven, gray at the temples with keen blue eyes and a strong jawline, there was nothing shifty about him. If there was a designer label for integrity, he would be wearing it. As a professional, he played by the rules and did exactly what was expected of him.

That said, some people may have wondered whether, or how, attorneys who defended alleged or already previously convicted criminals slept at night. Another way of wondering how Eldon Howell could live with himself. No one stood in line to get more guilt. Most people already had enough of it to last a lifetime.

As far as Wes was concerned, that was Eldon's business. Someone had to do the dirty work and make lemonade out of lemons.

Possibly that's why Wes never had a desire to become an attorney. It seemed so much cleaner and more clear-cut to get paid to pick up crooks rather than defend them. Less stress, less baggage in the overhead bins. Denial was another bitch.

"Shit sticks to your shoes when you step in it," Kim was fond of saying. "And it smells," she added, rolling her eyes.

Each to his own. Working the streets undercover and taking the physical risks of an agent weren't Eldon Howell's idea of an adventure. He'd rather take paid risks. Whether or not he won the case, he still got his retainer, so in many ways it was always a win-win.

"Where are we going with this, Dan?" Wes returned to the conversation. "I will sit with you during the trial and we'll do this together."

"Yes, you will sit with me during the trial," Dan repeated. "I just knew—"

"I wasn't going to like it?" Wes interrupted. "Hell, I don't have any opinion either way. I just want Masella to be convicted and sentenced. I just want to set a precedent. However we can make that happen, Dan, is fine with me. I'll be happy to stand on my head and pull counterfeit bills from my nose if we can make this happen!"

"Oh, I don't think that will be necessary, Agent Charles," Walter hee-hawed like a mule, "although it would certainly be an interesting act."

19

Where's the Beach?

Martin Seligman was bored and frustrated. For the past four months, nothing had happened. Not that this was unusual. For the past four years—change that to 10...11...12—nothing had happened. Which was why Sabrina had snatched the house from him—*her house!* The nerve of that bleached blonde bitch—and made him live in this prison of a room in this ugly neighborhood.

Her house. Just because she won it in the alimony battle with her ex-husband. *Who* had lived in it with her for eight years after her divorce? Hel-*lo!* And whose name had Sabrina Rosenblum taken over? *Martin Seligman's name.* She was now Sabrina Seligman.

The Lake Worth rooming house had roaches and rats and one of the renters was an alcoholic. He was passing counterfeit bills at the liquor store. Martin had overhead a phone conversation on the hallway phone. The guy, whose name was Orville, or at least that's the name he went by, was talking about "dubs" and "jacksons" and then a few seconds later, "serial numbers."

He hadn't heard from Sabrina in two months.

"Good-bye, Martin," she said cheerfully the last time they spoke. "I'll see you around."

Thank God for Father Ira. Thank God for the Catholic Church. The Fed-Ex packages arrived regularly by the first of the month.

Not that he wasn't doing his part for the Catholic Church and their charities. In the past three months he'd lined up five new clients and placed over 120 million dollars on the trade platform. By the Big Boys' standards it wasn't a whole lot, but once things started rolling, he'd have some of the larger denominations coming in.

"You'll be sorry, you motherfuckers," Martin swore daily at the long list of clients who were no longer speaking to him. "You'll all come crawling as soon as the trade starts. Mark my words!"

The only one who never seemed to be concerned was Father Ira. He was a saint. So cool, so calm. "Martin, relax," he said the last time Martin called him. "It'll happen soon. All good things take time. Our Good Lord taught us that..."

Martin turned off Father Ira when he started quoting the New Testament and speaking Latin shit to him. He hated Jesus Christ with a passion. The motherfucking liar. He stole all the good parts of Judaism and had the chutzpah to have himself nailed to a cross just to prove he was immortal. The whole thing stank of conspiracy. He'd always known it was a lie. He couldn't believe an intelligent man like Father Ira fell for all that shit.

"Enjoy the beach," said Father Ira before clicking off. "Get a tan for me."

Lester Worthington wanted out of the trade program. "Hey Les, it's only been four months," Martin reminded him. "The calendar year has twelve months."

"I don't get it, Martin. I've talked to scores of people about these bank trade programs and they've all been up front with me. They tell me that after the Certificate of Deposit is approved, it can take as long as six weeks to get the trade finished. Then at that point it's a 72-hour turnaround before the first tranche appears. Total of six weeks and three days, Martin. *Where the hell is my money?*"

"**Who told you those fucking lies?**" shouted Martin, lifting his plastic chair and turning it around so he could straddle it. He was John Wayne and the chair was Banner, Wayne's favorite horse. "**How many times do I have to explain to you Lester that nothing happens with the traders until they've got the right deal, until they get the right price from the buyers?**"

"**Right price, my ass, Seligman,**" Lester shouted back. "**The whole motherfucking program is a scam!**"

"**How could it be a scam, Lester? Your money is safe. It never left your bank. Shit, you've got the paper work. You signed the papers after your attorney reviewed them!**"

"**Let me tell you something, Martin. Let me just give it to you straight.** *You know shit!* **Do you know what's happening right now in the foreclosure market with robo-signing?**"

"**What's that got to do with an international bank trade program?**"

"**Everything!**" exploded Lester. "**The whole fucking mess is connected and it's all gonna get shit-canned together!**"

"Lester… Lester… who's telling you these lies?" Martin softened his voice. "Who's trying to make you believe our Hong Kong and Swiss bank trade programs are connected to the same U.S. bankers and crooks taking down the housing industry? The only thing that's connected is that all this confusion in the markets, all this foreclosure shit is causing delays in the trade programs. That's the only connection."

*"**Martin**, I wasn't born yesterday."*

"I know Les, we're the same age. We've been through a lot together. We even took Arthur Murray dance lessons together one time when we were both living in Dallas. **Listen to me, Les! You can believe fucking liars or you can believe me. I've been doing this for years. I'm not new at this game, Lester!"**

Click. Worthington hung up and dialed Josh Berman, one of his most trustworthy business associates.

"Josh, I need your advice, your input."

"Yes, Les, how can I help you?"

"Do you have a couple minutes?"

"For you I always have time unless I'm busy," answered Josh. "What's going on?"

"Did I tell you I took the plunge last January and called Martin Seligman?"

"Of course you didn't tell me because you know what I would have called you!" retorted Josh. "A first class schmuck. How many times do your good friends have to tell you that *a pusen fas hilcht hecher* (an empty barrel reverberates loudly)? Seligman's a fraud. A sociopath."

"Okay okay, but still, Josh, still, I felt I had nothing to lose," stammered Les. "After all, the money never leaves my bank."

"So he's telling you he's got special connections with God too, I suppose," said Josh sarcastically. And as long as he's got the money locked up with his trade program, you can't do anything with it yourself. That's the deal? How much did you have to pay him to get in?""*Kozebopkes* (Absolutely nothing)."

"So what's your bitch? You've got it tied up for a year and if nothing happens in a year, nothing happens. Right?"

"What I want you to give me, Josh, is, *die untershte sheereh* (the bottom line). Why the fuck hasn't it happened yet?", exploded Lester.

"Listen my friend, let me tell you something. If something sounds too good to be true—"

"It's probably good to be true," they both finished together.

"So tell me—I don't want to hear it, but tell me anyway—what's Seligman gaining from all of this? What's he asking you to do? What's your *oyfgabe* (problem)?"

"*Kozebopkes* (Absolutely nothing), except that I know he's using my name."

"And that's nothing?" exploded Josh. "He's telling others that Les Worthington signed in with him. Hell, you know what that looks like!"

"Yeah. It looks like I signed in with him," frowned Les.

"So you gave him some of your contacts, too—right?" Like people you do business with? Because he told you the more money that goes into the trade, the more money you're going to make? And you get a commission off each referral? Is that what he told you? Oh Marty boy, Marty boy. *Az Got volt gelebt oif der erd, volt men im alleh fenster oisgeshlogen* (If God lived on earth, all his windows would be broken). This man is a thief, a user."

"So what if the trade starts? What then?" Les demanded.

"Then you're a rich man and I'm still a nobody. Listen, Les," said Josh, "you're signed in for a year. There's nothing you can do about that part of it. He's got you goat-roped. You can put duct tape over his mouth, but unless you cut off his hands it's useless. Of course you could cut out his tongue instead, but that's messy.

"Look at it this way, friend," said Josh kindly. "Everything in life is a gamble. What's five million buckaroos to a man like you? I've never known you to be a tightwad. Just pretend to be a goy and turn the other cheek. Come January, the bank hold is up. Bank hold-up. Ha-ha! You learned your lesson. You're too smart to fall for anything like that again. Right? Listen pal, you don't drown by falling in the water. You drown by staying there."

"Yeah. I guess." Lester's voice was scarcely audible.

"Les, what the fuck! You sound like you actually believe this guy is going to come through! Let me see if I can get this through your head." Josh's patience was running out. "These prime bank debenture trade programs are a fraud. People have been sent to prison for running these schemes. Did you know that offering such programs, or claiming to be able to introduce investors to people who have access to such programs, violates federal law? I'm willing to bet that Martin is getting paid to give someone a chance to use your funds by borrowing against them for their own purposes. Believe me, Les, you got sucked in this time, but as soon as this is over, scratch Seligman off your list. Forget him. Don't take his calls."

Josh Berman always knew the right things to tell him, thought Lester, thanking him and hanging up. *So why did he still believe the trade program was legitimate, that it could really happen?* What kind of crap game was he playing with himself? *Fun loiter hofenung ver ich noch meshugeh* (Stuff yourself with hope and you can go crazy).

How the hell did all the wealthy people get all their money? According to Martin Seligman, through their secret trade programs. And that's why they were secret.

There's nothing wrong with being *meshugenah*, he reassured himself. Just don't talk about it to anyone else. It'll all be overcome next January. Life goes on. God forgives and forgets. If only other people would do the same...

Martin paced the 12 x 12-foot room. His cage, he fumed. "God damn weather. It was hot as hell in July and the landlord wouldn't turn the thermostat lower than 80. One small window, that's all he had. It was a box. The window might as well have bars.

His cell phone was ringing.

"Martin?"

"Tracy! Sweetheart, how are you? I've got good news for you! The kind of news you've been waiting for! Are you sitting down? Now don't be playing with yourself while we're talking, Tracy, or you know what's going to be happening to me over here in Palm Beach. Do you have your bikini packed?"

He felt much better after talking with Tracy. She was a love. She'd brought him three people already for the trade program and she never asked questions. Not like Barbara Bassett, that bitch. Barbara was getting on his nerves. Not only asking too many questions, but poking into his business. He took that back. She wasn't just a bitch, she was a nosey bitch.

It was past 9AM. The bank was open. The FedEx package from Father Ira aka Sendor Risgelt with twenty 100-dollar bills had arrived yesterday afternoon.

Picking up his ratty comb, Martin ran it through what was left of his hair, gray rapidly turning white. And no wonder. No one would live the way he was living. No one *deserved* to live the way he was living. It wouldn't be much longer. He glanced at himself in the bathroom mirror before he turned away. Old. Old looking. And that paunch in front. Too many whoppers and fucking 89-cent burritos.

What was happening to him? He couldn't cave in. So many good things were happening. He knew it. He could *feel* it, goddammit!

Consider how miraculous it was that the FedEx package with 2K in 100-dollar bills always arrived unopened. The bills could have easily been taken out and the package sealed up again. THAT was a true example of a miracle, Father Ira! Not some fucking virgin birth crap or Catholic bullshit about nailing up a guy on a cross and making a martyr out of him.

The true martyrs were people like himself, Martin Seligman. God knew who he was; God was looking out for him.

"Oh what a bee-yu-ti-ful morning, oh what a bee-yu-ti-ful day," he hummed to himself, locking the door of his room and starting off for the bank, three blocks away on 'M' Street. If any of those bums pounding the pavements right now ever realized he was carrying $2,000 in his shorts pocket...It was good to look and dress like a bum. No one would ever suspect who he really was.

"Everything's going my way!" he hummed. Life was good. The big money would be here soon. It was almost time.

Beverly, his favorite teller, was with another customer.

"Would you like someone else to help you?" asked the receptionist. "Katie" read her name tag.

"No, I'll be happy to wait," Martin beamed happily at Katie.

From the table he picked up a copy of the latest edition of *The Palm Beach Daily News*, fondly called "The Shiny Sheet."

During off season months, the paper only came out once a week. The winter calendar was already filling up. Shoshanna Rubesque was having a garden party for the Duchess of Domany and Gilbert DuBois of Parvelle November 13. The Sherilee and Ratibil Bumbermeyers' Ladebakk estate was undergoing a complete renovation for the December Conservation Ball. The Popcorn Gala would be moved from December to January at The Breakers and a special magic show by Murandagos the Miracle Man would be the featured attraction. Three cancer balls were scheduled for February: Cancer Research, Cancer Survivors and Cancer Future Survivors.

It made Martin feel good to read about all the celebrities who lived nearby, even though they weren't here in the summertime. Mid-April they started to flee to their New England, Colorado or offshore retreats. He'd already decided he was going to have places in Nantucket, Maui, Monaco, Belize, and the Solomon Islands.

He leafed through the Real Estate section to see if there were any ocean estates worth checking out with his realtor, Orin Formeister. He called Orin weekly. "When the time's ripe, I'll be ready to pay cash," he told Orin.

"Of course, Martin!" Orin sometimes wondered why he put up with this idiot. But then, there were so many idiots like Martin in Palm Beach, there was always a chance one of them was telling the truth. No shortage of money here, for sure... Business had been slow this year. He needed some big sales. Orin came from Mississippi but was sure no one could tell because he'd worked hard at cultivating a British accent. He'd bought some software "that Hollywood actors used," said the ad. It was on sale for $3.99 at Publix market in the bin outside the store.

Beverly was ready. "How's my favorite girlfriend?" Martin placed both elbows on the Formica strip in front of the teller's grill, winked and gave her a Signature Seligman Smile.

"How's the trade program going, Mr. Seligman?" asked Beverly in return. A plump dark-haired community college student with thick glasses and a crooked smile, Beverly reminded Martin of his deceased mother.

"Wonderful, Beverly! Everything is wonderful! You look more beautiful than ever today!"

"Well thank you, Mr. Seligman," said Beverly dubiously, offering him her crooked smile.

Trudy Seligman had died at age 54 of a brain tumor. She was a *kvetch* but she had a big heart in spite of the brain tumor, Martin said in his speech at the funeral. A kvetch was a Yiddish word for "whiny complainer." Maybe it was Beverly's crooked smile that reminded him of his mother. Trudy died with a full set of teeth but when she smiled she looked like a jack-o-lantern. It had something to do with the structure of her mandibles. Like his bitch wife Sabrina's overbite.

"We're almost there, Beverly, almost there!"

"Would you like to deposit all of this, Mr. Seligman, or would you like some cash back?"

"Hmmm. Deposit all of it. Yes, I think that would be a good idea." Martin did his usual 30-Second Pause & Ponder routine, just to make sure it appeared that a decision needed to be made.

The next day on his morning walk, he'd stop at the Publix ATM and withdraw $300. Then he'd wait a couple days and stop in at the convenience store, buy a lottery ticket and withdraw another $300.

"I'll be right back," said Beverly cheerfully.

Beverly disappeared into the room in back. To her horror she discovered her arms had broken out in large red blotches. There was something about that man that gave her the creeps. Maybe because of his fake cheerfulness, and the *ego*. He dressed like a bum but tried to give the impression that he was loaded. He was loaded all right, she decided several months ago when he first started coming into the bank to make his monthly cash deposits. Loaded with shit.

In the back room she placed two of the $100 bills under the scanner and checked them with the UV light. She was far from an expert at determining what to really look for besides the basics—the watermark bar stating the amount of the bill, the red and blue threads behind the engraving... She breathed a sigh of relief. Everything looked normal.

When she was hired three months ago she'd asked Mr. Muffit to sign her up for a training course in detecting counterfeit bills. He'd given her a strange look.

"So what's the madda? You don't trust the customers that come into this bank?" Barney Muffit shook his head, boring into her with his beady eyes. A short man with a hump and shock of salt-and-pepper hair, he talked with his hands and was always pushing a single strand of black and gray hair over his bald spot, as if to cover it up. It did not; instead, it only drew more attention to it.

"No, that's not really it, Mr. Muffit," said Beverly. "It's more than not trusting customers. It's a matter of being able to trust myself. I need to know what to look for."

"You think this is Wells-Fargo, B of A or Chase?" he scolded. "If you want to work for one of them Big Time Banks, go right ahead. Apply. Let me tell you, you're lucky to have a job, Beverly. Damn lucky. We're just a small outfit. Just a tiny chink-a-chink neighborhood bank. Of course, there *was* a time when we conducted training procedures on such matters, but after a while we found them useless."

Beverly wondered what it was about the training procedures that made them useless. "I don't think I understand, sir. How do you know if you're taking in counterfeit bills if you never check them to see if they *might* be counterfeit?"

"Yes, of course that's a good question," Barney waved his hands in the air and pushed back the strand of black and gray hair, "but frankly, we have no time for such things. We're too busy with other issues. With all the crime going on, the fraud with foreclosures and robo-signing... we've got our hands full and no time for such trivia. So is there anything else, Beverly?"

"No, thank you, Mr. Muffit. That's all."

She had never approached Mr. Muffit again about anything; she had a strange feeling her job would be in jeopardy if she asked too many questions. The problem was neither hers nor Mr. Muffit's. It belonged to someone else who ranked much higher than both of them.

Beverly returned to her teller's window and signaled to the next customer in line. *What's more important to you, Beverly Meddows—your self-righteousness or your job?* She chided herself. Okay, so what if Martin Seligman was a bit of a whacko? Lots of people in Florida acted strange. Lots of people everywhere acted strange. Maybe people thought *she* acted strange.

She deposited the customer's check and turned back to address him. "Would you like to have your balance?" she asked.

20
The Price of Redemption

Wednesday, July 14, 2010 – Cordova Rehab Center – Chicago Illinois

"Mr. Jay, on behalf of the Cordova Rehab Center we would like to express to you how very grateful we are to you for all of your time, energy and enthusiasm over the past year."

At the podium, the Director, Dr. Jorge Jacinto, turned to Jesse, who was standing next to him. The plaque Dr. Jacinto was presenting to Jesse made him an honorary member of the Cordova Rehab Center Executive Board. In the audience were medical doctors, social workers, addiction counselors and psychologists who had been invited to the presentation to learn more about Jesse and his work with the center.

"Mr. Jay, since you have taken charge of our counseling program and changed the program, we are experiencing a 99% recovery rate with no recidivism. That is unheard of! As you know, our goal at Cordova is to empower our patient-clients, to give them a new lease on life and give them an opportunity to recover their self-esteem as well as their health. You have done exactly that.

"Folks, Jesse Jay's generous contributions to Cordova have allowed us to sponsor many of our patients and pay for their therapists, since most of these therapies are not covered by health insurance. Mr. Jay, can you tell us a little bit about this?"

Jesse stepped up to the mic amidst a tepid round of applause.

"Actually, the program is very simple," Jesse began. "We just needed to take these people off their meds. If I offend many of you in the audience, I apologize. But at Cordova, we're into *healing*, not just into medicating pain or covering up the real issues."

Several people coughed and cleared their throats, shuffled their feet.

"Better Days, my nonprofit foundation is fully prepared to invest even more money in Cordova if we can continue to prove that recovery requires going to the source of the issue and giving people a chance to learn *why* they have become codependent on drugs, alcohol and other addictive behaviors that have sabotaged their health and a healthy lifestyle." Jesse's presentation was brief and thought provoking.

The next day, Dr. Jacinto called him. "Jesse, you did a magnificent job! We've really set a record, thanks to you!"

"I'm pleased that you allowed me to use your center as a testing ground or prototype," said Jesse. "Thank *you!*"

"Yes," said Dr. Jacinto. *Pause.* "However, we've run into a problem. Believe it or not, we have just received a call from the Cordova Board of Directors. Ironically, the Center's license may be revoked as a result of our high success rate. It may sound strange to you, I know, but the Center depends on the doctors and drug companies for their major financial source of revenues."

"Oh, but we can easily solve that problem, Dr. Jacinto," Jesse reassured him. "In fact, we are prepared to do exactly that, if necessary. Incidentally, another branch of our organization also administers job placement at no cost to the clients. No sacrifice of a week or month's salary, no money up front."

As soon as Jesse got off the phone, he dialed Father Ira and left a message in his voice mailbox.

Father Ira called him back promptly. "I'd love to meet with you, Jesse. I'll be available at 3PM today, at St. Anthony's. Can you meet me there?"

"You can go right into his office," said the receptionist when Jesse arrived. "Father Ira told me to tell you he'll be there in about ten minutes."

On the wall to the right of his desk, Father Ira had placed another Alex Grey reproduction. Jesse stood in front of it for a few moments, studying it carefully. It was a rendition of a full-bodied male angel. The colors were brilliant—orange, blue, green and gold. Male warriors' faces appeared in the multiple layers of unfolding wings.

As he turned away and was about to settle himself in one of the chairs in front of Father Ira's desk, his eyes lit on a photograph of a naked boy partially covered by a letter.

Jesse's heart skipped a beat. He stepped closer to the desk and lifted the letter to view the full photo. Father Ira, smiling broadly into the camera, had placed his hand above the boy's head with his index and pinky fingers lifted. *The Sign of the Devil!*

Jesse had read about satanic rituals in the Catholic Church that were condoned and even practiced at the Vatican and elsewhere. One of the rituals was The Enthronement of the Fallen Angel... *the body of Christ. To the antichrist, the crucifixion was a satanic ritual. Surely...*

Before he could cover up the photo, Jesse heard the door handle turning.

"Jesse!"

Father Ira was wearing a white embroidered surplice over his cassock and looked even more handsome than usual. His face was flushed and his long blonde hair had been corn braided with gemstones. Around his neck he wore a diamond studded cross with an overlay of rubies in the shape of the crucifix. *Ruby red, blood red.*

"I apologize for being late," said Father Ira. "This is such a busy time. We have visitors from Rome and it's been one meeting after another. I'm so *happy* to see you!"

The priest lunged toward Jesse, almost lifting him off his feet as he swept him into a warm embrace. Jesse could smell the alcohol on his breath, or was it more than that?

"I hope your meetings have been successful," said Jesse when Father Ira released him.

"*Highly* successful," smiled Father Ira. "Do you remember our first conversation when I commented this country is going to hell in a handbasket?"

"Yes, of course."

The priest seated himself opposite Jesse. "There was a reason why I said that, my friend. It was to let you know that I'm not on that trip. I'm on no one's trip but my own."

He was on a trip all right.

"Call it narcissism, call it selfishness," Father Ira lifted his arms, the sleeves of his robes flying outward, *like the wings of an angel.* "But let me tell you, the greatest fear of all is the fear of death. The Catholic Church is well aware of this, so for the more enlightened, it becomes an easy and more pleasurable—actually exciting—experience... to enact this death beforehand. Ahh yes, we must die for our sins, but what a wonderful death it can be!"

"Of course, in war there is always collateral," he chattered on. "It is the price that any empire pays... and the Roman Church is, after all, an Empire. A Roman Empire."

"I hadn't really thought of it that way," said Jesse. His head was throbbing. Somewhere deep within he could hear the sound of thousands of screeching birds. The pain in his gut was unbearable.

"We consider you one of us, Jesse. I think you know that." Father Ira's voice grew soft and dreamy, as if coming from a faraway place. Although his eyes were fixed on Jesse, he was gazing beyond him. "The death ritual can be *most exciting.* It is only through death and these rituals that we achieve salvation. The problem with most people today is that they're bored. They don't allow themselves to experience such pleasurable ablutions. They get caught up in frustration, despair and guilt... Yes, guilt..." Father Ira's voice trailed off as he closed his eyes and seemed to enter a trance.

Jesse shifted in his chair and waited.

After several minutes, the priest opened his eyes and continued. "The people forgive us," he said. "We know that with certainty. They realize we are the intermediaries between themselves and the Trinity. Yes, they do forgive us. They're even willing to accept our money as settlement and they look the other way, because God is on our side. That means He is not on their side *unless we say so."*

Father Ira's eyes glittered malevolently, "We can steal from them, and we can rob them blind! We can abduct their children, rape their daughters and seduce their sons... We can launder as much money as we want, and all they will ask from us is our blessing, "*Ut Deus tecum sit* (May God be with you)...

"Pawns! Parasites! We could skin them alive and roast them over hot coals and still all they would ask from us is to give them our blessing: "*Ut Deus tecum sit* (May God be with you)..."He laughed coarsely.

"Father Ira, I think you're giving me way too much information," said Jesse, hoping the mention of his name would break the trance. It did not.

"Once we remove ourselves from the issues and see them from this larger perspective—realizing that the power of Lucifer or Satan is greater than the power of God, things look different," Father Ira continued, ignoring Jesse. He fingered his diamond- and ruby-studded cross. "Lucifer the fallen angel. Lucifer the bearer of Light."

"There is so much evil in the world. But we must not get carried away by all the stories people tell. I'm sure you've heard rumors about the Pope, for example, and the Catholic Church. You must not believe them. We must always make sure the people know we're on their side, fighting for their cause. We are their legion, their army that fights all the evil in the world. We are the Warriors of the Light, the Warriors of Satan!"

"If there's anything I can do to help you, Father Ira, please know that I'm here to assist you," said Jesse, rising.

"Wait! Sit, sit! Don't go! You came here asking for more money. You have it, my friend. Just give me an itemized list of whoever needs to be fucked and we'll take care of it, ha-ha! And remember, as always, this conversation stays in this room."

"Yes, of course," said Jesse, his eyes filling with tears.

"It's a strange and wonderful world, isn't it?" smiled Father Ira, walking with him to the front entrance and kissing him on the lips before he could turn away.

Yes, indeed, it's a strange world, thought Jesse as he drove back to his apartment. The worst part of all was the desecration of a great artist's name. Alex Grey deserved much better than this.

He didn't feel personally betrayed. He knew what he was doing. It was his own fault. He was creating false bank documents in order to cover up computer blips that delivered a loaded debit card. Unlimited money... integrally linked to the printing of counterfeit money...

The part that was causing problems was what he'd known about all along but had refused to accept. *Father Ira and the Catholic Church were not part of the solution; they were a deliberate part of the problem.*

He went to the bathroom, scrubbed his lips with soap and washed out his mouth with hydrogen peroxide. Then he set to work researching the thousands of Catholic pedophile cases that existed in almost every country on the planet. If they weren't posted on the Internet he was sure it was only because the victims were too frightened to step forward.

He ordered a copy of *The Keys of This Blood*, by Dr. Malachi Martin, an Irish Catholic priest, distinguished scholar and prolific writer, who died in 1999 at the age of 78.

Whether or not one wished to believe that Dr. Martin's books reported the truth about satanic rituals practiced in the Vatican, it was a fact that Catholics believed in Satan. In the *Usus Antiquior*, they recited regularly the following prayer:

> Holy Michael Archangel, defend us in the day of battle; be our safeguard against the wickedness of the devil. May God rebuke him, we humbly pray: and do thou, Prince of the heavenly host, by the power of God thrust down to hell Satan and all wicked spirits, who wander through the world seeking the ruin of souls.

According to Catholic scholars the prayer is fundamental to the New Testament vision of the world and therefore to the Catholic faith. St. Peter himself said: "Be sober, be vigilant: because your adversary the devil, as a roaring Lion, walketh about, seeking whom he may devour."

When Jesse finally landed in bed at 3:30AM, he fell into a fitful sleep. Then the nightmares began. He was attending a masquerade ball and he was dressed as a woman, with a billowing red and orange polka dotted dress and hoop petticoats. The dress had a tight bodice. Styrofoam pads had been strapped to his chest to simulate two breasts. On his head was a blonde wig and his face was painted white with two red spots on his cheeks. His eyes were covered by a mask.

He was standing in the middle of a circle surrounded by seven priests in full regalia. They were also wearing eye masks. One by one each of them stepped forward, bowed low and asked Jesse to dance. It was all very elegant and proper until the seventh priest, a blonde-haired man wearing a large cross inlaid with diamonds and rubies stepped forward. He lifted is eye mask slightly to make sure Jesse recognized him. Father Ira!

Whispering in Jesse's ear, he took his elbow and guided him to a table in the middle of the room where he instructed Jesse to lie down.

"I am going to rape you," whispered Father Ira.

The other six priests crowded close, whispering and cackling among themselves.

"Jesse Jay—Daniel Hanas—I am going to prove to you that Satan exists in each of us," declared Father Ira. He reached underneath the table for a flaming torch.

Lifting the torch over Jesse's body, Father Ira started to pronounce a prayer in Latin:

"*Sancte Michael Archangele, defende nos in proelio, contra nequitiam diaboli esto praesidium. Imperet illi Deus, supplices deprecamur: tuque, Princeps militiae caelestis, Satanam...*"

Slowly he lowered the torch and as he did so, three of the priests stepped forward and removed Jesse's skirt and petticoats. They pulled down his pants. His penis was erect. Excited.

Jesse sat up, sweat pouring down his face.

In the second nightmare, he was on a guided tour in Rome. He looked up at the ceiling of the building they had just entered and realized it was the Sistine Chapel.

"This is where all the crime takes place," said his uniformed guide. The guide must have been a member of the Swiss Guard because he was wearing the official blue, red, orange and yellow Renaissance-style dress uniform. "You need to know exactly what happens in the chambers below the Chapel," the guide continued.

"Why do we need to know?" Jesse spoke up.

The guide hesitated, then glided over to Jesse and whispered in his ear, "You must never let on that I told you. Is that a deal?"

Jesse nodded. "Of course. But I do need to know before it's too late."

The guide frowned. "It is already too late, but I'm telling you this just so you will be prepared to experience being pleasured by so many members."

"Members?" repeated Jesse. "You mean members as in members of a group, or body members?"

"Both," smiled the guard. "Good! I'm glad you're catching on. They may let you live. It will depend on how useful you are to them afterward when they're through with you. It is a form of initiation that was ordered by Satan upon taking the priestly vows."

This time Jesse got out of bed, went to the kitchen and brewed a cup of coffee.

During her second year at Skidmore, Maya Hanas had run away. She was picked up by the police and arrested for possession of marijuana. From that time on, she was in and out of detention centers, getting into trouble again as soon as she was let go.

Jesse longed to visit her, but Rhonda kept Maya's whereabouts under lock and key. Her new husband, Evergood Krug saw to that.

According to Jesse's son Max, who was enrolled in a military academy in Virginia and who had stayed in constant touch with his dad, Krug was the kind of attorney people hired when they needed someone who knew how to lie in court and get away with it. He was also friendly with the right judges, i.e., the ones who could be bought.

"Dad, he's a crook. A nasty ass motherfucker," Max told him. "*Literally.* I do *not* want to have a military career. When I get out of here, I'm going to become an attorney and I'm going to prosecute the bastard."

Rhonda and Evergood had also cut off Max's communication with Maya.

Jesse tried to steer away from the subject of justice in his correspondence with Max. He also tried to stay positive. If there ever came a time when his son learned about his activities and who was funding them, he wondered whose side he would choose to be on.

My dear son, you may change your mind yet again about wanting to be an attorney when you discover how the game is played.

21

Intermezzo

"Hello, this is Shireen Fromarty. Is this Barbara Bassett?"

On lunch break from the library, Barbara had just placed her turkey and cheese sub sandwich and chocolate milkshake on a table. "Yes, this is Barbara."

"I'm sorry to bother you, but I'm just wondering, I'm just wondering, I've been wondering for some time, I'm really sorry to bother you... but do you happen to know a Dr. Martin Seligman?"

"*Dr.* Seligman?" Barbara repeated.

"Yes. He lives in Palm Beach, Florida. I'm calling from Theodosia, Missouri. Most people have never heard of Theodosia, Missouri. It's in the southern part of the state, near the border of Arkansas. Martin told me the doctor before his name is actually an honorary doctorate, from the University of Malabusta. I looked it up but honestly I couldn't find any university or even a college by that name, so I'm sorry to bother you—"

"What would you like to know about him?" Barbara crooked the phone on her shoulder and took a slurp of her chocolate milk shake.

"I'm just wondering, I've been wondering for some time—"

"**How can I help you, Shireen?**" *Out with it already!*

"Is Dr. Seligman married?" whispered Shireen into the phone. "He's about the most exciting man I've ever met, I mean by phone. I haven't met him yet, I mean, in person. He gave me your name to call. He said you'd known him for a long time. I'm divorced myself. Dr. Seligman, *Martin* said you could tell me all about him, I mean, his personal life. Frankly, if he's married, I'm really not interested, I'm not in the habit of dating married men, and in fact I've never dated a married man before."

Barbara's stomach started to churn. "Shireen, by any chance are you one of the participants in Dr. Seligman's bank trade program?"

"How did you know?" shouted Shireen excitedly. "I'm so glad we're talking! I've been meaning to call you, but somehow I hesitated, I just didn't want to bother you."

Well now you have, honey. "How much?"

"How much did I put into Dr. Seligman's wonderful trade program? Well, Dr. Seligman said the entry was ten million. He said he's expecting a fast turnaround. He shared some confidential information with me, he said not even the Big Men—the Rockefellers, Rothschild's, you know, the Warren Buffetts, Donald Trumps, and so on... not even these Big Wealthy Men have been invited into a trade program. Dr. Seligman—*Martin*—said he doesn't understand how he happens to be the one who was chosen, it's like he said The Man Upstairs seems to have a Special Mission for him."

"Yes," retorted Barbara. "A special mission all right. I'm certainly glad you called me, Shireen. Very glad. Thank you so much."

"Oh, you're so welcome, Barbara. May I call you Barbara? I really didn't want to bother you. So, about whether or not he's married... He says such funny things on the phone. They're so cute and clever, and frankly, sometimes he can be outrageous!"

"I believe he *is* married," said Barbara curtly. "I'm sorry to disappoint you, but I believe he's married to his bullshit."

"Ha ha! Oh that is so funny, Barbara! Married to his bullshit!" Shireen giggled into the phone.

"Shireen, I have another call coming in. Feel free to call me again, anytime."

Barbara didn't know where to place her anger. It was much too large to fit inside her mouth or any of her other orifices. It was much too large for this Subway restaurant or for the library where she worked, or for her apartment, or for any part of her life, in fact.

As soon as she returned to her apartment after work, she checked her bank account. Plenty of money to purchase a plane ticket to Palm Beach, hire a private investigator and reserve a room at a good hotel. She'd already concluded that Martin's "ocean front home" was as fake as he was.

She dialed Martin's cell phone.

"Barbara! What a treat! How are you, sweetheart?"

"I'm better than ever. In fact, right now I'm lying naked on the bed playing with myself. Martin, I am so hot to see you, I don't give a fuck whether or not the money has come in yet. It has nothing to do with the money. It's all about you, Martin. I want to see *you*. The money is just the final cherry."

"Barbara! Sweetheart! I'd love to have you come and visit me but I'm leaving for Hong Kong tomorrow and I won't be back for three weeks, possibly longer."

"Then I'll come tonight," she grinned mischievously. "I'll be on the next plane. I'll take a red-eye. As soon as I have a flight, I'll give you the number so you can meet my plane or send your driver—what did you say his name was? Mark?"

Martin's forehead was beaded with sweat. He paced the tiny room. It was a sweatbox. A prison. He was out of cash and he couldn't pull anything more out of his checking account. The FedEx package hadn't arrived last week. His cell phone was about to be shut off.

"Honey, you don't have to come to see me. DON'T COME HERE," he yelled. "I won't be here. I'll be tied up with meetings. **This is the wrong time to come.**"

"Tied up, did you say?" said Barbara sweetly. "How perfect! You know how I feel about S & M. Boots, whips, leashes and all that. I'm coming anyway, Martin. You have now excited me even more. You can't stop me! As soon as I get off the phone I'm calling the airlines to see if there's a direct connection between SEATAC and PBIA."

22

Surprise!

Friday, July 16, 2010 – West Palm Beach/Palm Beach, Florida

Barbara's heart was racing as she tripped down the ramp in her strappy silver 4-inch wedge sandals and into the Palm Beach International Airport. Her palms were sweaty. Her armpits were sweaty. Did she smell?? *Oh God, she hoped not.*

By the time she reached baggage claim, in spite of the over-chilled air, she was dripping.

No one was there to meet her. No man in a chauffeur's uniform, no printed sign: "Welcome, Barbara!"

No one searching through the faces of arriving passengers for a blonde 43-year-old babe who'd flown all the way from Seattle on her own dime. She'd even told him she'd be wearing a red pantsuit. "Red for hot," she'd joked angrily to herself.

Her Walmart Travelers Club matching zebra suitcases arrived on the designated carousel, but Martin did not—nor did Mark, his driver. Barbara took a deep breath. Stuffing—unless it was chocolate truffles or anything chocolate—was not one of her specialties. She was angry.

It's not that she wasn't prepared. Oh she had a Plan B all right. Homer and Penny, her brother and sister-in-law, had been only too happy to help her work it out. It's just that she never wanted to have to use it.

Maybe Martin was late. Or Mark the driver. Or both. She waited until all the other passengers picked up their luggage and departed. She'd already made a reservation at the Marriott on Okeechobee Boulevard, $199 a night, what the hell, just in case. She was blowing her entire savings account on this trip, so she might as well stay at a place that was comfortable and that made her feel like she was on vacation.

On vacation. The Marriott had an airport van and she'd also arranged for a rental car, just in case. It would be waiting for her when she checked in.

"*No surprises, were there, Barbara Bassett?*" With her fist, she wiped the tears from the corners of her eyes.

As she pulled her two zebra cases outside and waited at the curb for the Marriott van to pick her up, she stole a glance at the Barbie & Ken lovebirds also waiting for the van. Arms entwined, bodies pressed against each other, Barbi in a denim mini-mini-skirt, flip-flops and skimpy halter top that exposed her midriff—the kind of outfit she'd worn when she was eight or nine years old—and Ken all muscle and brawn: at least six feet tall, tanned, in a blue flowered Hawaiian shirt, white shorts and sandals... they were kissing and he had his hands on her breasts...he was feeling her up underneath her halter....

She felt like puking. Away from the air conditioning, standing in the humid hundred-degree South Florida heat, her one-piece latex body-suit—a polite name for a girdle—started to itch in all the spots she couldn't reach or scratch publicly. The damn straitjacket was cutting off her circulation. The pant legs of her red silk suit, tight to begin with, clung to her thighs. Her four-inch wedges were impossible. She kept teetering from one side to the other as if she were crippled or trying to balance on a sawhorse. Twice already she'd turned her right ankle. Now it hurt and was swelling.

Her hair hung limp and lifeless to her shoulders and the salty sweat on her forehead and cheeks glommed to her makeup. If the tears started in earnest, she knew her mascara would run and leave dark rings underneath her eyes. She was a wreck. Her life was a wreck.

At least the hotel van was air conditioned. As soon as she checked in and wheeled her zebras into her room, she double bolted the door, stripped off all her shackles, fell onto the bed naked and dialed Martin's cell phone. Busy. After a long shower, icing her ankle and watching *Luci-Desi Comedy Hour* re-runs on the free channel TV, she popped three Advil PMs and immediately fell asleep.

The next morning a hearty breakfast from the buffet (included in the room price)—cheese omelet, pancakes, muffins, Danishes, blintzes, do-nuts and three cups of coffee—restored her fortitude. Now that Plan B was already in effect, to her surprise, Barbara was starting to enjoy herself. Palm Beach County was a beautiful place, even in the summer. It was good to be away from Issaquah, and good to be doing something definite, at last.

Local news reported 90 degrees already, so she dressed sensibly. No latex armor, nothing underneath her flowered cotton moo-moo except a cotton cami and underpants. Not even elastic bra straps. No strappy sandals, just sensible tennis shoes, easy on the feet. She'd stuffed the moo-moo and tennis shoes into her suitcase at the last minute for "Informal Moments." Ha!

Pulling back her blonde hair and fastening it in a ponytail, she decided to go light on the makeup. Definitely no mascara. So what if she looked like the cleaning lady? Isn't that what she felt like—and essentially what she was doing? *Cleaning up her life?*

PI Albert Finger's office was only a short distance from the hotel, on Palm Beach Lakes Boulevard in a one-story brown stucco building with a red awning.

In the tiny cramped office, over the angry voices of a man and woman arguing in the next office and a bleating and trumpeting window air conditioner, Barbara shouted the answers to PI Finger's questions. Finger, a short stubby man with a brush cut, penetrating red and blue-webbed eyes and a large ruby ring on his right pinky, punched all the particulars into his smartphone, pausing every so often to fondle the large silver cross dangling out of the neck opening of his striped polo shirt.

In less than a half hour he'd located Martin Seligman, living in a rooming house in the town of Lake Worth.

"Do you want me to go with you?" Mr. Finger directed his gaze at Barbara's tote bag that was roomy enough to contain anything from knitting with several pairs of needles, a fry pan, hammer, butcher knife, or all of them.

"Oh no, I'll be fine," Barbara reassured him, paying him his $200.00 fee in cash. "You are a wizard, Mr. Finger. I'm so grateful to you! I should have called you from Seattle a long time ago."

"Good luck," shouted Finger, pocketing the money and standing up to give the air conditioner a bang.

Barbara programmed her rental car GPS for the address on South 'J' Street in the town of Lake Worth. It was off Dixie Highway, or U.S. 1. "Take Okeechobee Drive to Dixie Highway, turn right or south on Dixie Highway, and left on 8th Ave. S," said Delilah, the GPS Voice. It wasn't far away.

When she'd arrived yesterday, she was told by the concierge that the Paradise known as Palm Beach or "The Island," as it was fondly called by the natives, was "across the Causeway." On the map Barbara noted several connecting bridges.

Dixie Highway was everything Barbara had hoped to escape from in her life and more. Boarded up stores, warehouses, storage places, used car lots, check cashing stores, liquor stores, Denney's, Motel 8, a Goodwill store, McDonald's, Burger King, KFC, Jack-in-the-Box, Taco Bell… miles and miles of junk, trash and tinsel.

At the corner of Dixie and 8th Street, she stopped at a furniture rental store that had a payphone outside and dialed Martin's number.

He answered.

"Martin! It's Barbara!"

"Hello sweetheart, I have good news!"

"I thought you were supposed to be leaving for Hong Kong today."

"It was postponed because we just got more money in. You're not going to believe this, WHAT a surprise—we just added FOUR BILLION DOLLARS to our trade platform. But we have to complete the paper work first before we make the trip."

"That's wonderful, Martin! I have good news too! I'm right around the corner from you and I'll be there in less than five minutes!"

Silence. And then: "You're *here in Palm Beach*?" Martin ventured cautiously.

"*West* Palm Beach, Martin. Specifically, Lake Worth. Right near South 'J' Street."

"Are you alone, Barbara?"

"Of course I'm alone. And you WILL recognize me from my photos, of course."

"Well, well, well! Well well well! Come right over, Barbara. I can't wait to tell you all about the good news!"

She had to hand it to him. He had chutzpah.

It would have been difficult to determine which of the two was more surprised—Martin opening the door to a 5'6" 184-pound blonde cow in moo-moo and tennis shoes, or Barbara viewing in front of her a short, fat, partially bald-headed man no taller than 5'3" in an undershirt and Big Lots peach and yellow plaid seersucker Bermuda shorts.

Barbara registered dismay; Martin registered shock. He could do nothing less than let her in and offer her a seat on his plastic desk chair, the only chair in the room, while he perched on the bed. Even a perfunctory hug wasn't in order.

Barbara chose to stand. **"Martin, I am exposing you to your entire network of contacts, to every name you gave me as a referral,"** she shrieked.

"Could you kindly keep your voice down," suggested Martin. "There are other people—"

"I don't care WHO the fuck is around, Martin Seligman, and I don't care WHO the fuck hears what I have to say." Barbara's voice reached a hysterical pitch.

"Can we take a walk? Can we just talk a little? I told you I have some good news," Martin wheedled. "Come, I'll buy you some iced tea or a coke, or some ice cream," he urged, picking up a shirt from the bed and gesturing with his hands toward the door.

"Do NOT try to shovel me out of here like a piece of dreck!" Barbara sobbed.

Then, to her own surprise as well as Martin's, she stopped crying as suddenly as she'd started and obediently followed him out of his room, down the hallway and out the front door.

"Let's go to Charlie's Crab," she said her voice cold and brittle. "The treat will be on me. I have the directions keyed in on my GPS. We'll take the Southern Avenue Bridge so we can enjoy the ride along the ocean."

Martin shrugged. "Whatever you say, Sweetheart." He climbed into the passenger seat next to her and they drove though the side streets of Lake Worth onto Dixie Highway in silence.

"I can see why you like it here so much," said Barbara, breaking the silence as she stopped for a signal light and looked sideways at him. At the street corner was a pawn shop. A Neanderthal wearing only a loincloth struggled to wheel a rusty bicycle with an oversize basket filled with junk across the street before the light changed.

Martin didn't respond.

When they reached the Southern Avenue causeway bridge on U.S. 80 and Rte. 98, Barbara pulled into a service station and parked the car in front of the convenience store. "I'd like to stop here and enjoy the bridge for a few minutes," she said.

"What do you mean 'enjoy the bridge'?" repeated Martin, staring at her large handbag slung diagonally over her moo-moo and safely wedged in the space between her left hip and the car door.

"I thought I might enjoy jumping off," said Barbara, breaking into a hysterical laugh.

"You're crazy!" roared Martin, his hand already on the door handle.

Barbara pressed the automatic door lock and held her thumb on it. "No I'm not crazy, Martin. You're the crazy one," she said calmly. "You are the biggest motherfucker on the planet and I hate myself for falling for all your shit. I hate myself enough to jump off the bridge and end it all. You've made my life miserable. How many other women have you lied to? How many people have you ripped off?"

"Barbara, do you have a weapon in that handbag?" asked Martin as if he were asking if she happened to have a spare paperclip or rubber band.

His question cut through her tirade. Starting the car once again, she turned to him, knives flashing in her eyes. "I want to see Palm Beach. I want to see Worth Avenue and Neiman Marcus and Gucci's and Louis Vuitton and Tiffany's."

She headed across the causeway, turned left on A1A and let the car purr down the road. Martin's head was spinning. He couldn't jump out of the car. Barbara was on main control for the locks. He surely didn't want to make a scene, especially while the bitch was driving. She might swerve off the road and turn over. He didn't want to end up in the ocean.

"Martin, I think it would have been a waste of a good life if I had jumped off that bridge back there. If I were to kill you outright, I'd have to deal with homicide and possibly a prison sentence. Neither of those agendas agrees with me. It will be much more valuable for me to stay in circulation. I have important work to do."

She turned left onto Worth Avenue and stopped the car in front of Neiman Marcus.

"Before I drop you off, Martin, give me your cell phone, your money, your keys and your ID. Hand them over."

Wordlessly, Martin emptied the pockets of his shorts.

Barbara unlocked the car door. "Good-bye Martin. Good-bye forever!"

As soon as Martin placed one foot on the pavement, Barbara gave him a shove and pushed him out the door. She cruised away and did not look back.

Monday, July 19, 2010 – Lake Worth, Florida

Beverly Meddows was about to head out the door to take her lunch break when Barney Muffit asked her to come into his office.

"Beverly, we've received a call from a Mr. Albert Finger, a private investigator. It seems like he's been doing some checking on a man named Martin Seligman. Do you remember that name among your customers?"

Beverly froze. Of course she remembered him. But not for Mr. Muffit; she would never remember anything for Mr. Muffit. "Sir, as a teller I help so many people every day..."

"I know, I know. Names come and go," sighed Muffitt, raking a hand through his greasy strands of hair. "Just *think*, Beverly. Does the name Seligman mean *anything* to you? The bank receipt copies have your teller number on them, so you must have been the person who serviced him."

"No, Mr. Muffit." Beverly shook her head vigorously. She was reminded of the times when she was a little girl and she'd stolen a piece of candy from the candy jar and had flatly denied it. *I am a very honest person,* she repeated to herself as Mr. Muffit gazed distrustfully at her, his eyes blinking rapidly.

"Would you do me a favor and if someone by the name of Martin Seligman *does* come to your window, Beverly, would you kindly let me know? We are so busy, we have so much to do and I have no time for private investigators. Beverly, I'm holding you responsible for not reporting to me if a Mr. Seligman comes to your window while you are on duty. Do you understand?"

"Yes, of course, of course, Mr. Muffitt." Beverly bobbed her head up and down just as vigorously as she had shaken it from side to side several seconds before.

Beverly half walked, half ran down the street toward the Subway shop where she ordered her usual junior turkey and cheese on a whole wheat roll. As she paid for her sandwich her hand was shaking.

The article that appeared in the *Palm Beach Post* was sent to Father Ira by a woman named Barbara Bassett. It was mailed priority from Issaquah, Washington and arrived on July 24.

> July 21, 2010... The dead body that was found on Monday, July 19, 2010, at 8:38AM lying on the beach at R. G. Kreusler Park on South Ocean Boulevard in Palm Beach, Florida, was identified today as Martin Seligman by his estranged wife, Sabrina Seligman. Mr. Seligman was renting a room in Lake Worth and according to the landlord, Dwayne Maniff, Mr. Seligman's rent was four days overdue. "I knocked on Mr. Seligman's door and when no one answered, I contacted his wife, Sabina, who, until four months ago, signed the checks," said Maniff.

"May God be with you, Martin," prayed Father Ira, "and God help us all," he added, immediately reaching for his encrypted phone. Who else had received that article? How had Ms. Bassett obtained his contact information?

Most important of all: who the hell was Barbara Bassett?

Father Ira faxed a copy of the article to Peppi, and then dialed his number. *"Salve, mi amor."*

"Salve. Quid est?"

"Accepisti articulum?"

"Imo, mi amor."

"I'll take care of it, love. Consider it done."

Peppi dialed the Vatican. "Enrico, put me through to the Cardinal, please. Thank you."

"Securim, Cosi! NUNC!"

"Imo."

"Barbara Bassett. B-A-S-S-E-T-T. Issaquah, Washington."

> *"Imo."*

"Nunc! SECURIM!

> *"Imo."*

That evening in Issaquah, Washington, Barbara Bassett had just settled in front of her TV with a big bowl of chocolate brownie fudge ice cream to watch *The Manchurian Candidate*, one of her favorite movies that had just arrived in the mail from Netflix, when the doorbell rang.

"Who is it?" she called, peering through the peephole.

"I have a florist delivery for a Ms. Barbara Bassett." Through the peephole Barbara could see a uniformed delivery boy holding a large bouquet of red roses.

With the chain lock still on the door, she unbolted it.

A single push and snap and the chain lock fell off. The three masked men who surrounded her slammed a hand over her mouth, threw her down on the floor, pulled her hands behind her back, sprayed a chemical in her eyes and stabbed her arm with a needle.

The men dragged her to her bedroom, undressed her and placed her on the bed, pulling the covers over her as if she were asleep.

Martin's cell phone was on Barbara's desk next to her computer. The men scoured the apartment for any other information that could be useful.

Barbara never awoke. Media articles reported that one of the librarians called her on Monday after she failed to show up for work. When she didn't answer, suspecting something may be wrong, she called the apartment manager. Together they entered the apartment and found Barbara dead in bed. Cause of death was unknown. After a thorough investigation, said the reporter, homicide was ruled out. The coroner's report indicated it was cardiac arrest.

23
Leather-Bound Books & Lace

"And what do you want to be when you grow up?" Jesse held the mic close to the five-year-old black boy. He looked up at Jesse, his big brown eyes large and trusting, and said, 'My name is Derek and I want to be just like you, Mr. Jesse. I want to 'tain people and make them laugh."

The nurses and the rest of the children who had gathered in the St. Jude's Children's Hospital auditorium for Jesse's magic show clapped loudly for Derek. If the truth could be told, most of these children probably would not live to be Jesse's age. They had been diagnosed with cancer and other diseases declared "terminal." Many of the children had already lost their hair and they were in wheelchairs or using crutches and walkers.

"I think you have already started to make your dreams come true," said Jesse to Derek. "Do you hear everyone clapping and cheering? That's because of you, Derek!"

Jesse gestured for all the children to clap and cheer loudly once again.

"I don't understand," Jesse said to Sharon, one of the nurses who had gathered in the cafeteria afterward for an informal chat. "Why are you poisoning these children when you know there are other ways to deal with their health issues?"

"But Jesse, how can we be sure those other methods will work?" retorted Sharon.

"So tell me: are chemotherapy and surgery—and other toxic drugs working now?" countered Jesse.

"We are all doing the best we can, Mr. Jay." Gladys, another nurse spoke up.

Yes, I'm sure you all believe you are, said Jesse to himself. *God bless you for not conducting your own research and accepting the Voices of Authority without even blinking an eye.* He knew the name of the game. Money talks. The nurses were paid by the hospitals: decent salaries with benefits, including pensions.

He had a voice message from Father Ira. When he arrived home he called him.

"Jesse, can you meet me at St. John's tomorrow morning?"

"Of course."

"I'll be in my office."

Father Ira ushered Jesse into his office and closed the door. "Martin Seligman was murdered."

"WHAT?" Jesse sat down, suddenly becoming aware that another man was also in the room, a handsome, olive-skinned youthful looking gentleman casually dressed in a white open shirt, navy blazer and gray slacks. He was handsome enough to be a film star or model. Perfect features, perfectly coiffed hair... no, "handsome" was the wrong word, decided Jesse. "Pretty."

"This is Mr. Giuseppe Tubiano, 'Peppi' for short, a long-time friend, who is visiting from Rome. He was one of Martin's clients."

The two shook hands.

"Have I seen you in films, or are you a model?" asked Jesse. *GQ? Esquire? Numero Homme? Fantastic Man? Dapper Dan?*"

Peppi smiled slightly. "Hardly, Mr. Jay," he said in British-English with an Italian accent. "I am a dress designer."

"Ahh, forgive me, Mr. Tubiano, I'm not up on those things!"

"That is perfectly all right, Mr. Jay," demurred Peppi. "You do not have to be. And incidentally, you can call me Peppi, if it's all right to call you Jesse."

"Of course," said Jesse.

"We think it's an inside job," Father Ira continued, pacing the floor in front of the two and rubbing his hands together. "A mole."

"You mean someone didn't want Martin Seligman's bank trade program to succeed," said Jesse. "I'm confused. He's been soliciting clients for several years already. Father Ira, it's been over two years since you first told me about him. To my knowledge, unless something happened that I don't know anything about; his trade platform has *never* performed."

Jesse looked first at Peppi, then at Father Ira. Their expressions were impassive. "One would think Martin's failure to deliver might be cause for one of his clients to become angry and go after him," he continued. "But why would they do that? They always said they had nothing to lose. The money they were lending him to make the bank trade never left their banks. So in a sense it was like a lottery, only better. They didn't even have to pay a dollar or two for the tickets. If it didn't perform, it was business as usual."

"We think it's more insidious than that," said Peppi, choosing his words carefully. "But that is not our major concern. We want to make sure everyone is protected."

"What do you mean, 'protected'?" asked Jesse. "Is there some danger? A killer at large who may want to—"

"We don't know," said Father Ira.

"One never knows, does one?" exclaimed Peppi.

"So how does this affect the humanitarian projects and their funding?" Jesse was confused.

"Actually, it doesn't," Father Ira smiled. "It has nothing to do with them. Martin was merely an agent, a middleman. He knew how the bank trading programs worked and he had an impressive Rolodex, or data base of wealthy contacts. Investors with disposable incomes, people looking for tax shelters. Thanks to your excellent work in supervising the information packages that were delivered to Martin's clients..."

"Father Ira tells me you are one of the few persons who truly understand how important it is to keep spreading the gospel," said Peppi.

"I suppose that depends on which gospel you're referring to." Jesse's heart skipped a beat.

"The inside story about the Big Lie, of course," said Peppi, his eyebrows lifting slightly. "Or 'The Conspiracy,' as it is often called."

His mouth curved into a smile. "In Europe we are well aware of the power of the media. People believe what they read, see and hear. It is a well-known fact that the banking, government, media, health care and education industries are corrupt."

"You left out the Church," said Father Ira. "The Church is also corrupt. In addition to being a business man in Rome, Peppi is also a financial advisor for the Vatican. Two distinct factions of the Church are at war with each other. We cannot allow the level of corruption to be exposed, so we have formed a powerful lobby. We are doing everything in our power to raise the necessary money to silence the courts."

"And when we cannot raise the money, we borrow it," said Peppi.

"Yes," said Jesse. *Yes, of course. Or... print it, or create computer blips from the collateral that Martin's clients provided whenever they invested in his trade program.*

"It is an internal war," said Father Ira. "Corruption, like money laundering, is big business."

Jesse gazed around the office at the luxurious furnishings, at the leather-bound books, Alex Grey reproductions, original sculptures...

"I understand you are an outstanding speaker and performer who is in great demand in the Chicago area." Peppi addressed Jesse. "Your charity events have received great acclaim. Father Ira tells me you are also a professional banker, with considerable training and experience. What diverse talents you have!"

"We have obtained Martin's contact list," continued Father Ira. "For the good of humanity, for the sake of Church and to preserve the good name of His Holiness the Pope, we must do everything we can to win this war."

"Jesse, I'm not sure if you are familiar with some of the court cases Father Ira is referring to," said Peppi. "We have been trying to prove since 2002, for example, that the Vatican or Holy See is not an employer of priests who have been accused of pedophilia or molestation."

"The original lawsuit was filed in 2002 by a Seattle man who claimed that a Reverend Andrew Ronan repeatedly molested him in the late 1960s. The plaintiff tried to show that Ronan and all priests are employees of the Vatican. This would make the Vatican liable for the priests' actions."

"We have been attempting to show that there are no facts to create a true employment relationship between Ronan and the Holy See," continued Father Ira. "Other cases similar to this one have been dropped when the courts realized they were unable to produce the necessary facts. It has been pointed out by Douglas Laycock, a University of Virginia School of Law professor, that lawsuits against the Pope are usually dismissed on sovereign immunity grounds, with a U.S. court ruling that the Vatican cannot be sued because there is no jurisdiction in the U.S. to do so."

The Church is so clever, thought Jesse. *They've thought of everything!*

"The only way we can fight back is to insist on secrecy in child sex cases, and stopping or delaying the defrocking of pedophile priests," finished Father Ira softly.

"I think the deeper issue, if I'm not mistaken, and forgive me for pointing this out if I am wrong," said Jesse, "is to ask whether the Church is determined to put an end to these practices, or whether it is willing to continue to look the other way and let the court trials and claims mount up."

"But of course, no one wants cruelty in this world," Peppi declared. *"Questo è un dato di fatto* (That is a given). On the other hand, as I'm sure Father Ira has explained to you, there is another, er dynamic to all of this. Call it diabolic, or Satanic... or Luciferian. It cannot be dismissed. It cannot be *spazzato sotto il tappeto* (swept under the carpet).

"Yes, Peppi is right," declared Father Ira. "It would be foolish and naïve for us to assume that homosexuality does not exist everywhere. That is what the Vatican lobby is all about. We are trying to gracefully bring the Church into modern times. All of this is, of course, confidential and goes no further than this room. It is our understanding, for example, that the Pope knows nothing about the Gay Lobby. We trust you implicitly, Jesse."

"Of course," replied Jesse. *You bastards are recording everything anyway. I'm not that stupid! Naïve maybe, but not stupid.* Never had he realized that any other institution on this planet could be as corrupt as the banks. The Catholic Church won the gold medal.

"We do not want to condone pedophilia but also we do not want to dismiss medieval customs, a tradition that has always played such a profound role in the life of every member of the clergy," continued Peppi. "Our sacrificial rituals have been handed down for centuries from one generation to the next. Every person who is invited to participate in one of these rituals considers it a special honor.

"You see," he shifted in his chair, eyeing Jesse directly, "in order to fully understand the Passion of Christ, it is vitally important to understand the Passion of Man. Christ was, after all, a man. A human."

In his mind's eye Jesse saw before him a photo of two men vacationing in the Greek Islands. Both were handsome, well-built dudes. In swim trunks, their arms entwined, they were smiling into the camera... *They would never get caught because they had Cosa Nostra, the courts and people like Jesse Jay to protect them.*

"So, you are asking me to take over Martin's client base and continue the trade program so you can support your, er rituals. Do I have a choice?" asked Jesse slowly.

"You have already used the funds," said Father Ira.

"Large amounts of them," added Peppi.

"And you are doing such good work it would be a shame to have to cancel the debit card."

And cancel me, too, if I say no, thought Jesse. They had him trapped. *Good job, men.* Either he gives them the help they need and implicates himself even further in their counterfeiting and money laundering operations, or he gives them the help they need. His head was already on the block. *Call it blackmail. Call it business. He was screwed.*

That evening, Jesse googled Reverend Andrew Ronan and came up with the article in the Oregon Live.com news index:

http://www.oregonlive.com/news/index.ssf/2005/12/portland_prie st_abuse_case_aga.html

Process servers have crashed celebrity parties, donned disguises and engaged in car chases—whatever it takes to put legal papers into the hands of reluctant defendants.

But rough-and-tumble tactics won't work against the Vatican, an independent country located within the city of Rome. To sue a foreign nation, lawyers in an Oregon priest abuse case needed to spend $40,000 for a pair of Latin translators and wait more than three years to serve the proper Vatican official through the right diplomatic channels.

"I've never in 24 years of practice ever had the kind of obstruction, obfuscation, delays, difficulties, challenges and nonsense that I've encountered in trying to serve them," said Jeffrey R. Anderson, a Minneapolis attorney representing the plaintiff in the case.

But Anderson's persistence paid off. Thousands of lawsuits have been filed against Catholic dioceses and religious orders, but Anderson's suit is believed to be just one of two pending against the Vatican itself.

And Anderson's lawsuit, which involves a priest who molested a boy in Portland in the mid-1960s, is believed to be the first priest-abuse case to be successfully served against the Holy See in Rome.

Anderson, who has sued hundreds of dioceses and religious orders around the country, said he wants to hold the Vatican financially responsible.

"I have long come to the realization that there is a widespread problem that emanates from the top," he said. "And until it is addressed by the Vatican, it will continue to be a problem worldwide."

Lawyers for the Vatican dispute its responsibility for the actions of a priest in the United States. And they are fighting to dismiss the lawsuit, which seeks an unspecified amount of money.

Experts point out that it is very difficult to sue foreign governments, which have broad immunity with limited exceptions.
"It's the old principle of sovereign immunity," said Allen S. Weiner, a professor of international law and diplomacy at Stanford Law School. "The courts of one country generally can't sit in judgment of the actions of another state."

The 2002 federal lawsuit concerns the conduct of the **Rev. Andrew Ronan**, who was moved to Portland in the mid-1960s after admitting he molested children in Ireland and Chicago, the suit claims.

The plaintiff, who now lives in Washington, said he was a teenager when Ronan repeatedly molested him in Portland in 1965 or 1966.

Portland Archdiocese officials said they acted swiftly when they learned about Ronan, who was eventually defrocked and left Oregon. He died in the early 1990s.

In order for any suit to go forward, it must be delivered to the defendant. Delivery can be as easy as putting a copy of the suit in the mail, but lawyers sometimes hire process servers to track down reluctant defendants... But even if a process server could get past the Swiss guards, handing the pope a copy of a lawsuit doesn't count as service.

Because the Vatican is a foreign country, all documents must be translated into its official language. And Anderson also had to send the documents through the U.S. State Department to the proper Vatican official.

Jeffrey S. Lena, a Berkeley, Calif., attorney representing the Holy See, said his client simply demanded to be served legal papers like any other foreign government.

"It's in an extremely well-established framework in which the Holy See is doing and asking no more than the United States asks in its own international relations," Lena said.

Anderson hired two Latin scholars from the University of Minnesota to translate 41 pages—every word from "fraud" and "conspiracy" to "e-mail" ("inscripto electronica").
Lena, using his own Latin experts, argued that Anderson failed to meet the requirements. Twice, U.S. District Judge Michael Mosman told Anderson to try again.

Lena declined to contest the third try in November.

Anderson's next hurdle is the **Foreign Sovereign Immunities Act, which prohibits lawsuits against foreign countries with a few exceptions.**

Anderson says his suit falls under **the exception for injuries caused by certain foreign government officials on American soil.**

In this case, it's the molestation of the plaintiff by a Catholic priest in Portland.

In court papers seeking to dismiss the lawsuit, Lena claims the Vatican cannot be held responsible.

Experts say the case could hinge on whether a priest is considered an employee of the Vatican or a local archdiocese or religious order.

Jenny S. Martinez, a professor at Stanford Law School, said the courts have dismissed lots of suits over the years because they couldn't establish enough of a connection between the person who caused the injury and the foreign government.

"It is a high hurdle to climb," Martinez said.

Still, of all the cases she's heard of, a lawsuit against the Vatican for the acts of a priest on American soil might just work.

"This does seem to be a little different than most cases that have been thrown out," Martinez said.

Jesse also googled Attorney Jeffrey S. Lena. Even though Lena had become a hunted—and hated—man, he would survive. Just as the Church would survive. *Nessun problema* (No problem).

24
The Trial

Tuesday, November 16, 2010

"I would like to read a great quote to you," said Wes.

It was Kim's idea to invite W-2 to have dinner with them on the evening before the trial. W-2 had a calming influence on Wes, Sr. Even though he would be the last to admit it, during the past eight months before the case came to trial the pressure had been building. So much was at stake— and it was out of his hands. Whatever happened tomorrow depended on the whims of the people sitting in the jury box.

From his briefcase W-2 removed his Kindle and scrolled to the classic novel titled *The Trial* by Kafka. "Someone is speaking to K, the main character of the novel. The person says: 'It is not necessary to accept everything as true, one must only accept it as necessary.' 'A melancholy conclusion,' said K. 'It turns lying into a universal principle.'"

W-2 looked up from his Kindle.

"Brilliant," responded Wes. "If I remember correctly, this is a novel about a man who is the head of a bank who is suddenly accosted by two no-name agents from a no-name agency for a mysterious crime that the man knows nothing about."

"Right," said W-2. "He's facing a trial and that's all he knows. The piece I found interesting was when K's lawyer tells him that his most important task was to deal with the powerful court officials behind the scenes."

"I see what you're getting at, son," grinned Wes. "Real money has value. Counterfeit does not. Yet counterfeit money is necessary in order to make a case involving counterfeiting. This gives the counterfeit money a form of reality."

"And once counterfeit money is real and necessary, it has value," said Kim. "Pretzel logic. It's like an atheist saying 'I don't believe in God,' and merely by uttering that statement, they have affirmed their belief in the existence of God."

"What did I do to get such brilliant and crazy parents?" sighed W-2.

"Nothing to it, son," grinned Wes. "We did all the work."

"*I* did all the work," Kim corrected him, placing a large baking dish of lasagna on the table in front of Wes.

As anticipated, the courtroom was packed. All the agents from the field office were present. The Brush was particularly prominent; he was wearing a bright red and white polka-dot bowtie and a toothy grin that he flashed noticeably yet not without a touch of anxiety whenever the judge happened to look his way.

"Tell me we needed some comic relief," muttered Wes to Gordon as the SAIC seated himself in the front row of the gallery.

"The guy's a moron. What did you expect?"

Judge Jeffrey Peeler was presiding. Although Wes didn't know Judge Peeler personally, they'd met and talked at social functions. Both were black and at any law enforcement event they shared a mutual awareness that they were sometimes the only two black men in the room. If Kim were there, she might be the only black woman, making a total of three of them.

Relationships were not built on the sharing of color, religion, background or any other common denominator. Yet in some undefined, unspoken sense and in certain situations they were. If a black man or woman were running for president, even if some people who were black did not agree with that candidate's platform, they will vote for them. Sometimes they would even openly admit this. Life was strange and often unpredictable.

All heads turned as Tony Masella swaggered into the courtroom with the security guards. *As if he owned it,* thought W-2 from his gallery seat next to Rachel and Kim. Masella's face was impassive, his eyes cold. *A cool cat. Maybe they get to be so seasoned, so hardened, they take it for granted that one day they're going to be picked up and end up in the joint.*

No. After the research he and Rachel had been doing, W-2 was convinced this man had no intention of spending his life in prison, either from this crime or future ones. In and out. Revolving door. That was the name of the game, until finally the group that was running the show decided it was payola time and they disappeared altogether, with new identities.

AUSA Dan Walter surprised all of them, and possibly himself more than anyone else. Wes didn't want to guess how many tranquilizers he'd swallowed beforehand in order to get through the ordeal. *Whatever it took.*

Defense Attorney Eldon Howell was a pro. Impeccably groomed as usual, as Kim watched him glide to his seat she couldn't help thinking he would have made an excellent Arthur Murray dance instructor. He knew exactly how to deliver the right gestures at the right moment, how and when to use his hands... every movement was practiced and performed with precision.

Yet any savvy attorney knows that without good material, without a real argument that has meat—a case with tantalizing cross-examinations and plenty of sizzle—they're finished even before they begin. And this was exactly what Howell was dealing with: a heap of bones already gnawed clean after the first round.

Despite his well-rehearsed pyrotechnics, despite all the flapping and flopping in front of the judge and jury—his well-lubricated delivery with all the right pauses for charging up anger and self-righteousness from his attentive audience—after the first few speeches, it was evident to everyone in the courtroom that he was struggling.

The dearth of material from the defense was making Howell's interrogation of USSS Agent Mitchell Gordon sound like a broken record. The entrapment issue was rapidly becoming warmed-over hash.

Howell was well aware that he was up against one of the smoothest and most polished federal law enforcement agents in the country. Only someone like Mitch Gordon who'd worked the streets and knew a man's color inside and out, could pull this one off with even greater aplomb than Howell, thought Wes with amusement, already knowing each of Gordon's moves before he made them. The agent's 6'5" height alone was formidable enough, but everything that came with it was a package that no one wanted to reckon with.

Howell had no choice.

Gordon knew exactly how to work each play—when to fold and when to hold. And when he came up against actors like Eldon Howell who were only in it for the dough—who'd play any card they were given as long as there was enough money in it for them—he brushed them off like a piece of lint. No doubt about it, he was a cool cat, with an ego that never stopped and an air of self-confidence that was carefully nailed onto every word he uttered.

Each "yes" and each "no" in response to the attorney's questions were carefully aimed shots that Gordon simply tipped into the hoop. It was too much even for Howell. The agent was impervious to even the slightest innuendo that Howell attempted to deliver and then redeliver, just to try one more time to trip up Gordon. Just to make sure he wouldn't flinch even an inch. And when the attorney pounded on about the stupidity— the downright idiocy of the USSS to think they could frame a counterfeit case and get away with it—the expression on Gordon's face made Howell look like an idiot.

All this was bad enough, but when AUSA Walter, coached by veteran performer Wesley Charles, came up from behind and stole the ball away from Howell, popping it into the hoop when he least expected it, the game was over and the defense attorney was cooked.

This was the play. Facing the jury, Walter began in a pleasant enough yet somewhat patronizing tone: "I believe we've heard enough of the same old same old from the defense to the point of extremely redundancy. So before we continue with the prosecution, I would like the jury to have an opportunity to *actually see* the counterfeit money that the defendant ordered—that the defendant *contracted by payment of two thousand dollars,* to be printed and delivered to him."

Walter pivoted around and stepped back to let two of the court officers step forward and hoist up on the table in front of the jury a large corrugated carton similar to the size used to ship washing machines and kitchen sinks.

Ever so slowly, Walter opened the box and tilted it toward the jury so they could see the piles upon piles of counterfeit money. Dipping his hand into the box, the attorney pulled out several stacks of 100-dollar bills, stepped forward until he was standing directly in front of the jury, and riffled through them.

Just as Wes, Walter and Gordon anticipated, the actual display of the counterfeit bills made its own statement. An audible gasp could be heard from members of the jury. Even one side of Judge Peeler's mouth twitched visibly.

The rest of the trial bumbled on, with another play from Howell that caused even the judge to stifle a yawn.

Finally they reached the time for closing arguments. Eldon Howell took the stand for the defense. Adjusting his halfie reading glasses at the tip of his nose and straightening his documents, he cleared his throat, lifted his head and looked straight at Agent Wesley Charles, seated next to AUSA Dan Walter.

Howell stared intently at Wes for several moments. Then he turned to face the jury. "Ladies and gentlemen of the jury (pause): Doesn't it seem strange that Agent Wesley Charles, the case agent, never took the stand?

"You never heard one peep from Agent Charles. Nothing. He sat through this entire trial and said nothing. Nothing. In the history of criminal trials I have never seen nor heard of any case where the case agent doesn't get on the witness stand to explain his role."

Again the defense attorney paused, peering at the jury over his halfies. "Case agents know everything about the case. Everything. You the jury needs to hear from Agent Charles. What is the government hiding? What is Agent Wesley Charles hiding? You should know. This case is about entrapment and the government, about Agent Charles and his cohorts enticing my client to commit this alleged crime.

"They, the government, printed 50 million dollars in counterfeit money, gave it to my client and then, they have the audacity to charge him with possession of the counterfeit money they gave him."

The eyes of every member of the jury were riveted on Agent Charles. Wes now understood why the AUSA didn't want him on the stand. It was a clever strategy. Even Judge Peeler was gazing intently at Wes.

The only sound in the courtroom was the wheezing and ratcheting forward of the minute hand on the antique wall clock behind the judge's bench.

Then it was Assistant U.S. Attorney Dan Walter's turn. W-2 gently nudged Rachel. She nudged him back as Kim tilted her head in their direction.

The three already knew by heart the script Wes had prepared for Walter, and Walter delivered. With calmness and ease, the AUSA attorney proceeded to explain every detail of the case. He played the recording of Masella (Paul) and Gordon (Peter), showed the jury the $2,000 that Masella had given to Gordon, gestured toward the open box of counterfeit bills, showed the video that Wes had made from the surveillance van... and then smoothly he rebutted every point made by the defense.

"As for the answer to the question regarding Agent Charles not testifying... (Pause)... (Pause)... he didn't have to."

Beautiful, breathed Wes, feeling Kim's relieved eyes on his back. She was seated directly behind him.

The jury declared Masella guilty, convicting him of conspiracy to print counterfeit U.S. currency, and possession of counterfeit U.S. currency.

"Tony Massella is sentenced to two to five years in federal prison," pronounced Judge Peeler. "However," he continued briskly, his voice laced with anger, "I am *appalled* at the conduct of the agents' involvement in the printing of the 50 million dollars, then giving it to the defendant and charging him with possession."

"So I guess we need to eat this one," said Gordon glumly, placing an arm around Wes's shoulders as the two walked out of the courtroom.

"And you also know, this is not the end, my friend," retorted Wes. "There *will* be an appeal. Eldon and Masella are not going to let this rest. Whoever's paying Masella's bills has deep pockets. Very deep ones." Gordon well knew what that meant.

Later, Wes and Kim discussed Judge Peeler's comments. "Did you ever hear of Morton's Fork?" asked Kim.

"Nope."

"You know the expression 'between a rock and a hard place.'"

"Caught in a 'damned if you do and damned if you don't' dilemma."

"Right," said Kim. "Morton's Fork was a tax issue. Who could afford to pay taxes? In the late 15th century, John Morton, Archbishop of Canterbury, declared the answer to that question was 'everyone.' He reasoned that a man living modestly must be saving money and therefore could afford taxes, and a man who was living extravagantly was obviously rich and could also afford them."

"In other words," said Wes, "there is no accounting for the fact that 'a man living modestly' may still be struggling financially with a few little burdens such as college tuition, medical expenses/health insurance, possible job loss, a foreclosure crisis, et cetera... and living on peanut butter and spam... but the wealthy man may be living far beyond his means, without a penny to his name... in worse shape than the man living modestly yet delivering the illusion of being wealthy."

Kim sighed and did not respond.

"Maybe the issue was very clear-cut for Judge Peeler," Wes mused. "Remember, the media has really dug into this and chewed up the Feds. The USSS, FBI, CIA, all the alphabet groups are the same as 'the police' to many people. They don't make the distinction between what's been happening on the streets, with brutality, tear gas and other types of police violence that in many cases was clearly out of line—and between what we agents do to protect our country's leaders, its laws—*and* its money. It was a big thing for many people to learn that the Feds got actively involved in the printing of counterfeit money in order to make a case."

"Federal judges are appointed, not elected," Kim pointed out. "The media—the people's perception or how they're directed to perceive an issue—is not the last word. If the bottom line is supposed to be results, we got the results that were needed. Masella was arrested. Isn't that what really matters?"

"Federal judges are appointed by the president and the president is elected by the people. Ideally, the government is the people," Wes reminded her. "And there's also another issue at stake. If Judge Peeler should appear to show favoritism or even the slightest bend in a brother's direction, fair or unfair, you know what happens next."

"So I guess he played it smart, like a good politician, unless he really believed what he said," said Kim. "And of course, there's a slim chance that he did." She frowned. "He said he was 'appalled at the conduct of the agents.' You know what, Wes? Spinning our wheels in a pile of shit only makes the wheels grind deeper. What if you'd passed up the opportunity to find a printer for Masella? You don't have to answer that."

"We can only do our job, m'love, and then we can *do our job.*" Wes chuckled mirthlessly. "I always choose the second, and I know you do, too. It has something to do with making a difference in this world versus just pushing pencils and picking up a weekly or monthly paycheck."

"Don't forget the adventure part," teased Kim, lightening up. "It's not all altruistic, is it?"

"*Touché*. I am not a saint, never was and never want to be," said Wes. "And right now if you'll let me, I'd like to prove it."

"Agent Charles, I order you to show me your evidence."

Two years later....

25

La Festa di San Silvestro a la Peppi

December 31, 2012 - Rome, Italy

The famous couturier Peppi Tubiano's New Year's Eve party, or *La Festa di San Silvestro,* as it was called by Italians, was a major annual event. Only someone with deep pockets could stage such a bash. By all standards it was *l'evento dell'anno*–the event of the year. Invitations were hard to come by and prized by those who received one.

Father Ira always took a holiday leave from his Chicago duties in mid-December to help Peppi prepare for the party. The two meticulously worked out all the details. Father Ira had a vivid imagination—and so did Peppi.

When Rome's USSS SAIC Chris Mendoza received his gold-embossed invitation, he was both honored and flattered. One didn't have to be in Rome for long without knowing who Giuseppe Tubiano "Peppi" was. His exclusive dress shop had a prime position on Via Condotti, the Rodeo Drive of Beverly Hills, El Paseo Drive of Palm Springs, or Worth Avenue of Palm Beach. Peppi had a reputation for setting the trends in Rome and Paris. It was "the place" for finding that special gown or having it custom designed.

It was well-known that the famous *couturier* traveled in some of the most prestigious social circles and led an exciting social life. Photos of Peppi at well-publicized parties and galas were always a media draw. It was equally well-known that Peppi was gay. Even though he was now in his mid-fifties and had grown up during a time when most homosexuals, especially prominent ones, were afraid to come out of the closet, Peppi had never hesitated to let people know about his sexual preferences.

Since a large percentage of the male dress designers were known to be gay, it was perfectly acceptable for Peppi to be as flamboyant as he wished. And after all, was it not true that it was easier to hide in plain daylight?

Regardless, Peppi was known to be direct and outspoken. In fact, said many, it was one of his most likeable qualities. "He's very candid and open," was one of the most common quotes about Peppi.

That he was gay only added spice and speculation about his New Year's Eve event.

If SAIC Christopher Mendoza ever took a screen test, Hollywood probably would have hired him to play the role that he performed in real life. American born from Hispanic parents, with a flat nose and oily black eyes, all 6' 2" of his large symmetrically triangular body was muscle. Broad shoulders, impressive chest span, bulging quads and hamstrings exhibited serious dedication to a rigid workout schedule. Enormous bi- and triceps also indicated some unusual weight lifting capabilities. He was a behometh, a younger version of Hollywood's "Terminator" and California's former governor when he was in his prime.

Since Mendoza was totally committed to physical fitness when he wasn't working at the office or on duty, his free time was mostly taken up with sessions at a nearby gym. During off hours, he rarely accompanied the rest of the agents. It wasn't uncommon for SAICS to distance themselves from the agents under their charge, so no one questioned Mendoza's private life.

The gym near the U.S. Consulate, which is where the USSS Rome Bureau was located, provided an interesting mix of people that included many successful Italian businessmen, diplomats, government employees, and even several members of the clergy. One priest in particular, Father Rupert, was a devotee like himself.

In addition to their commitment to physical fitness, many of these men also shared their sexual proclivities. After the first few visits to the gym, SPAIC Mendoza was invited to accompany them to one of the nearby saunas or bathhouses.

Since discreetness was vitally important for these men, Mendoza felt comfortable joining them. He enjoyed their company, enjoyed the sex. Life was good. Very good.

Mendoza assumed he'd been placed on Peppi's party list for political reasons. His name and position had probably come down through U.S. diplomatic channels. The American agent, even though Catholic by birth, hadn't been to church in years and he'd never even heard of *La Festa di San Silvestro* before now. He was curious to learn how it was linked to New Year's Eve.

A quick search on the Internet for information about Saint Sylvester produced a Wikipedia article about a Pope Sylvester, who served a term from January 31, 314 to December 31, 335 A.D. He succeeded Pope Miltiades.

Although history has a way of substituting fiction for fact, it really didn't make any difference, as long as the fiction was harmless and could be used to the advantage of the ruling party. According to the Symmachean forgeries "emanating from the curia of Pope Symmacus, who died in 514, the Emperor Constantine was cured of leprosy by the figure of baptismal water administered by Sylvester at the time he was pope. The Emperor, abjectly grateful, not only confirmed the bishop of Rome as the primate above all other bishops; he [also] resigned his imperial insignia and walked before Sylvester's horse holding the pope's bridle as the papal groom.

"The generous pope, in return, offered the crown of his own good will to Constantine, who abandoned Rome to the pope and took up residence in Constantinople."

As one can well imagine, the legend gained immediate popularity among Roman Catholics. Hence, *La Festa di San Silvestro*, celebrated every December 31.

The gold-engraved invitation stated the party would be held at the Rome Marriott Park Hotel on via Colonnello Tommaso Masala, 54, and would begin at 9PM. Dress was black tie.

In 2012, an American in Rome, especially a law enforcement agent, was treated with suspicion and often outright hostility. Soon after arriving in Rome, the seven USSS agents who were assigned to the Italian foreign field office got the message that they were not particularly welcome. Since Mendoza was well aware that he was treated like an outsider, this placed even greater value on Peppi's party invitation. Immediately he sent back his RSVP.

Mendoza didn't mention Peppi's New Year's Eve invitation to the other agents. He had no reason to do so; he assumed word would spread around the office as soon as they received their own invitations. Several days passed and when no one mentioned anything about the forthcoming event, Mendoza assumed he was the only secret service agent who had been invited.

For the prestigious occasion, Mendoza treated himself to a new maroon silk paisley cummerbund, tie and handkerchief and a custom designed tuxedo. The outfit and accessories had set him back more than he'd anticipated, but it was worth it, he reassured himself. He needed to look smart.

At a socially correct 9:10PM, Mendoza arrived by cab at the Marriott Park Hotel. Paparazzi were already everywhere, squatting in front of, next to and behind the arriving vehicles; jumping over hedges and flower gardens; setting up tripods and other equipment wherever they could, in order to capture prize shots of the celebrities as they were escorted into the ballroom.

Mendoza had never been invited to such an auspicious bash; he would have felt lost if he hadn't recognized some of his gym friends. In fact, many of them were there. It was a relief to hang out with them and let down on some of their usual training rules. The champagne was flowing and the hors d'oeuvres were exceptional.

Promptly at 10:30PM, a formally attired young man wearing a tall white hat and white gloves tapped Mendoza on the shoulder. "Mr. Mendoza, sir, I would like you to come with me."

He motioned for Mendoza to follow him out the ballroom door and down a long hallway. At the end of the hallway was a room. The young man opened the door and waited for Mendoza to enter before he closed the door.

Inside the room were some of Mendoza's gym and sauna friends and many other men of various ages whom he'd never met.

"Ah, Welcome, Mr. Christopher Mendoza! Happy New Year!" Peppi, attired in a deep purple silk tuxedo with a flowered lilac-colored cummerbund and matching handkerchief, clasped his hand, giving it a hearty shake.

"Thank you, Mr. Tubiano, for inviting me!"

"Call me 'Peppi,' and if I may call you 'Christopher' or 'Chris'? You will not be sorry," Peppi promised him, kissing him on both cheeks and returning to the front of the room.

"*Se posso avere la vostra attenzione, signori* (If I may have your attention, gentlemen)," he began, speaking into his wireless mic.

"Some of you are newcomers. Welcome to the greatest show, the greatest *festa nel mondo!* (Greatest party in the world)!" Several of the men clapped and whistled.

Peppi held up his hand for silence. "Before I continue, may I make it very clear to the newcomers that whatever happens tonight never goes beyond the walls of these rooms. No one even knows this party exists as anything more than a traditional *Festa di San Silvestro.* Is that clear?"

All buzzing and chattering stopped. The room became completely silent. "You all know the penalty of disclosing anything that takes place this evening from midnight to dawn of the New Year." Peppi smiled beneficently on the group and raised his arms over them. *As if to bless them,* Mendoza couldn't help thinking.

"And now, I am going to ask you to remove your beautiful *oh così molto elegante!* (Oh so very elegant!) formal outfits and place them in the suitcases labeled with your names and contact information that will be provided for you upon exiting the room. When the party is over your outfits will be returned to you.

"As soon as you are naked, you will be provided a robe and escorted into our awaiting *Furgoni* (vans). You will then be driven to an undisclosed location where the party will take place."

Peppi paused and looked around the room, enjoying the shock and surprise from the newcomers. "This year's theme, my dears, is 'Leprosy,' he continued. "As soon you arrive, your leprosy costumes will be created by our highly gifted staff of body painting artists."

A round of laughter and applause swept through the room.

As Agent Chris Mendoza glanced around at the men who were already disrobing, his blood started to race and he got a hard-on just anticipating the pleasures that awaited him. Ring in the New Year! Bring on the good times! God *damn*, what a great idea! Hours and hours of debauchery with some of the wealthiest and most prestigious men in Rome!

Una autentica orgia romana... An authentic Roman orgy!

"Traditional menu will consist of lentils," Peppi was saying, "symbolizing money and good fortune for the coming year, and stuffed pig's trotter. The pork symbolizes the richness of life in the year 2013."

What the hell was pig's trotter? Mendoza wondered.

"The feet," whispered Salvatore Vacelli, one of his gym friends who was standing next to him and had already stripped naked. "The fucking feet of a pig. Don't even try to imagine what the damn things will be stuffed with!"

"It really doesn't matter, does it?" joked Mendoza back. The two men continued to banter until Mendoza was also naked and waiting for one of the servants to come by with a suitcase for his clothes. They put on the robes and waited for instructions.

"I hope we don't freeze our asses off in the *Veicolo* (van)," quipped Mendoza to one of the other men.

"Not to worry, sweetheart," he reassured Mendoza. "Our asses will always be covered. Don't forget who's in charge!"

So... who *was* in charge? wondered Mendoza, without really caring. Had he missed a beat?

The procession was already heading toward the exit.

When USSS SAIC Christopher Mendoza's RSVP to the Peppi's Festa di San Silvestro party arrived among the first batch to be returned, Peppi called

Father Ira. "Mendoza is the best damage control we could ever hope for," he gloated to the priest.

"Yes, but that doesn't mean we can be careless," warned Father Ira. "When you give to the needy, be sure you let your left hand knows what your right hand is doing. We cannot afford any slip-ups."

"Oh wise man, which version of the New Testicle is that? Or, as they say in French, '*Aimez vos ennemis comme vous, n'est-ce pas?* (Love your enemies as yourself, is that not so?')" joked Peppi. "If I were there right now, do you know what I would do to you?"

Father Ira was as excited and relieved as Peppi about the early arrival of the USSS agent's RSVP. It was, indeed, a piece of good news that they would be able to subject Agent Chris Mendoza to gross humiliation and unadulterated blackmail during the long evening of sadistic rituals that were a traditional part of the annual New Year's Eve event. Father Ira's physical accessories did a dick-flip just thinking about what a good time they were going to have.

Just in case they ever needed some evidence on tap, one of SAIC Mendoza's New Year's presents, a party favor, would be a video of himself in nude body painted performance indulging in the tasty dick juices of his fellow lepers, dancing cheek to cheek, tongue to tongue, graciously accepting the belt and the whip, then bending wa-a-ay over for his own delicious punishment. The last scene would be titled "The Royal Throne." Mendoza would be kneeling on a satin pillow, head bowed, and while each of the lepers lined up to spray him with liquid gold.

Enclosed in the video would be a note stating that several copies had already been placed in The Vault in case they ever needed to be used as evidence.

At the party, Peppi had his men implant a tracking chip underneath Mendoza's groin tattoo of a heart with two parallel bars and the scripted word "equality."

Just in case, Peppi smiled to himself.

And then it happened. A month after *La Festa di San Silvestro,* at the DaVinci airport, an Italian exchanged 12-$100 bills for Euros.

26
Avvitato (Screwed)

It was 1AM when the bills were passed. The regular night cashier had come down with the flu and the temporary cashier, an intern who had not yet been trained to examine U.S. bills, had been called at the last minute to cover.

Only after they reached the Alitalia bank did they raise suspicion. A bank officer had them checked and reported that the red and blue fibers embedded in the paper of authentic U.S. Treasury bills, were missing. The counterfeiter had cleverly printed red and blue lines onto the paper, using a multiple overlay process. The bills passed simple scan tests, but more sophisticated instruments had detected the fraud.

USSS Agent Fred Stillwell was alone in the Rome office when the Alitalia bank officer called. At once he had a courier send over the bills for forensic testing. Agent Stillwell did the testing himself and found the same problems with the threads. There were also some other issues with borders and images.

When SAIC Chris Mendoza arrived shortly after noon, Stillwell buzzed his office. Mendoza told him to meet him in the forensics lab immediately.

"In my opinion, it's a sloppy job, sir. Very amateur." Stillwell handed Mendoza an envelope containing the bills and the two forensic reports.

Mendoza reexamined the bills and the documents. Stillwell was right. "Shit. I dislike trouble with the Italians."

"But we have no choice, sir. We must send the bills to D.C.," said Stillwell.

In the back of his head, Mendoza heard a faint buzzing. A voice was speaking to him in Italian. *"E 'il tuo turno, Chris. Siete pronti per l'esperienza più emozionante in tutta la tua vita?* (It is your turn, Chris. Are you ready for the most exciting experience in your entire life?")

The New Year's Eve party... *La Festa di San Silvestro.* He was lying on his back on a wooden raft that was gently rocking him back and forth, back and forth, as it rode the waves. He felt so peaceful, so relaxed...

His naked body had been waxed and rubbed with fragrant oils and as a strobe of colored lights passed over him, they ejected delicate sprays of tiny luminescent particles. As the particles brushed over his skin they shot pangs of lust through every part of his body. His penis was so erect, so perfectly erect... it was beautiful... when he lifted his head, he could see it gleaming in the bands of light pouring from the strobes as they passed over his body, showering him with prisms of even more of the delicate particles, delivering to every part of his body the sweetest and most sensuous pain.

And now as he looked up on the ceiling, he could see a large convex mirror that allowed him to view himself in all his glory. He could see the heavy cords binding his arms and his legs and he could see his large stiff penis, very erect. He was tied to the raft and couldn't move. His penis had never been so large. He was so hot, so aroused and so erect... and he couldn't move... that was the joy of it... the agony was so sweet, so intense, he could only wish it would go on forever...

"If you turn in those bills you will be killed," warned a voice. It was his own.

Mendoza's tried to keep his hand from shaking. He smiled weakly at Agent Stillwell. "I'll handle this matter myself, Stillwell. Thank you."

"Fate attenzione," warned the voice again.

"And by the way, Stillwell..."

"Yes, sir?" Stillwell already had his hand on the doorknob.

"This matter will go no further than you and me. *Tell no one about the bills, Is that clear?"*

Stillwell shook his head, puzzled. "Not even the rest of the agents, sir?" he said. Surely they will want to—"

"**No**," said Mendoza sharply, his voice rising. **"Absolutely not.** "I will take care of this matter myself. I hope you heard me correctly, Stillwell. **No one else is to know about this. Is that clear? We will NOT have internal business that is SOLELY related to the USSS floating around the streets of Rome where it can be picked up by ANYONE, ABSOLUTE STRANGERS who will have NO FUCKING IDEA what to do with this information. We cannot take any chances.** *Queste informazioni non andare oltre te e me. Sono stato chiaro?* **(This information will not go further than you and me. Is that clear?)"**

"But sir, the Alitalia office already know about it, since they were the ones..."

"They know nothing," exploded Mendoza. **"You have told them nothing. They should have no reason to pursue this further unless we tell them to!"**

"Yes, sir," replied Stillwell meekly.

As he opened the door he almost bumped into one of the Italian translators who had been waiting outside. Maria Something... a *pomodoro calda* (hot tomato) according one of the agents. Stillwell could only imagine. If she wore her skirts any shorter they'd be over her head. And the flaming red hair and tattoos... *Yeehaw!*

"Sorry," Stillwill smiled timidly at Maria as his eyes undressed her. "He—he—Agent Mendoza will be free in a minute, I'm sure."

"Yes, I'm sure he will be, Agent Stillwell." Maria gave him a disarming smile.

Stillwell felt his knees buckling. *Shit! Any man would be damn lucky to have a piece of that broad...*

As soon as Agent Stillwell closed Agent Mendoza's office door, his phone rang.

"Christopher! *Come stai?* This evening at seven?"

"*Ma naturalmente!* (But of course)!"

How the hell did Peppi already know about the counterfeit bills?

"My driver will come for you at 18:40. He will also drive you home."

Peppi met him personally at the door. "Father Ira has already left for the States," said Peppi, kissing him tenderly. "We will be alone. I have a special evening planned for you. But first, if you will excuse me for a moment, Christopher, I have an important call to make. Ricco, bring Chris a drink. What would you like? Bourbon as usual? *Torno tra un minuto* (I'll be back in a minute)." Peppi smiled graciously.

In his study, Peppi pressed the speed dial for Cardinal Scatturo.

"*Adquiesce diligite* (Listen carefully, Love.)"

"*Imo.*"

"*Per i prossimi dieci giorni hanno ogni agente USSS seguita.* (For the next ten days have every USSS agent followed.)"

"*Imo.*"

Peppi returned with his own drink. "Ricco, some caviar," he smiled at the servant, who bowed and left the room. "Ahh, so, what's new at the office, Christopher? Besides the counterfeit bills that were just turned in? I have some exciting videos to show you tonight, that were taken at *La Festa di San Silvestro.* Our own party, of course! I have a feeling you will love the photos that were taken of you! Especially the ones during the waterboarding. *Mio Dio* (My God), you were terrified, but so brave! Or at least you put on a brave front. The videos—and incidentally, we've made a copy for you as a special New Year's gift. But they are only one of several things I have to show you tonight. I also want to introduce you to my staff of eunuchs."

27
Memory Jog

Monday, March 4, 2013 – USSS Offices – Chicago, Illinois

"Agent Charles, a call for you from Shane Burke in D.C."

Wes looked up from the pile of paperwork he was plowing through on his desk. "Thank you, Joanne, put him through."

"Hey, Wes."

"How's it going in D.C., bro? They treating you well?"

Thanks to Wes, Shane had been transferred out of Chicago to Washington 14 months ago, where he now had a cushy job with the U.S. Treasury counterfeit bureau. The counterfeit buck literally stopped at the D.C. office.

When USSS regional squads turned in the bills that had been identified as counterfeit, agents in Washington performed additional tests, then notarized and filed the reports.

Bureaucracy in D.C. had its perks. Wes was happy to have been instrumental in getting a plum position for Shane. "You deserve it, Bro," he told him when the transfer and appointment came through.

The two had stayed in close touch at first, but now it had been at least six months since Wes had heard from him. A call out of the blue meant something must be up.

"Things are good, I can't complain. Hey Wes, I'll always be grateful to you for all you've done for me over the years. I think of you as a brother from another mother."

"Same here, Bro. So what can I do for you?"Wes already knew from the tension in Shane's voice that this wasn't just a social call.

"Are you sitting down?"

"All right, Burke, cut the bullshit. Give it to me straight."

"Wes, do you remember the Masella case that we made a few years ago, back in February-March 2010, when we printed $50 million in counterfeit $100s?"

"Of course I do. How could I forget it—and after all that good work, Masella did only two years. What's up? What does it have to do with what's going on in D.C.?"

"You're not going to believe this, but I swear to God it's true, Wes. A bill with one of the same serial numbers was passed in Florence, Italy and arrived in our offices this week."

"**What?** You've got to be kidding!! Tell me you just won the lottery or that Snow White just gave birth to Seven Dwarves and I'll believe you, but that Masella's counterfeit bills turning up in Italy or anywhere else on the fucking planet... no way!"

"I'm not bullshitting you, Wes. Honest! I just looked at one of the counterfeit bills that were passed and it's an exact duplicate of the bills we printed, except not as perfect."

"No fucking way," Wes insisted. "They can't be! We sent specimens of the bills to headquarters after we arrested Masella. The rest of the bills are still in the box, stored away in our evidence room."

"Wes, I think you should look in the box. Now."

Wes was steaming. Shane Burke, of all people... his own protégé coming back on him like this with a fucking fairytale... *Who does he think he is? I trained that asshole and now he's trying to give orders to me!* "Okay, I'm on my way to the evidence room. I'll call you back."

Still fuming, Wes grabbed his set of auxiliary keys and headed down the hallway to the evidence room.

As soon as he unlocked the door, he spotted the box sitting on the same shelf where they'd placed it two years ago. Pulling it off the shelf, he flipped open the lid. The neat piles of counterfeit bills looked completely intact.

Wes dialed Shane's inside office number. Shane answered immediately.

"Shane, you're a fucking idiot. The counterfeit bills are still here in our evidence room. What the fuck are you talking about? You assholes in Washington made a mistake. Mistakes *do happen,* you know... even with you guys. Either that, or you've got the wrong serial number."

It wasn't an easy moment for Shane. He had no intention of angering Wes further, but at the same time... "Wes, wait a minute. Did you check for the plates and negs?"

"No, of course not," Wes retorted. "They have to be there. The box hasn't been touched in two years."

"Wes—*please check!*"

"Listen Shane, I'm in the evidence room and the box is sitting on the table in front of me. I'll put you on speaker." *Idiots, dickheads, dingbats,* *dufuses...*and Shane was leading the pack. *God help us if these are the kind of morons that work at D.C. headquarters...*

Wes dug through the box of neatly stacked bills, lifting them out and placing all of them on the table... $50Million worth of bills minus the five specimens that had been taken out and sent to D.C.

Except for the bills, the box was empty. Nothing else was in the box. Wes ran his hand over the inner surface of the empty box to make sure. Maybe the manila envelope with the plates and negatives would magically appear. It wasn't there.

Shane was waiting patiently.

"Shane, I'll call you back." The piss and vinegar in Wes's voice squirted into Shane's ear before the connection clicked off.

Shane gripped the sides of the desk until his knuckles turned white. *Shit.* The last thing in the world he wanted to do was upset Wes. He wasn't trying to *prove* anything. It wasn't an ego thing by a long shot. It's just that he had to do his job. Somewhere, somehow, Tony Masella's counterfeit bills were passed in Florence and turned up in the USSS D.C. office.

He stood up and started pacing the office. *It is what it is,* he told himself, half hoping Wes would come up with the plates and negatives, yet already knowing from the tone of Wes's voice that they weren't in the box.

Wes spent the next hour searching the evidence room for the missing manila envelope. Obviously, if not in the box, chances of it being anywhere else in the room were slim. Yet he couldn't take that chance. *God damn!*

Finally, he had to admit to himself that the envelope wasn't there. He returned to his office.

Kim knocked on the door, entered and placed a Starbucks Latte Grande on his desk. She took one look at Wes's face, crossed both hands over her chest and stepped away from the desk in mock defense. *"Lawd ha' murcy!* What's going on, Agent Charles? You look like you just got struck by lightning!"

Without responding, Wes dialed Shane's number and motioned for Kim to close the office door. She perched on the edge of one of the easy chairs.

"Shane, it's not there. Not in the box. And I scoured the evidence room. I didn't mean to go ballistic, but I have to tell you, I honestly thought you were either putting me on or something was seriously fucked-up over there."

"So do you think somebody in the office stole it?"

"Geez." Wes looked over at Kim, who was slowly piecing things together. Shane... box... evidence room... *The counterfeit bills! No wonder Wes—*

"The report came to us through the *Guardia di Financza*, the Italian Financial Guard."

The Financial Guard, a part of the Italian Army under the authority of the Minister of Economy and Finance, was in charge of many of the crimes that were under the jurisdiction of the Secret Service in the U.S.: tax evasion, financial crimes, smuggling, money laundering, anti-Mafia operations, credit card fraud, counterfeiting, terrorist financing, etc.

"I'll hold off reporting anything for now," said Shane. "I don't have to tell you what this could mean for both of us, Bro. Especially with Fuller Brush. Since I left the office I don't think he's changed his sentiments about you. You're the one who's going to get the finger on this."

Shane didn't have to remind him about SAIC Larson Fuller's fix on Wes. For months already, Fuller had been looking for an excuse to boot him out of the office. The scuttlebutt was that he'd been trying to cut a deal with the LA office, but Headquarters had quashed it.

"You can't trade in a BMW for a Chevy and expect the Chevy to perform like the BMW," warned the Director. "I know your issues, Fuller, and that's your problem, not ours. Wesley Charles is one of the best agents you've got. Hell, he's one of the best agents in the entire USSS!"

When Wes heard the outcome he was amused. At the same time he also knew it was a sign that his days may be numbered at the Chicago office. Prying open the coffin of the Masella case and finding a corpse still breathing inside when it already had a two-year-old toe tag on it was a custom-made nightmare for him—and a dream come true for Larkin Fuller.

"Thanks for keeping the lid on until I can dig into this further, Bud. I really appreciate it."

As soon as Wes hung up, Kim said quietly, "So the plates and negatives are missing from the box."

The two exchanged long woeful glances.

Wes dialed Gordon's inside line. "You busy?"

"At your service. What's up?"

Gordon strode into Wes's office and sat down in the easy chair opposite Kim.

"Something's rotten in Denmark and Florence, Italy." Wes drew up a third chair and briefly recapped the conversations he'd just had with Shane.

"Shit. You've got to be kidding, Wes." Gordon stood up and started to pace in front of them.

"First off, I can't imagine anyone in this office stealing the envelope," said Kim.

"I second that," said Gordon.

"Make that three," agreed Wes. "So what the hell went wrong, and where?"

"Let's do a memory jog," suggested Gordon. "When was the last time we saw the envelope?"

"It was some God-awful hour on a Monday morning. March first, 2010, to be exact. And it was around 2 or 3AM. We were totally wiped out. Johnny K. had been printing the damn stuff since Sunday morning early. We knew we needed a whole day to get the printing done, a time when the store was closed to the public—which is why I vividly remember the date.

"We put the envelope in the box with the money, right?" asked Wes.

"Right."

"Monday morning we drove back to the office and as soon as the boss arrived we took him to the van where we'd stored the box and showed him the paper, the plates and the negatives," said Gordon. "I remember The Brush commenting about what a good job the printer had done."

"I remember that too," said Wes.

"So," concluded Gordon, sitting down again, "we know the envelope contained the plates and the negatives and they were in the box when we delivered it to Masella. We didn't move the box from the van."

"Okay. Next—"

"The surveillance video," said Wes and Kim together.

They headed for the media room where Wes pulled the video out of the file. Gordon locked the door.

They ran it two times. Flawless operation. Nothing odd or unusual that stood out.

"Now let's run it in slow motion," suggested Wes.

Frame by frame, they re-viewed it.

Gordon drove up and parked behind Masella's blue Dodge Ram. Masella (Paul) climbed out of the van and went back to meet Gordon (Peter). The men glanced around the street; Gordon opened the SUV hatchback and lifted the lid off the box of counterfeit bills.

Masella leaned into the van to look at the bills while Gordon stood in front of the hatchback.

Paul emerged from the van, confirming that the paper looked good. The two lifted the box out of Gordon's van and carried it over to the Ram. Masella unlocked the trunk and they slid the box into the open space next to the van's spare tire. Masella then proceeded to dig beneath the spare tire for a white envelope containing 100-dollar bills, which he handed to

Gordon.Paul climbed partly into the trunk of the Ram to secure the box and cover it while Gordon counted the bills.

"WAIT! STOP!" Wes signaled to Kim, who was running the video. "Play that frame over again. STOP! Right there. What the fuck is Masella doing in the back of the van?"

"He's covering the box with some clothes while I'm counting the money."

Gordon leaned forward. "Stop the video again, Kim. Replay that frame!"

Once more they watched the segment in slow motion. And then they all saw it.

While Masella was throwing clothes over the box, he pulled out the manila envelope and hid it underneath the trunk floor mat. The action was performed so swiftly they almost missed it.

Three more times they replayed the same segment in slow motion, freezing the frame at the point where Gordon was counting his money while Masella removed the manila envelope from the box and slipped it beneath the floor mat.

"Shit," Wes pounded his fist on the chair arm. "We were totally focused on you. We were watching you counting out the money, Mitch."

"And you gave the van back to his wife," said Kim softly.

"We need to re-arrest Masella."

"Oh fun-fun-fun," chanted Gordon sarcastically. "Here we go 'round the mulberry bush..."

Wes's cell phone rang and Shane's ID came up.

"Anything?" he asked.

"Yeah, we've got it."

"Shoot."

"It's all in the video. Masella took the envelope from the box while Gordon was counting the money Masella gave him for doing the printing. Masella hid the envelope under the floor mat of the car that we returned to Patty, Masella's wife. I never checked the fucking box for the envelope when we arrested Masella. *How could I have made such a dumb mistake?*"

"Hey, don't beat yourself up, Bro. It's done. What is it you always say? 'It is what it is.' So now, what did you learn from the mistake? That's what you always taught me to ask. And you taught me well. You told me over and over again that *no matter how experienced you are, if you don't dot all your 'i's and cross all your't's during an investigation, you could miss something or screw up.*

"Just know, Bro, that *you* don't make any mistakes. You're as perfect as they get. But this case was unique because of the entrapment issue, and you let your guard down. Besides that, you guys were exhausted. Wiped out. You'd already gone a night without sleep—it's miraculous with all the stress you were under that you were still able to—"

"Thanks, Shane for all the golden talk," Wes interrupted him, "but you're wrong. I did make a mistake. You listened well to me and I didn't follow my own advice. I fucked up. I'm glad you let us know about this pronto. We're going to go out and arrest Masella."

"Hold on, Wes. I just talked to the Florence police and they've got a dude in custody with $20,000 of those bills. He may be getting ready to talk. I haven't let the cat out of the bag yet, so I'm going to issue a travel order for you to go to Italy to work with the Florence police on their arrest."

"So what are you going to tell my boss and your boss?" asked Wes.

"My boss is not a problem. We do it all the time. I just sent two agents from the New York Office to Bogota, South America on another case. Don't worry, I'll think of something to tell Fuller. He'd probably love to get you out of his hair for a while. So listen, Wes, hold off on arresting Masella until you find out what happens in Florence. Have a good trip."

"Thanks, Shane. I know you're putting your career on the line for this."

"You owe me, Bro."

As soon as phone conversation ended, Wes turned to Kim and Gordon. "I'm calling a meeting right now, at Jimmy Green's," he instructed. "Get W-2 and Rachel on the phone. Their attendance is mandatory."

Wes tried not to be hard on himself, but his pride wouldn't leave him alone. He'd done some foolish things in his life, but this blooper won the booby prize. It was inexcusable for him not to have followed his own instructions about doing impeccable checks on important evidence.

He knew this was one of those moments when only one being in the whole universe could help him sort things out. He dialed direct and as always, God was there for him.

"Hey God, did you ever make any mistakes?"

"Never," answered God, "And I certainly didn't make any mistake when it came to creating you, Wes. You're as perfect as they come. In fact, the best part about you is the kind of thing that just happened."

"What do you mean, God?" Wes demanded. "You mean there was something good about doing a dumb ass thing like taking for granted that those plates and negatives were in the box with the counterfeit bills?"

"Look at it this way," reasoned God. "First of all, you're human and it's human to err. How else would you learn? Another thing: even gods have to learn the hard way. For example, would I have ever made another Wesley Charles exactly like the one I already made? No way! I learned my lesson the first time—right?! Why should I repeat myself by trying to make another rascal exactly like *him*?

"Let's get a few things straight," continued God, "Number One: Wes is a risk taker. He never knows when to say no, even when he's got both toes curled over the edge of the cliff and it's a long way down with no net underneath. Who else but USSS Agent Wesley Charles would have dared print up all that shit money, knowing he'd end up in prison if the judge decided he had no fucking business trying to set a precedent for entrapment? No sir—no one but Wesley Charles would have done anything as smartass as that!

"And second," continued God, "Wes is someone who learns from his mistakes. Isn't that true? Wesley Charles, tell me and give it to me straight: is this something you would ever do again?"

"Hell no, God!" Wes exploded.

"So doesn't that make you a better agent today than you were yesterday? Isn't that one of the qualities I wanted you to have—besides good looks, a great body, more libido than at least ten men even when at your age you should be starting to slow down—and a mind like a steel trap? What other qualities do you want?"

"Forgiveness," answered Wes meekly. "God, help me forgive myself."

"Ahhh, that's easy," smiled God. "As long as *you* can forgive *me* for creating you with the ability to make mistakes and learn from them, you can easily forgive yourself. So now, let me ask you: can you forgive me?"

"Of course I can forgive you, God!"

"Good. Then we're halfway home. Now let me ask you: if I created you without any flaws and if one of your greatest strengths is being grateful to me for remembering to install a device inside your mind that allows you to learn from your mistakes—if I also installed a device that allows you to forgive yourself—how can you refuse my Mafia offer?"

By the time they were ready to go to Jimmy Green's, Wes had worked up an appetite for a Windy City Willy, double order of French Fries, and plenty of beer on tap.

28
Truth or Conspiracy?

Monday, March 4, 2013 – Jimmy Green's Sports Bar – Chicago

W-2 and Rachel were in the forensics lab working on a fraudulent credit card case when Wes's SOS came through.

Rachel was thumbing through a file cabinet when Kim texted her: "Jimmy Green's now. SOS." She glanced over at W-2 who was at one of the computers and texted: "My car or yours?"

In the two years since they'd met, W-2 and Rachel had become an item and a couple weeks ago they'd started talking about marriage. Rachel's older sister, Esther, was so happy for her younger sister. She knew that until she met W-2, Rachel wasn't having much luck with American men. She was eye candy all right, so that wasn't the problem. Or maybe it was. Men expected her to be that and nothing more.

"It's the black version of the dumb blonde syndrome," she complained to her older sister.

Esther had already been through this herself. "I'll give you a hint, Rachel. You're going to find the real men, the ones who respect you for who you are AND admire for your gorgeous bod—and face it, you really are drop dead gorgeous, Sis!—you're going to find those men not in top level white collar positions or in all the 'elitist' corporate places. These dudes are the plastic ones who only want to use you to drape over their arms. Take it from me.

"Another hint, if I may: stop looking. Just let it happen. You might be surprised to find someone right in your own back yard!"

And then it was Esther who was in for a surprise. In February 2010 when Mitch Gordon landed back home in Chicago for the Masella case and Kim made the introduction, the rest was history.

What was it about these Ethiopian Israeli women? wondered Gordon afterward. Like her sister Rachel whom Gordon had already met at the office, Esther was also a babe, and just as brilliant as Rachel.

Wes and Kim had never seen Gordon so happy. "For the first time in his life," said Kim, "Gordon's met a woman who's not going to try to emasculate him or interfere with his career."

"And that's because Esther's in charge, m'dear," was Wes's comment. "Which is the way it should be. She doesn't *need* to *need* Mitch. I'll let you in on a secret. That's what true love is all about. "

"Did I hear you correctly?" teased Kim. "Did you say Esther's in charge and that's the way it should be?"

"You are a goddess, a queen. I bow down to you." They were getting ready for bed. Wes got down on one knee before her, took her hand and kissed it.

"All right, all right, King Arthur. I get the message."

"Are you sure about that?" said Wes, lifting her up and carrying her to the bed.

"Try me."

———————————————

Jimmy Green's: five happy people eating and laughing their hearts out: who would have even suspected they had other things on their minds? The food was too good and the company even better. It was exactly the medicine that both Wes and Mitch needed in order to salve their smarting egos.

Afterward, Wes asked W-2 and Rachel to come over to their place for a while.

"While I'm gone, if you so choose—I have a project for you two. In your spare time." He glanced at both of them to make sure they understood the humor of what he'd just said.

"Spare. Time," echoed W-2, rolling his eyes. Both father and son got the laugh they were waiting for. Since W-2 had joined the USSS, seldom had he, Rachel or any of the other agents been able to work regular hours or put in what would be considered a normal 40-hour week. Hours were irregular; days were nights, nights were days... and who the hell counted hours?

"We're all well aware that during the two years that Masella was in the joint, we've experienced one of the most explosive crime waves in the history of this country," continued Wes. "The agency has been on overdrive ever since the economic crisis hit and tens of thousands of people lost their homes... fraudulent foreclosures, mortgage scams, bank and insurance scams...and as you well know, the forgery squad has also been dealing with a pandemic of credit card crime and identity theft like never before."

"You're right there," agreed W-2. "We've been buried. It's like we finish one case and we've got a dozen fresh ones landing on our desks."

"So the point being—?" asked Kim.

"In a sense we've all dropped the ball," said Wes. "Not intentionally. We all knew Masella was involved in Cosa Nostra, which in turn is linked to the Vatican. And we know Chicago, as one of the key Vatican banking cities, is in the midst of the fray.

"We started doing the research on possible Masella connections to the Vatican 'conspiracies'—banking, bankrupt dioceses, the large number of pedophilia cases, etc., and then, understandably, we got distracted. But now, the whole shitload of trouble is back again and in our face. U.S. counterfeit bills were found in Florence, Italy. We've got to find out what the hell's going on."

Wes turned to W-2 and Rachel. "My hunch is that our research should begin with the earliest Vatican connections to the Mafia and organized crime. One of the first questions to ask is how the Papacy became so filthy rich."

"Where should we start?" asked W-2.

"Don't go to libraries," answered Wes. "Go to the Internet for articles and books. Look up the work of Richard Hammer, for example, and Ellen White. Paul Williams and James Brant. Interview some investigative reporters who've been collecting this stuff for years. And don't forget to dig into the church history. Some of it may seem shocking. For example, you'll soon learn none of the so-called sacred texts are based on fact. Like over-the-fence gossip, or that popular party game—what's it called?— 'Telephone,' or 'Pass the Word'... whenever the Church Fathers—and yes, it was a religion that was always highly prejudiced against women, so it was the Church *Fathers*—whenever they wanted to change a rule, they created a new story or another version of the former one."

"Emotions are powerful," agreed W-2, reaching for Rachel's hand and clasping it tightly.

"Weepy, romantic happily-ever-after fairy tales did the sales job," said Wes, "and the written rules laced with these anecdotes —hand-written by their scribes—did the rest. Few people were literate. Females sure as hell weren't, or maybe this world would be a different place today. The people depended on the clergy for information—the truth. God and the Church were their protectors. This was well before Gutenberg invented the printing press, so you can see that rumors were the flavor of the day. The only books were those that were laboriously hand-written by the scribes."

"The Church and God were the authorities, just as they are today for most people," said Kim.

"And the Church also became a business," said W-2. "I can see why."

"It was a perfect control mechanism," added Rachel. "Information—'the truth'—in lock- step with emotions. Religion is an emotionally charged issue. Esther and I know all about that from growing up in Israel as Ethiopian Jews."

"Right," said Wes. "You two always had to deal with a double entendre. Black-skinned, but with a Jewish mother! How many people could not believe that black-skinned people could be Jewish?! It took science—the DNA test—to prove the bloodline.

"Much of early religious history has been discredited, but when academicians and investigative reporters dedicated to the truth expose their findings on the Internet, they're shot down and labeled conspiracy nuts," said Kim. "That's what we're up against, and that's why the best way to get the real information about Roman Catholicism is to read the latest books on the subject, and interview some of the reporters who've have been doing the research. I have a feeling many of them will be very willing to talk. If they haven't already written about it in their articles, you'll probably find they're convinced the corruption of the Vatican Bank is directly related to the large number of pedophile cases that either the Church has been hiding—or that the Church pays off the courts to dismiss."

Just as Shane predicted, SAIC Fuller offered no resistance to Wes's overseas trip. Wes was hopeful that possibly for the first time Larkin realized he'd been entirely wrong about the Masella case, that the decision to go ahead and print the counterfeit money and then do the sting had opened a can of worms that would have been otherwise unavailable.

"Truthfully, I still think he has no idea," said Kim.

"And maybe that's a blessing in disguise. The less he knows the better. That makes it much easier to do what we have to do," said Wes.

In a final meeting with the team, they outlined the initial plan, set up their communication system and then went through the usual ritual of discussing possible outcomes.

"You know something? This case is a hydra," commented Marc.

"So you've noticed," said Rombo. "Every time you cut off a part, it grows back. Like, we really thought we'd capped this case two years ago. How often does a ghost rise from the ethers and start printing the same fucking counterfeit currency with the same fucking serial numbers?"

"It's worse than a hydra," said Wes. "It's a cancer. Even though we can now explain how the fresh printing of Masella's counterfeit bills could have happened, we have no explanation for the fact that they are being passed in Florence, Italy."

29

Firenze

Tuesday, March 5, 2013 – Chicago to Florence, Italy

Theresa Sale, Wes's secretary, worked for several hours to book a short convenient flight, without success. "The best I can do for you, sir, is a 3:45PM coach flight tomorrow on Lufthansa, with a four-hour layover in Frankfurt, arriving at 12:50PM on Thursday in Florence."

Times had changed. He remembered how easy it used to be in the past to fly overseas. Often he'd be able to take a quick flight to New York that would take him directly to almost anywhere in Europe.

"Book it," he told her. At least it was Lufthansa. Even the seats in the coach section had plenty of leg room and the Frankfurt airport had comfortable snoozing chairs. He could also do some duty free shopping for Kim, W-2 and his prospective daughter-in-law.

Suddenly Wes was overcome by the realization that *one day he could be a grandfather*. The thought brought tears to his eyes. Age was a bitch, but it could also have some rewards.

When he checked in to security and identified himself as U.S. Secret Service, he readily forfeited his weapons to baggage claim in order to drink alcohol during the flight. One of the strict airline regulations for law enforcement officers dictated that drinking and carrying during the flight were forbidden. *Getting* loaded and *being* loaded didn't mix well.

Wes rarely found it difficult to make the choice between the two, and today, *kein Problem/ nessun problema* (no problem), since there was no charge for beer, wine and cocktails on Lufthansa flights. Ahhh, bliss. Plenty of booze and room to snooze. He'd downloaded some good films for his Kindle before he left, so he was well equipped.

On the last lap from Frankfurt to Florence, the young man seated next to him was also an American, from Des Moines, Iowa.

Since Wes was a U of Iowa graduate, he couldn't resist putting in a good word for the university.

"I'm a sophomore at IU," said the young man, who introduced himself as Larry Weeks. With several drinks and some shut-eye at the Frankfurt airport, Wes was in the mood to talk, especially to someone who was attending his former alma mater.

A few more lines of conversation about Wes playing first string on varsity football and some exchanges about the current football team brought forth the information from Larry that he was traveling to Florence to make arrangements to bring back his brother's body to the States. He'd passed away two days ago.

"Not a happy trip for you," said Wes, not knowing what else to say. "Was he visiting Florence or living there?"

"He was a priest," said Larry. "You did say you're a U.S. Secret Service agent, Wes. May I call you Wes? Is that correct?"

"Yes, I'm with the Chicago bureau," said Wes, wondering why this was important.

"Then maybe the story I'm going to tell you may interest you. Or it maybe it won't."

"Go ahead, try me," urged Wes, realizing at this point that nothing was going to stop the young man from talking anyway.

"My brother was younger than me. He was a quiet person and extremely sensitive. Very different from me and from the rest of the family!" laughed Larry. "He was also very smart and liked to write. One thing about him that my parents were never able to figure out... he loved to go to church. We were brought up Catholic and Frank and I went to parochial school, but as a family we didn't go to church regularly. Except for Frank. Even as a small boy, he never had any problems sitting still through services. I hated them! They lasted forever and I had a hard time not fidgeting. But Frank loved the Mass. He served as an altar boy, hung around the church after services and really enjoyed the catechism, or Catholic studies. Very unusual, I know. But my parents knew enough not to interfere. By the age of eleven, Frank talked about becoming a priest.

"Then one day after a youth event at the church—my parents drove him to these events and picked him up afterward—Frank got into the car and didn't say a word. I was in the car on that day because my parents were also picking me up from basketball practice. Frank didn't look at me, didn't look at my mom. He just sat there in the back seat in silence.

"'So how was it?' I finally asked my brother.

"'Huh? Oh. It was fine. It was good,' said Frank, falling into silence again.

"We didn't think anything of it. The incident was forgotten, life went on, Frank continued to spend even more time at the church, and then one day at the age of 17 he announced to the family that he was going to enter the seminary as soon as he graduated from high school.

"Obviously this came as no surprise. What *did* come as a surprise was when he said he wanted to go to Florence, Italy, to study and live at the Santa Maria della Pace monastery. Before leaving the country, he had to have a physical and get certain vaccinations and so on."

Larry took a deep breath. "It was then that we learned that Larry had AIDS."

Wes didn't know what to say at this point. Why was a perfect stranger spilling out this story to him?

"So he was gay and you didn't know that?" asked Wes.

"We suspected. But honestly, we didn't think... we couldn't even *imagine*... Remember, my parents are devout Catholics. Frank finally confessed that he'd been having sex with several priests already for several years. It was from the priests that he had contracted AIDS.

"My parents were devastated, especially since Frank was a minor when all of this started to happen—*and he was still a minor*... only seventeen! It was then that I remembered the day I was in the car when my mother picked up Frank after a church event and how strange Frank acted."

"How was he able to leave the country?" asked Wes, who knew how strict the health laws were both in the U.S. and other countries.

"We never learned who pulled the strings," said Larry, "although we suspected it wasn't that difficult. The power of the Church, as you may know, is unbelievable!

"One Sunday when we thought Frank was at church, he didn't return home afterward. That evening we received a telegram that he was in Florence at Santa Maria della Pace. We had no idea how he was able to get the U.S. and Italy to ignore his medical issue."

"But my brother didn't die of AIDs," said Larry. "Shortly after Frank arrived, he started to write letters to us telling us that he had sinned and that Christ would never forgive him. He wrote that he had failed himself, failed the Church and failed us. In letter after letter he poured out his grief and anguish about how God would never forgive him, that He was punishing him for his sins.

"We urged him to return home. We reassured him that a warm and welcome family awaited him."

"When did he take his life?" Wes asked softly.

Larry teared up. Wes placed his hand on the young man's arm. "Hey, dude. We all make our own choices. You didn't make those choices for your brother and you don't love him less for it. It has nothing to do with love, and for sure it has nothing to do with sin!"

Larry smiled gratefully, wiping his eyes. "Thank you, Wes, for listening."

"And thank you for sharing." Wes gave him his card and wrote down Larry's name, phone number and email address on his smartphone.

Wes was deeply disturbed by Larry's story. He was well aware of the suicide statistics related to pedophilia and the Catholic Church. It wasn't an isolated case by a long shot. It was also a well-known fact that Roman Catholic priests in the United States were dying from AIDS-related illnesses at a rate four times higher than the rate of the general population. Most of the cases were contracted through same-sex relations, and the cause was often concealed on their death certificates.

One of the most infamous cases was that of Reverend Michael Peterson, M.D., a priest of the Archdiocese of Washington, who was also an M.D. and psychiatrist. Reverend Peterson founded a center devoted to helping priests and other Catholics with their psychological issues. Hypocrisy 101: Rev. Peterson died of AIDS. *Guilt is the gift that keeps giving,* thought Wes, gazing out the window as the jet lowered over the rooftops of Firenze.

It was truly amazing... Florence, one of the most beautiful cities in the world, *"la culla del Rinascimento* (the cradle of the Renaissance"), had been inspired by a religion that was blatantly corrupt at the core, and always had been.

What was it about the Catholic Church that gave it permission to be above the law? How did the great artists, poets and musicians manage to avoid the obvious... what Wes, Kim, W-2 and Rachel had discussed only a few days ago, until the wee hours of the morning? All the lies, the centuries of persecution in the name of the Father, the Son & the Holy Ghost?

Magnificent works of art inspired by stories of the Virgin Birth, the Crucifixion and Resurrection, filled museums and galleries throughout the world. Great music, poetry, architecture and theatre were also birthed by creative artists and visionaries who embraced the teachings of the Catholic Church.

Possibly that was it, thought Wes. It had nothing to do with the dogma. Something else was at work here, something that had nothing to do with religion. Once we're born, from that time forth, life is all about longing to return to the womb, said Freud.

Whether or not that was true, "home," or "roots" were emotional ties to security. Fear is the opposite of love. Both are a human being's strongest instincts. A child's first safety net is love, parents, home and everything he finds there.

Wes was taken back to his childhood days and the small neighborhood Baptist church where he and his three brothers had attended services and Sunday school every week with their parents, Grace and Andrew

Charles. Grace sang in the choir and belonged to the women's auxiliary. Andrew was head of the Men's Club.

The words of "How Great Thou Art" and "Amazing Grace" floated through his head. How his mom loved to belt out those hymns! Grace Charles had a good voice, very melodious. Untrained, but rich and strong. *Mom, wherever you are, I'm about to land in Florence, Italy. I'm doing God's work, just as you taught me, but it's much fucking harder than I thought it was going to be. Excuse the swearing, Mom. I know you would have whacked us on our behinds if Sammy, Mark, Buster or I ever used that word in front of you!*

The landing wheels rattled and banged in the belly of the craft as the plane prepared for landing. Wes finished off his drink and handed the empty cup to the stewardess, a buxom brunette wearing a large diamond studded crucifix in the 'V' of her suit jacket, and matching crucifix earrings. Anyone who was tempted to take a bite from these young lady's Apples was asking for serious trouble.

A dazzling morning sun showcased the three major architectural masterpieces that dominated the Florence skyline: the large red dome of the Basilica di Santa Maria del Fiore, Giotto's free-standing campanile, and the famous town hall or Palazzo Vecchio, with its ancient clock tower and Michelangelo's Statue of David and Ammanati's Fountain of Neptune in front. In the past the fountain had been one of Wes's favorite meeting places.

All three structures rose high over thick clusters of brown and maroon rooftops. In the distance were the hazy blueish-gray peaks of the Alps and Apennines.

As the plane lowered and sped through layers of wispy clouds whose drops condensed on the window glass, Wes could now see the River Arno winding through the city, and the Ponte Vecchio with its colorful shops lining the banks. A wave of nostalgia swept over him as he remembered romantic times with Kim in this magical city of love.

For a moment he wished this was a pleasure trip and Kim was here with him. *No*, he told himself firmly. *That's not true at all and you know it, Wes Charles.* He was not in vacation mode. He needed to close the Masella case once and for all. That would mean getting Masella behind bars again—and just as important, finding out who was responsible for this second epidemic of bills bearing the same serial number as the first ones.

It was early afternoon by the time he checked into the Hotel Principe on Lungarno A. Vespucci, 34. As soon as he was settled, he visited the American Consulate, on the same street, identifying himself and giving the agent in charge the particulars of his visit.

From the Consulate he took a cab to the Florence USSS adjunct office. The field office was actually in Rome and the Florence adjunct was merely a suite of rooms in a large office building. Wes learned that all of the Florence agents were on protection detail nearby. Wes knew this was a common practice. When dignitaries of foreign countries needed more agents for protection detail, often they called on the USSS if they were stationed there.

The office administrator, Luigi Agostini, told Wes that the files on Emanuele "Manny" Scarpaci, the Italian man who had been caught passing $20,000 of counterfeit bills, were at the Financial Guard offices, located on Via del Pratello. Signor Agnostini arranged for a vehicle to take him to the Guardia di Finanza offices the next morning.

30
Social Justice

Jesse was elated about the success stories from the programs he had initiated at three substance abuse recovery centers. Before now, the centers had been subsidized by hospitals and clinics that administered *pharmaceutical* drugs to combat the use of *recreational* ones!

To help with the depression and other withdrawal symptoms, practitioners freely prescribed psychotropic or mood-changing chemicals that included antipsychotics, antidepressants, ADHD drugs, anti-anxiety medications and mood stabilizers.

As for alcohol, some people jokingly referred to the AA programs as "Alcohol Anon and on and on...." Jesse knew all too well that any program based on instilling fear, threat and punishment was doomed. It was just another Religion that preached The Fall of Man. The Nasty Apple story again.

In the case of an alcoholic, the only redemption from their "sin" was complete abstinence. The AA 12-step doctrine was merely another safety net or pacifier. All that was required for forgiveness and redemption was daily recital of the12-step "catechism." They had fallen, failed, and sinned and were guilty forever after for their trangression(s).

In the case of Roman Catholicism, penitence for the sin of having "fallen" meant abstinence from sex for the clergy. Physical intercourse was a tainted act. Alas, it was necessary in order to have children, but god forbids that it should be pleasurable.

What greater temptation for anyone practicing abstinence than to break out of their shackles and (drink/shoot up/masturbate/participate in) orgies? And what a perfect invitation for priests to be intimate with one another in the privacy of their own chambers!

Big pharma was "making a killing" on killing people's self-will, Jesse was fond of saying. And so were psychiatrists and other medical doctors. The name of the game was to keep the person (victim, addict) dependant

189

on any product or service that required payment. Tests, visits, referrals, drugs. "Anon and on and on."

Jesse's programs were free for everyone who enlisted. In the three recovery centers where he was underwriting the cost of full-time hypnotherapists and counselors to replace the use of pharmaceutical drugs and the AA program, the patients were getting well. Their health and zest for life were returning.

Recovered addicts started to develop strong goals. Their lives took on meaning and purpose. Relationships looked different when they were no longer laced with guilt and shame. Many of these individuals had applied for jobs and been accepted. Others had enrolled in vocational and academic programs, tuition paid by Better Day, Jesse's non-profit foundation. Return to a normal life and acceptance by those who had previously given up on them was now becoming a reality.

Jesse's other programs at hospitals, assisted living facilities, orphanages, women's shelters and prisons were also proving to be equally successful. Even if a person felt their lifespan was limited more than most, Jesse taught them to reframe their perception. "It is not the number of days you are alive that matters, but how alive you really are *during each of those days.* Invest in your life today and receive the benefits today!" was one of his favorite slogans.

Jesse's teachings made sense. His programs and presentations, whether humorous, inspiring or just plain fun, were dynamic. He was in great demand throughout the Chicago area.

Then one day the roof caved in. On Wednesday afternoon, March 6, at the conclusion of his magic show for children at the Lurie Comprehensive Cancer Center of Northwestern University, USSS Agents Wesley Charles, Jr. and Rachel Nahari approached him, waiting until the room had emptied and they were alone.

"You are Jesse Jay, formerly Daniel Hanas?" asked Agent Charles, after the two showed him their badge and credentials.

"Yes, sir," said Jesse.

"You are under arrest," said Agent Nahari.

Jesse was surprised to discover he wasn't angry, but relieved. He held out his arms for the cuffs and let the two agents lead him away.

Earlier that day when W-2 and Rachel realized the type of person they were going to arrest—a man who was known for his amazing work with cancer victims, suicidal veterans with PTSD, drug addicts, alcoholics and some of the so-called "dregs" of society—they had what W-2 coined a "come to Jesus meeting" with themselves.

W-2 wished Wes, Sr. was here and so did Kim, who met with the two after learning the particulars of the situation. She agreed with W-2 and Rachel that at this point the details were not to be shared with The Brush. "This is too sensitive. We need to develop a strategy."

The three gathered in the Charleses' family room.

"This is just plain fucking crazy." W-2 paced the room. "Here's a man who's really making a difference. We know what's going on in this country with the hospital and drug industry. You don't have to be a moron to figure it out. And this guy is setting a track record that exposes the scam."

"At the same time," his mother reminded him, "he's breaking the law. He has already allegedly committed at least one serious federal crime."

"*My* hunch is that Jesse Jay is going to be more than willing to talk in exchange for a lighter prison sentence," said Rachel. "He's a very smart man who made one big mistake. He got in bed with two groups that have paraded their invincibility before the world. Those two groups are the banks and the Vatican. Both are too big to fail. And even after outrageous media exposure of their crimes they're proving to be too powerful to be prosecuted and put behind bars."

"They're laughing all the way to the bank. *Their* banks, as they give the bird to the victims. The 99%." W-2 riffled through the 8-inch thick printout of pedophile cases and a second file of forged banking and financial documents. "This stuff makes me sick. I can't even read most of it... stories of how priests abducted young boys, seduced them during confession, and invited them to boys' club meetings that turned out to be orgies..."

"You two have done a great job collecting information," said Kim. "Take your feelings out of it, W-2, and let's get the job done. *We cannot cry over spilt milk.* Isn't that what I've been telling you ever since you tipped a jug of grape juice onto the new living room carpet? How old were you? Three? You bawled your eyes out! Your tears didn't clean up the mess. I have a strong feeling you're right, Rachel. Jesse Jay is going to become one of our best allies."

"How *did* you clean up the mess?" Rachel asked Kim, her eyes dancing with merriment. "Or did you decide to replace the carpet? Or maybe W-2?!!"

After arresting Jesse and bringing him back to agency headquarters, he sat quietly while W-2 and Rachel asked him questions and wrote up the report.

When they were finished, he said, "Agent Charles, Agent Nahari, I would like to speak with you as one human being to two other human beings. I like both of you. You are good people. I realize what I've done. My eyes are wide open and I see where I'm at. It's a dead end and I have no excuses for myself. So for that reason, I'm going to tell you everything I know. All that matters to me today and from this time forth is that justice is served in this world. Not the justices dished out by the courts—believe me; I know how corrupt they are—but human justice. Call it social justice."

He lifted his head and gazed at both of them. His eyes were filled with sadness and remorse. "First, you need to investigate a priest named Philip Tuma, who goes by the name of Father Ira."

Jesse proceeded to tell them the entire story of his relationship with Father Ira and how he had become involved with him.

"These men are corrupt," he finished, his voice breaking. "They're working with a large network of priests and lay people. The Vatican is heavily invested in this, from the top down. It goes many layers deep."

Jesse had to pause for a few moments to regain control before he could continue. "Believe me, I'm not angry at anyone but myself—yet I'm also ready to forgive myself, and I'll tell you why. *Yes, I'll tell you why.*"

His voice became stronger and took on a new tone. "The decision was mine from the beginning, from the moment I first met Father Ira. I take full responsibility for working with him and the rest of these men. But now, let me ask you: if you had to decide between working with this group of con men or the other group of con men—the bankers and corporate executives who are investing our taxpayers' dollars in foreign wars and sending our industries overseas—a group of white collar crooks who are cheating the government by hiding their assets in offshore accounts and who couldn't care less how they cheat and steal from the rest of the people—who turn their heads so they don't have to see those who are now living on the streets with no jobs, no homes and no food, *mostly because of them*—which group would you choose?

"How, may I ask, would I ever have been able to help any of those children get well if I'd allowed them to be drugged into submission with antidepressants and amphetamines... or allowed the ones diagnosed with cancer to be injected with toxic substances that not only would have destroyed the cancer cells but the healthy ones as well? And the elderly! Oh, let's talk about the elderly."

Jesse's eyes were blazing. "Living like drugged zombies in assisted living centers and nursing homes—another industry that bleeds the taxpayers. And then the veterans. God help us all, that's a story all by itself. Shall I tell you what's happening to these courageous men and women who've given their lives to defend our country? Do you want to know how much our government cares about these people when they return home, sick, disabled, often without jobs or a place to live? I don't want to go on. I can't. I've seen too much and I've been able to help too many people to believe my life has been in vain.

"I gave so many of them joy, and hope. I gave them back their lives. So I asked myself—yes, I asked myself—which is better: using Vatican mafia money and *actually helping people*, or playing a game of 'Let's Pretend'— lying and selling false hope to the young and old, to the disabled and dis- enfranchised—to people who'd already given up on themselves and their futures? I made the choice and I was fully prepared to pay the conse- quences if I had to.

"And now I'm selling out. I do not support narcissism and pedophilia. I do not support greed and deception. So where I do I stand? Do I stand alone with my grief and despair? This country is caught between two pil- lars of crime and deception. The global banks and corporations have cre- ated an octopus. A monster. *No one can deny this.* I know this better than anyone else!"

Again Jesse's voice broke. He looked away, shaking his head as the tears came freely. "I've said enough," he sobbed. "If you need any more information, if I can help you further, call on me. I have nothing to hide."

"Social justice and the Roman Catholic Church," said Rachel softly after Jesse had been taken away. She was visibly shaken. "So where do we start?"

W-2 swallowed hard and looked down at the gray cement floor of the conference room without speaking for several moments. When he finally raised his head and looked at Rachel, his eyes were red. "Number one, we need to get some input from Dad to find out where he's at. After he's had a chance to read through the information we've gathered about the ar- rest, I'm sure he'll have a plan."

Later that evening at Rachel's apartment, they studied Jesse's folder and reviewed the case once again. "Jesse's best shot was to align with the law," said Rachel. "He saw that clearly. Either way he's screwed, so he might as well go with the courts. If he can prove he was blackmailed at the outset—if he can prove he didn't know what he was getting into until it was too late, he may have something to work with."

"And if he *did* know what he was getting into at the same time he knew he was being blackmailed—what chance did he have for staying alive even then? One false move and they would have disposed of him. 'They,' referring to the group that includes Father Ira," said W-2.

"Which may include the Vatican, both here in Chicago and in Rome," said Rachel, "and everywhere else?"

"So he probably figured he might as well play it out until it came to this point. Because during that time it meant helping many people and possibly saving lives as well. That's what matters most to this man. Shit. This is a good man. Rachel, I have to confess that even though Mom's right about spilt milk and grape juice, at this moment I feel like bawling."

Rachel came up behind his chair and put her arms around him. "It's okay to feel, Agent Charles. We may be tough, but we're still human beings."

"Thank you," he squeezed her hands gratefully and kissed them tenderly. "You are the wisest woman I know, besides my mother. You are a queen."

"All Ethiopian women are queens," she reminded him. "Shall I prove it in hearts or in spades?"

31
Angela

Had Wes not been dealing with jet lag and exhaustion from loss of a good night's sleep—and unresolved anger at himself for allowing the plates and negatives for the counterfeit bills to pass by his scrutiny—maybe he would have been able to capture some of the usual excitement he felt when he was traveling out of the country to a place with such a rich culture and colorful history.

The story that the young man from Iowa had shared with him yesterday on the plane and the fact that only a couple weeks ago, Pope Benedict XVI had resigned—shock that had raised eyebrows and caused "the Ratzinger questions" to come out of the woodwork—were also pulling him down.

Who was Pope Benedict XVI—or rather, what was he? People were talking about the extravagant costumes—the sumptuous velvet robes and lace surplices, jeweled crowns, neckpieces, rings and bracelets... One of the most notable items from the Pope's wardrobe was a short cape known as a *mozzetta*. The winter version was fur-lined, ermine-trimmed and made of crimson silk.

Then there were the papal rings; diamond, sapphire and ruby pectoral crosses; the golden mitres inlaid with jewels... He had been described by some as a "truly bling pope."

In the midst of the Pope's weekly fashion show, hundreds of thousands of pedophile cases continued to be reported in every corner of the planet where Catholicism was practiced.

Those who engage in selective reading and listening are either senile or sociopathic, thought Wes. He shook his head as if it was a glass paperweight and the flutter of thoughts that had just surfaced were nothing but artificial snowflakes. If he shook his head violently enough, maybe the plastic flakes or thoughts would block out the image of the snowman/pope in white standing decorously in front of the crucifix in the nave of St. Peter's Bascilica, raising his hands to bless the multitude of faithful Catholics seated before him.

Via del Pratello was a long narrow street walled on either side by drab nondescript brick and concrete buildings—markedly different from the city's décolleté Renaissance churches, palaces, and museums. It also contrasted sharply with the open public squares and marketplaces, the colorful mélange of tourists, housewives and domestic servants shopping for fresh fruits and vegetables, housewares, handcrafts, jewelry, souvenirs and the cheaper form of bling.

No fountains here, no nude sculptures of perfect male bodies to distract the natives and visiting corporate multinationals from conducting their business. The only signs of life were the rows of tightly parked vehicles hugging the curbs that lined the deserted sidewalks; the only semblance of art was the graffiti on the sides of several of the buildings. What would archaeologists write in future centuries when they came upon these markings in a city that had also been inhabited by nymphs, cherubim, angels, gods and goddesses?

The reception room was empty. "I would like to see Agent Carlo Scelsi regarding the case of Emanuele "Manny" Scarpaci," Wes told the thickly mustachioed *adetta* or desk clerk as soon as he had identified himself.

"*Sì Sì*," said the clerk. "Agent Scelsi is on his siesta. He will be back shortly. If you would have a seat, *Senor*."

It is often said that the U.S. and Americans are different from other people on the planet regarding the way they conduct their business. "Americans are always in a hurry," complain Europeans, especially Latinos. "They need to get it done NOW!"

They were right. Americans were, after all, the inventors of fast food and instant gratification in a country that adored its shopping malls and drive-thru hamburgers/ coffee/ donuts/ drugs/ dry cleaners/ car washes/ banks/ notaries/ weddings/ divorces, etc., etc.

Tardiness, afternoon siestas, long lunches, multiple holidays and the inevitable chain of events that precludes the closing of any financial deal and that accompanies most business activities in other countries, did not exist in the United States... nor was it tolerated. The Austrians, Swiss and Germans tended to be more punctual, yet they also practiced lengthy foreplay—the establishment of a strong personal relationship—before the deal was consummated.

In Mediterranean countries business was even slower. *Everything* in life was to be enjoyed, especially wine and women. In Florence, Wes was already prepared for the usual delays. Fortunately he spoke fluent Italian; otherwise, he would have had to wait for a translator to show up and communication would have been limited to finger pointing, head nodding (yes) and head shaking (no - "*Io non ti capisco*" – "I don't understand you.")

Added to this were religious holidays. Roman Catholic countries probably had more religious holidays than any other, and in many places, conducting business on Sundays was *proibito* (forbidden).

Wes had nothing against wine, women or religion, but he did have priorities when it came to taking care of business. Bureaucratic self-importance was unforgiveable. While he was waiting for Agent Scelsi to appear, Wes got caught up on emails and text messaging. A half hour later, he approached the desk again. "Is there no one in the office who can help us besides Agent Scelsi?"

"*Sì Sì*," said the clerk, nodding vigorously and proceeding to go about his business.

"What I meant was, would you kindly have one of the other police officers show me the Scarpaci file?"

"I'm sorry," Salvatore Rizzotti shook his head. "Captain Scelsi is the only person who has the records. Would you like some cappuccino?"

"If you have a movie rental service, that might help," said Wes sarcastically under his breath.

At 2PM, Agent Carlo Scelsi, a porky-looking middle-aged officer with a perfectly executed Hitler paintbrush mustache and poorly fitting hairpiece bustled into the office. "Agent Charles, welcome to Florence! Did you have a good trip? How is your hotel?"

"*Sì, Sì grazie. Posso vedere il file per Emanuele 'Manny' Scarpaci?* (Yes, yes, thank you. May I see the file for Emanuele 'Manny' Scarpaci?) The man who was arrested carrying counterfeit American bills?"

"Ah, you haven't seen the file yet?" Agent Scelsi turned to the clerk at the desk and muttered something. "Agent Micele, would you please come to the front desk?"

At once a shapely well-endowed young woman with shoulder-length chestnut-brown hair and large brown eyes appeared.

"This is Agent Angela Micele. Agent Micele, Agent Wesley Charles from the Chicago Bureau of the United States Secret Service."

"*Piacere di conoscerti.*" I'm happy to meet you, Agent Charles," Officer Micele flashed Wes an engaging smile. Her olive skin was like velvet, her lips were plump and cherry red with no need for tint or gloss, and her delicate nose, high cheekbones and oval shaped face were a demonstration of God's perfection.

Underneath the frumpy agency uniform Wes could detect two large well-formed breasts, a tiny waist and hips that would come to life when liberated from their ugly gabardine trousers.

"Agent Micele, why have you kept Agent Charles waiting for three hours? Why didn't you show him the Scarpaci file? Agent Charles, my humblest apologies, we never keep anyone waiting in this office, especially not an agent from the U.S. Secret Service who has flown all the way over her to meet with us!" Captain Scelsi glared at Agent Micele.

"Agent Scelsi, excuse me, if I may interrupt. I was not informed that Agent Charles was waiting to see the Scarpaci file," objected Agent Micele. "Signor Rizzotti, did you not know that I was in the back?" She turned to address the clerk, but he had disappeared.

"It's true," Wes spoke up. "I was told by Signor Rizzotti that only you could show me the file."

"We have very inadequate clerical help these days," Captain Scelsi's mustache twitched irritably. "Agent Micele, I would have thought you would have taken it upon yourself and had enough initiative to check the front office to see if anyone was waiting, instead of sitting at your desk in back twiddling your thumbs or writing twits and tweets to your friends," he snapped.

Agent Micele was apparently accustomed to being dressed down by this idiot, thought Wes disgustedly. Without flinching or showing any trace of anger, she maintained her dignity and poise.

By this time Wes was well aware that he was witnessing typical Italian blowback in the workplace. Obviously Agent Micele had said NO to Agent Scelsi's advances, not once but several times. This was highly unacceptable to any officer with seniority or rank. In fact, it could even cost the young woman her job.

Another problem was also obvious. Agent Micele was holding down a position that was traditionally reserved for males. (Did he not recall his own reservation about hiring a woman?!) The job of a law enforcement officer was suitable only for *mascios*, males!

"I take it, Agent Charles, you also want to see Manny Scarpaci?" asked Agent Scelsi.

"Of course," said Wes, "but first I want to see the file. And since Agent Micele has permission to view the files as well, I would like to review them with her," he added boldly.

Agent Scelsi had been caught off guard. "*Sì, Sì Sì, certo. essere mio ospite* (Yes, yes, yes, of course. Be my guest.) Use the first room on the left. I believe Signor Rizzotti is already bringing the files."

Agent Micele smiled gratefully.

Wes followed the officer's seductively swaying hips into the appointed office, enjoying every serpentine movement of her body. In some ways she reminded him of a Latino version of Rachel with a touch of Sophia

Loren. She had the same smoky long-lashed hazel-colored eyes, large mouth and plump lips... *Kim sweetheart, I can enjoy, can't I?*

Of course, darlin'... you're all mascios... type AAA. That's what I love about you... even at your age my love, you act and look like a young 007... and did you know that you're probably old enough to be her father?

Wes concentrated on the information in the file. Emanuele "Manny" Scarpaci was an art restorer who worked in Florence on behalf of the Vatican Archives/Sistine Chapel art museum in Rome. He could easily have been a master printer, or if he hadn't used the plates and negatives himself, apparently he had access to good equipment.

The Vatican. Too many coincidences were popping up for Wes to continue to ignore the connections.

The records said that Scarpaci was gay and had been picked up once before on charges involving a large international male prostitution ring. He was let go when police could find no evidence leading directly to abduction, battery and assault, cocaine or drug trafficking. Headquarters of the prostitution ring were in the Vatican City.

All roads continued to lead to Rome, to quote fellow USSS agent Rombo and a perceptive sage many centuries ago during the time of the Roman Empire. Maybe today that saying should be changed to "All roads lead to the Vatican."

A cold shiver ran up Wes's spine. His head was spinning.

As soon as he examined the file, he asked Agent Micele to scan and encrypt the documents. She was a well-trained computer technician. It took only a few minutes for her to complete the work, send it to a secure IP on his laptop, and hand him a thumb drive that to anyone who didn't know the passwords would have appeared blank.

Agent Micele leaned across the table, picked up his smartphone, clicked on the notepad app and typed rapidly, "I have something to tell you. Can we meet at 7PM at the Bene Cibo Café... at the plaza in front of Santa Maria Novella?"

"*Grazie tanto*, Agent Micele," he nodded, pocketing his smartphone.

Officiously she gathered all the documents into a single pile, placed them in the folder, pushed back her chair, stood, shook his hand and smiled politely (for the cameras). "*Sono felice che potremmo essere di servizio a voi, agente Charles* (I am happy we could be of help to you, Agent Charles.)"

In the next instant she vanished. Wes knocked on Captain Scelsi's door on his way out. "Agent Scelsi, may I visit Signor Scarpaci tomorrow?"

"*Sì, sì, certo, agente Charles* (Yes, yes of course, Agent Charles)." Carlo Scelsi walked Wes out to the reception area. "Again I apologize for our inefficiency. Agent Micele is new here and she lacks, er the basic required skills for law enforcement, if you understand what I mean. It has been very difficult to train her. But you know, *abbiamo veramente le mani legate* (we really have our hands tied) with the new equal opportunity laws now fully operative," he sighed.

"Yes," said Wes without twitching a muscle. *Each of us has an equal opportunity to act like an asshole and dickhead any time we choose. You, Captain Scelsi, have just used up your coupons for both. I'm willing to bet Agent Micele is a ninja with a gun or any other weapon. And I bet she's a tiger when she's out in the field busting someone.*

What would it feel like to have your hands tied behind your back and have someone give you a kick in the balls? No, I take that back. Make that a few swift kicks. You are scum. Lower than scum.

Wes hailed a cab, fuming all the way to the hotel. Fortunately his room refrigerator was well stocked. As soon as he'd medicated himself with two shots of Jack straight up, he called Kim, took a cat nap and opened the files on the Roman Catholic Church and the Vatican that
W-2 and Rachel had sent him.

He learned that for many years the Vatican was integrally connected to the former Continental Bank of Chicago. In fact, it was known among inside circles as "the Vatican bank."

Before he died in 2006, Chicago-based Sherman H. Skolnick had done a masterful job uncovering fraud in the courts and in the Vatican banks. In 1984, when Continental Bank of Chicago was about to go down, the Vatican and Queen of England, both major owners of the holding company, sold their shares. How did they know in advance to get out? And then, Walter J. Cummings, who was Chief Judge of the U.S. Court of Appeals in Chicago—one step below the U.S. Supreme Court—stemmed the flood of damage lawsuits by threatening reprisals against the lawyers who were about to start action against the bank—his bank!

Skolnick wrote in his reports: "After all, Judge Cummings was a 'man of trust' for the Vatican, safeguarding their interests in his Bank and in his Court. He did not disqualify in related litigation. Guess who won in his crooked Court?"

The Bank of America was another of the pope's financial enterprises. Skolnick learned that "by the 1970s, Bank of America, the holding company, was owned principally by the Vatican and the Jesuits, the Pope's clever army who occasionally see fit to rebuff the Pontiff... Later in the 1990s, Bank of America and the Giannini family merged their interests publicly with Continental Bank, although the Chicago-based and San Francisco-based money ships had been more or less joined at the hip privately long before that."

Skolnick dug further into the Vatican connection with the Mafia connections. The Giannini family also operated the First National Bank of Cicero in Chicago, in the heart of the city's Mafia enclave. Bishop Paul Marcinkus, who was head of a Catholic Church in Cicero, eventually became head of the Institute of Religious Works, known as the Vatican Bank. Money laundering, counterfeiting and other nefarious bank practices were linked to Marcinkus, who fled from the Vatican to Chicago in 1991 after he was found out.

At the same time the highly secret Opus Dei, another Catholic organization that was rumored to practice Satanic or Luciferian rituals, established its North American office in Chicago.

Wes googled Marcinkus, known as "God's banker," and came up with dozens of additional articles about the bishop's corrupt practices. Right under their own noses, in Chicago!

Was it not feasible that *counterfeit money* was also deposited in a federally chartered bank that would deliver a recorded deposit receipt... and thus, placed on the books as legitimate currency? The counterfeit money could then be transported from within the federal system to an offshore bank where it could further be used as collateral or an asset against loans. Possibly much of the counterfeit money that was being printed and laundered through the system never even hit the streets. It was sent to the banks "just for show" or "just in case" it might be needed.

Probably it never was.

32
All Roads Lead To…

Friday, March 8, 2013

In the late afternoon Wes took a long walk to *Piazza della Signoria* to clear his head and think things through.

His mission here in Florence was specific, yet he couldn't help feeling it was only the tip of the iceberg—that the Masella case was connected to a highly organized crime syndicate that was so powerful, whatever he intended to accomplish would be quickly replaced by yet another operation just as lawless. Rombo had called it a hydra that day in the office. In response he had referred to it as a cancer.

He paused in front of Neptune's Fountain, recalling that he'd read somewhere that the Neptune figure's face resembled the facial features of Cosimo I de'Medici. The deMedici's, like today's Rockefellers, Rothschild's, Morgans, etc., needed to tell the world who was in charge. Neptune/Cosimo the Florentine was king of the seas at a time when maritime trade was at its peak.

The pedestal in the middle was decorated with the mythical chained figures of Scylla and Charybdis. There it was again: "damned if you do and damned if you don't"… the origin of one of his favorite phrases: "caught between a rock and a hard place…" Scylla, a six-headed sea monster, was a rock shoal on the Italian side of the Strait of Messina between the mainland of Italy and the island of Sicily. *Sicily, home of the Sicilian Mafia…* Charybdis, another formidable sea monster, was a whirlpool off the coast of Sicily. The two were close enough to pose a serious sea hazard to approaching sailors. To avoid Charybydis meant passing too close to Scylla; avoiding Scylla placed sailors in danger of losing their vessels in Charybydis's whirlpool.

He glanced down at the perimeter of the fountain with its river gods, laughing satyrs and marble sea horses. Here was another example of human creativity: *the work of our hands… and our hearts.*

It was a choice, thought Wes. Not an "either... or." War was not pitted against peace, or hate against love. It was war *and* peace, hate *and* love. Both together. One and the same. *Without darkness, there could be no light and without light there could be no darkness.*

Wes pulled out some coins from his pocket. Before he tossed each of them in the water, he knew he needed to make a wish, but his mind went blank. He flipped them into the water anyway.

What was he trying to accomplish, besides the obvious? He stared vacantly at the children gathered at the other side of the fountain. They were holding helium balloons. One of the balloons broke away and sailed into the sky. The little girl who had let go of her balloon let out a wail.

Who's holding the strings? Wes wondered, watching the escaped balloon sail high into the sky until it disappeared. *The church, the government, the media, the bankers... or all of them together? Why? What was their purpose? What did they intend to accomplish? Takeover of the world?*

How could it be any of these groups when each one was dealing with its own internal conflicts? And then, what about every nation on the planet fighting to protect its own identity? Was sovereignty the culprit? Sovereignty. Who had control over every group, every corporation, and every nation?

The Vatican was a sovereign nation, totally protected. Totally immune to reality. God help us all.

What was God's plan? Divide and conquer? Or was it not up to God after all?

A little boy came over to the little girl and handed her his balloon. At once she stopped crying. As soon as her mama securely fastened the balloon to her wrist, she started giggling and dancing around in circles, watching the balloon dance in the air with her.

Wes was so engrossed in the story playing out in front of him he didn't see the man on the other side of the fountain who had been following him. Now as he looked away from the children, his eyes lighted on the figure, a bald-headed man attired in priestly vestments. He was holding a small paper bag and was stooping down to feed the ducks. *Father Bartholomew, aka Adam Csonka!* What the hell was he doing in Florence, Italy?

Moving into a cluster of teenagers on skateboards, Wes glided to the curb, signaled to a waiting cab and jumped into the back seat. He called Agent Micele on his private cell phone. As soon as she answered, he said, "Changed location. Brown Sugar restaurant, Piazza San Firenze, on Via della Condotta."

Agent Micele was already seated at a corner table in the back of the restaurant when Wes arrived. *"Buona giornata,"* he greeted the waiter, nodding in the direction of Agent Micele's table.

She started to rise to greet him, but he motioned for her to remain seated. *Much lovelier to look at in street clothes,* he thought to himself. In a coral colored turtleneck sweater, matching blazer and slacks, her long brown hair falling loose around her shoulders, he was glad he'd told her not to stand up or everyone in the restaurant would have turned their heads to admire her. They would not notice the weapon cleverly concealed beneath her blazer. He was also carrying.

"Grazie per aver accettato di incontrarsi con me. (Thank you for agreeing to meet with me."

"Il mio piacere (My pleasure)."

"What happened and who was it? Do you know?" she asked in perfect English.

"I have some ideas, but nothing definite," said Wes. "Maybe after I know why you wanted to see me, I'll have a better idea. First, Agent Micele, may I call you Angela?—and you can call me Wes—I'm very happily married to another long term U.S. Secret Service Officer, so I'm no threat!"

Angela laughed merrily. *"Mi fidavo di te dalla prima volta che ti ho incontrato!* (I trusted you from the first time I met you!")

"Really? I wish I could say the same," joked Wes. "If I were a lonely, frustrated bachelor, for sure I wouldn't have trusted myself. Forgive me for confessing this to you, but I would have tried my luck, *signorina!"*

Angela eyed him with amusement. "Wes, you have such an unmistakable married look about you, it never would have even occurred to me that you were lonely and frustrated! Your wife is a Secret Service agent. Ahhh, so she's been through many of the same issues that I've had to face. I have to apologize for my boss, Agent Scelsi," she added quickly. "He doesn't know any better."

"You don't have to apologize for him. He's an asshole, forgive my language," said Wes. "His treatment of you was abusive. And you don't have to tell me why. It was a dead giveaway."

She blushed as Wes knew she would.

The waiter appeared. They ordered a bottle of Merlot Veronese and decided to split an order of Antipasto di Verdure and Bruschetta. When they were alone again, Wes continued their conversation. "If that dickhead tries to rape you, I'll kill him myself," he said vehemently. "I also know why you can't turn him in and make a case about it. We've got plenty of minority issues in the U.S."

"I know," sighed Angela. "I spent six years in the U.S. I have a degree in computer engineering from Carnegie Mellon University."

"Which is why your English is so good," said Wes.

"Yes. My real father was from Pittsburgh. My mother is Italian and she remarried when I was eight. So now, Wes," Angela eyed him intently, "let me tell you why I wanted to meet with you outside the office."

"Is it all right if I record this?" asked Wes, aware of the tension in her voice.

"Yes, I think it would be a good idea, in case you need it as part of an exhibit at any time. Thank you," she responded with relief. "If at any point we need to go off the record, I'll let you know in advance by signaling to you to click off your pen."

Clever girl, thought Wes. His pen was a recorder. It looked normal but had a switch on the side and she'd noticed.

"Incidentally, I have recorded nothing so far," Wes reassured her.

"Yes, I know," she said softly. "Besides being certain I could trust you to be a gentleman, I also knew I could trust you as an agent. That's why I asked if it would be all right to tell you this story. I'm hoping it will help you immensely with your case."

"I'm recording," said Wes, her signal to begin.

"Have you ever heard of a U.S. Secret Service agent named Eugene Burns?" Angela asked, her voice quivering slightly.

"Gene Burns? Of course!" said Wes. "I interviewed him when he applied for a position with the Chicago field office, where he was first employed. Eventually he was transferred to the New York office. I've been so busy, I've lost touch with him over the past few months. Gene Burns is like a son to me! Is he working on a case here in Italy?"

Her eyes filled with tears.

"What happened? Did something happen to him?"

"I apologize." Angela searched in her purse for a tissue and dabbed her eyes.

They waited until the waiter had poured the wine and placed the two platters of antipasto on the table, with a basket of bread and crackers.

As soon as he left, Angela launched into her story. "Gene was working in the Florence USSS adjunct of the Rome foreign field office on a case that involved counterfeiting that they believed was linked to the Vatican. We met when he first came to Florence; a mutual friend introduced us. Soon we were spending time together. Over the holidays on our vacation we went to the Greek Islands. *Molto romantico...* (Very romantic)..." Her voice trailed off for a moment.

She returned to her story. "At the beginning of February, Saturday, February second, to be exact, when Gene and I met after work for dinner,

I could tell he was very upset. Afterward we went back to my place and he told me in confidence that he'd learned that some counterfeit U.S. bills had been turned in to the Rome office. Apparently Fred Stillwell, one of the agents, gave SAIC Chris Mendoza the counterfeit bills to send to the USSS Bureau in D.C. and Agent Mendoza had no intention of doing so.

"Gene heard about the counterfeit cover-up from my good friend, Maria Pelino, a translator for the USSS who works in their office. She was waiting outside Agent Mendoza's office door to do a dictation with him and she happened to overhear a heated conversation between Mendoza and Stillwell. Maria knew Gene through me; we'd double-dated a few times. Maria didn't hesitate to call Gene to report the conversation.

"Agent Stillwell suddenly became very ill. He was on life support for four days at the Rome American Hospital and then he passed away.

"After Gene learned about the counterfeit cover-up and the news that Agent Stillwell was on life support, he decided to go to Rome to do some investigating himself. He went undercover on the street looking to buy some U.S. counterfeit bills. He soon learned he could buy some from a clerk who works at a dress shop called 'Peppi's' on Via Condotti. Via Condotti, as you may know is the most exclusive shopping area in Rome.

"Apparently the owner of the dress shop, a famous couturier by the name of Giuseppe Tubiano, 'Peppi' for short, is in tight with the Vatican, the Pope in particular. He is their favorite designer. Although Gammarelli is the traditional supplier for the Catholic priests', bishops' and cardinals' garments throughout the world, I understand Peppi is consulted every time they change a pattern or decide to use a new fabric. Peppi also chooses the patterns and fabrics for all the special ceremonial outfits, including the accessories.

"Maria told me she heard through the grapevine that Peppi was instrumental in advising Pope Benedict XVI to reinstate a papal pallium that used to be worn many years ago but had been discarded. This was an important change; anyone who has that much influence on the Pope is part of the inner circle, for sure."

Wes captured the meaning of Angela's words from her tone of voice. "What is a pallium, if I may ask?"

"Originally it was made of wool," said Angela. "It is a band of brocade decorated with four crosses and an eight-pointed star and it is worn around the head and shoulders. The new pallium is wider and longer and it has red crosses on it, representing the blood of Christ."

Wes lifted his wine glass. "Here's to the blood of Christ," he said irreverently. "Forgive me if you are a practicing Catholic, although I doubt it."

"You are correct," smiled Angela. "I left the faith a long time ago, but my entire family is extremely devout. It's Italy," she shrugged. "The Dark Ages."

"No different from the U.S.," Wes reminded her.

"Yes, I suppose you're right," she admitted, "although it's more noticeable here if you *not* a practicing Catholic than in America. Anyway, back to Peppi and my story. It's no secret that Peppi's gay. The *paparazzi* love him. He's all over the media all the time."

Wes nodded, already feeling sick. *All roads lead to Rome/The Vatican...*

He also knew what Angela was about to tell him that he needed to hear but didn't want to.

"Gene let his mind follow through to a logical conclusion. What if Mendoza was in bed with the counterfeiters? Otherwise, why wouldn't he have reported the counterfeit bills to D.C., and why would Stillwell have suddenly taken ill and then died from an 'unknown disease'?—Gene knew there'd be hell to pay.

Angela paused. "I think you know that Gene was the kind of guy who'd give his life to the Secret Service if he had to."

"Would give his life if he had to." Was that a slip? wondered Wes. Tensely he waited for her to continue.

"Gene realized he needed SAIC Chris Mendoza's permission to set up a sting operation, but under the circumstances, how could he spill the beans to the man who may be trying to cover up the counterfeit operation—and for god knows what reason—although one could guess." Again, Angela's voice became shaky.

"He took a chance, a risky one. Guessing that the other agents had no idea that counterfeit bills had been turned in—surely Mendoza wouldn't have told them, and Agent Stillwell was already taken care of—he met with two of the other agents, Roger Whalen and Eli Lemberton. He told them he'd been sent by the D.C. office to do some investigating about a counterfeit operation going on in Florence that may be connected to some action in Rome.

"Gene was familiar with another case in Rome with actual names and a case number, so it was easy for him to ask the agents to write a memo to SAIC Mendoza, reporting they would be covering for Agent Burns from the Florence office, regarding 'such and such case,' just for an evening.

"Gene already knew Mendoza was a careless kind of guy when it came to details. Mendoza is a body builder. Everyone in the agency was aware that to Mendoza the measurement of his triceps meant much more to him than his USSS administrative duties.

"What Gene didn't count on..." Angela took a deep breath, "now hold on when you listen to this, Wes... is that the two guys he chose to cover him were both bigoted assholes, excuse my French.

"It doesn't make any difference that their prejudice against blacks originated during their childhood in the U.S. It doesn't ever leave their psyches simply because they're overseas on duty. It's still in place, believe me! Gene witnessed it everywhere, although, like me with the female issue, he tried to make light of it.

"The agents sent the memo to Mendoza and everything was fine—or so Gene thought.

"Meanwhile, I did my share as well. I asked my friend Maria to do some snooping. I wanted to see if we could get the serial numbers and a few other specifics on the counterfeit bills that had been turned in. I knew Gene would need this information in order to show a connection between Florence and Rome operations."

"Good thinking!" Wes praised her. Any evasion to report counterfeiting operations was serious, and if there was a connection in Rome with the Masella bills that Manny Scarpaci had been caught with, that information would be invaluable.

"Through one of his informants, Gene arranged to meet with the seller at Peppi's where he planned to make the arrest," continued Angela, "with Agents Whalen and Lemberton covering."

33
Cover but No Cover

Friday, March 8, 2013 – Brown Sugar Restaurant - Florence, Italy

While Angela was talking, another scene was playing out simultaneously before Wes. Eugene Burns was fresh out of Northern Illinois University when he applied for the Secret Service. Gene was brilliant, a real nerd if there ever was one.

Clean-cut, soft-spoken, he was a math major... a really nice guy. Truthfully, the USSS was hard up for black undercover agents. The shortage was creating a problem. Chicago South Side, the ghetto, was a drug den and it was also known for prostitution, counterfeiting and money laundering. Wes had already made many cases in the ghetto working undercover. He had a special talent for working on the streets; he loved the performance part of it.

He also liked the risk. It was another reason why he'd been so smitten by Kim. She was one of the gutsiest undercover female agents in the country. She shared his sense of exhilaration whenever he found himself in a perilous situation that required fast thinking and the ability to "fake it to make it."

Wes was on the hiring review board and after he read Gene's credentials and interviewed him, he gave him a resounding affirmative vote.

"We need young men like you," Wes told him when he was asked to tell Gene he'd been accepted.

"And I can only hope to earn a record for making as many cases as you, Agent Charles," was Gene's response.

They'd spent a great deal of time together and Gene had come a long way since his first months at the agency. He mimicked many of Wes's best tricks and was a quick learner. Gene also became a risk taker. He didn't hesitate to go the extra mile when he had to. Wes often commented to his colleagues: "Nothing will hold back Agent Burns when he's got something hot going."

Angela's voice had started to quiver again. She paused and tried to steady herself. "The date was Monday, February twenty-fifth. Gene was on his way to the shop—if you know traffic in Rome, you can easily get caught in a jam, especially if there's an accident. Agents Whalen and Lemberton were supposedly following him to the dress shop.

"I had taken a train to Rome to be there after Gene made the arrest. We planned to celebrate together. I arrived in Rome early, so I decided to while away some time at Moma Restaurant, on Via San Basilio. Gene and I used to go there whenever he came to Rome. It's diagonally across from the American Embassy where the USSS Rome adjunct field offices are located. It's a favorite hangout for the agents.

"As soon as I entered the restaurant, I spotted Agents Whalen and Lemberton having dinner and engaged in an animated conversation. Fortunately they didn't notice me.

"It was by pure accident that I ran into them—but then, there are no accidents, are there? *Why weren't they already on their way to the dress shop?*

"At first I thought maybe the sting was called off. Maybe they decided not to take Peppi down after all. Maybe something happened that ruined the setup. Maybe two other agents had been assigned to the case at the last minute. A thousand thoughts raced through my mind."

"And so?" Wes felt a tightening in his chest.

"I texted Gene, knowing already that I wouldn't be able to reach him, that he would have cut off all regular communication channels.

"I did get a message back." Angela looked away. "The message said, '*È già troppo tardi* (It's already too late.)'"

Wes placed a hand on her arm as the tears rolled down her face.

"The official report was that the agents lost Gene in traffic," Angela continued as soon as she had control of herself again. "They said they were right behind him and then there was an accident and they lost him. The traffic jam was so bad, they couldn't get through.

"The next day..." Angela removed a pack of tissues from her purse. "...A package was waiting for me at my apartment that contained..."

"Don't tell me," said Wes hoarsely. "Has anything about Gene appeared in the Italian media?"

She shook her head. "No. And on Tuesday, February twenty-sixth, the Florence and Rome field office US Secret Service agents were sent on special protection detail. On February eleventh, if you remember, Pope Benedict XVI announced his resignation and February twenty-eighth was his last day. The media was saturated with speculation about who would replace him.

"The entire front page of every newspaper was devoted to stories about the Pope and prospective candidates, details about when the cardinals' conclave would be begin—details and more details, ad nauseum. The Vatican City was already swarming with reporters, dignitaries, cardinals, tourists… it was bedlam.

"Gene had told me to let him know if anything suspicious got turned in to the Florence Financial Guard office while he was in Rome, and to make sure it was sent directly to Washington, D.C., to the counterfeit bureau of the U.S. Secret Service. He gave me the name of an agent by the name of Shane Burke.

"On Tuesday, February 26, our office did, in fact, receive some suspicious $US100s that were passed at one of the smaller banks.

"Since I'm the only one in the Florence Federal Guard office who's trained to do advance forensic work, Agent Scelsi was forced to assign the job to me. The tests indicated they were, indeed, counterfeit. As per Agent Scelsi's instructions, I couriered the bills overnight to Agent Burke in D.C., who confirmed our findings.

"Immediately we went after the counterfeiter, Emanuele 'Manny' Scarpaci, who had passed the bills that were turned in. He also had more of the funny money in his possession, since he was the printer. We arrested him that night."

Angela paused for breath. "As you know, Gene had no family. Both of his parents died several years ago and he had no brothers or sisters."

"And the USSS in Rome *and* Florence are covering up the fact that Gene is missing and another USSS agent died of unknown causes?"

"Yes and no. The scuttlebutt around the Rome agency is that Gene was murdered and they've already started to conduct an investigation. Because of the sensitivity of the situation, nothing can be publicized. The U.S. State Department is very clever. They don't have to tell anyone anything they don't want them to know. We're living in terrorist times. Americans are hated over here by many people, and after 911 the world has changed, and so on and so forth.

"As for Agent Fred Stillwell, the medical report at the hospital took care of that. The truth is the truth. When he arrived at ER he was on oxygen and they ran a full battery of tests. They did everything they could."

Wes was furious. One USSS agent possibly poisoned and definitely dead and the other one gone missing since Monday, February 25—over a week ago. The only evidence that he was probably no longer alive was the contents of Angela's package.

Whoever killed him had a perverted sense of humor. The woman Gene was dating, an Italian police officer, would be forced to publicly disclose the evidence she had received that Gene was murdered. The whole affair would be chalked up to a *scandalo romantica*—a romantic scandal. Jealous lovers, etc.., etc.—and Angela would be caught in the middle of it.

"This is unconscionable!" he fumed.

"Yes, it is," said Angela.

"So is there anything else you need to tell me?" asked Wes, sending her an expectant look.

"Yes." Angela leaned forward, laid her hands on the table and eyed him directly.

"Here's the part that I think explains why no one knows what happened to Gene. Peppi, the owner of the dress shop, is a very powerful man. The Mafia is extremely dangerous and as you know, it is directly linked to the Roman Catholic Church, to the Vatican Bank.

"I think something's going on that involves the USSS here in Rome—specifically SAIC Chris Mendoza. Why didn't he turn in those counterfeit bills that Stillwell brought him? I think the situation is global, without any boundaries because there don't have to be. It's everywhere. They're everywhere."

"'It' and 'they' meaning...?" asked Wes.

"Well, you know," said Angela. "Remember the film '*V*' for 'Vendetta'? How about '*V*' for 'Vatican'?

"Angela, to date, you are the only person who knows for sure that Gene is dead. Is that correct?"

She nodded. "Who would do such terrible things?" Again her eyes filled with tears.

The question was rhetorical. She was a Federal Guard officer and Wes was a Secret Service agent.

34
Puzzle Pieces

Friday, March 8, 2013 – Florence, Italy

Back at the hotel, after a stiff drink and a long shower, Wes stretched out on the bed and called Kim on her cell phone at the office.

"Kim Charles, I'm missing you," he said as soon as she picked up.

"Bullshit," she snorted. "You're probably having the time of your life with one or more of those smoky-eyed Sophia Loren babes, one on each arm... I know you, Wes Charles!"

"Actually, I did spend the evening with a babe who looks very much like Sophia Loren. No joke! She's a Federal Guard officer. Kim, honey, I have some news to share with you about Gene Burns."

The joking stopped; Kim could hear the heaviness in his voice.

"He's been missing since Monday, February 25. No missing persons report has been filed and the woman I just mentioned is, or was, his girl-friend."

"Wait a minute. *What did you say?* Sorry, Wes honey. Give me a mi-nute."

Wes could hear her blowing her nose. He knew she'd take it hard. Kim had also served as a mentor for Gene. She'd become very fond of him. The three had shared some good times together when Gene was in the Chicago office.

"Okay, tell me what happened," she said finally.

Briefly Wes outlined the story.

"So, how are they covering this up? What about Homeland Security? Isn't anyone looking for a body?" demanded Kim. He knew she was shaking with anger, as livid as he was.

Wes didn't want to tell her about the package Angela had received the next day. "I'll have more information soon; that's all I know at the moment."

"Wes, W-2 and Rachel have just made a forgery arrest that may be connected to the counterfeiting in Italy. That's my news of the day but

215

you certainly topped it. They'll be sending you all the files. They arrested a man by the name of Jesse Jay. Have you ever heard of him?"

"I don't think so," said Wes. "Send me the info. I'm off to the prison tomorrow to visit Manny Scarpaci. Interesting fellow. An art restorer working in Florence on famous paintings that belong to the Vatican. He had a restoration studio in the Sistine Chapel."

"And he's the printer? asked Kim.

"I don't know that yet."

"And if he is, you plan to get the plates and negatives back."

"Of course."

"If I were a Catholic I'd start reciting the rosary," said Kim. "Wes, this is too close for comfort, based on the arrest that W-2 and Rachel just made and on the dirt they uncovered. If the mother lode turns out to be named Mary, I think it might not be such a bad idea for you to rent a Holy Ghost."

"How about an unholy one who's a martial artist and expert marksman?" joked Wes drily. He knew what she was thinking because he was thinking the same thing. She wanted to tell him to be careful but it was an unspoken vow between them that it would never be said aloud.

"Holy ghost, holy shit," said Kim instead.

"I love you, babe."

"And I love you, too, Big Man."

35
Too Much Information

Saturday, March 9, 2013 – Florence, Italy

Wes was to report to the Federal Guard office at 1PM for his visit with Manny Scarpaci. He spent the morning reading through the latest material W-2 and Rachel had collected. He also reviewed the charges against Jesse Jay, Director of the Better Day non-profit foundation. The file included several media clips portraying a man who had received numerous accolades for his exceptional humanitarian work throughout the Chicago area.

Jesse Jay was formerly Daniel Hanas, a bank executive at a prominent bank in Chicago. White, 51years old, divorced, two children. Maya, the eldest, was serving time in a correction facility on drug charges and Max was attending a military academy in Virginia.

Jay's major benefactor was Father Ira, whose real name was Philip Tuma, well connected to Cardinal Francis George, head of the Chicago Archdiocese, through Father Elmo Rigardi, Secretary for Cardinal George.

In Kim's note she wrote that she, Mitch, Marc, Len, Kevin, and Rombo had already set to work looking for connections between Father Ira and Tony Masella—and then for a link to Florence, Rome and the Vatican.

Jesse Jay had given W-2 and Rachel the name of an "intimate" friend of Father Ira's, a world-famous Italian dress designer, Giuseppe Tubiano, who owned Peppi's, an exclusive dress shop in Rome on Via Condotti.

Peppi!!! Giuseppe Tubiano!!! The hairs on Wes's arms stood up. The pieces were starting to fit together.

It was easy to collect information about Peppi, wrote Kim. He was all over the Internet, at major Hollywood, Bollywood, Dubai and London events showing off his seasonal styles on celebrity models and movie stars.

"Here's some real dirt written by someone who must have had a bone to pick," wrote Kim. "I'm guessing he's a jilted lover. It'll be scrubbed from the Internet soon, I'm sure: " 'Youthful looking with a full head of curly brown hair, medium-height, clean-shaven, olive skin and amber-colored eyes... only the more intuitive could detect the cruelty in his set jaw and a certain glint in his eyes. One could easily guess that if anyone ever double-crossed him, Peppi would be merciless and unforgiving. Those who know him intimately would identify him as a power bottom.'"

The article went on to describe some of Peppi's idiosyncrasies: "One of Peppi's favorite costumes was tight-fitting troubadour pants, a colorful beret and a cape that he flung over one shoulder. Whatever he did was done with panache."

Rachel and W-2 learned that Father Ira's deal with Jesse Jay involved sponsoring or underwriting Jesse's nonprofit programs in exchange for use of Jesse Jay's expert banking knowledge to forge bank instruments—certificates of deposit (CDs), bank guarantees (BGs), standby letters of credit (SLCs), bonds, etc., that were used as collateral or assets against loans.

"It is my guess," wrote W-2, "that this is a clever way for the Vatican Bank not to feed the hungry and clothe the poor but to feed their own coffers to pay off pedophile cases and keep them out of the courts. They're probably also using this money to pay off priests who are continuing to practice pedophilia, so they can get them to resign.

"Isn't it absurd—chutzpah, for sure—that, like the big bank execs, these crooks retire from the priesthood with lifetime pensions... because why? Because the church feels sorry for them and they don't want them out on the streets begging, or living under cardboard boxes? No. I think there's much more to it. These perverts would snitch the first chance they had. They'd make a worse hornet's nest for the Church. So they pay them off and swear them to secrecy with big fat pensions. Just like the banks and other miscreant financial institutions pay off their executives to keep them quiet.

"In some instances," W-2 continued, "although we have no proof of this, they may even be paying off judges.

"One of the most damning pieces of news that has appeared recently is the Vatican's claim of immunity. In a July 20, 2011 article that appeared in the *New York Times*. Irish lawmakers accused the Vatican of encouraging Roman Catholic bishops not to tell the police about priests who were suspected of being pedophiles and of flouting Irish law."

Another report gave details of a confidential letter dating from 1997, written by a senior Vatican official, the late Archbishop Luciano Storero, Pope John Paul II's Apostolic Nuncio to Ireland. A copy of the letter obtained by Irish broadcasters RTE and provided to AP, warned Ireland's Catholic bishops not to report all suspected child-abuse cases to the police:

A 2009 Irish state report found this actually happened with Tony Walsh, one of Dublin's most notorious pedophiles, who exploited his role as an Elvis impersonator in a popular *All Priests Show* to get closer to children. In 1993, Walsh was defrocked by a secret church court, but successfully appealed to a Vatican court, and was reinstated in the priesthood in 1994. He raped a boy in a pub restroom that year. Walsh since has received a series of prison sentences, with a 12-year term imposed last month. Investigators estimate he raped or molested more than 100 children.

Catholic officials in Ireland and the Vatican declined requests from the Associated Press to comment on the letter, marked "strictly confidential"; RTE said it had been given it by an Irish bishop.

"The letter is of huge international significance," said Colm O'Gorman, director of the Irish section of Amnesty International. "It shows that the Vatican's intention is to prevent reporting of abuse to criminal authorities. And if that instruction applied here [in Ireland], it applied everywhere."

According to the article, this was the "smoking gun" that a U.S. advocacy group, the Survivors Network of Those Abused by Priests, had been looking for. Lawyers for the victims who were seeking to pin responsibility directly on Rome and the Vatican and not on the dioceses, would now be able to cite this incident. W-2 quoted:

To this day, the Vatican has not endorsed any of the Irish church's three documents since 1996 on safeguarding children. Irish taxpayers, rather than the church, have paid most of the €1.5bn to more than 14,000 abuse claimants dating back to the 1940s.

Wes read further that "in a 2010 letter to Ireland condemning pedophiles in the ranks, Pope Benedict XVI faulted bishops for not following canon law and offered no explicit endorsement of child-protection efforts by the Irish church or state."

As predicted, this didn't go over very well in Ireland. The pope had received a great deal of bad press after that weak attempt to put an end to the hanky panky. He was widely criticized in Ireland. Did he not realize what this meant to the Church? Why wasn't he coming out with open condemnation? Some even went so far as to ask "why isn't he coming out himself, if he's defending these crimes?" (Was the Pope gay, as so many people suspected?) This appeared only once, according to W-2, who found the source, which was then scrubbed from the Internet.

W-2 provided the gruesome pedophile statistics easily obtainable, with sufficient footnotes and citations on the Wikipedia website. "In the United States the 2004 John Jay Report commissioned and funded by the U.S. Conference of Catholic Bishops (USCCB) was based on volunteer surveys completed by the Roman Catholic dioceses in the United States. The report stated there were approximately 10,667 reported victims (younger than 18 years) of clergy.

In the 56 cases that were investigated, priests were reported to deny the allegations.

> The 4,392 priests who were accused amount to approximately 4% of the 109,694 priests in active ministry during that time. Of these 4,392, approximately: 56 percent had one reported allegation against them; 27 percent had two or three allegations against them; nearly 14 percent had four to nine allegations against them; 3 percent (149 priests) had 10 or more allegations against them. These 149 priests were responsible for almost 3,000 victims, or 27 percent of the allegations.

> The allegations were substantiated for 1,872 priests and unsubstantiated for 824 priests. They were thought to be credible for 1,671 priests and not credible for 345 priests. **298 priests and deacons who had been completely exonerated are not included in the study.** [Boldface mine – W-2]

> 50 percent were 35 years of age or younger at the time of the first instance of alleged abuse.

What type of abuse was the report describing? Fondling, forced acts of oral sex and intercourse or attempted penetration.

> Although there were reported acts of sexual abuse of minors in every year, the incidence of reported abuse increased by several orders of magnitude in the 1960s and 1970s. There was, for example, a more than sixfold increase in the number of reported acts of abuse of males aged 11 to 17 between the 1950s and the 1970s.

The next all-important piece of research pertained to lawsuits and settlements. Most sex abuse cases were under the jurisdiction of state law. As of April 2010 many sex abusers associated with the Church in several countries had been tried by secular authorities and some were convicted and sentenced to imprisonment.

> According to Donald Cozzens, "by the end of the mid 1990s, it was estimated that [...] more than half a billion dollars had been paid in jury awards, settlements and legal fees." This figure grew to about one billion

dollars by 2002. Roman Catholics spent $615 million on sex abuse cases in 2007.

From that time forth, incident, lawsuits and settlements continued to multiply exponentially. Predictably, settlement money was bankrupting the dioceses, forcing them to close churches and schools throughout the country. Although many of the accused priests were forced to resign, others were defrocked—unless they were grouped among the elderly. When a priest reached a certain age, according to canon law, they could not be defrocked! Instead, they were sent to retreat houses. Rather a soft life after all those offenses, thought Wes. If they were not priests, they would be spending the rest of their lives in prison. *They had committed crimes; they were criminals!*

The more Wes read, the angrier he became. One case in particular, drew his attention:

Bernard Francis Law, Cardinal and Archbishop of Boston, Massachusetts, United States resigned after Church documents were revealed which suggested he had covered up sexual abuse committed by priests in his archdiocese. On December 13, 2002 Pope John Paul II accepted Law's resignation as Archbishop **and reassigned him to an administrative position in the Roman Curia naming him archpriest of the Basilica di Santa Maria Maggiore, and he later presided at one of the Pope's funeral masses.** [Boldface mine-W-2]

Wes archived the information and headed for the jail.

Wes could have already guessed that Emanuele "Manny" Scarpaci bore none of the characteristics of a hardened criminal. Clearly, Scarpaci was the patsy, or fall guy.

Throughout the ages, artists have depicted Jesus Christ as white-, black-, brown-, red-, yellow-and olive-skinned, with characteristics or features that match their own. Without a doubt, thought Wes as soon as he was seated opposite Scarpaci in the meeting room, Manny would have qualified as an Italian version of the great prophet/messiah/savior. His facial features and olive-colored skin were sensitive, his clear green eyes, sorrowful and compassionate; and his high cheekbones and firm jawline with its ragged beard, depicted a man who would have flinched had he been given a whip and instructed to injure someone. Probably, thought Wes, Manny Scarpaci would first ask to take the punishment himself. This was what, in a sense, he was doing right now.

Wes saw all this in the counterfeiter's eyes. Years of experience had taught him what to look for and what to expect from alleged felons, crooks, hard-core criminals and so-called "bad guys."

Wes also suspected he was not a homosexual but that he'd been seriously raped and molested, possibly even tortured into submission. The report about the prostitution ring was a way of adding fuel to the fire, to make sure he had enough brownie points to be convicted.

In broken English, Manny told his story as Wes listened. "They" had come to him at his studio in Florence where he was restoring some paintings of the Madonna and Child rendered by Giusto de' Menabuoi, a Florentian 14th Century artist.

Manny was also a certified journeyman printer, he told Wes. "I had never printed counterfeit bills before they came to me and told me it was for the benefit of the Church. I am a good Catholic." Manny crossed himself.

"And who are 'they'?" asked Wes. When Manny clammed up, Wes tried again.

"Manny," Wes said gently, "I know nothing about Fine Art and I have no idea what is involved in restoring famous paintings, but I want to tell you this. I know you are a master at what you do. I do not think you would have printed that counterfeit money had you not been forced to do it. Am I correct?"

Again silence. His sensitive green eyes clouded over.

"If you cooperate with us," said Wes, "if you tell us exactly what happened and if you tell us the truth, we'll get you out of this. I promise you that."

"*Non si può fare quella promessa. credetemi, non avete idea* (You cannot make that promise. Believe me, you have no idea)," Manny's voice quivered. He stared down at his hands.

"I believe I do have an idea," answered Wes firmly. "Do the following names mean anything to you? Father Bartholomew, aka Adam Csonka; Father Ira, aka Philip Tuma; and Giuseppe Tubiano, known as 'Peppi'?"

Tears splashed down Manny's face. The pain was too great. He could not contain it any longer. Wes realized it must have been a long time since anyone had spoken kindly to this man. "*Se parlo* (If I talk)," he said in a low, scarcely audible voice, "*Io sarò ucciso. un'offerta di mafia è, come sapete, uno che non può essere rifiutato* (I will be killed. A mafia offer is, as you know, one that cannot be refused)."

"You have already said enough," said Wes. "You'd make a lousy liar."

Through the tears came a smile. His eyes were webbed with pain and doubt.

"I'm not going to ask what they did to you," said Wes. "I just want you to know that no one, positively no one can take away your dignity, nor can they shame you in any way, regardless of how they try. I think you know who said, 'The kingdom of God is within you...' and 'Be perfect, therefore, as your Heavenly Father is perfect.'"

"Mathew, Chapter 5, verse 48," said Manny hoarsely, crossing himself again.

"You would make a good preacher, Wesley Charles," Wes's mom used to tell him. In some ways, Wes knew Mama Grace Charles was right. Law enforcement, justice, was another way of doing the work of God.

"Agent Charles, the printing operation is underneath the Sistine Chapel in Rome," said Manny. "I have just placed my life in your hands, but I want you to know that I forgive you— *Io non ti biasimo se non mi puoi aiutare* (I will never blame you if you cannot help me)."

At the hotel, Wes called Kim to deliver a full report of the meeting and then he texted Angela. He made arrangements to meet her at 6PM at the Brown Sugar for dinner.

36
Getting Even

Saturday, March 9, 2013, Brown Sugar Restaurant Florence, Italy

The moment Angela entered the Brown Sugar Restaurant, dressed in a bright flowered print mini-dress with a 'V' neckline, her long chestnut brown hair tied back with a matching flowered scarf, all eyes turned to admire her.

She really did resemble Sophia Loren with her flawless olive-colored skin, the smoky eyes, dazzling smile and seductive way of moving her parts, especially the well-developed ones. She was a tempting goddess and serpent of the feminine sublime. No wonder Gene Burns had been smitten.

"*Possiamo sedere a quel tavolo in un angolo?*" (May we sit at that table in the corner?") Angela asked the maître d', pointing to a secluded area of the restaurant.

"*Sì, certo.*" He led them to the same table where they had sat before. They ordered a bottle of Brunello di Montalcino, engaging in small talk until the wine arrived, the waiter had poured their glasses and left them alone.

Angela listened intently as Wes told her everything he had just learned from Manny.

"The printing operation is in a chamber underneath the Sistine Chapel."

"The Sistine Chapel," breathed Angela, her eyes narrowing. "That's where the cardinals are having their conclave to choose the new pope. The conclave starts on Tuesday. The Vatican City is already overrun with media, dignitaries and tourists."

"Perfect timing, don't you think?" Wes grinned mischievously.

She smiled and shook her head, clicking her tongue as their eyes met. They both knew all too well that distraction was both a crook's and police officer's best friend. Now she realized why Wesley Charles was such an exceptional agent. Life was an adventure. *What's done is done.* It was time to move on and do the clean-up work.

"I can sign up for Rome duty. Captain Scelsi will be only too happy to get rid of me for a few days. It's going to be a regular circus in Rome... a perfect opportunity for riots, looting, bomb scares, abductions... Every branch of the police and military has already been instructed to assign their men and women to the Vatican City until the new pope is elected."

"Exactly what I was thinking," beamed Wes. "Good girl!"

At once Angela texted her friend, Maria Pelino, the USSS translator, and made plans to visit her in Rome. Maria was part of a large Italian family with connections that could be helpful.

"*Ti rendi conto quanto sia pericoloso questo è.* (You do realize how dangerous this is)." Angela eyed Wes intently.

"*Naturalmente. Pericolo non mi ha mai spaventato. Ora una bella donna—questa è un'altra storia. Loro mi terrorizzano!* (Naturally. I have never been afraid of danger. Now a beautiful woman—that's another story. They terrify me!)"

Angela laughed heartily, just as Wes wanted her to. "*A volte non abbiamo scelta. È che non è vero?*"(Sometimes we have no choice. Is that not true?" said Wes, eyeing her intently.

They ordered a second bottle of wine and dinner, choosing two house specialties: *ravioli du pecorino e pere su creme di barbabietole* and *tagliatelle al ragu Bolognese.* Wes learned more about Angela's experiences in the U.S. and about the shock of returning to Florence, where "females are not yet as liberated as in America, to put it mildly."

Wes entertained Angela with stories of some of the cases he'd made, hilarious anecdotes about The Brush and some of his fellow agents' office antics. It was the type of camaraderie that could only be possible when two people had shared the same bond with a person they'd loved and lost. It was a way of salving the pain and accepting the bitter-sweet reality that Gene Burns would still be with them, even if only through their memories.

The next morning Angela took a train to the main terminal at Piazza di Cinquecento and cabbed to Maria's Pelino's apartment on Via Ludovisi. She lived near the American Embassy and USSS field office, housed in the Palazzo Margherita, on Via Vittorio Veneto 119A. The U.S. Government had acquired the Palazzo Margherita in 1931.

Since it was a Sunday, Maria was free. She also had more time than usual the following week because the USSS agents had been assigned to protection detail, undoubtedly related to the anticipated crowds in Rome that week.

"*Buongiorno! Come stai?*" Maria opened the door and gave Angela a warm hug and kiss on both cheeks.

Agent Fred Stillwell, R.I.P., had not been incorrect about Maria's sex appeal. He'd pegged her correctly. Her Matisse print mini-dress was as flamboyant as her flaming red hair worn in a pixie cut, and generous array of body tattoos. When she bent over, the skirt deliberately exposed matching bikini underpants.

Maria held her new friend at arm's distance. "I mean, how are you really doing?" She eyed Angela anxiously.

"Okay. *Beh - davvero non bene, Maria*. (Well really, not well, Maria)," admitted Angela, tearing up and wiping her eyes with the back of her hand, "but I do have some juicy news for you."

"Sit, sit. What would you like to drink? Water, soda, wine, caffé?"

"Just water is fine. Thanks."

Maria stuck her head in the refrigerator and emerged with two bottled waters. She placed a bowl of fruit, some nuts and a cheese plate with crackers on the coffee table. Handing Angela one of the bottles of water, she sat down opposite her friend, lifting one knee over the other to expose the parade of outrageous tattoos that marched up her thighs and beckoned toward tantalizing territories hidden beneath her panties. "*Bene. Dimmi tutto.* Tell me all!"

Briefly Angela recounted the episode at the Federal Guard office with Agent Wesley Charles last Friday, their private meeting afterward, and then yesterday evening when they'd met again for dinner.

"Agent Charles—Wes—is one of the kindest and sharpest intelligence agents I've ever met. He's also a really decent human being. He knew Gene personally. In fact, he was Gene's mentor in Chicago when Gene first jointed the USSS Counterfeit squad."

"*Sul Serio!* No kidding Tell me more! So I'm assuming you told him everything?" Maria leaned forward eagerly.

Angela nodded. "I also told him that I saw the two USSS agents, Whalen and Lemberton, who were supposed to be covering for him having dinner at the Moma Restaurant."

"And that the counterfeit bills that were not reported here in the Rome office have the same serial numbers leading to Tony Masella." Maria's eyes filled with mischief. "And did you tell him how you got that information?"

"*Maria, amico mio! Dio ci aiuti!* (Maria, my friend! God help us!)" The two looked at each other and exploded in gales of laughter.

"*Che bello sentirti ridere, il mio amico!* (How wonderful to hear you laugh, my friend!)" gasped Maria.

The two women had planned this one carefully. Maria managed to steal the key to the Top Secret computer room while she was giving Agent Whalen a blow job in his locked office.

"I must admit, I'm an expert multi-tasker," joked Maria afterward.

"You don't have to give me a blow by blow account, unless you want to," Angela had quipped.

As soon as the agents were off duty and had signed out for the evening, Maria told security she was staying late and entered the computer room. Within a matter of minutes she'd obtained the information she needed. Both the Florence and Rome counterfeit bills had the same serial numbers and flaws, indicating they'd been printed from the same plates.

"*Eccellente, ottimo,* Maria! You did a good job!" Angela toasted her with her water bottle. "And now, girlfriend, we have another important task to perform. Last night Wes also told me that Manny Scarpaci, the counterfeiter, snitched big time. He told Wes the printing operation is in one of the chambers underneath the Sistine Chapel. Wes was going to go back today to get more definite directions."

"*Gesù! Madre Maria!*" exclaimed Maria under her breath.

"It appears that the entire operation is connected to the Vatican through Father Ira, Giuseppe Tubiano—'Peppi'—and god knows who else," continued Angela. "This is a hell of a time to have something like this going on, but Wes didn't think it was a problem at all. In fact he said it may very well be to our advantage. I think he's right! What could be a greater distraction than the election of a new pope?" she chuckled.

"There are never any ideal conditions," agreed Maria, winking at her friend. "We always have to create them, yes? Although I do know that I work best under conditions of revenge."

"I've noticed that," retorted Angela, "and come to think of it, I do too. But I wonder if Wes knows what he's asking for if he's planning to explore the Sistine Chapel during a cardinal's conclave."

Maria held up her hand. "Suggestion, *amica mia.*"

"*Sí Sí.*"

"Tonight we will have dinner at Piacere Molise on Via Candia, 60, near the Vatican. We will invite Nicky Denzler, a Swiss Guard. He's one of the toy soldiers who stand in front of the you-know-what. Every hour on the hour, if you wind him up, he turns, lifts his gun, salutes—"

"I think you've got your childhood memories mixed up, Maria dear. The soldier that clicks and turns is a Swiss clock and the one that stands at attention at the entrance to the Apostolic Palace is a Swiss—"

"Oh my dear, you are so right!"giggled Maria. "I think I'm trying to juggle too many balls in the air! I'm getting things confused!"

"So how do you meet these Swiss cocks—Swiss men, Maria?" grinned Angela. "Or, shouldn't I ask?"

"This one was easy, no mystery," Maria winked and dipped her head coquettishly. "Another bottle of water or something harder?" She stood up, did a runway walk across the room and posed in front of the fruit plate to pluck off some grapes and pop them into her mouth. "*Mio caro,* Nicky Denzler is my cousin. We are the same age; we almost grew up together. My aunt married a Swiss watch maker. No joke! Uncle Gustav makes very fine Swiss clocks and watches.

"Nicky is a computer engineer, a genius. He can easily develop some type of *dispositivo* (device) for Wes that will give him the access and protection he needs. Believe me, once he knows Wes is a U.S. Secret Service agent who's making a case that's possibly linked to the Vatican, he will be more than happy to help."

"*Eccellente!*" So tell me," asked Angela, "why the sudden change of heart for your cousin?"

Maria shook her head sadly. "At first Nicky was really excited about his job; he was honored to have been chosen to be a guard because his family is *molto Cattolica* (very Catholic). But as soon as he was there for a couple of months and discovered some of the shenanigans that were going on, he was ready to quit. He'll probably serve out his term, just because, like a true Swiss, or I should say like a true Teuton—the family is German-Swiss—he's not a quitter.

"I've heard that the lower levels of the Apostolic Palace, especially below the Sistine Chapel, are very weird—very *medieval.*" Maria shuddered. "Maybe they're only rumors... I don't know." She shuddered again. "If any of them were true... *inquietante...terribile* (creepy... terrible).

Angela clucked sympathetically. "I've heard the same stories and I wouldn't be the least bit surprised if they are true."

As a police officer she had already been exposed to all kinds of atrocities that people were capable of performing on one another. At this stage in her career, nothing seemed out of the range of possibility, especially when it involved the Catholic clergy.

Also, after hearing stories about what went on at American Bohemian Grove gatherings in California and Skull & Bones Club initiations at Yale University, it seemed perfectly logical that Roman Catholicism with its long well-documented history of inquisitions and other forms of persecution seemed capable of conjuring up their own sadistic party games.

"So now, I see the plan," said Maria. "Agent Charles gets clearance, Nicky takes him below—Angela, *do you know how fucking dangerous this is?*" She interrupted herself and stared at Angela as if realizing for the first time that she was speaking in English and not Italian.

"Am I going to be a coward? Gene wasn't a coward," was Angela's immediate response.

"*You?* How do you enter into it, Angela?"

As she gazed intently at her friend, her eyes filled with tears. "You really loved Gene, didn't you, Angie? But that doesn't mean you have to sacrifice your own life just to get even."

"Really?" Angela's hazel eyes narrowed and her voice became brittle. "Maria, if I can contribute in some small way to helping Wes and the rest of the Feds get to the bottom of this, I'll feel as though I've served a purpose. I grew up as a Roman Catholic. My entire family is Roman Catholic, like yours. I am disgusted and ashamed of what's going on today among Catholic priests and with the Vatican Bank. The worst part of all is the fact that if my parents realized the level of corruption and the decades, *centuries* of cover-up—they'd put on ear muffs so they wouldn't have to hear about it, and next week, as always, they'd promptly show up for Sunday Mass.

"Here's an example of what sheep the Catholics are, including my family. This story appeared in the *Los Angeles Times* only last month. Cardinal Roger Mahony of the Los Angeles Diocese robbed the cemetery maintenance fund—he robbed the dead!—in order to help pay a landmark settlement with molestation victims. The cardinal took 88 percent of the fund—115 million dollars! Could the dead object to being robbed?!!

"The abuse settlement itself amounted to 660 million dollars, so that was just a drop in the bucket. Where do you suppose they found the rest of the money?

"Ha! I think you already know the answer to that one," said Maria. "So how about the living? The relatives of these poor dead people? What did they have to say about it? Or were they not consulted?"

"Not until after it was a done deal did they learn about it. The article said that since the 1890s the families of those who were buried in church-owned cemeteries had contributed to the cemetery upkeep fund. Maria, what would your family say if the church came to you and told you they were using the cemetery upkeep fund to help pay off the courts and settle pedophile sexual abuse cases? What would they say?"

"I know exactly how they would respond. They'd say, 'If that's what the Church needs to do, then that's what should be done. We are good Catholics.' Then they would genuflect and go about their business, just like your parents."

Angela nodded. "Right. And you know what? Even though the dead don't have a chance to object, I'm sure they would have delivered the same response if they'd had a chance. Do you know that for years, Cardinal Mohony and the rest of the leaders of the Los Angeles Diocese have contrived ways to keep the police and other law enforcement officials from learning about rampant sexual abuse among their priests—and they have been successful?

"Here's another interesting story. In 2002 Reverend Donald O'Connor in the Diocese of Jolliet, Illinois was accused of sexual abuse and removed from his position. This didn't mean he couldn't conduct mass at another location, which is exactly what he did—and the Catholics continued to *pay him to pray for them*! Now how perverted is *that?*

"The Church also gives these criminals stipends. It continues to support them financially because they feel sorry for them, since they no longer have a job! Why are so many Catholics in denial? The answer to that is easy. Number One, my parents, for example, would probably fall apart if they allowed themselves to accept the truth. And Number two; do you know how many people have been murdered for trying to expose what's going on? My parents aren't the martyr type. And Number Three, if they quit the Church and stopped going to Mass, 'people would talk.' That's just as bad as being labeled a whistleblower."

"I can come up with a fourth reason, which may be more powerful even than your three," said Maria. "It is my understanding that there are a significant number of priests inside the Vatican and elsewhere that worship Satan, the 'Fallen Archangel. It is an exciting—exhilarating type of ritual that requires sodomy of little boys as well as adult males. They also perform ritual sacrifices on the same altars where they conduct traditional Catholic rituals! These perverts actually sodomize and kill little boys and they get off on themselves while they're doing it. *They blame Satan for their evil appetites.* Satan gives them *permission* to practice cruel sado-masochistic rites, to have 'religious' orgies."

"It's cathartic, is it not? They literally go out of their minds," said Angela. "Imagine how much testosterone is released after months and sometimes years of abstinence. It's like going into hormonal overdrive.

"The Devil takes possession of them and the only way they can release him is to submit. Through submission comes redemption. It is a well-known fact that popes perform exorcisms. The Devil or Satan takes possession over someone and only a priest or higher clergy can 'pull out' the evil spirit and cleanse the person's soul. It is an exciting battle between good and evil. If you believe that people can be possessed by the devil, if you're programmed from birth to believe in the power of Satan, you need to cling to religion, to Catholicism, in order to make sure you don't get attacked! What does it take to change this programming? That's the big question!"

"Right," agreed Angela. "Emotions are the key. The programming takes place from birth at the subconscious level. Have you ever argued with someone about the Word of God... the 'Literal' Word of God in the Scriptures? How do they know that God actually spoke those words when there are hundreds of thousands of versions of the bible and other so-called sacred books, each one quoting God yet using different words? Now how stupid is that?"

"My way is the highway," said Maria. "Catholics roll the rosary beads through their fingers and mechanically recite their prayers...

"Exactly!" exclaimed Angela, her eyes flashing. "And these crooks in the Vatican have their number. They know how to keep priming the pumps, how to pay off the right people in order to cleverly cover up their crimes. The same type of programming is at the source of bigotry.

"During the time I met with Wes, he told me some interesting, really wicked stories about what it's like to be black, meaning African-American, in the U.S. and working undercover as an agent in the ghetto areas. That's why he's so furious about what happened to Gene.

"'Honey, you ain't seen nothin' if you haven't been to South Side Chicago,' Wes told me. He said it was common for him to be working undercover and for the white agents to be backing him up or covering for him—only to discover they never showed, or they showed too late.

"After he witnessed Agent Scelsi's behavior at the police station, he guessed that because I'd refused to let that douchebag into my pants, I pay the price every day. Just because I'm a female doing what's considered male work."

"No, Angela. It's even worse than that. Scelsi would treat any woman the same way, regardless of *what* they were doing or *how* they were employed. They are chattel. Property. Especially a piece of property as *attraente* as you!"

"I'm going to be Agent Wes Charles's cover," declared Angela. "A *woman* will serve as a cover for a *black agent.* I will be waiting to whisk him away as soon as he emerges with the plates and negatives from the printing press."

"Then I'm coming with you, my dear," declared Maria, standing up and performing a few Taekwondo kicks that fully revealed her colorful bikini underpants. "You know how I love to practice my martial arts skills when I have to. Especially on dickheads."

37

'Jeannie'

Monday, March 11, 2013 – Rome, Italy – The Vatican

Before Wes left Florence for Rome, he had the counterfeit squad in Chicago develop a shadow report of his whereabouts, for the benefit of amateur snoopers with pecker trouble, such as former priest, Father Bartholomew (Adam Csonka). When he was out walking yesterday afternoon before meeting Angela for dinner, again he'd caught sight of the bald-headed former priest pretending to gaze at the items displayed in a shop window as he followed Wes down the street.

That pesky old mosquito never gave up. If he remembered his biology correctly, it was the females who were the bloodsuckers. "It figures," he said to himself. "Pedophiles would suck both cocks *and* blood. And they suck to kill."

The Masella case was over two years old. That's when lover boy Csonka first showed up... at the Elite Restaurant when Kim and he were celebrating their anniversary. Amazing. How did he fit into the picture? Who was his Daddy?

Silly question, he told himself. *It's like what they say about a CIA agent in the U.S. Once a spook, always a spook.*

The shadow report stated he was on his way back to the States, with confirmed ticket purchase by the agency, confirmed hotel checkout, confirmed airport shuttle, etc. The squad detailed the report with receipts for gifts at the duty-free shops, sandwiches; drink at the airport bar... the works.

"Just for you, Father Bartholomew," Wes sang to himself as the report came flying back through the wires.

Wes winked at his new self in the mirror. "Hello, Russell Morgan, goodbye Wes Charles. Have a good flight. *Buon viaggio, bon voyage, Gute Reise...*"

On the train, Wes tried to fit together more of the puzzle pieces. The Vatican Mafia had learned about the counterfeit bills landing in D.C. and they'd guessed that once Wes learned about it, he'd be on his way to Italy. Not too difficult to figure out.

How much did they think he knew? Wes wondered. Were they aware, for example, that he knew about the counterfeit bills that had been turned into the Rome USSS field office and had never been reported to D.C.? Did they know he knew that Jesse Jay had been arrested? Of course they did. *But did they know that both Jesse and Manny Scarpaci were talking?*

And then the big question: how important was it to retrieve the Masella plates and negatives? In 1976, the Foreign Sovereign Immunities Act or FSIA established limitations as to whether a foreign sovereign nation or its political subdivisions, agencies, or instrumentalities may be sued in U.S. federal or state courts. It established specific procedures for service of process and attachment of property for proceedings against a Foreign State.

Since the counterfeiting had not occurred in the U.S., Wes had no physical proof that the Italian operation was directly connected to Tony Masella without obtaining either the printer, on which the counterfeit bills were made, or the plates and negatives from which they were printed.

Wes knew he would never be able to obtain the printer, but if he could obtain the plates and negatives that were used to print both the first batch of bills in the U.S. as well as the latest batch of bills in Italy, he could easily proceed with the arrest and prosecution of Masella. It would then be up to the Italian government to prosecute the Italian counterfeiters who were involved.

He still had so many unanswered questions. Why the hell didn't SAIC Chris Mendoza send the counterfeit bills to D.C.? And why did they have to kill Agent Fred Stillwell? Who did it? Mendoza or "Them"? Whoever "Them" was. What the hell was Mendoza involved in?

The whole thing stank. It was rotten. *Evil.* Wes never liked to use that word, but in this instance, no other one sufficed. Just like the word "Satan." Just because he didn't believe in Satan didn't mean that others didn't.

For many years he'd heard stories about the underground chambers beneath the Apostolic Palace, but until now, he'd never put much stock in them. They seemed more like the kind of tales that people told around campfires... Satanic rituals were medieval, reminiscent of witchcraft and ancient tribal rites of human sacrifice.

Evil. Sadistic. Masochistic.

If the stories were true, he needed to see the altars where the sacrifices took place.

Yes, he told himself firmly. It would be well worth the effort to retrieve the negatives and plates for Masella's counterfeiting operation. And yet... who was Masella, after all? Just another patsy, another fall guy. He was only a symptom of the cancer. Wes already knew that sending Masella back to prison would not remove the tumor, nor would it prevent the disease from spreading.

Yet even though Wes knew that arresting Masella and having him serve another prison sentence may seem meaningless when looking at the bigger picture, in the long run for his own peace of mind, it had to be done.

In Rome "Russell Morgan" rented a car and on the GPS he punched in the directions for the location on the outskirts of the city where he had agreed to meet Angela and Maria.

It was a balmy spring day in the low sixties, with just a few stray cotton candy clouds in a pale blue sky. A nice change from March in Chicago, Wes couldn't help thinking. No snow, no lake effects. Just a gentle breeze from the Mediterranean riffling through the trees and kissing the grass... *Kim, honey, I do miss you...*

He turned on the news and drove for several kilometers on the main highway past the city limits. The only news in the entire world today was the event that was happening only a few miles away. According to reporters, the Vatican City was already overrun with Catholic dignitaries, the media, tourists and natives from other parts of the country. Preparations were well underway; the Vatican reported that 5,600 journalists had been accredited to cover the event. Red curtains would unfurl from the central balcony at St. Peter's, the spot where the world would meet the new pope once he was elected.

The newscaster delivered a detailed report of the minutiae: tailors had competed sets of clothes in three sizes for the new pope to wear as soon as he was elected. *Interesting*, thought Wes, smiling to himself. *Either the cardinals had already narrowed it down to three choices, or God's Pope only came in three sizes.*

Over the weekend a pair of stoves had been installed inside the Sistine Chapel. One would be used to burn the cardinals' ballots after they were cast and the other, to send up the black or white smoke signal—black to signify a vote that had not yet delivered a new pope, and white to celebrate the news that everyone was waiting for.

As Wes turned off the main highway onto a country road, it started to become more isolated. Soon the towns and villages disappeared and the countryside was dotted with just a few lone houses. Then there was nothing except fields, trees and overgrowth on either side of a road that was paved only in patches. The parts that were dirt hadn't been rolled in several months.

Angela had told him to look for a dark blue Fiat parked under a tree by the side of the road. He was relieved when at last he saw it ahead.

"Have I died and gone to heaven?" wondered Wes, as he parked the car, climbed out and saw standing before him, in addition to a gorgeous well-endowed smoky-eyed babe with chestnut brown hair, another young woman more petite but well-rounded, with a fiery red pixie haircut, pert nose and pouting mouth.

The second woman removed her sunglasses, stepped forward and held out her hand. "*Wes, io sono Maria. Sono lieto di incontrarmi con voi!* (Wes, I'm Maria. I'm delighted to meet you!")

Nothing shy about this goddess, thought Wes, gazing into Maria's bedroom eyes and clasping a hand that he had a feeling knew a few interesting tricks. It was one of those enviable moments that any man could wish for, to find oneself in an unidentified location with two gorgeous females. If not for the nature of the meeting, it would have seemed like perfection.

Both were attired in khaki fatigues and matching hoodies. Hardly fetching outfits, but easy cover-up for a bulletproof vest and concealed weapons. It was a well-known fact that women dressed for themselves. Wes was reminded of that classic joke that circulated often on the Internet. When women were asked what they wanted in a man, the list went on for pages. When a man was asked what he wanted in a woman, the answer consisted of two items: "Come naked; bring food."

"*Benvenuti in terra di nessuno!* (Welcome to No Man's Land!)", laughed Angela.

"Did you say you were into archaeology, Agent Charles?" Maria smiled invitingly. "You wanted to see some ancient Roman crypts, am I correct?" Right this way! But first, we need to hide our cars. Follow me."

With her flaming red hair and curves that even the military garb couldn't hide, she was one sexy babe, thought Wes. A gutsy one too. He was reminded of Kim. Agent Kim Charles wouldn't have hesitated to use whatever accessories she had in order to get what she wanted. It had worked on him, hadn't it?!

He followed Maria's blue Fiat down a ramp that led to a grotto that was an ancient burial ground, grown over with bushes and tall grass. As he parked the car and stepped out, Wes looked around him in amazement.

"Welcome to our secret garden!" Angela pulled a large picnic hamper from the trunk of the car and gestured toward a wooden table with benches.

"An amazing place with two amazing women!" declared Wes. They were completely hidden from the road. Beyond the burial ground on every side was a thick forest. Amidst the tall grass were clusters of small stone slabs that poked up crookedly from the ground. He walked over to examine a couple of them. The carved lettering was scarcely legible. On a few he could make out the Star of David. An old Jewish cemetery! He brushed away the overgrowth on a couple more of the stones and was able to make out some Hebrew letters.

"How did you find this place?"

"We didn't," answered Maria. "It found us. Or rather, it found my family. One day, several years ago, when I was a little girl, we were driving through this area and looking for a place where we could picnic. Suddenly I told my parents we needed to stop because I had to pee. You know how kids are! My dad saw a dirt road ahead so he decided to follow it. We stopped at the place where we met you, and it was so charming, we decided to walk around a bit and do some exploring. That's when we came upon the ramp. It's been a family picnic place ever since."

The sun was bright and the air was even fresher-smelling here in the country. Birds twittered and chirped as they flitted among the trees. Wes lifted his arms and stretched as he grinned at both women. *"Un posto magnifico!* (A magnificent spot!) Angela, Maria, I want to tell you how grateful I am to both of you. You have been immensely helpful. I'm sure I would have had to return to Chicago without the kind of evidence I hope to find tomorrow when I go to the Vatican."

"Remember, Wes, we have just as much invested in this as you," said Angela softly.

Maria opened the picnic hamper and spread out a tablecloth. "The wine is chilled just right... a *molto buono* chianti from our very own Tuscany."

"'A Jug of Wine, a Loaf of Bread—and Thou/ Beside me singing in the Wilderness—Oh, Wilderness were Paradise enow!'" quoted Angela from *The Rubáiyát of Omar Khayyám* as she unwrapped the meats, cheeses and condiments. "The bread is still warm! Mmmmmmm, smell!"

Wes didn't realize how hungry he was. Or maybe it was because everything always seemed to taste better in the open air, away from civilization. No one would have even guessed that they were only a few kilometers away from one of the busiest cities in Europe.

When they were finished eating, Maria reached into her purse and produced an electronic device the size of a smartphone. "Wes, after Manny Scarpaci gave you more information about the location of the printing press beneath the Sistine Chapel and you transmitted that information to Angela, my cousin Nicky Denzler, a Swiss Guard at the Vatican, integrated that information with his own knowledge of the underground tunnels and stairways. He then programmed this device with everything you will need in order to get into the chamber where the printing press, plates and negatives can be found."

Maria turned it on, punched in a code and handed the device to Wes. He held it in his palm and looked at the row of icons that appeared on the screen.

"Let's go over the exit strategy first," said Maria. "Once you're down under and in the chamber where the printing is done, we want to make sure you can escape."

Wes looked the two women. "I should hope so," he joked wryly, suddenly realizing even more acutely than before what he was getting into. This was not the kind of adventure one read about in novels or saw on the Big Screen. If anything happened, all three were well aware that he may never be heard from again.

"Of particular importance in each of the chambers are the invisible exits that lead up several flights of stairs to the street level," said Maria. "The entire structure was built centuries ago, according to the laws of sacred geometry."

"What that means, Wes, as you may know," Angela explained, "is that the entire underground area, which is actually as large as the Vatican City itself, was energetically patterned."

"Yes. You mean, according to frequencies," said Wes. Like the pyramids in Giza."

"Exactly!" said Maria. "Like all the pyramids, in fact. Bosnia, Peru, Russia, China... actually there are thousands of pyramids on the planet, and we now know they are generators. They were built to provide energy. Free energy," she grinned. "Nicky can explain it. He's not only a Swiss Guard. He is also an engineer and physicist.

"One of the walls in every chamber has an invisible door that opens when the right frequencies are accessed. When you wave this device in front of the walls, it will light up to show you where the exit is. The only piece you have to commit to memory is the code that you will voice out loud. You won't hear yourself speak. Your voice will be muted for your protection. You can also tap the code onto the keypad. No one else knows the code except you. We will now set that code. What would you like it to be?"

Maria handed Wes a keypad for him to enter the password. Wes didn't have to think about that one. At once he coded onto the keypad the letters 'K,' 'I' 'M' and the number '33' for the 33 years they had been married. The code appeared as dots on the keyboard.

When he had finished, Maria uploaded it to the device. "As soon as you voice the password to the device or tap it onto the keyboard—whichever is faster and easier for you—the door will open.

"It will close behind you after the sensors no longer detect your energy field. The area you are approaching will start to glow as you move forward.

"Can I give the device a name?" joked Wes, holding the device in his palm and admiring it.

"Of course!" laughed Maria.

"Well then, I will call it Jeannie," said Wes, "for Gene, genie, jinn, *and* Jeannie."

Angela reached over and gave him a hug. "Thank you, Wes." Her eyes filled with tears.

"*Mi piace che* (I like that)," said Maria, smiling and squeezing Angela's hand. "Jeannie will also vocally deliver your GPS directions and all other details—but without headphones or earbuds. No cumbersome wires or other equipment."

Maria proceeded to demonstrate how the device was used.

"*And*," said Angela when Maria was finished, "at the same time you're reading, listening and talking, Jeannie is live streaming a video directly to your offices in Chicago for your other agents to view. If you want one agent to be in charge, Maria will help you set this up. Of course it is also recorded."

"Set it up for Agent Kim Charles," said Wes.

"Security phone?"

Maria showed him how to upload the number and send activation instructions to Kim.

"*Magnifico!*" Wes continued to be amazed at all the advances in modern technology that could now be used for communication and surveillance. His entire career as agent may have been different had these devices been available several years ago.

"Only one caveat," said Maria after they'd finished the setup.

"Caviar, did you say?" joked Wes lamely.

"No, seriously, Wes, there's only one thing you need to be aware of when Jeannie and you are alone in the dark." Maria was trying to match his playfulness, but Wes realized she was dead serious.

"She bites? Pinches? French kisses?" he asked lightly, almost afraid to hear what she was going to tell him.

"None of the above. *You must listen to Jeannie and do everything she says.* No ifs, ands or buts about it. Remember, she's not human. She's a programmed computer. An electronic device."

Both Maria and Angela eyed Wes intently.

"So, in other words, if Jeannie tells me to go left and I go right, I'm in deep shit," said Wes, his jaw tightening.

"Exactly," said Maria. "You must *ABSOLUTELY obey her.*"

The three sat quietly for several moments, listening to a flock of birds chattering back and forth.

"You women are all alike," Wes retorted finally.

Nicky had done a great job with Jeannie, but even a Swiss Guard who was commanded to know everything about the Vatican inside and out in order to properly protect it, could be vulnerable. Loose ends, things he might not know, could ruin even the best laid plans.

"What you're telling me is that I still have to think on my feet, even though Jeannie is in charge."

"No, Wes. Actually, it's better that you *don't* think," corrected Angela. "*That's* what Maria is trying to tell you."

"So even when I think I know what to do—"

"There you go again," sighed Maria. "Wes, please just follow Jeannie at all times. I know it's difficult for a man to let women take the lead, but just this once..."

Wes threw up his hands. "I surrender. I get it. Is that good enough?"

"We hope so," chorused the two women.

"So now, shall we continue where we left off? Fresh air, delicious food, perfect wine... and Jeannie." Wes deliberately changed the subject by finishing off the second bottle of wine, closed his eyes and rubbed his stomach. "Angela, Maria, my two Italian Sirens."

Maria countered, "And you, Agent Wesley Charles, are our—"

"Agent Wesley Charles," finished Angela. Wes smiled at her.

"Angela, if I may ask a foolish question—why wasn't a tracking and recording device like this used a few days ago when Gene went undercover to make the arrest?"

"That's not a foolish question, Wes," she answered. "Actually Maria can answer it best. Nicky is way ahead of the pack with his cutting-edge technology. I'm not sure what takes so long for devices like these to be used by law enforcement. It would be *rivoluzionario* (revolutionary) if we could all have Jeannie's. I'm guessing the USSS might also be dragging their feet. I think it has something to do with politics, *È che non è vero* (is that not true?)" We're still living in the Dark Ages with much of our fossil based energy technologies, for example. I'm sure you're also aware that if the Powers That Be permitted it, we would have clean air, pure water and plenty of food for everyone. There's a nasty game going on."

"One of the rules of that game," continued Maria, "is to make sure we remain ignorant of the fact that we are not material or physical beings."

"So we are—?" prompted Wes.

"Energy beings," said Angela. Holograms. The universe is a hologram. Quantum physics is far different from Newtonian physics. Everything in the world is vibration. Frequency is the name of the game and INFORMATION is the key to what gives us life and sustains us."

"All of this is over my head," admitted Wes, "but I need to learn more. The main thing right now is that Jeannie performs as she's supposed to. Is it not possible, however, that whoever kidnapped Gene has a similar device?"

"Of course," said Maria, "and Nicky has accounted for that as well. The Vatican may or may not have Jeannies, and also they have many other ways of apprehending intruders. If you should encounter anyone while you're on your mission, Jeannie will take care of them. And that's what I've been trying to tell you. Here is the final instruction. Wes, what is the command you give a dog when you want them to attack?"

"SIC!" said Wes at once. Kim and he were on the move too much to keep a pet themselves, but they loved animals and had many friends who had dogs.

"Right!" said Maria. "You will hold up Jeannie in front of that person and say "SIC!" Jeannie will then deliver energy waves of *grave confusione* (serious confusion)—that will, how do you say—*discombobulate* the person. They will be unable to see, think or hear correctly for at least an hour afterward. Usually they get very dizzy, their eyes start to roll and they sway from side to side until they fall to the floor and lie there without moving."

"What if I want to use my fists and do a KO instead?" joked Wes.

"If they're armed, I think Jeannie is a safer choice," Angela grinned. "Although once they've been sic-ed by Jeannie, of course you can do whatever you want."

"*Caro Amico,* you can stand on top of him and pound him into sausage meat if you want," said Maria, "but he won't know the difference. And what fun is that? You'll never have that *maschile*—how do you say it?— masculine—macho, machissimo—pleasure of winning or getting even."

Wes knew Maria was right. A fight or attack was all about self-pride and self-pride depended on recognition. A tree could fall in a forest but if no one heard it, who cared... and if no one heard it, who would know what caused it to fall? Yet sometimes it might still be a good idea to simply get rid of the pest once and for all.

"Never before have I felt such a need for revenge," said Angela suddenly.

"It's understandable," exclaimed Maria.

"There's more to it than just what happened to Gene and I think that's what's bothering you," said Wes. "As a law enforcement officer, there comes a time when you get sick and tired of witnessing so many instances where someone either pays off the courts or finds another way to duck out of being punished like the rest of us. The Catholic Church has been getting away with serious crimes—either directly or indirectly.

"Take the case of the young woman in McAllen, Texas, who was allegedly raped and murdered by a priest back in the '60s. Her body was thrown into a nearby canal and when the police drained the canal, near her body they found items that belonged to the church as well as a Kodak slide photo viewer with the priest's name on it. Shortly before the priest allegedly raped and killed this girl, he was investigated for attacking another young woman.

"This priest was never indicted," Wes continued. "He was merely investigated—and the district attorney never called him to testify before the grand jury! When asked why he wasn't called, the DA answered, 'If I make him a target, he's got the right to tell me to go to hell.' The DA threatened to prosecute the McAllen Police Chief if he revealed the whole story with the evidence, because the DA claimed 'there are some things that have to be kept secret and just cannot be put into print.' The DA was reelected, incidentally. The priest was merely sent to another church facility.

"Now in his mid-seventies, he's still living as a free man. Another piece is just as important," Wes finished, "and that's the issue of justice and forgiveness. The DA told the media that if the priest did commit this crime, 'I hope he will atone for his sin.' Wow! Wouldn't every alleged murderer like to get off that easy! Then the DA went on to say that if the victim died after leaving the church, she 'died in a state of grace and she should be in heaven.'"

Angela and Maria shook their heads in disbelief. It was yet another example of Catholic immunity; the Catholic Church was impervious.

"Even the victim's sister didn't want the murderer brought to justice," said Wes. She told the press: 'I feel like that's between the person who murdered my sister and God. If the murderer asked God for forgiveness, he's going to heaven like anyone else who asks for forgiveness.' In other words, true Christians forget and forgive!"

"God help us all," sighed Angela.

"The repercussions of these crimes are just as tragic," said Wes, "like the large numbers of suicides, when young boys can't live with themselves after they've been abused. The guilt is unbearable."

"It's similar to what's happening with the big banks both in Europe and the U.S., is it not?" said Maria. "Take Greece, for example. The people are suffering terribly. They are treated like slaves who are being forced to sacrifice all their property and income in order to keep the big banks in business... as the big banks continue to sell off their antiquities and take over the country's wealth."

"Then, whenever the courts prosecute, it's the lower executives instead of the ones at the top, that are forced to confess or resign," added Angela. "Maria and I just had a long discussion about this yesterday. We know we can't count on the older generation. They're already brainwashed. We are the ones who have to deliver the wakeup call. And that's why I chose a career in law enforcement. It's also why I chose to return to Italy. And possibly, just possibly, it is why I happened to get involved in a case that's linked to the Vatican, which I have believed for as long as I can remember, is corrupt from the top down and the bottom up."

Wes was thoroughly enjoying the conversation. These two women were very smart, *Women really were amazing, damn it*. He was missing Kim even more than ever.

All the way back to the hotel with his check-in under the name of Russell Morgan, he hummed "Genie with the Dark Brown Skin and Coal Black Hair..."

38
This is Faith, Baby!

Tuesday/Wednesday, March 12/13, 2013 – Rome, Italy

It was 1300 or 1:00PM in Chicago when Wes called Kim and related the details of his meeting with Angela and Maria. "Jeannie will give you full instructions for tuning in livestream. The whole enchilada will be record-ed for The Brush, the courts and posterity. Jeannie does it all."

"So who the hell is Jeannie?" demanded Kim. "I've got a billy club right here by my desk and I'm ready to smack you one—"

"You've got a serious challenge my dear. She is all of 4 inches tall and 2 inches wide," chuckled Wes. "She is the smartest device I've ever met. If you check our encrypted emails you'll already find everything for getting your secure phone set up as a receiver. You'll also be able to watch it livestream on video."

"A device? Since when have you started to call females devices? Where'd you find this babe?"

"One of a kind, m'dear, just like you. Mitch will be the other witness in Chicago. Number three witness will be Shane in D.C. Call him and tell him what's up. Then forward the instructions. It's all good, Kim baby. I'm pumped. It's beyond exciting!"

Wednesday, March 13, 2013 - Noon - Vatican City

The papal conclave was already in session. Earlier the cardinals had cele-brated a morning Mass at St. Peter's Basilica. Just as the service began, the sky clouded over and erupted with huge rolls of thunder followed by jagged forks of lightning.

The devil's pitchfork, grinned Wes. From his hotel window he watched the storm boil up. Maybe there was a connection after all... the power of the satanic forces was not to be underestimated. The sky darkened, the lights flickered and the skies opened up, delivering a heavy downpour that weathercasts predicted would last for several hours before it started to let up. Anyone standing in St. Peter's Square without an umbrella or raincoat would already be drenched.

At 6PM, Wes made his final preparations, closed his suitcase, packed his laptop and checked out of the hotel.

Not even a thunderstorm could hold back Roman Catholics, the media and the curious when a papal election was the *plate du jour*. On the streets, huddling under their umbrellas and makeshift waterproof tents, people were laughing and shouting; excitement was high. Angela and Maria picked up Wes at the hotel in a rented vehicle and wove through the crowds heading toward the square. They stopped by the side entrance of one of the buildings near the Apostolic Palace behind a waiting cart. Wes slipped out of the back seat of the vehicle and hopped into the waiting cart.

He didn't even have to press the ON button for Jeannie. She was already starting her instructions in his ears. "Fasten your seat belt," she purred. As soon as Wes buckled the straps around his shoulder and waist, the cart rolled down a ramp. The door closed behind him and he was enveloped in darkness, with only a thin beam of light in front of him.

"This is faith, baby," he whispered to Jeannie. "At this moment, you are my one and only."

Back in Chicago and D.C., Kim, Mitch, and Shane had a single thought that did not have to be voiced aloud. Like Wes, they were well aware that as high tech as Jeannie may be, one blip in the system and Wes might be lost forever.

"We love you, Jeannie and we're counting on you," prayed Kim. *"You're the best, babe!"*

Wherever he was, it was damp and cold. Wes was glad he was wearing his winter jacket. He slipped on the hood and pulled up the collar flaps.

As the cart rolled forward, Wes couldn't help thinking of the days when Kim and he used to take W-2 and Loretta to the Funhouse in Chicago at the Navy Pier. He could still hear the kids screaming as the cars unhooked and started to roll... lifting, falling, gliding and sliding, stopping, starting, bumping and jerking to the right and to the left... *Yes, Jeannie, I'm back in good old Chi...*

Not exactly. His heart skipped a beat as something wispy floated directly ahead of him. There it was again... now there were two... three... *What were they?*

Maybe it was only steam, the condensation of water, Wes tried to reassure himself as his teeth started to chatter. And then he saw it: a tall white-robed figure with a skeleton head and hollow eyes—and another—and another—Joining hands, they made a circle in front of the cart and performed a series of weird movements. Wes had seen enough horror movies in his lifetime and didn't have to be told that he was watching a *danza della morte*...a death dance.

I am not imagining this," Wes whispered to himself as the circle of dancing skeletons moved closer, surrounding the cart. *This is actually happening. So help me God, it's true. I have no way of proving this, but I know without a doubt—"*

The cart rolled down a steep ramp. The air grew colder. He must be in some kind of basement or sewer; the stench was overwhelming. A gas mask would surely help. Dead bodies? Garbage? Mold and road kill? Yagggghhh... he felt like puking.

After several minutes he came to a hallway lined with doors. Two of the doors were half-open. The cart stopped in front of the second door. The ghosts, death dancers or whatever they were had apparently been following the cart. Now they stood on either side of the doorway. *Like Walmart greeters. This isn't part of the script, is it? Talk to me, Jeannie!*

Jeannie didn't respond. The cart rolled into the room.

Jeannie!

A body was lying on a bed of ashes on the large altar in the center of the room. A wreath of roses had been placed in front of the altar. On the wall was a floor-length painting of a naked man with silvery wings. His eyes were fiery coals. Blood dripped from his testicles.

Lucifer!

The body on the altar was a young boy. His eyes were open. He was still alive.

Wes felt nauseous. His head was spinning as he started to piece together everything he'd read about the Illuminati, all the conspiracy theories about robed and hooded romps in the woods at secret gatherings where world leaders and government heads gathered to pay homage to Lucifer, the Fallen Angel. *So it was true. Here was the evidence.* Yet who would believe him? How could he ever tell anyone about this? Why didn't the boy climb out of the bed of ashes? What was going on?

"Help me," said the boy, turning to look at him. "Please!"

Jeannie! Wes called out helplessly. He was already unfastening his seat belt.

"Do not leave the cart, Wes," Jeannie instructed.

"Please help me," begged the boy. His eyes filled with tears. He turned his head toward the cart. "I can't see you," he said. "Where are you? Who are you?"

Was it a trick? Wes's pressed his hands over his heart and bowed his head.

Jeannie, I've got to rescue him, he pleaded.

"Do not leave the cart," repeated Jeannie sharply.

"Please!" begged the little boy.

"I think you can climb down from that altar yourself," said Wes lamely.

"No. I can't," sobbed the little boy. "Please!" he pleaded.

Was it his imagination or was Lucifer moving his wings and stepping out of the painting? Before the words even entered his head, Wes spurted out: "Show me who you really are!"

To his horror, the boy disappeared. Only the bed of ashes remained on the altar.

"You see," said a voice in his ear with a distinctly British accent, "this is the problem with conspiracies. Now you see it, now you don't. People don't know *who* or *what* to believe. This should give you a clue of what's going on in the world, especially here in the Vatican.A wave of despair swept over him. There was so much he didn't know about... yet wasn't he a USSS Agent? Why wasn't anyone clueing him on any of this horrible stuff?

"I just did," said the man in a white ermine trimmed purple robe and tall three-cornered hat standing in front of him.

Stepping forward, he unbuckled Wes's seat belt and lifted him out of the cart. Wes felt a sharp prick in his left thigh. A needle. They had injected him with...

His head felt heavy, his eyelids were drooping...his arms, legs, shoulders, head, and every part of him went limp.

"WES!" Jeannie screamed from somewhere in the back of his head.

In Chicago and D.C., as soon as Wes had entered the room, the screen flipped into a display of arcs and rainbow-colored fractals.

Wes was swimming in a pool of thick red liquid. *It's only cherry Kool-Aid*, he reassured himself. *It couldn't be blood. Blood is too thick and too heavy, yet the smell...* His body was sinking...

"WES! Come back!" shouted Jeannie.

In the distance he could hear the sound of tapping, like keys tapping on a computer. The sound grew louder. His head started to clear. He opened his eyes.

"Wes! Can you hear me? We were intercepted. I need you to answer!"

Yes, Jeannie, yes!

"Listen carefully to everything I tell you," commanded Jeannie. "Get up!"

He tried to move but discovered he could not. Heavy ropes had been wound around his body. When he looked down he discovered to his horror that they were not ropes but snakes. Live ones. One of the snakes reared its head and stared coldly at him. With his fingers he could feel their slimy bodies as they slithered over him, binding his arms and legs tightly to his body.

"You have to get up!" ordered Jeannie.

What the hell! Wes wiggled his toes just as a snake took a nip at them.

"Lift your head," ordered Jeanie. "Look long and hard into the eyes of one of those snakes. Count from 1 to 10. Then suck in your breath and hold it until I tell you to release it. Take a deep breath because you're going to be holding it for at least 60 seconds. Keep staring at the snake while you're holding your breath. I'll tell you when to exhale."

Obediently Wes chose the snake that was lying on top of his chest, and stared into its beady eyes. He counted to 10, and then sucked in his breath. Deep within he felt something give way. His body felt weightless; he seemed to be rising from the floor. He heard a strange buzzing in his ear.

"You're doing beautifully, Wes!" Jeannie encouraged him. "Keep holding your breath. **Do not let it out!"**

The snake's eyes started to glitter and grow larger until they were two round globes the size of vehicle headlights.

"Don't breathe out yet!" commanded Jeannie.

The snake's eyes had become two convex mirrors. He saw a reflection of himself floating above the body of Wes Charles, writhing on the floor as the snakes slithered over him.

"OK... BREATHE OUT!" shouted Jeannie.

As Wesley Charles's breath poured out into the room, the snakes fell away from his body.

"Into the cart. Quick!" Jeannie ordered.

Wes scrambled to his feet just as the room flooded with armed guards. He leaped into the cart.

"Password!" yelled Jeannie.

Wes held up the device. "K-I-M-3-3!"

The door opened and they took off down the hallway, the guards in hot pursuit.

39
Thirteen Stories Deep

Wednesday, March 13, 2013 – The Vatican, Rome, Italy

Sirens shrieked through the corridors followed by a series of clanging bells. The guards had triggered the alarm system.

"Hang on tight!" ordered Jeannie.

Yes, ma'am! They rolled forward and headed straight for a solid wall. Just in time the cart jerked to the right and sped down a narrow ramp. At the bottom of the ramp, reflecting in Jeannie's light beam, Wes could see an oily swirl of water.

"Close your eyes and hold your breath again!" commanded Jeannie.

He felt himself falling. The cart landed with a loud splash. He sank into icy water.

"Keep holding your breath!" ordered Jeannie.

"*NO PROBLEM, JEANNIE. THIS WATER IS SO F-FUCKING COLD MY PARTS ARE GOING TO FALL OFF!*"

Seconds later the cart popped up to the surface.

"Breathe out!" commanded Jeannie.

The cart leaped onto the concrete and took off. Behind him Wes could hear the loud stomping of boots. The cart was jerked around as once again he was surrounded by guards.

"Breathe in again and hold it," commanded Jeannie. "As long as you don't inhale you are invisible. The guards can't see you."

Wes could feel hot meaty breath on his face as the guards closed in on him. They reached for him, clutching the air, but could feel nothing.

"**Do not move,** and do not breathe until they go away," ordered Jeannie. "I've just sent out a false clue. **DO NOT MOVE!**"

In the next instant the guards fell away and the cart raced forward down the hallway.

"We're here," Jeannie said finally into his ears. "We have to act fast. The guards are now everywhere down here. Unfasten your seat belt, climb out of the cart and take three steps to your right. You will find a wall directly in front. When you touch the wall, you'll find you can only go to the right. Keep walking until you come to a door that opens to a staircase. I'll be right in front of you with a light. Open the door and go down the stairs. There's a banister for you to hold onto. **Quickly... NOW!"**

The video screen had flashed no again. Kim, Mitch and Shane followed the beam of light through the corridor to the stairs. They watched the outline of Wes's form as he descended 13 levels.

"Thirteen stories deep," breathed Kim.

Thirteen stories, counted Shane. *Jesus. Hail Mary, Full of Grace...*

"Now keep walking," instructed Jeannie. A half hour later, Wes found himself standing in front of a large cement wall.

"Hold me up to the wall," instructed Jeannie, "and use your password."

"K-I-M-3-3," breathed Wes.

Kim closed her eyes, her fists clenched in her lap. Mitch reached over and placed his hand on her arm.

The entire wall gave way from the top, opening to a room.

Holey moley! Kim let out a gasp, Mitch's eyes grew wide with disbelief, and Shane looked like he'd been struck by lightning. "This shit is straight out of *Star Trek* or *X-files*," he muttered.

Wes stepped inside the room—and there it was. Printer, inks, cutting table, dye drum, packing cartons.... the full operation.

When Wes's eyes acclimated to the dimness, he saw the plates and negatives lying on a table. Without wasting a second, he pulled out the metallic security sack from the inside pocket of his jacket and scooped the plates and negatives into the sack.

Just as he was about to place the sack in his jacket, the room exploded in a blaze of light. Wes jumped back from the table.

Standing directly in front of him with a gun pointed at his head was a short bald-headed man with deep-set eyes, sunken cheeks and a large misshapen nose. *Adam Csonka. Father Bartholomew.*

"Well, Russell Morgan, what kind of cheap trick was that? You seem to think we're morons or that we haven't progressed with our own technology over the past 30 years!" Csonka's cruel cackles filled the room. "You should know better than that, you old fool, you old has-been. *Agent Wesley Charles!* Hands up, *Agent Charles!"*

"Here's your moment, Wes," instructed Jeannie in Wes's ear. "Hold me up and wave me directly in front of you. Yell "SIC!"

Wes did as he was instructed and yelled **"SIC!"**

The weapon fell from Csonka's hands. His bald head started to bob back and forth like a bowling ball tipsily wobbling down the alley, heading toward the gutter. Just as Maria had described, his eyes started rolling from side to side. Then, like a plant that had just been sprayed with a toxic insecticide, his body wilted and dropped to the floor.

All of this happened in less than ten seconds.

Wes snatched Csonka's gun, tucked the security sack into his jacket, gazed momentarily at the pathetic looking heap on the floor and overcame a temptation to give Csonka a kick in the balls. Then he changed his mind.

This time in Chicago and D.C., the video screen went dark.

Wes knew he wasn't the kind of guy who would ever kick anyone when they were down. He wouldn't even do this to a hard-core criminal who'd almost taken his life. No, this guy needed much more than that. Rolling him over and laying him out flat, Wes reached for his gun, firing three shots that hit Csonka squarely in the pineal gland, heart and genitals.

"Thank you, Jeannie," he said, sliding the gun back in his holster.

"You're welcome, Wes," said Jeannie. "Any time."

Wes held up Jeannie in front of the left wall. Nothing. He tried the wall next to it. Nothing. Third wall. Still nothing. Maybe the room was so light, he couldn't see Jeannie's light…Fourth wall…

"Not to worry," said Jeannie. *Beep! Beep!* The light started flashing in front of him.

"K-I-M-3-3," breathed Wes.

Nothing happened. The room was sealed shut. It was a tomb. Again it was pitch black.

40

A New Pope is Elected!

Wednesday, March 13, 2013 – Chicago, Washington, D.C., the Vatican - Rome, Italy

Shane was already calling Kim and Mitch. **"Jesus!"** he shrieked. **"What happened?"**

"**Shane!**" sobbed Kim.

Mitch texted W-2. "KTs office. Now."

As soon as W-2 entered the room, tears streaming down her face, Kim wordlessly handed him the smartphone.

"What's this?" he asked. "What's going on? Wh—"

W-2 stared at his mother's anguished face and then at Mitch, who had also started weeping. *Mitch Gordon sobbing like a baby?*

"Please," begged W-2. "Tell me what's going on. Tell me wh—"

W-2's jaw flew open as the device in his hand started beeping loudly. Once again the screen lit up and then, as if going through a digital reconfiguration, projected a series of jumbled numbers and letters in rapid succession followed by snow and static.

The screen cleared. "7:06PM Vatican Time," read a placard in large black letters.

A thin curl of white smoke poured out of a chimney and twisted high over the Sistine Chapel and St. Peter's Square. A loud roar could be heard as the cameras panned over the massive sea of humanity huddled under umbrellas, dancing and hugging each other hysterically.

"*Un nuovo papa è stato eletto!* (A new pope has been elected!)" read the lettering on the screen in Italian and English."8:30PM Rome Time, 2:30PM Eastern Time."

Cardinal Jorge Mario Bergoglio, now Pope Francis I, was stepping out on the balcony and lifting his hands to greet the solid mass of uplifted faces in St. Peter's Square.

The cheers were deafening.

"He's gone," wept Kim, turning her head away from the screen and rocking back and forth. "Gone," she repeated. W-2 held her tightly and let her cry. When she stopped for a moment, he murmured in her ear, "Mom, how the hell do you know that? Just because you can't see him on a computer screen?"

W-2's words made Kim come to her senses. "You're right, son. We don't know shit—but that's exactly that's the problem!" Again she started weeping.

In Washington, D.C., Shane was getting the same image of the new pope lifting his arms and turning to the left, right, center, left right center, blessing his flock.

Where the hell was Wes?

From their monitor in Rome, Angela and Maria were dumbfounded. What went wrong? How could this have happened? Maria dialed Nicky's number but just as she expected, she couldn't get through.

41
Physics or Miracles?

Wednesday, March 13, 2013 – Rome, Italy

Wes clasped Jeannie tightly in his hand. In the hallway he could hear the guards approaching. "Jeannie, you can't let me down," he whispered. "Please, I need a door so I can get out!"

The windowless room was hot and stuffy. His nostrils filled with toxic fumes from the printing inks and chemicals used to make the bills. His head started to hurt. He felt faint.

"*I am not giving up,*" he told himself. "*There has to be a way out of this room!*"

His voice held no conviction. His inner mind was in turmoil. Strangely, it wasn't fear that he felt, only regret.

"*Kim baby, we may never be able to celebrate another anniversary. Please know how much I love you! W-2, Rachel, I will never be able to see you kiss each other at your wedding and if it's a Jewish wedding, break the glass. I will never be able to hug my grandchildren.*"

"*Loretta, sweetheart, I miss you! You're going to be a celebrity one day; I know it. It's in the stars! I will never see you in your leading roles. I will never see the films you direct...*"

In the midst of his litany of regrets, another voice started to speak to him.

"Wesley Charles, do you believe in God?"

"Of course I do!" he retorted.

"And do you believe God can speak to you directly?"

Wes thought for a moment. "Do I have to answer that?" he said finally.

"I think you do," said the voice. "Because this is God speaking to you. I want you to tell me flat out, no holds barred, Wesley Charles, that you love me."

"Oh God, I love you. I do love you, God... and let me put it on the line. Let me be absolutely up front with you. My love for you has nothing to do

257

with what's going on right now down here in this hell hole, in this godforsaken place," said Wes without hesitation.

"So do you understand who the most powerful being in the universe is?"

"You are, God," said Wes again without hesitation.

"No, Wes," said the voice. "Tell me: aren't you as powerful as God?"

This time Wes didn't answer at once. "God, is this a trick question?" The sweat was pouring off his forehead.

"Excuse me?" said the voice.

"God, I am as powerful as God!" said Wes aloud.

"Yes!" said the voice. "And why is that? Is it because *you are God*? *Because all of God's people are gods?* Wes, do you remember who said, 'Ye shall be as gods'?"

"You did, God, or man did, in Genesis the Old Testament of the Bible," stammered Wes.

"Exactly!" said the voice. "Now get the hell out of here with those plates and negatives and make this case!"

"One more thing, God," pleaded Wes.

"Go ahead."

"Do you love all of your people equally?"

Beep beep! Beep! Beep! On the wall in front of him, the outline of a door appeared. It opened to a staircase leading upward.

"Watch your step," warned Jeannie.

In her officer's uniform, Angela was waiting for Wes in an Italian Army Corps vehicle at the southwest corner of St. Peter's Square. Maria's head appeared. She ushered Wes into the vehicle next to Angela who was driving, and hopped into the back seat. Angela took off through the back streets of Rome, lights flashing, sirens blaring.

"Slow down, woman!" shouted Wes. Goddess Angela with her smoky eyes and gorgeous curves expertly maneuvered the vehicle through the thick lines of stalled traffic. The go-cart ride beneath the Sistine Chapel was nothing compared to Angela's demonic driving. Later she told Wes she had a kid brother who was a race car driver. "He taught me a few tricks."

He surely had. They nipped off street corners and wove through the traffic as if the vehicle had wings.

"I have news for you, Wes," shouted Maria, leaning forward.

"Like we're going to arrive in one piece at my hotel?" shouted Wes.

"All that and a bag of chips, as you Americans say," she yelled back. "I just checked my messages. We have a new pope and the boys are coming back tomorrow. They'll be in the office on Friday."

"Shucks. I wanted to see the white smoke emerging from their anal chimneys," shouted Wes, "and now it's too late!"

"*It's never too late,* Agent Wes! The timing for everything is perfect!" crowed Angela. She turned off the siren and flashing lights and wheeled into the side street leading to Wes's hotel. As she spoke the words, "It's never too late," *Wes was seeing the lovely woman seated across from him at the Brown Sugar Restaurant in Florence, describing the note and then the package she had received, after Gene went missing.*

"I need to send off this package tonight," said Wes, returning to the present. "I'll call Agent Scelsi and make an appointment with him tomorrow. I'll tell him that you are to be at that meeting, Angela. Then I'll take a train to Rome and show up at the USSS Rome office Friday morning. Unannounced."

"Excellent plan," said Angela. "Rather than take a train to Rome on Friday, Wes, I can drive you there in one of our vehicles. The courier pouch is waiting for you at Hotel Duilio on Corso Italia 13 in the center of the city. You're registered at the hotel under the name of Russell Morgan."

Wes called Kim first.

"Wesley Charles reporting to headquarters."

"**WHO? Did you say Superman, Batman, Captain Marvel, *and Wesley Charles?!!!*"** she shouted into the phone.

"Honey—"

"Whatever you're about to say, save it, Wes. Is that really you? I thought, we thought... oh God, Wes! Wes, you're alive! **I love you!"**

"Burke, do you believe in miracles?" asked Mitch, putting the phone on speaker.

"Cut the crap, Gordon."

"No, I mean it," Mitch insisted. "It's a miracle."

"Physics. Not miracles but physics," insisted Kim, holding back her tears. "Thank God for the laws of physics!"

"Whatever it is, thank God he's safe and the plates and negatives are in D.C. with you, Shane," said Mitch. Shane had just called them to report that Wes's package had arrived from Rome.

"But I want to tell you one thing, man. Jeannie has just performed surgery on my testicles. She takes all the balls out of an orgasm. I'm wiped out. *Crap!*"

"You don't have to marry her, dude," was Shane's comeback. "You don't even have to sleep with her if you don't want to."

When they clicked off, Mitch gave Kim a high five, and then hugged her tightly. The two waltzed around the room openly crying. The hell with what other people thought. Who cared? Wes was safe!

42
Saving Jesse

Thursday, March 14, 2013 – Florence, Italy

"So what did you think of Jeannie's star performance?" asked Wes when he was back again in Florence.

"I think we ought to hire her. Who's the genius behind the genie?"

"A cousin of a woman who works at the American embassy here. She's a good friend of Angela's. The two women arranged everything. Sometimes I wonder if there's anything a woman can't do—especially when they're hell bent on revenge."

"I hope you're not first discovering that," Kim teased. "Mitch and I just played the Jeannie video for the whole squad. And of course, we're saving you the honor of playing it for The Fuller Brush. We will also make a point of telling him that the entire operation was arranged by a Secret Service Agent's girlfriend, a Secret Service agent who used to work in the Chicago office."

"An agent who happens to be black, did you say?"

"Shane has suggested that Gene should get a special citation. We've already discussed it."

"For sure," agreed Wes. "But first, it looks like we have some serious issues that need to be resolved. The crew is back again from protection detail. I'm not presenting my calling card in advance."

"I'm sending you even more ammunition from Jesse Jay. Wes, he is a very decent human being and he's not hesitating to be up front with us. But he's very depressed. W-2 and Rachel have spent considerable time with him.

"Depressed, like—"

"Yes, very much like. He's on suicide watch."

"Give Harold Strong a call and arrange to have him stay with Jesse 24/7 in comfortable quarters. We can't afford to lose him. I think Jesse already knows him. He hired Harold previously to work at the Cordova Rehab Center." Harold Strong was a well-known hypnotherapist and counselor who had helped many PTSD veterans and victims of sexual abuse.

43
Spirit of the Law

9:00 AM – Friday, March 15, 2013 – USSS Secret Service Office, American Consulate - Rome, Italy

Robed in white with a white skullcap, Argentina's Archbishop, Jorge Mario Bergoglio—Pope Francis I—stood on the balcony overlooking St. Peter's Square and lifted his arms to bless his flock. The square was a solid mass of people hovering under umbrellas. Even if they had no protection from the rain, they were oblivious to the rain and their drenched clothing. All that mattered was this one historical opportunity to witness Pope Francis's first appearance.

In the media room of the USSS offices in the American Embassy, Agents Roger Whalen and Eli Lemberton were clustered around the TV watching a rerun of the big event as they nursed their hangovers with mugs of steaming black coffee. Neither of the agents was feeling up to snuff. It was only 9AM but at least they were there in body, joked Lemberton.

"Jesus. My head feels like the batting cage of the Yankee Stadium during warm-up," complained Whalen.

"Whenever you feel like carrying your head under your arm just ask yourself if it was fucking worth it," moaned Lemberton.

"Yeah, thanks a lot. Like no. Like yes. Shit," retorted Whalen, his face twisted with pain. He grumbled something incoherent as he popped two aspirins into his mouth, took a swig from his coffee mug and threw back his head to force the buggers down his throat.

"He looks like a fucking bride posing for wedding photos," joked Lemberton, watching the Pope turn slightly to one side and then to the other, as if to make sure his lifted hands covered the entire throng.

While the two agents were glued to the TV set, SAIC Mendoza entered his office unnoticed and closed the door. At once he pulled out his private cell phone and punched in a number.

Lewis Feathercornn, Father Ira's administrative assistant, was waiting for his call. "Chris! Welcome back! Are you coming to the bash tonight? You'd better damned well show your ass!"

"Yes yes yes, of course. I wouldn't miss it. Same place as usual?"

"The car will arrive at 9PM. So I assume everything's copasetic? Father Ira wanted to make sure. He's been so busy with all the preparations..."

Mendoza popped a handful of vitamins in his mouth and threw back his head as he took a swig of bottled water. "Yes. Agent Charles was taken care of two days ago and we have everything under contr—"

"Smile! You're on candid camera!" Agent Wesley Charles strode into SAIC Chris Mendoza's office, holding up his smartphone and snapping a photo. Wes held out his hand, his face wreathed in smiles. "Agent Mendoza, I am Wes Charles from the Chicago bureau, USSS Counterfeit Squad. I am the agent who made the original case in 2010 with Tony Masella regarding counterfeit bills that were printed in Chicago. Masella served two years."

Mendoza stared at Wes as if he were seeing an apparition.

"It's good to meet you at long last," Wes chattered on. "And incidentally, we're on livestream right now in the Chicago and Washington D.C. offices. Agent Shane Burke, are you there?"

"Yes, Agent Charles, I'm here." Shane was having a hard time controlling his laughter as he watched Mendoza squirming.

"Agents Kim Charles, Mitchell Gordon, Leonard Eastwood, Marc Green, Kevin Gerr and Romeo Gonemo, are you there in Chicago?"

"We are all here, Agent Charles," said Kim.

"The reception is excellent, Agent Charles," grinned Mitch.

"SAIC Agent Larkin Fuller is out of the office today, but we will have a video showing for him tomorrow when he returns," said Marc.

"Excellent!" beamed Wes. "Agent Mendoza, yesterday I met with the officer in charge at the *Guardia di Financza* on Via del Pratello in Florence where counterfeit bills were handed in and sent to the USSS Washington D.C. office. Incidentally, copies of the files containing scans of the counterfeit bills from the Rome office are also in D.C. All of the bills bear the same serial numbers tracing back to the Masella counterfeit bills printed in 2010."

USSS SAIC Chris Mendoza turned white as Italian police officers from the Financial Guard streamed into the office and surrounded him. He was well aware that misdemeanors in a foreign country were punishable by that country's legal system. Penalties could be extremely severe, especially if the countries held any grudges against each other. He could easily become a bargaining chip.

One thing was certain: his career with the USSS was over... as if it mattered. When the Italian courts got through with him, he may never see the sun again except in a prison courtyard.

Lewis Feathercornn was puzzled by the sudden phone disconnect from Mendoza. No big deal, he told himself. It happened all the time with encrypted phones. No need to call Mendoza back, he decided. He'd delivered the message about the party tonight, and that was the main reason for the call.

Agent Wesley Charles was on a roll, although now that the Italian police had started to stream through the doors, his lighthearted mood was shifting. Like the spring storm that had hurled itself into the Vatican City on the day the new pope was elected, dark clouds had already gathered in the bottom of Wes's belly as he wound up to fire the first lightning pitchfork across the bow.

Apparently the Italian police corps, freshly released from duty at the Vatican City, had decided not to spare any numbers on today's showing at the USSS offices. A major portion of the Florence precinct of the Financial Guard corps was there.

Agent/Officer Angela Micele was at the head of the pack with Chief Agent Carlo Scelsi. Thanks to Wes, Scelsi had no choice but to give the honors to Agent Micele. At yesterday's meeting, Wes had read the riot act to him. Humbly he acknowledged her outstanding service to the corps and agreed to a citation as well as a promotion.

The Italian police hustled Whalen and Lemberton into the room. The other three USSS Rome agents who had arrived for what they thought would be a normal day of work were also present, standing at the back of the room in shocked silence.

"What we have here," Wes began, first addressing Mendoza and then turning to address the rest of the officers and agents assembled, "is one of the greatest travesties that has ever been committed in the name of the United States Government, the United States Secret Service, and in particular, the counterfeit squads of Chicago and Washington, D.C.

"In 2010 in the U.S. District Federal Court of Chicago, Anthony Masella was convicted of conspiracy to print counterfeit U.S. currency. Masella served a two-year prison term and was released on November 21, 2012.

"On Thursday, January twenty-third, 2013, Rome USSS Agent Fred Stillwell, **now deceased,** handed several $100 allegedly counterfeit bills to you, Special Agent in Charge, Christopher Mendoza.

"You, Christopher Mendoza, failed to report the suspicious bills to the USSS counterfeit bureau in Washington, D.C. and send them samples. Since Agent Fred Stillwell is **unable to be present and therefore, cannot speak for himself,** we do not know what you told him. We have no records of any conversations that took place between you, Agent Mendoza, and the late Agent Stillwell.

"It is highly unusual, however, that Agent Stillwell, who was perfectly healthy according to his medical examinations before reporting for duty in the Rome USSS office three months ago, suddenly became seriously ill immediately after he turned in the suspicious bills to your office, Agent Mendoza. He was rushed to the Rome American Hospital and passed away shortly after."

The room had become completely silent. Police were guarding the doors. The offices had been sealed off from outsiders and yellow security tape with the lettering "*crimine* (crime)" had been wrapped around the entire building.

"Agent Mendoza, did you not think first before deciding not to send those purportedly counterfeit bills to D.C.? Did you not realize what that meant to the rest of the USSS? To have an agent in a prominent foreign location, who, for some fucking reason, chose to hide evidence from his own colleagues and from the U.S. Government? Do you realize how fucking embarrassing this is to the rest of us who work our tails off to make cases and turn in evidence and honor our country, our fellow workers and all Americans, by representing them intelligently, conscientiously, ethically and morally...."

Wes's voice had reached a hysterical pitch. "Jeannie" was capturing the performance on video. In Chicago the entire office staff had gathered. In D.C., Shane, several other agents, and some of the top brass were also watching.

"And speaking of embarrassing, I think maybe it's time for *you* to be embarrassed. At another time, all of you will have an opportunity to view the entire video—I will just show you a few brief clips that have been extracted—actually, Agent Mendoza, we weren't sure which part of the video would be juicier or more entertaining: the scenes showing your back side, front side, mouth, testicles... so we decided to give the viewers a buffet. I believe this is called a preview or trailer in the movie business."

Wes snapped his fingers and a video screen rolled down. Maria positioned the video from her laptop and clicked on the "Start" arrow.

The next three minutes were impressive. The video editors had done an expert job of showing Mendoza at his best, or worst. No comments were necessary. The group sat in frozen silence.

SAIC Mendoza's body had gone rigid. His expression was impassive. The only sign of emotion were the tears streaming down his face. He didn't bother to wipe them away.

"Agent Mendoza, I must commend your colleagues for their expert demonstration of blackmail," Wes continued. "This video is excellent. I trust it is the same one they showed you after the late Agent Stillwell brought you the funny-looking U.S. bills.

"If not for our colleague, Agent Eugene—Gene—Burns, who happened to hear a rumor in the Florence USSS office where he was stationed—notice I said 'was'—when he heard information passed on to him by an Italian employee of the USSS in Rome, who happened to overhear a conversation between you, Agent Mendoza, and the late Agent Stillwell—if not for Agent Burns's decision to act and get to the source of the issue—we would not be standing here today pointing our fingers at you and showing this video, Agent Mendoza. We would have no knowledge of this counterfeit money that was passed in Rome. Nor would we know that the bills bore the same serial numbers as the Masella counterfeit bills printed in 2010. And incidentally, in case you're wondering, Agent Mendoza, we do have samples of those counterfeit bills that were turned in at the Alitalia cashier's office in Rome, so we can prove they have the same serial numbers as the original Masella bills.

"It is the job of every conscientious USSS agent to follow every clue they get, and do what they need to do if it may involve crime.

"Notice, I referred to 'the late Agent Burns.' We have no proof that he is still alive, since we have not heard from him in two weeks. Yes, that's right: **two weeks!** You in Italy are aware that Agent Burns has gone missing, but the USSS in the United States has heard nothing. Why is that? Is some kind of cover-up going on that we don't know about?

"Is the State Department aware of this little slip-up? Is there so much excitement about the papal election here in Rome that this matter has somehow gone by the wayside? A USSS Agent missing for two weeks! Except that we do have one clue which leads us to believe that he is dead. That he was murdered."

Wes paused and looked around the room. In Chicago and D.C., the agents were grateful that all of this was being recorded.

"A note along with evidence that I care not to discuss publicly because it would be highly inappropriate, was sent to one of the Italian police officers who is a member of the Financial Guard in Florence, and who was a close friend of Agent Burns.

"That woman, Officer Angele Micele (Wes pointed to Angela) is the brave and dedicated person who disclosed the Agent Gene Burns story to me after having met me at the *Guardia di Financza* on Via del Pratello in Florence where U.S. counterfeit bills were also handed in. Those bills, incidentally, WERE sent to Washington D.C. after Office Micele conducted the forensic work on them. In fact, that is the reason why I came to Florence. I met with the man who is now being held as the guilty party for having printed them. The reason why I was assigned to this case is because these counterfeit bills also have the same serial number as the 2010 Masella counterfeit bills.

"Like a dedicated agent, Burns located one of the alleged sellers of the counterfeit bills and set up a sting operation with two of your agents, Mendoza, who would be covering for him while he approached the seller to buy some bills. Those agents were Agents Roger Whalen and Eli Lemberton."

If Whalen and Lemberton looked sick and green around the gills from their night-after hangover before, now their faces had become death masks. All eyes were focused on the two men.

"Agents Whalen and Lemberton covered for Burns all right," Wes's voice trembled, and then took on a shrill pitch. "Officer Micele, on her way to Rome to meet with Agent Burns after he had made the case and arrested the seller, happened to stop by at Moma Restaurant, across the street from this building. As you agents know, it is a favorite eating place for people from the Embassy and agents working in this office. Florence USSS agents also eat at the Moma Restaurant when they visit.

"When Office Micele entered the restaurant that night, she saw, seated at one of the tables, Agents Whalen and Lemberton.

"**What were they doing there, besides feeding their faces—the obvious?**" screeched Wes. "**What the fuck were they doing at Moma restaurant when they should have been out on the street, covering for Agent Burns? I ask you: WHAT THE FUCK WERE AGENTS WHALEN AND LEMBERTON DOING, CASUALLY SEATED IN A RESTAURANT HAVING DINNER AT EXACTLY THE TIME WHEN THEY SHOULD HAVE BEEN FOLLOWING AGENT BURNS AND KEEPING A CLOSE WATCH ON HIM AS HE APPROACHED THE DESTINATION WHERE HE WAS GOING TO MAKE THE CASE AND ARREST THE SELLER OF THE US COUNTERFEIT BILLS?**"

Wes's eyeballs bulged; sweat poured down his face. He was a black man in white heat. "**DO YOU KNOW WHAT HAPPENED TO AGENT EUGENE BURNS? HAS ANYONE EVEN BOTHERED TO FIND OUT?**"

Wes stormed over to the two agents, glowering at them. "**Do you have one moral bone in your bodies, you motherfuckers, you pieces of shit?**" he screamed, lifting his right arm and swinging it behind him to gather momentum. "**DO YOU HAVE THE SLIGHTEST IDEA WHAT YOU DID? DOES IT EVEN OCCUR TO YOU MORONS—**"

Angela stepped forward and placed a firm hand on Wes's elbow. "Wes, Agent Charles, please...! Stop!"

Wes shook her hand off. "**I THOUGHT I HAD MET SCUM BEFORE, BUT YOU TWO MEN—AND YOU, CHRIS MENDOZA—YOU ARE A DIS-**

GRACE TO THE HUMAN RACE, NEVER MIND THE U.S. SECRET SER-VICE!"

"Its okay, Wes, it really is," said Angela gently, pulling harder on him and holding his arm in a firm grip so he couldn't move it. "You've made your point!"

Angela stepped away from Wes as he backed off. Then with all the dignity and poise of a woman who knew exactly what to say and how to say it, she jumped in before Wes had a chance to continue, and proceeded to address the group.

"Ladies and gentlemen, justice *will* be served, both here in Italy and in the United States. If these three men are murderers or accomplices, the evidence will turn up at the court trial. If they are innocent, they will be returned to the United States. Based on Agent Wesley Charles's remarks, I'm confident they will receive what's coming to them.

"I would like to personally thank Agent Charles for his courage and determination to get to the bottom of this case. We are also grateful to those who helped us obtain a copy of the video that was used to blackmail SAIC Mendoza."

Angela yielded the floor to her boss, a beaming Officer Scelsi, who cleared his throat, shifted from one foot to the other and lamely thanked everyone for being present at this auspicious event.

"God help us," Kim shook her head. "What an asshole. I'm guessing that Angela has another set of stories to tell about *that* poor substitute for a man."

"I don't believe any of us wants to make this into an international incident," said Wes, now in control of himself once again and stepping up next to Officer Scelsi. "When we have located Agent Burns's remains, they will be flown back to the U.S. where we will conduct a proper burial for him, awarding him posthumously for his service to his country."

As the Italian police shoveled Mendoza the Iron Man into the waiting van, he was sobbing loudly and muttering some unintelligible gibberish.

Wes drove back to Florence with Angela to visit Manny Scarpaci. As anticipated, he wasn't faring well in prison. For the past three days he'd gone on a hunger strike.

"Manny, I have two requests," said Wes when they were in the visiting room alone.

Manny didn't lift his head.

"You are an educated man. I'm sure you know the difference between the letter of the law and the spirit of the law. As a Christian you also know the story of the Good Samaritan. There is a way out for you because you chose to help us get to the source of the issue regarding the Masella case and its connection to the Vatican. We have much work to do; it has only begun with the prosecution of those who were directly involved in this case.

"People have started their lives all over again when given a new identity," said Wes. "You are a gifted artist and there are some beautiful places here on the planet where you would help restore important artifacts."

Manny reached out a hand to Wes, tears streaming down his face.

Wes planned to stop off in D.C. to meet personally with Shane before returning to Chicago. He would then make preparations to go back to Rome for the trial.

"Why don't you take a direct flight to D.C. from Rome," suggested Angela. "I can drive you to the airport. Maria invited me to spend a few days with her to recoup."

"Thank you! Yes, indeed, that would certainly be much more convenient."

44

Liza

As Wes strode out of elevator into the hotel lobby followed by the bellboy with his luggage, at once he spotted Angela in full uniform. She flashed him a smile, stepping forward to greet him. He hugged her warmly, kissing her on both cheeks.

"*Angela, angelo mio! Sto per perdere voi!* (Angela, my angel! I'm going to miss you!)"

She laughed and rolled her eyes dramatically. "You will always be welcome here, Wes. We can always conjure up more drama and excitement here in Italy, if you wish!"

"Not exactly what I had in mind," grinned Wes. "Anyway, I look forward to seeing you again, I hope, when I return for the trial."

"*Ma naturalmente* (But of course!)

On the way to the Rome airport they regaled each other with a recap of the past few days' events, embellishing the narrative with "what if" versions at varoius points that sent both of them into spasms of laughter.

"Laughter is the best medicine on the planet," declared Angela as they turned into the long drive leading to DaVinci Airport.

"You'd better believe it, especially after what we've been through," said Wes. "Angela, by far this has been one of the most life-changing events I have ever experienced, bar none."

"Even more life-changing than that moment when you popped your head out of your mama's belly?" teased Angela as they headed up the ramp toward Lufthansa Airlines. Again they both enjoyed a good laugh.

Before Wes opened the car door, he reached into one of the pockets of his vest and removed a small golden charm on a chain. He turned to face Angela, handing her the necklace.

"I want you do know, my angel, that maybe in another lifetime under different circumstances, things could have been way different between us than they are now. I sensed that from the moment I met you.

"This charm was given to me by my father, Andrew Charles, before he died. It is a replica of Liza, the African god or goddess of protection and divination. It originates in a country in West Africa that was once called Dahomey that is now known as Benin. My father's ancestors came from Dahomey, where they were slaves. The area used to be known as the Slave Coast."

"Thank you, Wes," said Angela softly, her smoky gray eyes filling with tears. "I will treasure this gift."

Wes jumped out of the van, pulled his luggage from the trunk, blew her a kiss and disappeared inside the revolving doors.

45
Small Potatoes

Saturday, March 16, 2013 – Washington, D.C.

Shane didn't wait for his mentor and colleague to come to the office; he met Wes's plane. "Congratulations, Bro! Great job!"

The two men eyeballed each other after a warm hug. "Shane, I know I should feel some sense of victory, but to tell you the truth, I'm not sure what we've accomplished," admitted Wes. "Sure, we nabbed Masella and he'll go back to prison. That part of the mission is accomplished. But it's such small potatoes.

"In Italy while I was standing in St. Peter's Square and witnessing the mobs of people who waited for hours in the pouring rain for white smoke to emerge from the rooftop of the Sistine Chapel—just to be able to get a glimpse in person of the man who would come out on the balcony in a white robe—the man who had just been pronounced their new leader in an election in which they did not participate and over which they had no control—I realized the enormity of the situation.

"Do you realize how many millions of people are actually aware of the crimes committed *daily* even at the highest ecclesiastical level of the Roman Catholic Church, yet somehow, *it doesn't seem to matter to them?* It seems to have nothing to do with them unless they've been personally raped, molested, kidnapped— I only hope the new pope can start to change things around. He has so much work to do. The Church is so corrupt."

"You're wound up, man. Let's go talk somewhere before going back to the office," Shane suggested. "Are you hungry?"

On the jet flight back to Chicago, high in the sky, Wes had another talk with God.

"God, tell me if you will, what happened the other day when Jeannie went blank. According to Kim, Mitch and Shane, my underground mission was replaced by the announcement of the new pope and his appearance on the balcony. They never saw me escape. What was that all about?"

"To tell you the truth, Wes, I'm not sure myself," said God. "It might have had something to do with bandwidth, or satellite interference with all the drones over the Vatican City, monitoring for terrorists and assassination attempts. You know how it is with big events…"

"Yes, that's true. Anything can happen," Wes agreed. "Say listen, God, if you can spare another minute, there's something else I'd like to ask about. I don't like to use the word 'upset,' but you know what? *I really am fucking upset* about all the crime and corruption in this world—excuse the f-word, God. Its like things have gotten *completely* out of hand. Take the Catholic Church, for example. You know better than anyone else how much pedophilia and other sex crimes have gone unpunished by the Vatican and the courts. What's wrong with this picture? How can the Church get away with merely "forgiving" these crimes as if they were merely *sins,* when other non-Catholics get sentenced and sent to prison for such felonies? Why has this travesty not been exposed? *The safety of our children is at stake!"*

Wes took a deep breath and wiped his eyes with the back of his hand. "Add to that all the corruption in the banking and financial world… and *outright violation* of this country's Constitution and Bill of Rights, *the law of the land!* As a law enforcement officer, that really gets me in the gut. Then on top of that, the inequality. Wherever you look, in this country and abroad, *pandemics* of hunger, disease, poverty…"

"Oh I know, I know all too well," sighed God. "You're right, Wes. I still have so much work to do…"

Lightning Source UK Ltd.
Milton Keynes UK
UKOW03f1845020517
300357UK00001B/291/P